Sorciére
Born of Shadows Book 2

J.R. Erickson

ISBN-10: 1979419566
ISBN-13: 978-1979419567

DEDICATION

For Kyle and Avery – my guys.

ACKNOWLEDGMENTS

Thank you to all of my family and friends, who have been my avid beta readers, and to my wonderful husband who has supported this re-commitment to my writing. Thank you to my amazing editor Michal Anderson who made this book better and wasn't afraid to give me real - and often funny – feedback. Finally my gratitude to Rena at Cover Quill who designed my beautiful covers for the Born of Shadow's Series.

CHAPTER 1

"Gently..." Helena cooed.

She wrapped her hands around Abby's and helped her guide a delicate paper bird into an intricate wooden cage.

The lovely, but simple, bird held Abby with its two shining, black eyes. Helena had crafted it from fine, white rice paper and though its eyes were merely flecks of obsidian, they bore into her with life.

"Did you create a prayer, love?" Helena asked squeezing Abby's elbow and closing the cage door.

"Yes. I gave it to Sebastian last night," she murmured, taking the bird cage and lifting it before her.

Abby had never performed a death ritual, but Helena, an elder witch at Ula, insisted after Sydney's funeral that Abby and Sebastian would benefit from the consummation. She looked forward to a day alone with Sebastian, but her heart beat oddly at the thought of releasing Sydney's spirit.

She had returned to the Coven of Ula the day before with Oliver and Dafne. When they had crossed through the passageway beneath the cliffs to enter the sparkling lagoon that flanked the castle, Abby felt a great weight lift from her body. For the first time in days, a peaceful calm stole over her.

She had driven home to Ula in silence with Oliver and Dafne. Oliver seemed intent on giving her space to grieve and Dafne simply preferred silence, generally the uncomfortable kind. Abby preferred it as well simply because she needed time to process. While at Sydney's lake house, now her mother's lake house since Sydney's death, she had learned that her Grandma Arlene had also been a witch and had visited the Coven of Ula sometime in the past. Abby pictured the box that her grandmother had left for her, more than a decade before, and considered retrieving it before her ritual with Sebastian. She wondered again what had transpired in the years before her Grandmother's death that made her so sure that Abby would become a witch.

Sebastian's appearance pulled her from her thoughts.

"Hello, my witchy woman."

He strode into the room and kissed her hard on the mouth, jostling her cage and eliciting an anxious groan from Helena. Abby pressed her fingers into his mop of black curls, and kissed his cheeks and eyelids.

Abby had met Sebastian less than three months before and yet in the short time they'd known each other, the experiences of a thousand lifetimes had transpired. She had gone from being an ordinary young woman, unhappy with her life, to an emerging witch living in a magical castle on a secret island in Lake Superior.

"I've missed you," he told her, nuzzling her neck.

"She was sitting in your lap at breakfast," Helena laughed and hugged them both together. "Young love is intoxicating. I'm drunk just standing here with you two."

"Thank you for this," Sebastian told her, growing serious. He gestured to the tiny bird and kissed Helena on the cheek.

"Are we ready?" Abby asked.

"Ready when you are." He held up a canvas bag.

"What is it?" Abby asked, but he closed it before she could peek.

"It's a surprise," he whispered and kissed her again, softly this time and, when he pulled away, Abby almost refused to let go.

They both wanted so badly for the day to go well. Abby felt their stifled energies bouncing back and forth between them. They had never had a real romance--only stolen moments flung into the tumultuous world of death, witchcraft and mystery that they now both inhabited. Sometimes Abby wondered what their relationship might have become if there had been no Devin, no Vepars and no witches. She ignored the possibility that, without those elements, she and Sebastian would never have met at all. Perhaps, without her inner calling, she would have stayed with her ex-boyfriend Nick and moved through the world as his soft and pliable shadow.

"Let the adventure begin," he said, carefully taking the cage.

Abby nodded and accepted Helena's quick, fierce hug.

****

Abby and Sebastian walked away from the castle, meandering beyond the second lagoon. The island that the Coven of Ula inhabited in the Upper Peninsula of Michigan was sprawling and picturesque. In October everything shimmered in gold. Amber colored leaves and the sweet golden light of autumn created its own magic.

They followed a trail that Helena had described in detail the night before. A large forest of old-growth cedars stood at the southern tip of the island. The dense canopy of trees blocked most of the light from their footpath. Abby walked mindfully, carefully side-stepping any signs of life on the forest floor. As she grew more connected to the energy of the earth, she felt spirit in everything. At times she shuddered to squish a blade of grass.

"Hey, check it out," Sebastian exclaimed, pointing ahead.

An ancient-looking stone stairway curved up out of the forest floor, roughly chiseled into a corroded limestone wall. The stairs were moss covered and crumbling. A delicate braid of flowers and vines created an archway over the stairs. Handmade chimes hung from a low-hanging branch. They tinkled softly in the breeze.

"Shall we?" Sebastian asked, holding out his hand.

She took it and bit back the warning that the steps looked ready to collapse.

They walked slowly, pebbles sliding underfoot and toppling to the leafy forest floor. Overhead orange and gold leaves shimmered in the mid-day sun.

Abby felt her heart rise into her throat when they left the stairwell and emerged into the cliff-top meadow that Helena had described the night before.

"The floating garden," Abby murmured and knew that she had plucked its name from a collective mind that was not her own, but a dozen cumulative witches' memories.

They were not in a field and not in a forest, but a lovely marriage of the two with twisted trees that plunged into the earth, their branches rose ecstatically toward the blue sky. The ground was a dazzling parade of violets and yellows and reds, the flowers in full blooms of magenta and turquoise. Radiant gold reeds floated next to heaps of glossy ferns. In October, the flowers should have been dead, dried and crumbling onto beds of browning leaves, but in this enchanted garden, the plants lived on. The flowers, however, held only a piece of the charm. The whole garden appeared to genuinely float. The meadow flowed into blue sky and Abby steadied her hand against Sebastian's back to calm the sense that she'd left solid ground.

"Whoa," he laughed, teetering momentarily to the side. He moved hastily to one of the gnarled trees. He placed a palm against it and then quickly pulled away.

"Touch it," he told her.

She did and a thousand voices converged in her mind. Not human voices, but the twittering and whispering and laughter of some other life. She leaned into the tree and rested her forehead against it, an overpowering sense of love embracing her. For an instant, she swooned and then the sensations subsided and she returned, sort of, to reality.

A narrow red stone path wound through the garden and, when they both felt confident of their footing, they picked their way along, single file, neither wanting to crush even a petal.

Abby could not see the cliff edge ahead. The trees' hanging branches blocked their view, but Helena said that they would know the right spot when they found it. A blue and black butterfly drifted lazily ahead of

Sebastian, alighting briefly on the bird cage before she took flight.

"A blessing," he said, clearly delighted by the small creature as she danced away.

Abby felt a strong surge of Yes and grinned as the butterfly disappeared into a mass of purple chrysanthemums.

"Whoa, careful," Sebastian called back, stopping abruptly. The flowers did not end, but trickled over the steep cliff edge. The rock wall plunged one-thousand or more feet, ending at a platoon of jagged rocks that drowned again and again in the surging dark water.

Abby turned in a slow circle, looking behind her, but as she shifted her gaze, she spotted an outcrop twenty feet below them. It was a flat rock ledge, heavy with flowers and, in its center, stood a still pond. Beside the pond lay an enormous starry quilt.

"That must be for us..." Sebastian said, taking Abby's hand and starting along the cliff.

Abby felt the tiniest prick of fear at the thought of getting to the blanket. It was such a long way to fall. One small slip of a foot and... But before the fear could take hold, her heart swelled and she felt overwhelmed by the power within her and more, by the power surging from the enormous lake below. She felt light enough to fly.

They discovered another stairway, this one significantly cruder than the last. It was cut into the side of the cliff and reminded Abby of that dark hole in the earth where the Lourdes of Warning lived. She blinked the memory away.

"Okay, let's do it," she murmured and picked her way down the stairs. She demanded that Sebastian let her carry the bird cage, despite his insistence that he could handle it.

Once settled comfortably on the quilt, Abby pulled the small scroll that contained her incantation from her pocket. She unfurled it gently, holding it flat against a rock on the pool's edge. She glanced down and caught her reflection. Her curly hair was wild and the blissful smile on her face rendered her momentarily unrecognizable. When had she ever smiled like that?

Sebastian moved behind her and wrapped his arms around her waist. She sighed heavily, happily and they stood for a moment letting time ebb away. She breathed deeply and savored the scent of cinnamon on his breath and the steady pressure of his chest as it rose and fell into her back. A lump moved into her diaphragm and her throat caught and she resisted the urge to turn around and sob uncontrollably against him. The dark mood passed and, when he released her, she returned to the scroll.

Abby shrugged off her boots and turned towards the sky, opening her arms wide. She moved ankle-deep into the soft, cold water of the pool and began to chant. Sebastian murmured in unison, looking to his own copy of the prayer.

Her chant was written in Latin, translated by dictionary, but as she whispered a final call to her beloved Aunt Sydney, the words grew into giants reaching into the sky to bring the spirit of her aunt back to her one last time.

She turned in a circle counter-clockwise and the water began to turn with her.

Behind her, Sebastian opened the bird cage. The tiny paper bird rested on his hand and he looked uncertainly at Abby. She nodded and he held it toward the sky.

The water churned faster, whirl-pooling up to her knees.

Overhead the blank, blue sky swirled with the water beneath her. A flash, white and blinding, streaked down to them.

Abby heard paper wings gently rubbing and turned to see Sebastian watching the paper bird, transfixed.

He moved to her and she cupped her palms around his. The paper wings flapped and fluttered and the tiny, inky eye blinked once before the wind caught her and she took flight.

"Oh," Abby reached out, and almost thought of clutching the bird, but Sebastian stopped her, pulling her closer to him. They watched the paper bird glide high and then drop and spiral back down to them. It lit just above their heads, skimmed across the garden and then turned out to Lake Superior where it quickly disappeared over the horizon.

"Goodbye," Abby breathed.

****

"What is it, love? You seem so...far away today?" Elda asked Bridget gently.

They were in the elixirs room, bottles stacked to the ceiling, all with tiny neat labels in Bridget's perfect calligraphy.

Bridget's brow furrowed and she stood on a step stool, hovering over satchels of dried herbs. Her round body held the grace of someone much more proportional.

"It's something, some sign..." She trailed off and Elda moved closer, sensing her distress.

Bridget nearly always exuded a supreme aura of tranquility and any agitation in her energy immediately alerted Elda.

"Tell me," she prodded her. Bridget, one of the coven's most intuitive witches, was also one of their most unsure. She came to her powers late in life and never truly felt at ease with them.

"Twice now, when I've been mixing the elixir of Samhain, a symbol has appeared."

Bridget did not look Elda in the eyes, but instead hurriedly began crushing herbs in her mortar, sprinkling in bits of cacao.

"What symbol did you see, dear?" Elda continued, gently.

"Well, I cannot be sure, but it seemed to be a...a black widow spider."

Elda frowned and immediately opened herself to the coven. Could she sense some treachery? Bad tidings? Nothing, nothing out of the ordinary. Somewhere, far away, she could feel Abby and Sebastian bidding farewell to Sydney. Closer, she felt the heat of Lydie, angry with Max for pressing her into her astral-travel, but doom? She did not sense that.

"Are you sure, Bridget? Might it not have been some other symbol?"

"Well, of course it might have been." Bridget flustered, wringing her hands. "It might have been a flower, for Pete's sake. I mean, you know how off I can sometimes be..."

But that wasn't true. Not really. Bridget was rarely off, but Elda could nearly always validate her intuition. She had merely to tune into the symbol, the premonition, and it would rise up from its shadow and be known. This time, she felt nothing strange at all. In fact, she felt a profound sense of peace and good tidings.

"Knock, knock," Helena called. She walked in behind them, holding a bundle of dried sage.

Bridget hurried over and took the sage. Elda understood that, for now, the subject had been dropped.

****

Sebastian had packed them a picnic, including Sydney's favorite coconut cake, which he had baked for the occasion. They ate sandwiches and fruit and talked about the good times that they had both spent with Sydney in their earlier lives. Abby hung on Sebastian's every word, loving the stories of Sydney that he alone claimed.

"Oh, she was a nightmare around my dad," he sighed, leaning back on his elbows and grinning at the sky. "A terrible flirt, and it drove my mom wild. I still remember one summer we went to visit her with Grams for a long weekend, and Sydney came trotting out to our van wearing high heels and a white bathing suit. White, practically see-through! I swear I could see smoke coming out of my mom's ears."

Abby giggled and took another gulp of sweet cherry wine. The alcohol softened the edges of the world and she felt dizzy and buoyant.

"Yeah, she had no filters. When she met Rod, I think she finally found her match."

Abby had liked Rod and, more, she liked Sydney with Rod. Sydney found in Rod a kindred spirit. Abby remembered them always laughing, and when they weren't laughing they were kissing and openly groping each other.

"To tell you the truth," Sebastian laughed, "I had a crush on her until I was a teenager. She was just so...sexy."

Abby nodded. "Oh, I know. I practically had a crush on her, and not just because she was beautiful, but so alive. When she walked into a room, she lit it on fire. My mom loathed her."

"Really?"

"Yeah, she was insanely jealous of Sydney, had been since childhood from what I gathered."

Abby pictured the sour face that her mother made whenever she spoke of her sister.

"I get that," he said, taking a drink directly from the bottle. "Siblings that are so different are bound to clash."

"How about you and Claire? Ever fight?" Abby had almost not asked the question, afraid that the mention of Sebastian's murdered sister would send him into a funk, but he smiled and shrugged.

"Sure, when we were young. We fought over the remote control and who got the toy out of the cereal box and dumb stuff like that. There was never real animosity though. She was four years younger than me so we spent most of our lives in different phases. By the time she hit the hard part of puberty, I was a young adult and so on. When our parents died, everything changed. She became this innocent child that I had to protect and then, when she learned that she was a witch, our roles were almost beginning to reverse. She grew defiant and, honestly, stronger than me. It freaked me out, but still we didn't fight. We just started to grow apart."

Abby nodded, understanding, but not. She didn't have siblings and, though she longed for them as a child, she felt grateful too. Her mother always appeared so preoccupied or worse, too occupied. Abby moved from the white-hot beam of her mother's gaze into the cold, dark shadows without a lot of happy medium between the two.

"Isn't it strange that we were all in the Astral Book of Shadows?" Abby said, chewing a strand of hair. "I mean Claire, Devin and me."

Sebastian nodded.

"Yeah. Do you remember Adora, the witch I told you that discovered Claire? She constantly stressed paying attention to synchronicities. Those conversations have stuck with me more than anything else she said. It didn't have the same effect on Claire though, and I think if it had..."

"She wouldn't have fallen for Tobias."

Sebastian grimaced at the sound of his name.

"Yes, she might have recognized how eerily convenient it was for him to come into her life and be so comfortable with the witch stuff."

"Maybe she just wanted to believe that she could have that too--the magic and the love."

He looked up sharply at Abby and she frowned down at her hands.

"Are you afraid of that, Abby? That you can't have both?"

She bit her lip and returned his gaze, not wanting to admit that she felt exactly that.

He rubbed the stubble on his chin, frowning and then seemed to change his mind. He scooted across the blanket and pulled Abby into his lap. He wrapped his arms around her waist and she caved into him, watching a seagull swoop towards the water far in the distance.

His breath was hot in her hair and, when she tilted back to look at him, his lips found hers and pressed hungrily against her mouth. She kissed him back, suddenly feeling as if he might slip away and be gone forever. They both grew more desperate, tugging at clothes, until they were nearly naked, legs and arms encircling the other. He slid on top of her and his eyes looked starved as he pressed his face into her hair and breathed her in.

****

Dafne watched them making love, but felt nothing. Their bodies were one, a single trembling flesh and, had she wanted to, she might have remembered a similar love in her own life so long ago that it no longer belonged to her at all. Instead, she closed her eyes and began to chant. She drew the heavens down to meet her outstretched palms and the earth up to her lips and wove the beginnings of their collapse.

In the empty space before her, she stitched their souls together and then, forcefully, she tore them apart, flinging their beams of light to the furthest reaches of the darkest night.

"Not lost, but alone," she whispered. "Together no more, no more, no more."

The fates had spoken and Dafne had taken it upon herself to rid Ula of the toxic parasite that had stumbled into her womb. She would eradicate it and cast the evil far, far away where it could find them no more.

For an instant, the sky grew dark and venomous and Dafne jerked her head once to direct that shadow into the lovers. She saw it slip between them, undetectable, like a breath of air.

The wind blew her cloak around her and something poked at the back of her head. She batted it forcefully away. It struck the ground and her eyes followed the crumpled shape of the paper bird as it tumbled over the cliff's edge to the rushing water below.

CHAPTER 2

Lydia wandered into the dining hall the following morning. A tired Sebastian stared irritably into his coffee.

"Where is everybody?" she yawned, grabbing a cinnamon roll and plopping down across from him. She eyed him wearily, taking note of his rumpled t-shirt and tousled hair. It was typical Sebastian attire, but somehow that morning he seemed even more disheveled than usual.

"Not a clue," he told her, picking at a plate of scrambled eggs and not looking up.

"Long night?"

He glanced at her, as if seeing her for the first time and then gave a curt nod. "Nightmares."

"I get that," she told him, pulling her knees to her chest and hugging them tightly. Her pajamas were covered in small red monkeys, a Helena purchase, and she picked absently at their glittery faces.

"Do you ever feel like something comes in and takes over at night? Some night monster just creeps in while you're off swimming on the moon and you wake up with this whole other being inside you?"

Lydie crinkled her brow and shrugged.

"Sometimes Oliver sticks my finger in water while I'm sleeping to try to make me pee," she told him, pretty sure that she was missing the mark.

Sebastian didn't respond, but instead stood abruptly and left the hall, taking his plate with him.

He returned to his room and sat on the edge of his bed, considering his drawer of tinctures, but not feeling moved to take anything. The dream had been vivid and terrifying, but, in the light of day, its edges were blurred and grainy.

Claire had come to him. She pleaded for help, insisting that she was trapped, until he avenged her. Where had they been? In a cave? He knew only that it was dark and wet and he had been afraid. It was a strange dream, like nothing he had ever experienced, and he could not shake the feeling that it was real and that Claire had been calling out for his help. He held tightly to her plea.

Abby had been gone when he rose from sleep. She had stayed in his room the night before, both of them clinging a bit longer to the sweetness of the previous day, but when he awoke to an empty bed, he did not go find her. He needed to contemplate the dream and Abby wouldn't get it. In fact, he felt strangely convinced that she wanted to prevent him from helping Claire. It didn't make sense. She had never implied such a thing, but something in the pit of his stomach demanded that he keep the dream a secret.

****

"So, what does this mean for Sebastian?" Abby asked. She had cornered Elda in the scallop-shaped greenhouse that bordered the second lagoon.

Elda, a superior witch at the coven of Ula, and Abby's often mentor, pursed her lips and picked up the envelope that Abby had dropped on the table before her.

It contained an invitation given to Abby the previous week by Oliver, while she attended the funeral of her Aunt Sydney. She had tucked the invitation into her grandmother's wood box and not removed it until she had an opportunity to speak with Elda alone. It had been difficult not to bring it up with Sebastian the day before, but she didn't want to taint their day with a party that may or may not include him.

Elda picked up the envelope and lifted it to her nose, inhaling.

"Heliotrope," she whispered. "Every invitation is scented with the coven's themed flower. Sorciére uses heliotrope abundantly." Elda waved the envelope in the air sending wafts of the floral scent into the room. "We get this delightful smell for years and years. You know, Abby, I have All Hallow's invitations that are decades old, which still smell of their coven's signature flower."

"Sebastian?" Abby asked again, not allowing the change of subject.

"Sebastian is not a witch."

"So he can't go?"

"That's not what I said."

"Please, can we cut the cloak and dagger?" Abby's patience with the elder witch was running thin. She was tired and, honestly, a bit grumpy. Her night had been restless and plagued with nightmares and a tossing Sebastian beside her. She'd welcomed the dawn so that she could slip out of the bed that felt too small.

Elda avoided Abby's eyes, returning to the flowers that she meticulously trimmed. Her fingers were shock blue from the violet petals that she lovingly touched.

"If Sebastian were to go, we would have to conceal him very carefully. If anyone were to find out..."

"What?" Abby asked. "What would happen?"

Elda frowned, but did not shift her eyes from the flowers.

"Anything could happen. But, as you know, anything can always happen and we can't live our lives fearing the possibilities."

"Would the other witches be angry?"

"Perhaps. Dafne, for instance, is already angry, but she is part of our coven and won't act on those feelings. I cannot say the same for other witches."

"But what about the oath 'harm none'?"

"Well, there are witches who would flip that question back to us. We are bringing a human into a magical world, a world that he can barely fathom, let alone survive in. We are exposing other witches to his weakness when we bring him into their covens."

Elda wiped her blue fingers on a white rag, but no inky prints appeared.

"Vepars have very strong powers over regular people, Abby. I know that you believe Sebastian is immune, but has he ever really faced one alone? Does he truly know that they are unable to penetrate his mind? Is he sure that they could not seduce him with the promise of bringing his sister back from the dead?"

"That's absurd," Abby snapped. "He would never help them."

However, Abby did not know if she believed her words and neither did Elda who sighed, but said nothing.

"You don't know what Sebastian would do and neither does he, for that matter."

"So, what then? He shouldn't go?" Abby asked, brushing her index finger along the blue plant. It burned and she pulled her hand away quickly, but before she could stick the throbbing finger into her mouth, Elda jerked it back.

"That's poisonous."

She picked up a small glass bottle from the table and squirted Abby's finger twice.

"You always put a neutralizer on before touching the plants. I'm sure Bridget has told you that."

Abby nodded. Bridget had told her, but she'd forgotten.

"You seem distracted," Elda murmured.

Abby nodded.

"I'm just really tired and, honestly, worried about this party."

"He can go, if that's what you want. But think on it first. Our decisions do not merely affect us. On a separate note, Faustine went to Trager City and had Danny released from jail."

"Really, that's great. But how?" Abby asked, surprised. Danny was the adopted brother of Devin, the girl that Abby had found murdered several months before. The discovery of Devin's body had seemed to trigger the events that led to Abby uncovering her own powers. Danny had been framed for Devin's murder by the Vepars that killed her.

"He brought some potentially damning errors in the investigation to the new Chief of Police's attention. He said it was quite easy actually. He barely used any magic at all. The man is so concerned with his career, he would move mountains to keep the issues from coming to light."

"What issues?"

"Well that's where the magic came in. Suffice it to say that Danny is free."

Before Abby could ask more, Elda had turned and disappeared deeper into the greenhouse.

****

After leaving Elda, Abby circled the edge of the lagoon several times, considering Sebastian. She loved him deeply but, upon waking that morning, she felt strangeness between them. It did not make sense. They had spent the most wonderful day together and fallen into bed, drunk with their love. Still, that morning, she had watched him sleep, unable to shake the feeling that he was deceiving her in some way.

She knew that the other witches felt uneasy around Sebastian. Human emotions were volatile, and often fear based, as Oliver had told her a million times. Their emotions made them weak, which Abby found vaguely hilarious since, lately, emotions had been consuming her every moment. According to Oliver, the more emotional humans were, the more easily Vepars gained control of their minds.

She felt sure that Helena's suggestion of the grief ritual grew from the hope that releasing Sydney would help Sebastian find peace. Twenty-four hours earlier, Abby would have agreed, but in the light of a new day, she felt less secure. Had it been a dream or some sign in the night that triggered this anxiousness in the pit of her belly?

When she found no solace in the lapping water, she returned to the library, hoping that some book might hold the answer to her growing unrest.

She found Helena, seated next to the fire, staring intently into an unfamiliar mirror that was partially draped in a dark afghan. The mirror stood at least seven feet tall. The gilded edges were carved with tiny howling faces.

When Abby stepped before it, her image trembled in waves. Her body undulated a long sigh from her curled hair to her bare feet. Her shifting image reminded her dreamily of the county fair fun-house mirrors. In one mirror you were tall and skeletal, while another revealed a warped ghoul with a pinched face and squat body.

"Mirror, mirror on the wall" Helena murmured cheerfully, waving her hands so that her bracelets chimed.

The fall days cooled the castle considerably and made the library's enormous fireplace a frequent stop for the coven's inhabitants, even during the daytime. It was not unusual to see Helena warming by the fire.

Abby stood next to her, allowing the flames to bake her skin through her pant legs.

"Your hair looks lovely," Helena told her, not shifting her eyes from the mirror image.

Abby touched it absently, fingering a fat curl. Her cropped hair had grown much longer since arriving at the castle and, weeks earlier, it had suddenly begun to curl in thick waves. Her previously short hair, which she'd chopped off in a rage only a month and a half before, now fell to the center of her back.

"Thank you; it's strange though, isn't it?"

"Not so strange," Helena smiled, reaching back to her own thick, auburn ponytail and giving it a tug. "Mine was blonde, platinum blonde, when my powers first appeared. Then one morning I woke up and it was a little darker and each day after that until I got this."

"Platinum blonde?" Abby stood in front of the mirror examining her image.

"Yep, it's like puberty for a witch. But instead of getting acne and cramps, your hair has a midlife crisis and people start asking why you're wearing wigs."

"Any other changes I should be aware of?"

"Oh, there are loads." Helena scooted along the floor and rested her back against an itchy purple loveseat. "My nails grew really long, toenails too," she rolled her eyes, "but there are spells to slow those down."

"Yuck, toenails too."

Abby looked at her hands. Her fingernails did look better--no more stubby, broken ends.

"So why do we have this magic mirror?" Abby asked. It took time adjusting to the idea that she was a witch and that she belonged at Ula. Saying things like 'we' and 'us' used to make her look around self-consciously and wait for someone to correct her. Each day the coven became more familiar and her space within it more a fixture and less a decoration.

"It's for All Hallows Eve," Helena told her. "We walk through it."

There it was again. All Hallow's Eve and the big party at the Coven of Sorciére in Bordeaux, France. The party that Sebastian had not been invited to and Abby had been keeping secret from him.

"We walk through it? How?"

"Well, whoever throws the All Hallows Party each year is under obligation to provide mirrors to all of the participating covens. They create a fold in space on the night of the event and we just walk right through."

Abby leaned into the mirror until her nose nearly touched it. She wanted to stick a hand forward and see if it slipped through the glass.

"What do you mean create a fold in space? How is that possible?"

"Anything is possible," Helena quipped, standing and walking to the mirror. "But space is especially malleable. You see, when we go to France we are simply moving energy through space. If we drop the illusion that we are here and they are there, we can jump right to them. Let me not reduce it though," Helena added quickly. "These are spells that take the energies and commitment of a dozen powerful witches and the gateway is opened over time. The thinning of the veil is like a decrease in tangible reality. It's the perfect night to enact such a spell."

Abby still didn't understand but, in the moment, she was too entranced by the mirror to ask for clarification.

"Can I touch it?" she asked.

"Absolutely, but you won't get much out of it today. The mirrors are bewitched on the day of the party."

Abby reached a finger forward. Solid, the glass felt cool and did not bend beneath the pressure of her touch.

"Can anyone walk through it?"

"Sure, though the experience is not for everyone."

****

Sebastian heard Abby's voice as he passed the library. He quickened his pace, but did not glance behind him. He needed to find Claire's journals. It had been gnawing at him for hours, this feeling that the answers lay hidden there.

He walked along the curving, stone staircase that led to the dungeons of Ula. He had visited the dungeons only once to help Max carry several boxes of crystals to the room that Elda called The Circle. It was here that Sebastian spied the journals. Prior to that, the lowest level that he had visited was the Healing Room when Abby had nearly died after traveling in her astral body, but that was two floors above The Circle and on the other side of the castle. The bowels of the castle seemed to be calling him. Invisible fingers guided his journey down.

He felt confident that Elda kept important information in the stone room and he was intent on finding it. He had relinquished The Astral Book of Shadows to her when he first arrived at the castle and now regretted it. She had also asked for Claire's journals with the promise that she would return them, but she had not mentioned them since.

He rarely wandered the castle and sneaking into the dungeons made him feel almost criminal. More so, he felt angry that he should have to seek out the journals in secret, but they would question his motives if he asked for them. Even Abby would scrutinize him. She wouldn't understand. She had lost Sydney, yes, but a sister? And she was one of them, a witch, a powerful being who now served the earth.

Even as these thoughts skidded through his mind, growing in strength, he felt incredulous that overnight he had undergone such a fierce transformation. The day before he had been ready to release his vengeance and devote his life to Abby and to uncovering her new world. Now he felt only a mad desperation to avenge his sister. Claire had come to him, she needed his help and no one would stand in his way.

The stairs wound down and narrowed until his shoulders nearly touched on either side. Fewer doorways lined the walls and the candle sconces appeared less and less. Soon he moved in almost total darkness, carefully planting each step and keeping his right hand pressed against the wall for guidance. The silence was almost unbearable and twice he stopped, turned around and nearly went back.

****

That evening the coven ate dinner on one of the many stone porches that jutted from the castle's foreboding exterior. Candles flickered and everyone's faces wore the grotesque orange shadows of Jack-O-Lanterns. The wrought iron table was littered with dried flowers, and incense wafted from two wooden gargoyles at the table's ends.

Abby shifted in her chair, casting anxious glances at Sebastian who sat next to her, his eyes vacant. He wore the same rumpled t-shirt and sweats that he'd gone to bed in the night before.

"Corn bread?" she asked him, holding up her uneaten bread and hoping desperately for some small recognition.

He blinked, gazed toward it and shook his head.

"I'm full."

He had barely touched his chili and a full glass of spiced cider sat at his elbow. Nothing gave Sebastian away like food. He ate more than a pack of wild dogs and Helena teased him for it incessantly.

Abby caught Elda's eye and looked quickly away. She did not want to alert the witch to any curious behavior. Lydie let out a high-pitched giggle at some comment from Oliver who looked relaxed and happy as usual.

Only Dafne seemed irritable and, when she caught Abby looking her way, she arched her eyebrows and glared back at her. Abby held her stare, growing angrier with each passing second, and then she flashed on a similar evening little more than a month earlier when her unkempt rage had destroyed a set of wine goblets. She returned her eyes to her food and picked absently at her napkin.

A red moon had begun its ascent over the water and all of the witches turned to watch as it climbed the night sky.

"The autumn moon," Helena cooed lovingly, stretching her fingers toward the rising orb. Everyone seemed to sigh in unison as the cosmos came alive with the night.

Abby watched the stars and sipped her cider. She tried to block out the strained energy between her and Sebastian. Fireflies began to appear at the table's edge and their glowing bodies made Lydie hoot with glee as she dashed from her chair to scoop one up. She did not cage it, however, as Abby had done as a girl. She leaned her face close, whispered a secret and released it. Oliver joined her, and soon Abby could not sit any longer and followed them from the table, making ever widening circles, until they had left the porch and wandered into one of the many gardens.

****

"Abby."

The whisper barely registered. In her dreams, Abby stood in a dark forest where snow fell in huge gusts. She felt the ice biting into her legs and blinked rapidly against the freezing gale. She saw Sebastian, almost lost in the blizzard before her. She tried to call out to him, but her voice made no sound. From the darkness, a shadow emerged. A small woman deeply enveloped in furs took his hand. Abby screamed again, sensing danger, and tried to run through the thick snow to stop him. He followed the woman and, despite Abby's efforts, they disappeared into the storm.

"Abby," the whisper came again, louder, and Abby felt a hand on her arm, cold fingers splayed over her bicep.

She groaned and rolled away from the touch, needing to stay connected to the fleeting remnants of their footprints.

"Hey, wake up." The voice grew familiar, Sebastian's voice, and Abby finally allowed the images to fade.

She blinked the room into focus.

"You were moaning," he told her, pulling the comforter gently from her clenched fists. She grabbed him and hugged him against her, burying her face in his shoulder.

"Well, good morning to you too," he laughed, pulling away and looking into her face. "Are you okay?"

"Yeah, I'm just..." She closed her eyes and shook the dream away. "I guess I was having a nightmare."

"Do you remember it?"

She shook her head but, in fact, she did remember the dream. She remembered the feeling that if he disappeared into the woods, he would be lost forever.

"It took a long time to get you up. I thought maybe you were traveling."

Astral-traveling, he meant. Which Abby never did while sleeping. They were not the same thing, but Sebastian was not a witch and thus often confused many of the powers. He called high jumps flying and seemed to believe that her night vision equated to x-ray goggles. More than once he had asked her about his boxer choice, as if she could see through his pants.

"Can't remember any of it?" He asked again and this time she detected a note of suspicion in his voice.

"No," she sighed, rolling away from him. The night sky was a sickly green, storms approaching, and Abby knew that the next day she was supposed to work on her element at the second lagoon. The lagoon held a large stone slab that directed each of the witches' power in their given element--in Abby's case, water.

"Do you want to talk?" Sebastian asked and Abby, tired, almost said, "No." But then Sebastian had been acting so strange, and she longed to rekindle the connection that had been so strong only a few days before when they'd said their final goodbyes to Sydney.

"Of course." She rolled back to him and pulled him toward her by his t-shirt. He kissed her on the forehead and then slid back.

She moaned and started to pull him again, but his t-shirt slid up and Abby could see the initials tattooed on his bicep--COH for Claire Olivia Hull, his dead sister. The tattoo looked fresh, the black calligraphy more pronounced than she remembered.

"Did you get that touched up?" she asked, knowing that he couldn't have. He had not left the coven since their arrival nearly six weeks earlier.

"I did it yesterday," he said simply, touching the skin near the tattoo, which Abby realized looked red and slightly puckered.

"With a needle?" she asked, surprised.

"Yeah, a needle and some ink that Helena gave me."

"But why?"

He looked at her strangely and pulled his sleeve down, covering the inflamed skin.

"To remember. That's why I got it in the first place."

Abby sucked her cheeks in and bit back the words on her tongue. It was not appropriate to be jealous of Sebastian's dead sister.

"Why is it an issue?" he demanded, stepping from the bed and dropping to his hands and knees.

"What are you doing?" she asked, peering over the side.

"What does it look like? I'm getting my shoes so I can go back to my room."

"Oh, come on, Sebastian. Just stay, I didn't mean anything..." But that was not true. She wanted him to stop obsessing over Claire. She wanted him to behave differently at the coven and stop talking about the Vepars, but she hadn't said any of that to him and felt as if she couldn't. More strange, she'd barely thought of Claire in weeks, but suddenly the dead witch seemed to be filling all of the chasms newly erected between her and Sebastian.

"Just get some sleep," he told her, grabbing his sweatshirt off the floor and leaving the room. He didn't slam the door, but still she jumped when it clicked in the frame.

rcié

CHAPTER 3

For two days, Abby did not see Sebastian. The approaching All Hallow's
Ball, combined with a seemingly endless list of distractions, left everyone at
Ula surprisingly busy. Abby spent the day in the dungeon memorizing
mantras to invoke the spirit. She sat on the stone floor and meditated, but
the cold bit into the back of her legs and she wriggled uncomfortably. Elda
sat on a stool nearby, her eyes closed and lips parted. She too was
meditating, in addition to giving Abby directions.

"Ommmmmmmn," Abby began again, making the sound deep in her
belly and allowing it to continue long after breath had left her.

Elda joined in the chant and Abby felt the vibrations that they each
emitted traveling the length of her body. It took her away from her mind,
but as soon as she returned to silence, her thoughts took hold again--mostly
thoughts of Sebastian and her inability to accept his chilly behavior.

"Concentrate, Abby--not on your mind, but on the stillness of this
moment," Elda directed.

Abby closed her eyes again.

"This time, begin with the mantra HRIM. When you make the sound,
lose yourself in it. The thoughts in your mind are not real, just let them go
and be here now."

Abby started again. "Hreeeeeemmmmm."

As long as she held the chant, she felt energetically charged. Her body
pulsed and goose-bumps prickled along her neck.

"Now," Elda began. "Without stopping your mantra, bring rain into the
dungeon."

"Hreeeeeemmmmm," Abby continued, though she did not imagine a
dark cloud bursting with rain. Instead envisioned droplets on her face and
the electrical current of the storm. She stayed there, but the more she felt
those imaginary droplets, the more she thought of Sebastian. She
remembered the night at Sydney's lake house, when they'd run along the
beach during a spontaneous rainstorm. She knew now that the storm had
been a manifestation of her growing power, but she was less concerned
with that than Sebastian's hand in hers and the exhilaration at their decision
to search for Devin's killer.

"Abby? Abby, come back?" Elda demanded.

Abby opened her eyes to Elda who looked mildly perturbed.

"I'm sorry," she said, exasperated. "I have a lot on my mind."

"Clearly. Let's finish here for today, but you must work at the lagoon. I have a ritual to prepare you for tomorrow's summoning that will probably take you until late tonight."

Abby nodded, but hated the thought of spending the rest of the evening locked in her room chanting and waving incense. She wanted to have a conversation with Sebastian, but feared his response to the questions in her mind.

****

Sebastian pushed the swinging door into the kitchen. Bridget sat on a high wooden table, both feet propped on a stool in front of her, an open cookbook resting in her lap.

"Lured by the sweet scent?" Bridget asked, waving toward the enormous antique oven where several pots released tendrils of steam.

He could smell ginger and garlic, maybe some cinnamon.

"Mmmm, what's cooking?" he asked, lifting a lid and peering into a black gelatinous pool that smelled of vinegar.

"Bad choice. That's a potion for Faustine," Bridget laughed. "He's suffering from an especially persistent foot fungus."

Sebastian wrinkled his nose and pulled away.

He had only been in the kitchen a couple of times, but found that he thought of it often. He missed cooking, a hobby that had also become a lifeline for him in the time before the coven. When he cooked, he turned off his thoughts and focused entirely on the meal. His mother had taken great pride in teaching her only son how to cook. Later, when his entire family lay dead beneath faceless tombs, he found solace in preparing food. Sometimes he made elaborate dinners that only he enjoyed. His masterpiece had been a Paella Valencia, which he prepared during a two-month stay in Texas before he finally booked his flight to Panama in search of his sister's killer.

He had cooked daily in Texas while renting a small efficiency that lacked everything except a functional stove and refrigerator. He gained twenty pounds during those two months, which he lost in three short weeks in Panama fighting constant diarrhea and nausea after being stricken with malaria. The malaria persisted throughout his stay and the staple food that he survived on during the trip--rice--now made his stomach churn at the thought. His trip had been a disaster. In addition to not finding a single clue as to Tobias's whereabouts, he spent most of his time occupying bathrooms until he finally flew home and spent three days in the hospital recovering.

Sydney's home on the lake had symbolized a new hope.

"Which sounds better? Red velvet cupcakes or black forest chocolate?" Bridget asked, holding up her copy of A Million Cupcakes to Make You Smile.

"I like the one shaped like a spider," he said pointing to the cover.

A strange look crossed her features, but then she flipped the book over and grinned.

"Dark chocolate cake with chocolate ganache. It's rich, but I like it," she said, nodding her approval.

"So do you need any help?" Sebastian asked hopefully, knowing that Bridget, a witch, did not need any help.

She looked at him for another moment and then opened her hands wide.

"Of course, the cook needs a vacation sometimes too. Why don't you whip up a couple of sides for dinner?"

"Really?" he asked, not bothering to hide his relief. Finally, a space to feel useful.

"Yep. We're looking at Minestrone for the main dish so whatever sounds good with that."

"Awesome, yes, okay." He immediately started getting familiar with the kitchen, opening cupboards and drawers. "This place is fully equipped," he said scanning a shelf lined with at least two hundred spices.

"Then you should have all you need," Bridget chirped, hopping down from the table. "I will be off to the garden then to collect a few things for Faustine's potion."

She patted Sebastian motherly as she left and he sighed happily, staring at the empty counter space before him.

****

"So why haven't you told Sebastian about the party?" Oliver asked, burrowing his bare feet into the cold sand.

They stood near the stone slab at the second lagoon where Abby had been trying to concentrate for the better part of an hour after Elda had finally released her from the dungeon. The new goal that Elda had given her was to turn the lagoon solid enough that she could walk across. It was not an easy feat.

"Because..." She blew a puff of air out of her cheeks and dipped her hands again into the frigid lagoon waters. Ice cold at first, the water gradually grew hot. She stood again when she felt sufficiently revved up and returned to the slab. "I got the feeling from Elda that he shouldn't go."

Oliver smoothed the sand around his feet and considered.

"You wouldn't know it, but Elda plays a mean devil's advocate."

Abby nodded, sitting on the edge of the slab and not bothering to even look at the water, let alone focus her power there. She was too distracted. On top of that, for days she had felt agitated and quick to anger.

"Have you ever seen a human at an All Hallow's Ball?"

He wrinkled his forehead and picked up a handful of sand.

"If I have, I didn't know it."

Abby bit her lip and thought again of the possibility of sneaking Sebastian into the party. Elda implied that it was possible, but she had not seemed enthused.

"Would Dafne reveal him if we brought Sebastian and pretended that he was a witch?"

Oliver laughed and looked at her sideways.

"It's not that simple, Abby. He can't just wear a costume and hope nobody notices. These are witches, many of whom are clairvoyant. They're not easily deceived."

"Well, Elda said..."

"Oh, I'm not saying it's impossible," he interrupted. "Just that it will take work. You'll have to put a lot of energy into the spells and that means stating a clear intention. Don't try to cloak him when you're having all of these mixed emotions or you're liable to cast him as something worse than human, something dangerous."

"Dangerous." Abby repeated.

Rather than think more on it, she turned her eyes to the lagoon and pushed all of her power into solidifying the dark mass. Ripples broke across the water and then steadied.

Abby walked to the water's edge and put a foot tentatively over the surface. It was solid, sort of, so she stepped onto it completely. Her feet sank down, but she was able to teeter out onto the lagoon. She felt like she walked on firm pudding and, though she expected Oliver to howl and break her focus, he remained quiet.

She walked a few feet further, staring through the gelatinous water at the sandy floor as it sloped beneath her. A white crayfish crawled along the lagoon bed.

"Hey," she yelled. "There's a crayfish right here."

"Yeah?" Oliver called. "Think the water will hold both of us?"

"Sure," Abby said, but didn't really know.

Oliver walked carefully toward her, holding his arms out to both sides and intentionally swaying back and forth. When he reached her, he paused and stared down.

"That fish looks cray," he joked.

Abby laughed.

"It's almost transparent."

"Yeah, how would you like that? To be invisible?"

"I would love that," Abby told him, wishing that more than invisible, she could just disappear altogether. Then she wouldn't have to tell Sebastian anything.

"There are spells you know--to make you invisible."

"Really?" she asked turning to face him. "I think I've done it, accidentally."

"I believe it."

She smiled and returned her gaze to the crayfish that had begun a slow crawl deeper into the lagoon.

"Let's lay on it," Oliver suggested. "Face down."

"Okay," she said, excited by the prospect. In her shoes, she could not tell what the water would feel like. She dropped onto her knees and then placed her hands on the surface expecting something cold and wet. Instead, her palms met a sheet of cold, firm silk that sank a few centimeters when she put her weight on it.

Oliver lay down next to her and they both rested their foreheads against the surface.

"It feels like Jello," Oliver mumbled. "I wish I was a water element."

"Yeah right. You can manipulate earth, that's amazing."

"Nature's waterbed," he laughed and rolled back and forth letting his fingers trail over the undulating surface.

"My opinion is that you don't invite Sebastian," he said. "Just make up some reason that he can't go and leave it at that. I can tell you've already wasted a lot of thought on this."

Abby started to disagree, but she had devoted countless hours to whether Sebastian should go. It had been a constant distraction since Sydney's funeral and Sebastian's growing agitation only amplified her doubts.

Above them, gray storm clouds drew closer. Abby turned onto her back feeling the water dip beneath her, but still the surface stayed firm. She looked up into the bulbous clouds and felt their magnetic energy, the very energy that she had tried to draw in the dungeon earlier that day. They were filled with water, vibrating with the intensity of it and she could almost see the filaments that connected her own energy to that of the rain.

Oliver reached over and squeezed her hand before climbing back to his feet. He helped her up as the first droplets hit the tops of their heads. A crack of thunder snapped Abby's focus. Beneath them the water became liquid again and they both plunged down.

It was icy and Abby felt the breath sucked from her lungs. They were in over their heads, but they both laughed and choked as they struggled back to the beach. When they emerged, Abby spotted Dafne. She stood in the greenhouse, watching them from a circle, smoothed clear, in the fogged windows. Her black eyes locked with Abby's and then her face was gone.

****

"Sebastian?" Abby knocked again and, when he didn't answer, she pushed his door with her foot. It opened and she called his name once. "Sebastian? Are you in here?"

No answer.

Sebastian's room was similar to hers, except the windows faced the lagoon and it was decorated with medieval torture devices that made her shudder whenever she visited him there. One wall held five different axes, their blades revealing slivers of her face in the candlelight.

Sebastian was not an organized guest. His duffel bag lay open on the floor, his clothes a plume of debris surrounding it. An enormous oak desk stood beneath one of his windows covered in books, many lying open, their spines bent back. She walked to the books and glanced casually through them. Every title spoke of Vepars or demons.

Abby knew that Sebastian continued to hunt Tobias, at least in his mind. He had stopped speaking of it with her, but occasionally slipped and let out some Vepar fact or trailed off about some secret location that he wanted to investigate. Abby hated his obsession with the killers. She wanted to forget them, but her opinion seemed of little matter to him lately.

She wanted to bridge the gap, but simply could not find a way. Part of her felt deeply in love with Sebastian, but another part of her felt utterly detached from him. She thought of his beautiful blue eyes that glittered with a mystery that she could not begin to comprehend. She could sit and stare into his eyes and never grow tired of the light that she saw in them. At least she had felt that way a week earlier, but doubt had taken her love hostage and she could not shake it off.

She sat on the edge of his bed and took his pillow in her hands, lifting it to her face and inhaling his scent. Her feet did not reach the floor, but her heel knocked against something hard. She hopped from the bed and squatted, reaching below the hanging comforter. Beneath the bed, her fingers sought an edge and she gripped it and pulled it towards her.

As she tugged, a large wooden box emerged. It was lidless and inside, items and photos were carefully placed, many pinned to the box's walls and others glued to the base. There were photos of Claire. Claire in a red prom dress posing in front of a park swing set. Claire bikini-clad on a beach towel. Claire as a young girl with her arms wrapped around a stuffed turtle and two fingers stuck in her mouth. Around the pictures, Abby saw twigs, herbs and pieces of cloth. Several small containers glued to the bottom of the box were filled with liquid, one that looked strangely like blood.

"What are you doing in here?"

She paused with her hand above the box, only seconds from dipping her fingers into the brownish liquid, and took a deep breath.

Sebastian stood in the doorway, his face empty of emotion, but his arms crossed defensively over his chest.

"I was just looking for you," she started.

"I was in the Healing Room getting a tincture for Bridget."

"What tincture?" Abby desperately wanted to distract him from her snooping.

"I don't know. Something for mosquito bites." He looked perturbed, his eyes moving toward the box, but he said nothing. "Are you ready for dinner?"

She nodded and stood, following him out of the room.

****

"So what costume will you wear to the All Hallow's Ball, Abby?" Elda called down the dinner table.

Abby stopped, her forkful of chicken poised halfway to her mouth. All of the witches looked at her expectantly and her face burned. She noticed that Sebastian was staring intently at the garlic mashed potatoes he'd prepared earlier that day. He had been spending more time in the kitchen with Bridget, which relieved Abby because it meant that he was not stalking the library for more titles on Vepar destruction.

"Ummm, well..." she choked and found herself looking to Oliver for help.

His lips were folded in a grimace and when they made eye contact, he shrugged as if to say 'guess you're telling him after all.'

"Well, I've been so busy, I haven't given it much thought." An absolute lie. "By the way, Sebastian, I forgot to tell you about the All Hallow's Ball."

"Oh." he mumbled, finally looking up. "Lydie mentioned it last week."

Abby sucked in a breath and felt her blush deepen.

"Yeah, I told Sebastian that he should be the Goblin King from Labyrinth," Lydie quipped, spooning potatoes into her mouth.

She had recently dropped the clichés and Abby loved the change. She was much more like an adolescent girl than Abby had realized.

"Ha, the Goblin King, Lyds?" Oliver laughed. "You want poor Sebastian in spandex pants and a pirate shirt?

"I wasn't sure if it was a witch only thing..." Sebastian said, ignoring Oliver.

"Well, I'm not totally sure either," Abby said looking at him apologetically. She reached beneath the table to squeeze his knee, but discovered that he was sitting too far away.

"I'm sure that he can be concealed," Dafne muttered and Abby glanced toward her, bewildered. Oliver too seemed shocked at Dafne's comment, but her gaze had drifted back to her plate and no one else seemed to notice.

"It can be done," Faustine said simply. He rarely spoke more than a few words at dinner, sometimes none at all, and Abby was surprised that he chose this moment to tune in. He looked down at her sideways, but his expression remained a riddle and Abby could not perceive his intentions.

"Great," she said with feigned enthusiasm, but Sebastian did not mirror the sentiment.

"It's so much fun," Helena mouthed at Sebastian, grinning.

He nodded at her, but his eyes wandered to the windows at the far end of the room.

"Last year," Helena started, "I went as Medusa. Elda enchanted real snakes for my hair. It was amazing."

"Yeah, that was cool," Lydie perked up. "Elda, could you enchant wings if I go as one of the winged monkeys from Wizard of Oz?"

Elda smiled and dabbed her mouth with her napkin.

"We'll see, Lydie."

****

After dinner, Abby and Sebastian returned to her room. He had brought a book about Vepar venom and said nothing as he settled onto Abby's bed and flipped it open.

"Do you want to talk? she asked.

Despite her growing intuition about the emotions of others, Sebastian's continued to elude her. Was he angry that she had not mentioned the Ball? Or merely so preoccupied with thoughts of Claire that he'd barely considered it?

He glanced at her over his book and shrugged.

"If you feel like we need to."

"I'm sorry I didn't tell you about the party. You've just seemed so...distracted."

The rain grew louder and Sebastian looked at the window and then at Abby expectantly.

"It's not me," she said.

"It's fine that you didn't mention it. We've both been busy with more important things."

His words stung since most of her energy as of late had been directed at the party and the conundrum it had created in her life.

"Honestly, Sebastian, I chose not to mention it because you haven't seemed interested in much of anything these last few days."

He cracked a cold smile and stared hard into her eyes.

"What does that mean?"

She hesitated.

"Okay, I said that wrong. You haven't seemed interested in the coven or in me."

He closed the book and rested it on his lap.

"I love you, Abby. I'm crazy about you, but this..." he held the book up, "...is my purpose in this world. I doubted it, but now I know and I have to pursue it all the way to the end."

"What does that even mean? Your purpose is to kill Tobias? Come on, Sebastian, what kind of purpose is that?"

"Could there be any greater?"

"Sure, how about love, Sebastian? Taking all of that energy and pouring it into love."

"This is about love," he whispered.

Abby felt her chest thicken, but she stifled the tears.

"Okay, fine. I'm going to run a bath." She left him in the bedroom where he had already returned to his book. She sat on the edge of the bathtub, watching the water pool, and wondered what had happened to their love.

****

"Dafne has been blocking me," Faustine said suddenly.

He and Elda were seated in the dungeon oratory. It was no longer a place of prayer, but an enchanted space meant to bind the energies of their coven.

"Dafne?" Elda asked, peeling her eyes from the Book of Shadows she had been vigorously scribbling in.

"Yes, I wasn't sure even a few days ago. But today I am. Her mind is not available to me."

"Even in the tower?"

He nodded.

"Perhaps you should ask Helena if she is sensing anything in Dafne," Elda told him.

She looked down at her book where she'd been writing Bridget's new anti-fungal remedy, but suddenly she could not concentrate.

"The energy has been off lately," she murmured, setting a palm out as if collecting rain drops.

"Yes. I thought that it was Abby and Sebastian and all of the chaos of late, but now..." he trailed off.

Elda set her pen down and stood, moving into the circle in the center of the room. The Magic Circle, marked by the runic symbol X, was a sacred space that the witches used to call forth and join their powers. It had been months since they had last performed the ritual, largely because they had all been preoccupied.

"Yes," Faustine responded to her thoughts. "We should gather and call the Magic Circle. We need to bind Abby into the coven."

Elda nodded, but felt uneasy. She was not sure that Abby was content at

Ula and she knew surely that Sebastian was not.

"It is simply young love," Faustine concluded reading her mind. "It is volatile. I would not give it much thought."

"What about their connection? Helena witnessed Sebastian ripping an arm off a chair when Abby became upset."

Faustine furrowed his brow and nodded.

"I know, but I'm not so sure that the connection transcends the most basic link of loving one another. Have we not all experienced the passion, rage or pain of our partner?"

"Yes, of course, but to physically act it out?"

"It is worth investigating in the future, but right now my focus has shifted to Dafne and why she is putting a wall in front of my eyes."

"I will speak with her," Elda said, nodding in tune with her thoughts. "I will try to discern her intentions."

Both she and Faustine knew that Dafne was a powerful witch whose mind, when closed, would not be penetrated.

****

Dafne whispered a hurried incantation and the pile of items on her desk vanished. Technically they did not vanish, but became the exact color of the cherry wood, knots and all, making them nearly impossible to detect.

"You busy?" Elda asked, pushing open Dafne's bedroom door.

Dafne had one of the only dungeon rooms. She preferred it because the earth's thermal energy strengthened her own fire element.

"Uh, no, writing a spell in my journal." She held up her journal, a tattered old thing that was legible to no one but her.

"Anything interesting?" Elda asked sweeping into the room and scanning it quickly. She did not detect the flurry of items on Dafne's desk.

"Hardly. I've been trying to pull from the sun at night, but the energy is just...weaker."

Elda nodded, sensing that Dafne was eluding her, but did not want to give her suspicions away.

She lifted a pile of books from a leather club chair, one of two in Dafne's room, and sat down. Dafne, seated in the other chair, seemed unperturbed by Elda's visit and gave nothing away.

Elda felt the first stinging fingers of a headache behind her eyes and lifted her thumb and forefinger to massage the bridge of her nose.

"Not feeling well?" Dafne asked

"Just a little headache," Elda trailed off. She lifted one of the books and eyed its title. It was not unusual, a memoir written by a witch in another coven.

"Remedy?" Dafne asked, pointing toward a chest kept at the foot of her bed filled with tinctures and poultices.

"No, thank you, dear." Elda fingered the fabric on the chair and stole glances beyond Dafne, again searching for anything out of the ordinary. However, Faustine was right. Dafne had a steel wall up. Elda could not get a sense of her emotions nor could she catch a fleeting thought. It was intentional, she was sure of it, but why she didn't know.

Dafne was a moody witch and had been since her arrival at Ula nearly a century earlier. Despite her devotion to the coven and her steadfast adherence to the witch's rule, harm none, she never fully opened up to any of the witches, except for maybe Oliver, but Elda could sense that crumbling as he grew closer to Abby.

"How are you doing?" Elda continued. "I feel that we haven't spent a moment alone in ages..."

"Fine. I'm preparing for All Hallow's and trying to stay out of everyone's way," Dafne said shortly, glancing at her journal with a growing looking of impatience.

"Hmm...," Elda searched Dafne's face, but she returned Elda's gaze dispassionately.

"Was there anything else?" Dafne asked.

"No, I don't think so," Elda said standing with a flourish of her dark robes. "But I'm here, Dafne. You can always come to me if you need to talk."

She left the room slowly, stealing another long glance around the space, but she saw nothing out of the ordinary.

CHAPTER 4

Late one afternoon, Lydie climbed the steep sand dune that served as the westernmost border of the island. It was no more than fifty yards across, but it seemed to rise forever. The top offered a blow-out view of the vast lake beyond. The nearly vertical dune on the other side, long eroded into sandstone, was a dizzying drop.

"Into the clouds," Lydie whispered with a grin and a mostly unconscious thought of her dead mother whom she often imagined as residing in the clouds, but only the really white fluffy ones. The gray clouds never held more than rain.

Her feet were cold because she had foregone shoes to feel the sand a final time before fall took hold completely. Sand wedged beneath her toenails and it hurt, but she forged on, her ankles slicing through sugar and her feet creating small divots as she ascended.

The sky was blue and clear. She felt her breath growing short as she trudged up the dune. Generally, her superior strength made the climb easy, but nightmares had plagued her recently and she felt tired. She did not remember the nightmares exactly, only that Sebastian's face floated before her when she woke. She wanted to tell someone about the dreams, but everyone in the coven had seemed preoccupied and Oliver, her usual confidante, was spending all of his time with Abby or patrolling the mainland.

She reached the dune peak and dropped to her knees, lowering her face to the sand and resting her cheek against it. It felt like home, the home she'd shared with her parents in the Sleeping Bear Dunes National Forest, and sometimes she climbed the island dune to return there. She sank both hands deep into the sand and massaged it with her fingers. With her eyes closed, she concentrated on one of the more poignant memories of her childhood home. In her memory, her father carried her up a sand dune on his shoulders. It was spring and cool so she wore fleece pajamas. Her mother laughed and ran ahead, cart-wheeling back down the dune to meet them.

As she guided energy into the image, she felt the stirrings of her astral body. It broke away from her physical body and a wave of seasickness washed over her as she traveled at light speed to the terrain of her childhood. She did not travel back in time. No, that was a feat that even witches, as far as she knew, could not accomplish. But suddenly she was there again at the wide expanse of sand dunes that dipped and soared like a great desert. In the distance, she saw the rippling waters of Lake Michigan, but she turned her astral body south and began to float back down the dune that she had climbed with her parents so many years before.

At the base of the bluff, she came to a dense wood. She wound her astral body through it easily. She had visited it before, several times, and though Max still believed that Lydie could not travel in her astral body, she could actually do it quite well. If she knew more about the capability of witches outside of her coven, she would have learned that very few witches could take their astral body to far away locations at will. Most of them could visit the sacred caves and areas nearby, but to travel elsewhere was a special skill which Lydie had mastered years earlier, but told no one.

In the woods, she paused, pulling memories out of the mind that rested peacefully on top of the dune at Ula. She remembered learning to climb trees in the forest. Her mother often climbed with her in a small sack that wrapped across her chest. Lydie knew what it felt like to be a monkey, a koala bear, an animal baby whose mother could leap from branch to branch. Her parents were not like the witches at Ula. They were lovers of life and they were kids in their hearts. They danced and ran and climbed and kissed. They inspired in Lydie the magic of life that had nothing to do with their powers as witches. Perhaps they were careless as Lydie had once heard Faustine call them, but she missed them desperately.

Lydie knew that Elda and Faustine were unaware of her memories. They did not realize how clearly etched in her thoughts were the years that she spent with her parents. They did not know that she longed to live a life very similar to theirs, a life that was not part of a coven, that had no rules and that considered joy to be as sacred as a Book of Shadows.

Moving out of the woods, she came to the small house that they had occupied as a family. The yard, if it could be called that, was overgrown with long stiff grass that would have scraped Lydie's feet if she'd been walking in her body. When she was a child, a baby really, her mother filled the yard with flowers and herbs. Much of the vegetation was magic, the types of plants that humans did not grow, but none of her parents' friends, many of who were non-witches, knew the difference.

Now there were 'No Trespassing' signs nailed to the trees, which had not been there when Lydie's parents owned the house. The signs were marred with bullet holes and the nails were rusted, but they clung on, making Lydie sad for the pain that the trees had to experience for some flimsy signs.

Lydie remembered playing in the yard at night and falling asleep to the cacophony of crickets and mosquitoes that inhabited the woods. Now, in autumn, they were all gone, back to their beds to sleep the winter away.

The house was a small two-bedroom cabin constructed of hand-hewn logs that Lydie's great-grandfather had cut himself more than a century earlier. Lydie drifted onto the wide porch that wrapped around the lower level of the cabin, noticing the sagging eave overhead and remembering the brilliant display of bird feeders her mother had hung there. She stopped at a window, thick with dust, and looked into the open space where the sitting area and kitchen remained. The house was mostly empty, except for the dust balls and a few pieces of old, moth-eaten furniture. Lydie scanned the walls, but no pictures hung there and hadn't for years. No one lived in the cabin because Lydie owned it, though Faustine kept all of the details private and Lydie never had the nerve to ask for more information.

She looked at the kitchen and the peeling white counter-tops dotted with tiny red flowers. She could see the rim of the heavy porcelain sink that her mother washed dishes in when she felt like being domestic and not using her magic. Lydie's dad always used magic when doing dishes. A simple incantation and the water became a churning well of suds. He often used the same spell when Lydie was in the bathtub and her rubber sea monsters all but came to life.

She floated along the exterior of the house, but felt her body pulling her back to the island. At first she resisted, wanting to enter the house and return to her room and to the crawl space that she had been rescued from, but already the vision was growing blurry. With a jolt and another wave of dizziness, she returned to the sand dune at the coven.

She was lying face down in the dune and, when she sat up, her back hurt from being folded in half. She shook her head and scanned the horizon, wondering what jarred her travel. At first she saw nothing except a few seagulls flapping angrily against the wind, which had picked up. She looked back toward the second lagoon, her gaze passing over the greenhouse and the cherry blossoms. From her vantage point she could see the castle rising a hundred feet above the highest island peak. There she saw a strange image.

Dafne was emerging from a high window on the one of the turrets that twisted into the sky. Lydie knew the turret as Faustine's tower, the space that he went to connect telepathically to the witches in Ula and to witches in other covens. He spent most of his time there, but the other Ula witches rarely visited the tower.

Now Lydie watched as Dafne climbed out of the window and stepped onto a tiny stone ledge, pressing her body against the castle walls and skirting the perimeter of the tower. When she disappeared around the back, Lydie lost sight of her.

She would have to tell Elda. She had sensed tension in the castle and though she hated to tattle, she felt a strong urge to relay what she had seen to one of the elder witches.

She began to climb down the dune, but saw Oliver racing up, his muscular legs pumping beneath his athletic pants.

"Ha, I thought I'd find you up here," he laughed, diving into the sand next to her.

She giggled and sat down beside him.

"Let's go down that side." He pointed to the cliff side of the sand dune where the dune was a straight drop nearly thirteen hundred feet to the water below.

They had done the drop many times. Usually they started off running and jumping, but soon their legs scissored too quickly and they just fell the rest of the way. Oliver would hold her hand the whole way down and his lightness spell made their bodies practically dissolve into the water so that they barely felt the impact. The water would be cold, but they had only to grab a few bites of Bridget's Flaming Pepper Plants before they went in and they wouldn't even feel it.

"We better get the pepper plants," Lydie started, but Oliver interrupted her.

"Already got 'em." He held up two of the flaming peppers, both black, and handed her one.

"Down the hatch," he said and stuffed the pepper into his mouth, his face immediately glowing.

Lydie followed and forgot entirely about Dafne's strange trip outside of the tower.

****

Sebastian lay on the floor of his room and reached beneath the bed, pulling out the box that Abby had discovered. He was not happy that she had stumbled across it. He had barely looked at it and he didn't want her uncovering something that might prove valuable. He set the box on the bed and returned once more to the door, listening for footsteps on the stairs. There were none and, though he hated to do it, he turned the heavy bolt and locked it.

He had discovered the box in the dungeon in a strange room stuffed with unfamiliar artifacts He still did not know what led him to the box-- intuition he thought--but something had drawn him to the room that day and it could not have been luck that it was unlocked. He wondered if Claire was communicating with him from the other side. His dreams of her had grown increasingly regular.

It was a simple wooden box without a lid. He peered in at the peculiar arrangement. Claire's journals were stacked in the bottom and photos of her, along with incense and dried herbs, were pinned to the sides. It appeared to be a shrine, but knew little of what that meant. Who in the castle would have made a shrine for Claire? And to what ends? Beneath the journals, he discovered a simple silver band. The inside was etched with tiny inscriptions that he could not read. He slid the ring on his pinky.

He suspected that Elda had created the box. After all, he had given her Claire's journals, but something in that thought didn't sit right. Elda had implied that his preoccupation with Claire's death was natural, but not truly helpful, a belief that he disagreed with. A belief that also made it less likely that she created the shrine. Unless the shrine worked as a magical tool that helped Elda and the other witches of Ula to discover the whereabouts of Tobias. Were they intentionally keeping him in the dark?

He carefully reached into the box and lifted Claire's journals out, setting them on the bed beside him.

A muffled scrape drew his attention up from the box and his eyes darted to the door. The bolt firmly in place, no one could barge in; however, the light beneath the door was marred by two shapes--feet.

He quickly stuffed everything back into the box and shoved it under the bed. His heart raced and he wiped his clammy palms on his pants. A sense of suspicion plagued him and he could not seem to shake it.

It had to be Abby. The other witches rarely, if ever visited his room. Still he did not open the door. He couldn't. They, the witches, Abby and the others, would suspect him. She would sense his evasion. She would know that he was hiding something. Already in the previous weeks she had come to suspect him. He knew it. He felt her suspicious gaze follow his every move and he hated that she was right. He lied to her and crept into the dungeons. He concealed the box concerning Claire. He hid his dreams. He had no other choice. Claire needed him.

He looked back at the door, but the shadows were gone.

****

"I have something to show you," Helena twittered, dancing into Abby's room with a pile of garment bags.

Abby finished copying the spells that Elda had requested into her notebook and set it aside. Her hand ached and her eyes were nearly crossed from shuffling through all the old texts on incantations for strengthening the goddess.

"Ooh, the Goddess," Helena said peering over Abby's shoulder at the spell book. "It's your power, know it well."

Abby yawned. She enjoyed learning the Goddess spells, but longed for a break. Elda had kept her so busy with practicing and learning and training and repeating that she had hardly eaten in two days.

Helena set the bags on her bed and pulled out a hunk of tin foil.

"Pecan roll from Sebastian," she said with a wink. "He's quite the little chef, you know?"

"Yes, I know," Abby said a bit too sharply. She smiled apologetically at Helena. She wasn't mad exactly, just worn out. She missed Sebastian and wanted to cook with him. She wanted to set the books aside and spend the day doing anything that didn't involve study.

"It gets easier, honey," Helena said, pulling the chaise across the room and settling onto it. "Right now, you're building the foundation."

"Great. What's it like to build the whole house?" she asked, exasperated.

"Easier, believe it or not."

"So what have you got in here?" Abby fingered the edge of a bag preferring to change the subject. "Dead bodies that I have to conjure back to life?"

Helena grimaced and Abby realized that maybe her comment was out of line. Elda had once told her that Vepars could do just that thing.

"No bodies here, love. Just marvelous costumes for All Hallow's Eve!" She stood and swept off her maroon robe. Beneath it, she wore a shimmering orange dress with bright red and orange wings that curved seductively against her bare back.

"I have chosen the Phoenix," she gushed. "It's far from done, but what do you think."

Abby grinned and touched the silken fabric.

"It's breathtaking."

Helena replaced her robe and gave Abby a hug.

"I will design yours as well. It will be magnificent. This is, after all, your first All Hallow's Ball."

Abby munched on the roll and lolled her head from side to side trying to stretch the kink out of her neck.

"I don't think I'm going to have time to do any costume planning at this rate." She held up the stack of books on the bed beside her and grimaced.

"You won't have to." Helena smiled. "Just leave that up to me. Your focus is best served right here." She tapped the pile of books.

"Why so much preparation?" Abby asked. "I mean, I get the impression Elda is trying to prime me for something."

"The Ball is an initiation of sorts, honey. It will be your first real experience with other witches, beyond your coven, of course."

"Will I need to know all of this though? Am I going to be tested?"

"No, no. Not a test per se, but witches often perform magic when they're gathered. I mean, why wouldn't we, right?" She grinned and blew a puff of air into her palm. A dusting of sparkly powder flew into Abby's face.

Abby sneezed and wiped the sparkles from her nose, but there was nothing on her hand.

"Where did it go?"

"It was never there."

****

"Something is wrong," Faustine sighed, rubbing his tired eyes.

"Wrong?" Max was meticulously separating a pile of tiny stones, his face only inches from the table.

"My vision is suffering." Faustine blinked hard once, twice. "It started with Dafne, but now..."

Max picked up tweezers and plucked a bright green stone, the color of jade, but more crystal-like, and set it aside.

"Your connection?" Max stopped and peered at Faustine surprised. Was his old friend changing? Perhaps growing weaker with age?

"Yes, my connection. It's as if there's interference."

Max scrunched his eyebrows and listened intuitively for the barrier. Sometimes answers simply appeared in his mind, but now nothing.

"Strange weather lately and we are approaching All Hallow's Eve," Max said absently scratching his head.

It was true that All Hallow's Eve muddled the witches' powers. It was a mysterious time of year--the thinning of the veil between the living and the dead--and all of the witches experienced it in some form. Some years Max found that he could not astral-travel in the weeks before October thirty-first. In nineteen ninety-eight, Elda lost her ability to manipulate water for two weeks, and that same year all of Helena's insomnia tinctures became toxic.

"I hadn't considered All Hallow's," Faustine said, nodding his head slowly. He did not fully believe it, but he understood better than most the strange and magnificent changes that arrived with the October holiday.

"Surely that's all it is," Max added, returning to his stones. He lifted a magnifying glass up to one and held it towards Faustine.

"Look like diopside to you?"

Faustine touched it, but the stone did not reveal itself to him. Strange. He looked at it more closely.

"Yes, it's diopside."

Faustine stared up at the stone ceiling. Opening his mind, he scanned the library, but he felt none of his witches. It may have been empty, all of the witches tending to matters elsewhere, but he didn't think so. He bowed his head and reached into the space, but no heartbeat sounded in his ears and no thoughts found him. If the room was not empty, he was even more disconnected than he had realized.

****

"Melusine," Helena laughed triumphantly pushing into Abby's room the following day.

Abby sat on the floor, a spell book open in her lap and two empty bottles of Concentrate resting by her knee.

She peered up at Helena through clear, agitated eyes.

"Melusine?"

"Yes, it is your persona for the Ball, your creature, your mythology. It came to me in a dream last night and I have already begun your costume." Helena's eyes sparkled and her auburn hair was wild in the morning light.

"I don't know who Melusine is," Abby snapped, and then put a hand self-consciously to her mouth. "Sorry, I may have overdone it last night." She pointed at the bottles of Concentrate.

"Half of one bottle is more than adequate for a twenty-four-hour period, you know?" Helena said, plopping onto Abby's bed. She pushed a toe against the book on Abby's lap and it toppled to the floor.

"I know, but I kept thinking that I needed more."

"Well, that is because you're concentrating on something other than your studies. The potion works, but your mind tells it where to go."

Abby ground her teeth and stood, pacing the room and ringing her hands anxiously.

"I don't have time for costumes, or for a party or for a life," she muttered, glancing angrily at the spell book and fighting the urge to boot it across the room. "Elda has me studying constantly, and you know what? I am completely exhausted."

Helena smiled sympathetically and patted the bed next to her, but Abby was too wound up for sitting.

"This is only a brief time, Abby, and all new witches must experience it. You have to be capable of the spells, of performing your rite. As your coven, it's our responsibility, and Elda as your mentor's responsibility to prepare you. And remember what I told you about puberty for witches? A little irritability comes with the package."

Abby had heard versions of the same thing from Elda and Oliver, though she appreciated Oliver's version most of all. He had described his first two months of training as Catholic Reform School run by nuns who had magic powers.

Abby groaned and threw her hands up.

"I still don't see why this is so important. Will there be sorcerers at this party throwing fireballs in my face that I have to turn into canaries?"

"Ha, wouldn't that be something?" Helena giggled and shook her head. "Nothing like that, but it's a powerful night, a night where strange and wonderful things happen. Usually the events are lovely and fun and mysterious, but they are also dangerous and you must be capable of protecting yourself in all moments."

"Why can't anyone actually tell me more about the party itself? I feel like I'm walking through a dark tunnel wearing a blindfold."

"Because it is part of your initiation. It's as simple as that. I know that the modern world pays little heed to ritual, but witches know the importance of it. If you do not receive a proper initiation, the world will make up for it in other ways."

"Like?"

"How can I say what is to come if you are not initiated? Those answers only exist when fate brings them into your life."

"Fine," Abby said dismissively, knowing that she would only get more ambiguities. "Tell me about Melusine."

"Well," Helena started, clearly moving into her arena. "Melusine, most importantly, was a water spirit. She is mythically known as the daughter of Pressyne, a lady of the forest. Pressyne punished Melusine for betraying her father by turning the lower part of her body into that of a serpent."

Abby grimaced.

"A serpent? "

"Yes, but you will have both the serpent's lower body and two bat-like wings."

"This sounds a bit morbid for a Ball."

"No, no. All Hallow's is a costume party. It is a tribute to the dead, to the spirits of the other world, and we honor them by taking their form."

"And you dreamed this?"

"Yes, and so it shall be, my dear," Helena chimed. "Dreams of this kind have great significance."

Abby nodded her head gravely. She had not yet begun her study of dreams, but Elda had warned her it was lengthy and imperative for all witches to grasp the basics of dream divination.

****

Dafne stared hard at her reflection in the mirror and wiped off her red lipstick for the second time. She would not bother with makeup for dinner because there no longer seemed anyone to please. Oliver had aligned himself with Abby and, though Dafne felt an empty prickling in her stomach when she thought of them together, she had to admit that it aided her plan. With Oliver close, Abby was distracted. She barely registered Sebastian's growing distance. The others, Dafne felt confident, were attributing the blocks to All Hallow's and would not realize the true culprit behind their weakened powers until long after the Ball and, if all went well, never.

She dropped the lipstick into the trash and glared at it until the red tip melted into the can and formed a crimson glob. Returning to the mirror, she met her dark eyes and ignored the flickers of guilt at the betrayal of her coven. It was not a betrayal, not truly, but if they were to know her intentions, they would see it as thus. So she cloaked her behavior, buried her thoughts and muddled them with distractions. Smoke and mirrors, as a common person would say. But Dafne relied on much greater strengths than illusion to lure their focus elsewhere.

She took a moment to clear her room of all lingering thoughts and energy, ensuring that no other witches would detect anything amiss if they passed through. Elda had been lurking about and Dafne sensed her inquiries, but knew also that she had discovered nothing. Dafne's naturally suspicious character heightened her powers of deception--she could hide in plain view. Even her own coven could not sense her thoughts if she turned away from them. Of course, she would lift that veil of secrecy in time, but only after he was gone, purged from the castle and toppled from the evil throne that she felt sure he was destined for. She would never receive thanks for her great feat, for none of the witches, save Indra, would ever trace the threads back to her. She knew how to cover the silken lines of her web, how to weave the pattern so that it became chaos to any eye but her own. She had gone beyond befuddling Sebastian and Abby. She had included all of her coven and guaranteed her success by using All Hallow's as her supreme cloak.

Her dreams had grown more urgent, more terrifying, and despite the fast approaching Ball, she longed to will the sun to set earlier each night and rise sooner each morn. Her blood raced and even in that moment, in the cool sanctuary of her dungeon room, a fever prickled at her hairline, creating a crease of sweat-matted hair that she didn't bother wiping away.

She returned her gaze to the mirror and blessed the Goddess within before darkening the glass.

She waved her hands over her vanity table and then cast the same spell across her room.

"Conceal," she whispered. "Mote it be." And it was. Only her eyes drew out the shapes and shadows of her secrets. Her eyes lingered on a painting that hung above her armchair. A raven with dark probing eyes perched on the gnarled branch of a tree from her youth, a youth that existed before her tender heart had broken. She still remembered his hand sweeping along the canvas, oily paint smeared on the cuff of his yellowing shirt. He had turned to her, eyes gleaming, and laughed at the macabre beauty of this bird, which had seemed to follow them everywhere. "It is our guardian angel," he'd told her.

But of course, she knew now the message of the raven--death.

"Dafne?" A small voice squeaked from the doorway and Dafne turned to see Lydie, her hands shoved deep into the pockets of her sweatshirt.

J.R. Erickson

CHAPTER 5

"Crabby Abby? Knock Knock," Oliver peeked his head through her door, knocking gently on the wood frame.

Abby looked up from her Mystical Herbs Reference Guide and yawned. Stretched out on her bed with a cup of Bridgett's super strong Turkish coffee, she'd been reading about the psychoactive properties of nutmeg.

"Did you know that you can get stoned with nutmeg?" Abby asked, pointing at a picture of the large nut.

"Myristica insipida," Oliver said knowingly. "But I don't recommend it."

"Really?" Abby was intrigued. "I love nutmeg. I wonder how much you have to eat."

"A lot and it's not pleasant."

"You've tried it?" Abby rolled onto her back and looked at Oliver upside down.

"Let's just say that I received training by a very interesting witch whose teaching philosophy was 'No physician is really good until he has killed one or two patients.' I think he told me that was a Hindu proverb, but the jury is still out."

Abby laughed and sat up, swinging her legs to the floor.

"But, alas, you live."

"That I do, barely after the nutmeg incident, but that is a story for another time."

"Oh, come on. I feel like my learning here is a series of anecdotes that I never get the full story on. Tell me about him or her? Was it Elda that nearly killed you?"

"Ha, yeah right. Have you met Elda? No, but consider this, if you will commit to three hours of library study with me, I will tell you about my teacher."

Abby grimaced. "What are we studying?"

"Vepars."

Abby gazed at Oliver's face to see if he was serious. Despite having encountered several Vepars and even killed one, most of the coven had avoided answering her questions about their mortal enemy. Curiosity compelled her, but Sebastian's growing obsession with the creatures made her reluctant to know them.

Oliver smiled gently and sat on the edge of her bed.

"He's not joining us. Elda asked him to spend the afternoon with Lydie and Max in the dungeons."

"Why?" Abby asked keeping her eyes firmly on the window across the room.

She knew why, of course. The other witches were no more interested in fueling Sebastian's fire than she.

"If you're wondering about what she told him, it wasn't a complete put off. Max is teaching Lydie to communicate with animals. It's truly amazing and Sebastian will no doubt enjoy it."

"Animals?" Abby asked incredulous. "Speak with them?"

Oliver smiled, amused.

"Not in English, but yes, in the language of the earth. There are many ways to communicate. I think humans are the only ones that forget it."

Abby paused and remembered the terrified squirrel from her last meeting with the Vepars. No words were exchanged for her to know his fear.

"I think I would rather do the animal teaching too." She grinned and looked at Oliver from the corner of her eye.

"You and me both," he sighed and squeezed her knee.

She stared at his hand, but said nothing, enjoying the warmth through her jeans.

"It's strange having had that relic," Abby murmured, remembering the tiny Goddess lighter that had forged a connection for Devin to stay in the world of the living. It also allowed her to see life through the eyes of a Vepar. "I could see through Vesta's eyes. I didn't have access to her thoughts, but I was right there. Now I'm in the dark again and, honestly, I prefer it that way."

"Of course you do," Oliver assured her. "I have spent most of my life hunting Vepars, but I would never want that kind of window into their darkness. I need distance in order to destroy them. You're an empath, Abby. Had that relic stayed with you, Vesta would have become a doorway for them into you. That's the reality for some witches. You're a healer, you would have wanted to help her."

Abby remembered the final glimpse that the relic had shown her of Vesta observing the corpse of her brother Tane. Black tears were smeared across Vesta's pale cheeks and Abby had felt her grief and loss.

"So what exactly will I be learning?" she asked him, changing the subject and releasing those final images of Vesta.

"For starters, how they operate. How their venom affects us, what their deeper motivations are, and how to sense their presence. There's a lot to cover, more than a day or even a year's worth of study, but we have to start somewhere..."

A year? The idea of devoting a year to Sydney's killers made her hot with rage.

"Why should I learn about them? Why should we spend any time thinking of them?" she muttered angrily, again ruminating on Sebastian's infatuation with the murderers.

"Because they're learning about you right now. They're learning about your human history, the people that you loved, the places you might hide. They teach their recruits to hunt us, to kill us, to steal our power. You would be doing yourself and your coven a great disservice by choosing ignorance over knowledge."

Abby felt a lump begin to form in her throat as she flashed on Sydney's dead face in the Pool of Truth. Her beloved aunt could never be returned, but other deaths could be prevented.

Oliver saw the gleam in her eye and nodded.

"That's it. Hold onto that feeling, Abby. That's the witch's power, the desire for justice at all costs. Not revenge," he quickly added, "but an end to evil."

****

Lydie squealed in delight when Max pulled the silver cloak from an enormous golden cage in the center of the dungeon. Inside, a small orange kitten stood, his fluffy tail puffed in exasperation.

Sebastian laughed, momentarily caught in the glee of Lydie's excitement.

"Oh, Max, he's adorable. Is he mine?" She turned her big glittering eyes on Max and he looked briefly dumbfounded.

He seldom got carried away by Lydie's girlishness because it rarely appeared. Since dropping the clichés, she had seemed to regress to a sweeter childhood self, a girl of seven or eight, and though it brought some trepidation in him, he enjoyed her innocence.

The cat and all of the animals he had brought to the castle for the day's lessons were from an animal shelter on the mainland. He had cast phantom replacements in their cages, but intended to return them by the following day. However, her joy was intoxicating.

"You can keep him," he said, resigned. "Though I'm not sure Kissy will approve of his new housemate."

Kissy was the only pet at Ula. He had been wandering the castle halls for well over twenty years, searching for food scraps and belly rubs. Max did not actually know who originally brought the chubby gray cat to the island, but he felt confident Helena had a hand in it.

Lydie rushed to the cage and pulled open the door, gathering the puff-ball in her small arms and clutching him desperately.

Max had given little thought to such frivolities as kittens and toys during his years with Lydie. Though he had been her teacher throughout her time at Ula, from a very young age, she exhibited advanced powers and an aged cynicism that left little space for coddling.

Helena and Bridget had still managed to baby Lydie during her first years at Ula. Grief and fear had rendered her, for a short period of time, quite impressionable. They cooed and pampered her but, within a year, a hardened shell seemed to encase her. She no longer entertained baby talk, refusing to speak to them in response. She used her powers to light her stuffed animals on fire during an especially stressful time at the coven when a witch had fallen at the hands of the Vepar Tobias. To Bridgett's dismay, Lydie even refused birthday cakes after her seventh year and would tolerate only witch-related gifts--few toys or girlish items.

Max had not brought up Lydie's change with the other witches. They were all so preoccupied and she was in his charge, after all. Moreover, he wanted to cultivate Lydie's innocence, bathe it in loving acceptance so that she might let it live for a while. He ruffled the fur of the cat's head and rather enjoyed the thought of another kitty in the castle.

There had been a time when the coven was overrun with pets. They were both a necessity and a fancy. Faustine's cat Black was nearly thirty years old when it died while chasing a fireball produced by the witch Julian. Of course, that had been another time and Max rarely traveled into the past. The present was all that existed, but sometimes, on an especially sunny day, he could not help but remember a time of such intense light that it nearly brought him to his knees.

****

"Sit still," Oliver barked lovingly, placing his hands firmly on her shoulders.

Abby had been squirming since their so-called lesson began. She shifted in the chair, crossed and uncrossed her legs and tapped her feet. It was not the subject exactly, though the Vepars certainly made her antsy. Mostly it was a feeling that lingered in the room, a sense of something amiss.

"Don't you feel it? Something's off," she said for the second time, but again Oliver simply shrugged.

"Abby, you've been going at break-neck speed for weeks. That, combined with Sebastian's...well, you know. It's going to make you feel anxious."

Abby bit her lip and let her argument die. He might have been right, he probably was, but still she couldn't shake the unease that crawled into her bones and made everything jittery and tight.

She stood up and paced to the fireplace.

"Okay, keep going. The Vepars venom," she told him, nodding that he should continue.

"The Vepar's venom," Oliver continued, barely glancing at the book in his hand, "induces a nearly immediate state of unconsciousness. This occurs when their teeth make contact with flesh, puncture the skin and it enters the blood stream."

"What is it, the venom?" Abby asked. She had felt the Vepar's venom first hand, but she did not understand why it appeared to have less impact on her than other witches.

"Well, that's the thing. We don't know. Witches have been trying to collect Vepar venom for thousands of years, but it's virtually impossible. We can't find it. It's not stored in their teeth, gums or lips. When we try to isolate it in a witch who has been bitten, there's no trace of any foreign substance."

"How do you know it's venom then?" Abby asked, pulling a chair closer to the fireplace and perching on the edge, still too anxious to fully relax.

"We don't. The venom label has come from Vepar's themselves. It's what they call it. We don't actually know what it is."

"Then how did you create an antidote?"

"Trial and error. Not an easy process, to say the least. Bridget makes our antidote here at Ula, but the original creator was a witch in rural Ireland. He wasn't part of a coven or anything. A hermited witch, according to Helena."

"A hermited witch?"

"Yes, he lived in isolation, away from other witches. Apparently, he was a genius chemist. Half of the elixirs in Bridgett's stores are from this guy."

"Really?" Abby imagined a witch with long graying hair and tattered leather sandals staring intently into a boiling pot and seeing the future.

"Yeah, we have books on him in here. But don't worry, Elda will send you there soon enough. For now, let's talk Vepars."

Abby shrugged and leaned back, letting her hands fall on the arms of the chair. A light shock, like touching a low voltage live wire, ran up her forearms and she ripped them back.

"What, what is it?" Oliver lifted her arm expectantly.

She stared at the chair and tried to conjure the vision that had come to her. It was brief, nearly incomprehensible, but there had been a dark wood and a face lost, searching. Sebastian's face.

****

"Shh..." Dafne's eyes darted around the cave, but no other presence appeared.

She had traveled within her astral body to meet Indra, a witch from the coven of Sorciére, that she had been communicating with regularly.

Dafne and Indra had met at an All Hallow's Ball two years previously and their painful pasts, combined with a general suspicion of all non-witches, immediately connected them. Indra, like Dafne, was a hunter and she thrived on the study and annihilation of Vepars.

"I dreamed of him again last night," Indra whispered, when she felt confident that no other witches were present.

"And?" Dafne did not enjoy drawn out conversations. Learning of Indra's dreams and visions often took more patience than she could gather.

Indra took a deep breath and closed her eyes.

"I am walking in a dark forest and the leaves are whispering a warning of danger. My skin, hair and eyelids prickle with fear, but I do not waiver from my path. Where am I going? I know not. Only that in my palm, I clutch a tiny red flower and I must deliver the flower for healing. From the shadows to my right..."

Indra crouched as she spoke and waved her hands to the right.

"A venomous whisper steals the wind for his own. He tells me that his transformation is nearly complete. That he, the Great One, will soon rise, and all of the witches of Gaia will cower beneath his gaze."

Indra shuddered and took another deep breath.

"I look into my palm and the flower is your coven of Ula, smoldering and ruined. The man steps from the brush and I see a hint of blue eyes and then...nothing."

Dafne let out a long breath and bit the knuckle of her right hand. Indra's dreams were coming more and more frequently. They were prophesying a great change. Dafne's dreams were much more gruesome, but foretold of similar catastrophe.

"Did you tell your coven?" Dafne asked, but she knew the answer.

No, Indra did not tell her coven. She had become estranged from them and spent all of her hours in the dungeons casting out for Vepars. She hunted them at night, alone, and when they fell, her coven celebrated, but she refused to participate. Instead, she returned to her solitude, her dreams and her visions and, more than all of that, her obsessions. Vepars had stolen more from her than the earth might ever replace. Her lover, her children and her closest friends had been sacrificed on their altar of blood lust.

Dafne knew a similar tale of anguish and, though she had never revealed the details to Indra, Indra had dreamed of them in pieces.

"Have you begun?"

"I have." Dafne reached into her robe, her ethereal body shimmering and pulled out the enchanted scroll that carefully bound her spells. Indra leaned eagerly toward it, her eyes widening. Dafne felt a strange sense of satisfaction knowing that the witch, superior in many ways, appeared enthralled by her casting.

****

Abby returned to her room to retrieve a wicker basket of tinctures she had made. Part of her lessons with Bridget involved mastering human healing.

For a week, she had pored over worn texts and journals searching out remedies for a list of ailments provided by Bridget. If she had mixed everything correctly, she now knew how to develop medicine for nausea, PMS, paranoia, headaches, diarrhea, and the flu.

Bridget taught her in the healing room, where many of the coven's tinctures were stored. Two walls rotated to reveal shelves of potions that could help mend broken bones, clot the blood, and protect against the venom of Vepars. Abby longed to sit on a stool before the shelves and read every title. However, time rarely permitted such investigation. Between lessons, practicing her power, and Sebastian, she was amazed that she remembered to eat amidst the constant shifting.

"Forgot the prickly lettuce here in the premenstrual syndrome tincture," Bridget told her.

"Oh, shoot," Abby moaned, remembering the green thorny plant sitting on the workshop table. She had taken it down, two days earlier, to add to her pestle, and then Sebastian had arrived hungry. They went to the dining room and she completely forgot about her final ingredient.

"Don't worry, doll," Bridget bubbled. "We're only on round one."

Abby looked forward to learning about remedies, but the upcoming party at Sorciére still consumed most of her thoughts. They only had a week before the party and Elda, who promised to give her details, had left to visit a coven in Canada where an old friend of hers was nearing death.

"Any news on Elda's return?"

Bridget looked up with a sly smile. "Excited about the party?"

Abby sighed and nodded.

"Yes, and nervous. It's just Sebastian is worried so..."

"So you're worried."

"Yeah."

"Well, let me help you," Bridget pulled a bottle from the shelf and set it in Abby's palm. The glass bottle, only half full, contained a mint-colored liquid.

"What is it?" Abby tilted the bottle on its side and the light green amoeba inside broke into tiny balls and floated along the glass.

"For your worries."

Bridget did not let on much. Though always friendly, chipper in fact, Abby knew little about Bridget who kept to the kitchen and greenhouse most of the time.

"These look just about perfect?" Bridget chirped, inspecting the contents of each bottle with a large magnifying glass. The glass was held in place by silver taloned claws that extended to a long spiraled handle. "Wanna see?"

She held the glass out to Abby who took it and peered at the contents of her headache remedy. Through the magnifier, the liquid became thousands of tiny particles zipping around the bottle, their colors and shapes each distinguishable.

"That is amazing," Abby whispered, staring harder as a heart shaped lavender speck jetted by.

"Yes, you can see every feature. You come to know how the energy dances. If the dance is off there is something missing from the potion."

"That makes the remedy useless?"

"Not useless," Bridget replied, placing Abby's tinctures on the shelves and making her heart swell considerably, "but not useful for the ailment. They can also be dangerous, which is why I check them myself."

"You've checked all of these?"

"Yes, every one."

Abby's eyes scanned the rows of tiny bottles, there were thousands of them. She shuddered at how long it must have taken for Bridget to examine every one.

After meeting with Bridget, Abby left the castle, welcomed by a fat, full moon dangling overhead. She wanted to wander the grounds. She had already spent a good deal of time getting acquainted with the large island that Ula inhabited, but the coven's grounds were deceptively large. She entered the cherry blossoms and veered off the path, stepping over the remnants of leaves and blossoms turned brown and brittle.

She pulled the tincture from her pocket and lifted the rubbery dropper from the top. Squeezing the tip, a small blob of sour liquid plopped onto her tongue and she swallowed it with a grimace. It tasted like rotten fruit.

From the blossoms, the castle looked as tall as the sky itself. The windows were small, orange orbs of light drifting in the low hanging clouds overhead. Abby had not been to any of the castle's highest turrets. They were used, as far as she knew, by Faustine and Elda only.

Sebastian had grilled Helena about them, but she pretended that nothing more significant than loud snoring went on in their high walls.

The thought of Sebastian made her heart hurt and she licked her teeth and gums and swallowed, wanting the entire worry potion to work its magic.

****

The days leading up to the Ball were harried and exhausting. Between last minute lessons, costume preparation, and Sebastian's concealment, not a single moment of down time could be found. Helena and Bridget were non-stop designing, sewing, plucking, and forcing all of the witches into their costumes again and again until everything fit perfectly. They had chosen to outfit Sebastian as a dragon, to complement the mythical Melusine's many figures, and Elda had spent a great deal of time casting the spells that would conceal his human identity. Abby had participated in nearly all of the spells since she would be the one most likely to give him away if something went awry.

Abby collapsed into bed each night with aching eyes and sore limbs. Her brain was full to bursting and she slept the sleep of the dead, having made an agreement with Sebastian that they would retire to their separate rooms for the week before the party to be fully rested.

On the morning of the Ball, Abby found all of the witches, save Dafne, in the dining room talking excitedly over plates of fruit and pastries. She grabbed a Danish and pulled a chair next to Oliver whose bronzed skin had been sprayed with a sparkly sheen by Helena the night before. He looked like a handsome Greek statue.

"You like?" he asked, leaning in and pecking her on the cheek.

She grinned and nodded.

"California girls, eat your heart out," she laughed, rubbing a finger along his forearm, but nothing streaked away.

"What? You think this is fake?" He shook his head, blond hair falling over his forehead. "This is the real deal baby. No tan in a can for me."

"Tan in a potion," Helena teased, miming a spraying motion.

"I think it looks awesome," Lydie said, shoving a handful of raspberries into her mouth. "I wish I had colored my skin."

****

"Don't be afraid," Helena told Abby and Sebastian as they stepped toward the mirror.

For a moment, they surveyed themselves in full costume. Abby's long darkish curls shone with bright red and green scales. Her cascading red dress revealed the black serpent's tail beneath and behind her, huge black vellumous wings rose from her back, casting her in shadow. Sebastian wore her counterpart--the dragon. He held the dragon's head mask in his hand. It covered his face, only from the nose up, and Elda had enchanted it to breathe fire when he coughed.

Sebastian gripped her hand and she felt a jolt of terrified energy at his touch. She envisioned a languid stream and cast the calming energy into his palm. His shoulders relaxed. They both stepped into the mirror and then the world vanished.

CHAPTER 6

A suffocating darkness took hold and Abby started to resist, pulling back toward the room that they had left. Before she could cry out, her body landed sweetly on the other side. Her feet found solid ground and Sebastian's strong hand materialized in her own. Their eyes locked and she saw the fear in her own reflected there, but also relief and maybe even glee.

Abby got lost in the throng of people pushing through the hall doors. Sebastian's fingers were in her own, light, barely grasping, and then they were gone and she held only emptiness. She did not immediately notice, caught instead by the dazzling foyer that she'd stumbled into on the heels of hundreds of other witches, whose costumes only added to the chaotic fervor of the moment.

She stared, mouth agape, at the soaring ceilings that did not end, but continued into a vacuum of space punctured by glittering stars that pulsated in a rainbow of silver and gold.

"Isn't it glorious?" Helena enthused, sweeping into Abby's path and steering her towards an enormous golden archway.

"Wait." Abby remembered Sebastian and felt the first pinpricks of panic at her empty hand.

But then he was there, white teeth gleaming from his face, sooty and red and colorful. His blue eyes were as enormous as hers felt and he laughed, squeezing her waist and leaning into her ear.

"Thank you," he whispered.

She clutched his hands and pulled him in for a quick hug before Helena dragged them off to another brilliant room. In the center of the space, streams of golden liquid fell from the sky. It spewed down and swirled onto the stone floor and disappeared. An orchestra stood on a star-shaped balcony twenty or more feet above the witches who danced and twirled below.

"Now we dance," Helena cried, linking her arms through Sebastian's and Abby's and whirling them onto the floor. The three of them danced, and then a witch who Abby did not recognize, clutched Helena from behind and pulled her into him. She laughed and waved and off they went.

Sebastian pulled her tight against him and reached a hand up, sinking his fingers into her glittery curls streaked with red and blonde and black.

"You are so beautiful."

She smiled and buried her face in his neck and allowed the ripples of gratitude to pour through her as he spun her again and again. Whatever had lain between them in the previous weeks vanished in an instant.

They danced for an eternity and then fell into the hallway, flushed and laughing. The halls were dazzling with iridescent bubbles gently floating from the ceiling, their bodies alight with candle flame and the magnificent colors of costumes. Raised platforms, sheathed in burgundy velvet, held golden tents, slightly parted to reveal a witch inside. Some of the witches consulted sparkling globes, others shuffled tarot cards, and Abby wandered awestruck along the aisle staring in wonder. Sebastian was equally amazed, his grip loose in hers and, when they came to a tent with the words Diviner of Dreams in black script along the platform base, Abby stopped.

"This one. Let's do this one." She stared at the tent with a sudden urgency that she did not understand. The witch at the table wore a long hooded, black robe and her eyes did not shift from the black lace tablecloth before her.

"Yeah?" Sebastian asked quizzically, glancing along the row. "Are you sure you wouldn't rather have your tea leaves read?" He gestured to a tent, two platforms down, that smelled of chai spices. The witch inside threw her head back and laughed while pouring a cup of steaming tea for an older male witch whose enormous flowery cape barely fit in the tent.

"You go there. I'm going to try this one," Abby insisted, letting go of his hand and stepping onto the platform. She gave Sebastian a quick wave and ducked inside, ignoring the look of uncertainty that had settled on his handsome features.

The golden flaps closed behind her and she sat carefully into the chair across from the witch who did not look up. She started to clear her voice, but then the witched lifted a finger, slowly and held it to her lips.

Abby studied her face--pale white, chalk white, but her lips were red as if bloody. She looked both very young and very old, skin soft and smooth, but milky saddened eyes and thin gnarled hands. Her head hung heavily on her shoulders and the bit of hair that Abby could see beneath her robe was a silvery gray.

After minutes that resembled hours, during which Abby felt less like a witch and more like an adolescent waiting in the Principal's office for punishment, the witch looked up and settled her cloudy eyes on Abby's face. Her lips parted, as if dry, and she began to speak.

****

After their readings, Sebastian gushed about his tea leaves. His reader saw a miraculous future for him, rich with love and family and magic. Most of all, Sebastian loved that the witch did not know him to be a 'mere mortal' - his words. When he asked about her own reading, Abby lied. She did not know why she lied, only that Sebastian's joy meant more to her than any desire to disclose the terrifying mystery that the witch had laid before her. That, and she feared speaking it aloud might make it real and in that moment, with the world more magical than she'd ever known it, she chose silence.

She danced with Sebastian and then Oliver, and then witches she did not even know. Sebastian was stolen by Lydie and cut in by Bridget and when Abby finally stumbled into the hallway to refill her champagne, it had been nearly an hour since she'd even seen her dragon companion.

"Food now," Oliver whispered, surprising her from behind and guiding her towards another space. They walked out into an open garden where witches lounged on wooden benches and sat at wrought iron tables heaped with small round cakes, each stamped with a cross. Every inch of stone-wall crawled with vines, heavy from the bloated purple and blue flowers that clung to their skinny bodies.

"I'm starving," Abby told Oliver, reaching immediately for one of the cakes, already salivating at the smells of ginger and cinnamon emanating from it.

"Nope, not those," he laughed, pulling her hand back. "Soul cakes. Those are for the dead."

She momentarily recoiled.

"Are you serious?" She shot a glance toward the night sky almost expecting to see swirls of ghostly faces watching from above.

He grinned mischievously

"It's All Hallows. Tonight everyone's invited to the party."

He kept laughing as he steered her toward the long buffet tables draped in glittering pink linen.

"Will spirits come tonight?" she asked. "Really?"

He smiled and she could not tell whether he was laughing at her or not. Clearly, they both knew that the subject of the dead returning was nothing to scoff at in the mystical realm. On the other hand, Oliver found few subjects that he couldn't joke about.

"Yes, they come. But you don't always know it. They're usually tricksters and you're none the wiser until you're engaged in some deep conversation and they just disappear."

"Honestly?" she asked, taking a bite of a baguette.

"Swear. Scouts' honor." He held up two fingers and then three. "Never a scout."

"I figured."

They ate and watched the spectacle of witches dancing and drinking. Their costumes offered a promenade of fantasy and fright. There were witches on fire, witches with glowing, iridescent skin, and some who wore drab gray robes and kept mostly to the periphery, watching, but not engaging in the festivities. They were young and old and everything between. Their costumes masked their ages, but not nearly as well as their witch youth. If Elda was hundreds of years old, there might be witches at the Ball who were in the thousands. She smiled as she tried to imagine a young man dressed in the silvery robes of a sorcerer as having lived for centuries.

"See anything you like?" Oliver teased, pinching her forearm.

She rolled her eyes.

"I already have a date, thank you," she told him. "Speaking of Sebastian, where is he?"

She craned her neck and turned full in her seat, but had no real hope of spotting him in the crowds pulsating in and out of the castle doors.

"Don't worry. He will appear at the perfect moment. Come dashing through in that fire breathing get-up that Helena's got him in, and sweep you off your feet."

He downed a glass of champagne as he spoke and smirked at her, but she heard aching in his words. Was Oliver jealous of Sebastian?

"Isn't it miraculous?" Elda appeared mysteriously from behind two witches and sat at their table with a flutter of emerald skirts. It was the first time that Abby had seen her since the party began.

"It's unreal," Abby agreed, stretching back in her chair and breathing deeply the mingling scents of fruity desserts, night-blooming flowers and a thousand incense all wafting in some perfect symphony of sweet, sugary bliss.

"I remember why I look forward to this all year," Oliver added, snatching another glass of champagne as a tall slim waiter passed them by. All of the waiters were skinny men dressed in black silken tuxedos. They wore little expression and Abby found she felt slightly unnerved by them.

"They're not real people," Elda told her.

Abby turned to her, wondering if she had read her thoughts.

"Not real? How so?"

"They're animals. Cats to be exact, though lord knows why Andromeda insists on using her cats. I've seen them get quite beastly at these things."

"Wait, cats?" Abby stood to watch the back of the waiter who'd just passed them by. She looked at Oliver to see if they were playing a joke on her.

"Andromeda," Oliver butted in, "is kind of like a crazy old cat lady in witch world. She has spent most of her one hundred and fifty years on earth creating spells to make her cats human. I'm convinced it's so that she doesn't have to pay to crate them when she flies...."

"Oh, phooey," Elda laughed swatting at him. "She did it to protect her coven originally. Of course, that was well over fifty years ago."

"Cats?" Abby asked again, watching as another waiter hunched to the ground and began gathering the shards of a broken plate.

"Wait. Look at that one." Oliver elbowed her and she turned to the buffet table just in time to see one of the waiters scoop a finger-full of tuna pate into his mouth.

"See," Elda sighed, smiling. "Cats."

****

Abby wandered back into the castle in search of Sebastian. She had expected him to appear on the veranda, flushed and hungry, but then she realized that the castle boasted at least half-a-dozen banquet halls, indoors and out. She spun as she walked, eyeing the crowds for signs of his fiery garb and ran smack into a furry witch.

"Victor," the black fox told her, thrusting his hand into Abby's and boring into her with intense dark eyes, brown, but almost black.

"Abby, or Melusine tonight," she told him with a shallow curtsy. She was unnerved by his eyes.

"Melusine, my favorite of all the water goddesses. Quite a frightful choice though. Will you be turning into the serpent tonight?"

She pulled her dress up to reveal the scaly fins beneath and grinned. "Perhaps..." She started to add that her dragon half was around here somewhere, but he pushed a finger to her lips.

"Shh. Do you hear that?"

She listened. She heard everything and nothing. Her ears caught witches deep in conversation, laughter, falling water, clinking glasses, and on it went.

He laughed, tilting his head back and let his laughter carry high in the sparkling room. The ceiling glittered with constellations and darting spirits. Not real spirits, but phantoms conjured by the coven of Sorciére who, according to Helena, was putting on the best All Hallow's Party to date.

"Listen right here." He pressed two fingers against the space just above and between her eyebrows--her third eye or, as Elda called it, her pineal gland.

When he did so, she felt a slight jolt and suddenly she did hear something. Laughter, low and haunted, echoed in her ears.

"The laughter of the dead," he told her, leaning in so that his lips brushed her ear. She trembled and rubbed her arms against the goosebumps prickling.

"Join me, Abby?" Victor asked, taking her elbow in his furred hand and steering her into an adjacent room, this one much smaller than the Grand Hall. The walls curved, closing the circular room at two French doors that were open to the night. The bowl-shaped ceiling was spun with silvery cobwebs.

"Oh," Abby gasped, placing a hand to her mouth. The cobwebs were being spun by millions of tiny spiders.

"Stunning, aren't they? On loan from The Sky Mothers in Australia. There is a witch there who speaks to them. She's brilliant."

A breathtaking witch, costumed as a flamingo, with glowing violet plumage streaming behind her, disembarked from a round coffee table where several other witches had assembled on a jumble of comfortable silk couches, talking intimately. She came to Victor and kissed him softly on the lips.

"What do we have here?" she asked, eying Abby mischievously. "A sea nymph? A bewitching Siren?"

"Melusine," Victor whispered, squeezing Abby's elbow and cocking an eyebrow.

The flamingo's eyes lit at the mention of Melusine and Abby felt she was missing an inside joke.

"Join us?" The flamingo asked, pulling Abby toward their table.

She glanced behind her, knowing that she should find Sebastian, but felt instead the urgent need to know these young witches that seemed so together, but also younger than the other witches she had met and, perhaps, more alive.

She sank into one of the chairs and took the glass of rose wine thrust into her hand.

"I'm Kendra," the flamingo told her. "This," she pointed to a young man on her left in a silver-sequined leotard with dazzling black wings and red, sparkling eyelids, "is Dante or Cupid's Shadow tonight."

Dante arched his eyebrows and leaned toward her, kissing her outstretched hand gently.

"Ezra," said the girl to Abby's left. Her voice was low, rough–hewn, and hardly matched the periwinkle fairy costume frothy with chiffon. Her brown eyes were big and kind and she did not shake Abby's hand, but placed her hands in prayer before her chest and gave her a slight bow. Abby could see tattoos creeping from her dress along her neck and down her arms.

"And our final comrade," Victor told her with a nudge, "is Marcus, but as you can see he's currently unavailable."

She followed the line of Victor's finger to the French doors and there, on the stone ledge, she saw a witch walking ever so casually on his hands. He gripped the beam beneath him and, monkey-like, moved along. His reddish waves brushed his biceps and he grinned, despite how difficult the maneuver must have been. Upside down, his legs were one, held stiff with toes pointing toward the sky.

"Whoa," she breathed, leaning forward in her chair as if to somehow peer out over the ledge, which she knew dropped to water far below. Though Sorciére was not an island as Ula was, it was at the outermost speck of a peninsula that jutted into a rushing river, The Garonne according to Helena.

Marcus, as if feeling her eyes, looked up and, for a moment, they stared across the room at one another. He winked and then powerfully shoved himself upward, flipped once and landed on the ledge with both feet. He dropped to the floor and strode into the room, bowing to Abby.

"Is the circle complete then?" he asked, eying Victor and then moving his gaze to the other witches.

"Shut up Marcus and sit," Kendra told him, flicking champagne from her fingers at his face. He licked it from the edge of his lip and leaned backward into his chair, nearly folding his body in half so that his legs dangled behind him

"Marcus is our acrobat." Victor shrugged. "You can't believe how he comes in handy."

"Yes, I can," she said. "I've spent enough time avoiding death in trees that I would kill to be an acrobat."

Victor nodded and Abby noticed the significant glances that they all seemed to exchange, somehow casually enough that she almost thought she imagined it...almost.

"What? Is that off limits?" she asked, when no one spoke.

She suddenly wanted desperately to talk about some of the things that she had experienced since becoming a witch. For the first time since it all began, she felt like she sat with people who understood.

"I totally get it," Ezra chimed in, "and there are no off-limit topics--not with us. Now those old vultures out there," she gestured toward the lobby where two older witches in gray robes ambled by, "mum's almost always the word."

Abby smiled and relaxed deeper into her chair.

"I feel that," she admitted. "That silence. My coven is so quiet sometimes..." She trailed off because at the first mention of Ula, color had begun to climb up her throat and into her face. Was she betraying her coven by speaking about them to these witches?

"Abby," Victor interrupted her thoughts. "We're a lot alike. You feel it, don't you?"

She did, of course she did and, as a witch, she had begun to allow those feelings first priority. That was the whole foundation of intuition that Elda had taught her, an unexplainable knowing. She felt like she belonged with these five witches.

"We're all new to this, Abby," Kendra told her, sweeping her long hair over her shoulder. Kendra looked young as did the other four witches.

"How new?" Abby asked, regretting the question almost immediately. What if young turned out to be decades into the life rather than centuries?

"Two years," Kendra stated simply.

"Three," said Victor. And on they went--Dante two, Ezra four and Marcus one and a half.

"Just months for me," Abby told them. "Not quite three."

Marcus whistled and slowly rotated so that he sat upright.

"Those are some hard months."

"The hardest," Ezra added, reaching over to give Abby's hand a supportive squeeze.

"Made harder when you go the traditional route," Victor said, staring at Abby sympathetically.

"What do you mean the traditional route? Are there other options?"

"Of course," Kendra chimed in quickly. "There's life in a coven and life on the outside."

"Also known as freedom," Victor said seriously, contemplating Abby as he traced the rim of his wine glass with his finger.

"How so?" she asked, but of course she already knew--freedom from Elda, Faustine and her other teachers, freedom from the heavy stone walls and the constant expectations and the learning that some days felt a bit like torture.

"I don't think you need me to answer that Abby," Victor said.

"Let's show her instead," Dante added, reaching a hand into one of his long black boots. He pulled out a silk cloth and unwrapped it slowly on the table in front of them. Inside lay a scattering of small bones. Dante's deft fingers swept the bones and Abby saw what looked like the skull and first several ribs of a fish with the bent points of wings emerging from its sides. He took a small silver pouch from his pocket and set it next to the bones.

He closed his eyes, spoke too low for anyone to hear and then swept the bones into his champagne. He tilted the pouch above his glass and sprinkled a dusting of green flakes into the shimmering liquid. The other witches drained their glasses and then passed the empty ones to him.

"You too, Abby," Victor nodded at her glass. "Join us."

She looked at their expectant faces, swallowed the last of her wine and passed the crystal goblet to Dante.

He twirled his glass and then poured a small sip of his champagne into each of their glasses, mindful that the bones did not slip out.

When she took her glass back, she noticed that the champagne had turned darker, muddy almost.

"Cheers," Kendra said, conspiratorially leaning in. The others followed her and their glasses met in the center of the table. Abby took a deep breath and clinked her own against the others. She closed her eyes and took a drink...

****

Have you seen Abby?" Sebastian asked coming up behind Dafne who stood, staring moodily through one of the castle's windows.

The witch gasped and stumbled back as if he had burned her.

"Sorry, sorry, I didn't mean to startle you," he said quickly backing away, but still looking at her.

Her dark eyes looked stormy and glazed as if she'd had too much to drink, or something else entirely.

"Hittin' the bottle pretty hard?" He meant it as a joke, but of course she only glared at him silently.

"Never mind," he sighed, holding his hands up and backing away.

****

It happened immediately, before she even tasted the acrid liquid in her glass. The room and the other witches fell away. She spun in a giant vortex seeing only blurred colors and shapes. And then all was still and Victor's dark eyes were close to hers.

"She's here," Victor said. The other witches gazed at her, their expressions gleeful.

She looked around and gasped, but the water that should have flooded her mouth did not. She sat on an ocean floor, her legs tucked beneath her, and the sand spread out in gentle ridges. The other witches sat as well, cross-legged, and they appeared to be more interested in her reaction than their own.

"We're at the bottom of the Atlantic," Kendra told her, spreading her arms out to either side and laughing.

Abby realized that no words were actually being spoken. Their conversation consisted entirely of their thoughts.

"Probably two-hundred feet deep here," Dante thought.

"The ocean?" Abby asked.

The others laughed and Victor grabbed her hand.

"Look." He pointed overhead where a school of stingray drifted along. Their white bellies turned and caught shafts of moonlight. As they crossed over the group, their shadows cast everyone in darkness.

"How?" Abby asked, when her amazement had abated enough for words.

"Magic," Dante said, moving from his knees and darting straight up into the water. Marcus followed, back flipping and then diving back to the sand.

"Have we astral-traveled then?" she asked, feeling the sand which felt like sand. She could also feel the cold in the water, though less intense than it should have been.

"Sort of," Victor told her. "We haven't exactly named it yet."

"You discovered it then?"

"We created it," Kendra corrected her.

"Well, that's a little dramatic," Ezra interrupted, earning a scowl from Kendra. "There are a lot of witches who have discovered unheard of magic and never written of it, so we don't know..."

"Oh, come on," Kendra snapped. "Let Dante have his victory."

"Hush," Victor laughed, moving to his feet. He pulled Abby up. She could feel the great pressure of the water around her and above her. Her ears popped and Victor laughed at the look of horror that briefly crossed her face.

"It's okay," he said, slipping a finger into his own ear. "Happens all the time." He stuck his tongue in his cheek and made a loud popping noise. "Shall we swim?"

She followed him as he pushed off and her costume did not feel wet or heavy, but merely floated. They swam towards the surface, but then Victor broke to the side. He kicked his feet gently, barely parting the water and kept his hand in hers, gently pulling her along.

She gazed at the seabed, dotted with gray shells and low slithering fish. The sand sloped down and then dropped away where below them an enormous shipwreck slid into view.

She jerked her hand from Victors, shocked at the enormity of the ship, rising like a hulking corpse in the dark water. Its hull pointed up, but still it lay far beneath the surface.

"Don't be afraid," Victor told her. "Nothing can hurt you here."

She nodded, but her chest felt tight and she grasped his hand harder as they swam down into the dark cavity. It was like the pirates' ships she'd watched in childhood movies. The sails were long gone, but a few tattered ropes still clung to the mast.

The ship seemed to undulate with the water, its presence feeling sinister and, when Abby began to kick her legs and propel herself back in the water, Victor grabbed her hand.

"No, come on," he told her, leaving no room for resistance as he gripped her arm and swam down towards it.

As they drew closer, she began to see small schools of silvery fish darting through the decayed portholes in the ships sides. The ship was tilted, its stern lost in the debris field scattered along the ocean floor.

"It's amazing, isn't it?"

"Spectacular," she thought, and this time did not resist when he pulled her towards the main deck.

****

When she returned to her body, swooning with the secret of what she had just experienced, Abby felt desperate to find Sebastian. She wanted him to meet Victor and the other witches and she could barely wait to describe their ocean journey.

She left her new friends and returned to the Great Hall, realizing that she needed a bathroom break before she hunted for her missing sidekick. Abby found the latrine, a vacuous space of stone and mirrors with giant sunken tubs adrift in rose petals.

Her head swam and the champagne and the thousand new faces all masked and adorned in feathers and glitter only added to her light-headedness. She leaned her hands on the edges of a stone basin, breathing deeply the perfume of the space and sneaking glances at her own unfamiliar face. Her cheeks, flushed pink, made her brown eyes appear darker, sparkling beneath painted silvery black lashes and candlelight.

She grinned and shook her head in disbelief at the good fortune of such an inspiring night. Never had she experienced anything like it and, as crystal glasses were thrust into her hand and handsome witches in strange costume whisked her onto the floor and twirled her beneath the dazzling night sky, she grew exuberant and tipsy. Now, to top it all off, she'd met other witches who actually understood her and they lived in Chicago, a city that Abby loved.

A toilet flushed and she spun around, unaware that she was not alone in the bathroom. Soft footsteps padded from behind a copper door strung with garlands of fresh flowers. The witch was young, strikingly beautiful and hauntingly familiar.

Abby searched her face. When had she met the young woman who stared at her now as if they were old friends?

"Abby," she breathed, and took Abby's hands into her own very pale, very cold fingers. Abby studied the wide-set hazel eyes and small girlish mouth.

"Do I know you?" Abby asked, but the face before her slid into place in a photograph that Abby had seen, a photograph of a young woman in a red dress standing in front of a wooden swing set.

"Claire," the girl said before Abby could find her own voice.

"Claire?" For a moment she still could not place her and then..."Wait, Sebastian's Claire? But how?"

Claire laughed, high and strange, and then snapped her long slender fingers.

"Magic, silly."

Abby leaned heavily against the sink. The rush of the evening was moving in another direction and she had begun to feel dizzy, black dots sparkling in front of her.

"No time for that now," Claire demanded, gripping Abby's forearms in her hands and squeezing hard.

"We have to go to Sebastian," Abby said suddenly, realizing that she held his most coveted prize only inches away.

Claire shook her head and her image twitched and faded. Her touch on Abby's arms lost its intensity.

"Follow the smoke," Claire whispered, but as Abby watched, Claire's eyes grew wide with fear and she let out a tiny, guttural sound. Abby turned to the mirror where Claire's gaze had locked. In the back of the latrine, a witch dressed in a Native American costume stood watching them. Her thick, black hair fell in a heavy braid over her shoulder. She wore a long, deerskin dress with a heavy pelt wrapped around her neck, the dried feet of the thing, a fox, hanging by her waist.

Abby spun around, but the woman and Claire had both vanished completely.

****

Sebastian leaned against a golden column wreathed in bundles of purple flowers that smelled almost like cherry pie. His eyes swam from the booze and he took a bite from the sloppy sandwich that he held in his hand. It had been at least an hour since he'd seen Abby and figured that he should find her, though no urgency arrived at her absence. He knew that she could take care of herself and, more so, she needed time apart from him to connect with other witches. He did not want to be the albatross that denied her the full experience as a new witch.

He watched a group of child witches conjuring phantom monsters. A girl costumed as Cleopatra pulled a handful of sparkly dust from her pocket and threw it into the air. A winged canine with human eyes emerged for an instant looking so real that Sebastian's arms slid off the column and he nearly fell onto his back. He caught himself as the dust broke apart and rained down on the young witches.

"They're talented, aren't they?" the voice came from behind him.

He turned to see a beautiful woman with long, flowing purple hair watching him playfully. A smile curved her dark, glossy lips. She wore a tight, black dress that hugged every curve and nook of her body, wrapping so tight across her chest that he could see the white slopes of her breasts.

"Have another," she flirted, handing him a glass of champagne.

He opened his mouth to decline, but instead took the glass and drained it in a single gulp. When he finished, he stared at it in wonder as if he couldn't understand where the flaxen liquid had gone.

Down the hall, a large wooden door swung shut and the movement caught his eye. He saw her for only an instant. Her short, dark hair hung above her pale neck. It was her tiny shoulders that gave her away. Years of his life had been lost, or perhaps gained, tormenting Claire for those narrow shoulders.

"Claire," he called out, but the girl did not turn. She disappeared into one of the many ballrooms.

He started to lunge after her, noticing that his feet felt heavier and that the gold pillar seemed to hold the entirety of his weight.

The purple-haired witch looked amused and lifted her soft fingers to his lips. She cupped his chin and looked deep into his face. He stood, riveted by her eyes that were the lightest green, almost without color. He pitched forward, but not with his body, only his mind, and fell into the crystal of her eyes. He surrendered to the darkness.

****

Abby sat on the floor and shoved her head between her knees, sucking in breaths that didn't fill her chest, but got lost somewhere in her throat. As she breathed, the champagne's effect dulled and she began to regain some of her composure.

She had foolishly believed that as she came into her power, panic and anxiety would simply disappear. She would blast it away with a geyser or something. Instead, she felt heightened by everything, including anxiety, and the black spots behind her eyes were like moon eclipses.

When Lydie walked into the bathroom, talking merrily with another young witch, Abby could only stare at them, imagining how insane she looked, but unable to fake it.

Lydie immediately ran to her, squatting down and pushing her hair back from her face.

"What happened? What is it, Abby?" The smile drained from Lydie's mouth and Abby felt guilty. The other young witch, dressed as an insect of some sort, looked equally unhinged.

Abby shook her head and frowned.

"Have you seen Sebastian, Lydie? I really need to find him."

"Only earlier when you two were dancing," she said, continuing to look concerned.

Abby struggled to her feet and smoothed out her dress, avoiding Lydie's puzzled stare.

"You looked so scared, though. I mean, are you sure there wasn't something else?" Lydie glanced around, studying the high, dark corners in the bathroom. Candlelight only made more sinister the unseen crevices and Abby understood that as much as Lydie loved All Hallow's Eve, it also terrified her.

When she left the bathroom, Abby felt the first wave of panic wash over her. Ghoulish, masked faces leered at her as she stumbled down the hall. She stared into faces and at the backs of heads, seeking only one, but his familiar blue eyes did not meet hers in return. When she finally found Oliver, her panic was bordering hysteria.

"Sebastian's missing!"

CHAPTER 7

Abby sat on the salmon-colored chaise beneath her window and stared numbly at the black storm moving across the water. There were tears, but they were far down, imbedded in the dark places too deep to dig free, so her eyes remained dry while her heart split again and again with no physical release. Sebastian was gone.

Gone? But what did that even mean? She couldn't seem to reach the bottom of that thought, the place where it ceased to be a boiling stone in her stomach and turned into a facet of the mind--a logical piece of information that she could work with.

How had they talked her into returning? She had wanted to stay and the witches at Sorciére had more than offered their assistance and their coven, but somehow the witches of Ula rallied around her and, before she could protest, Oliver practically carried her to the mirror and back to the suffocating isolation of Ula. They force-fed her calming tea and brainstormed their strategies as Abby watched in utter shock and disbelief. Faustine would track him from the tower, Oliver and Dafne would go on the hunt, they would contact other covens, but all for what? They had left him there. He could have merely wandered into a dungeon and gotten lost, but Abby knew better than that. Superior witches with powerful skills had searched the castle for him. He had vanished without a trace.

Now she sat in her empty room and watched the white caps on the lake below. Every watery surge thrust into her like steel pokers jabbing at the soft flesh of her heart. Still she did not cry and when Helena brought her more tea, she did not drink it, but let it sit on the windowsill and grow cold in the approaching twilight.

She slept in fits, waking again and again to the emptiness of her room, only to remember a much greater emptiness--Sebastian. The clock chimed and she knew that twenty-four hours had passed since she'd last touched him, last seen the candlelight flicker in his blue eyes while he whirled her around the Sorciére castle, looking happier than she had ever seen him.

"You have to eat something, love," Oliver told her, pushing in her door with his hip. He balanced a tray on a single hand and Abby smelled orange juice that made her stomach turn.

"Were you a waiter in a previous life?" she asked dryly.

"In this life actually, one of my many pre-witch talents."

Abby sighed and leaned back into her pillows. It was nearly six pm and she could already see the sun in its gradual descent. She had not left her room since they had returned early that morning and Oliver had tried twice to coax her down, but each time she refused. This time, he brought the food to her.

"Come on, spoonful of sugar?" he asked, pointing to a bowl of sugar next to a halved grapefruit.

Her stomach rumbled a hallow cry, but she ignored it, feeling only a knot where hunger usually lived.

"I'm genuinely not hungry, Oliver."

"I know that." He propped the tray on the bed and sat down next to it. "But you still need to eat. You're skin and bones as it is, Abby."

Not true exactly, though the healthy weight that Abby had gained when her powers initially surfaced had suddenly subsided. Stress was a mighty force and it had rendered her skeletal in hours.

She picked up a piece of toast and lifted it to her lips, taking a tiny bite. It scraped the inside of her mouth and took several minutes to chew, but she finally swallowed it with scratchy reluctance.

"There. Happy?" She knew that she sounded bratty, but she didn't care. She felt horrible and wanted to pay it forward to anyone insane enough to enter her space.

"How could I have left him? How could we have left him?" she asked Oliver, not for the first time. He was the only one who really seemed to agree with her that they should have stayed.

"He never should have been there," Abby added, shaking her head viciously. "Why did I ask him to go? Why did I convince Elda to conceal him?"

"Things happen, Abby," he said. "There's a reason for all this. We don't know what it is, but have faith that it will work out."

She bit her cheeks to refrain from snapping at him and stared out the window instead.

He sighed and took a bite of the croissant on the tray, smiling apologetically as he chewed.

"No, eat it. I can't." She rubbed her hands on the side of her head as though it might relieve some of the pressure building there.

"Elda and Faustine are taking action. I know it feels like they're not right now, but they actually are."

"Why can't I act? What's the point of being a witch in a coven if I'm shoved aside when the person that I love is in danger? Am I just supposed to swallow this?"

"Hey." He set the tray on her bed and took a seat beside her, placing a hand in hers and gently rubbing her fingers. "I get it. I know that you're ready to explode right now, but you can only help Sebastian if you're calm. Irrational stuff will just put you in danger. You know that it's true."

She knew that he referred to her frantic middle-of-the-night rescue attempt, little more than six weeks before, a choice that sent her into the lair of an evil witch, at the bidding of the ghost Devin, all in an attempt to save her family who, it turned out, were not even in danger. He was right, but she could only get behind that on a logical level. Her heart, her soul and her body told her to move, to get off the couch, out of the castle and back to Sorciére while the last of Sebastian's trace still remained.

"Tell me this," she demanded, jerking her hand from Oliver's and turning to face him. "How would he even get back here? How?"

"You heard what Elda said. She enchanted the charm to send him here, to bring him back to the castle."

Abby shook her head in disbelief.

"She said that after he was gone. She never told us that before the party. I thought he would simply be outside the castle, in the city or something."

Oliver held up his hands in surrender.

"That was my impression also, but she has no reason to change her story. They would never leave Sebastian. Abby, we searched the grounds outside the castle. He wasn't there."

It was true, they had searched. After the Ball ended and Sorciére had cleared, they searched every inch of the castle and the grounds surrounding it. Faustine and Elda rallied the witches who they'd known for centuries, who they could trust with their secret, and together they hunted.

They did not merely look for him, though. Powerful witches could see with much more than their eyes. They consulted tools of divination. They had scraped beneath Abby's fingernails and removed things from her dress, but did not find enough of Sebastian to work with. Faustine had returned to Ula through the two-way mirror and retrieved articles of Sebastian's clothing, his hairbrush and pair of his sunglasses. In a room that felt oddly like a bubble, the witch Demetrius lit five cauldrons. In each, he dropped an article that belonged to Sebastian. Every cauldron revealed images of Sebastian at the Ball and then only darkness. Both the Ula and Sorciére witches were dumbfounded.

"I just feel trapped here. They insisted that I come back and now I'm sitting here biting my fingernails, which just grow back to spite me." She held up her fingernails, still long, but jagged in the spots that she'd just bitten.

As Abby watched the incoming storm slowly rolling toward them, she thought back to the previous night.

"We'll find him," Oliver had reassured her, for the seemingly hundredth time. They stalked the castle together, most of their costumes pulled off and left in a heap on one of the many hallway floors. She'd been peeling off layers for hours since the first inkling deep in her belly that something terrible had happened. She wore only the black dress that acted as a sheath beneath the dazzling Melusine costume. When she glanced down, she realized that it looked like a dress for mourning.

At first, she had merely believed that Claire's warning had struck a chord and the ominous tone continued to reverberate through her, but after nearly an hour looking in ballrooms and banquet halls, on verandas and in sitting areas, she started to recognize that her fear was for Sebastian. She could not feel him. Even when they fought and he grew very distant from her, she always sensed his presence. Now, as she combed the castle painstakingly, the emptiness chilled her to the core. Oliver visited bathrooms and when that too turned up no trace, they tracked down the witches of Ula and each individually began their own search. Twice they had reconvened, but not a fragment of him remained. They could not even find a witch who had seen him in the previous hours.

Abby and Oliver took the steps two a time, climbing one of the castle's several wings. The halls were dark, not meant for party goers, but most of the guests had departed and those that remained belonged to Sorciére and many of those witches too had begun to look for Sebastian. Only a few witches close to Elda and Faustine knew that they searched for a human. Elda believed it unwise to let the secret out to everyone.

Oliver waved his hand and a tall mahogany door, previously locked, popped open. Beyond, lay only a dark room stuffed with paintings and antiques. If Sebastian hid in that space, they'd never find him amid the towers of art and statuary. They encountered Helena in the next room, frantically ripping blankets and pillows from a linen closet in search of him. When she turned to them, she looked wild, but immediately pretended to be unruffled when her eyes fell upon Abby.

"You can't feel him either?" Abby asked, though she already knew the answer.

The night went on that way. Abby watched Demetrius with the cauldrons. Then she sat in one of the All Hallow's tents as Helena and then Bridget consulted a crystal ball. Max astral-travelled throughout Sorciére and then back to Ula. Faustine used Sorciére's Crystal Tower to seek Sebastian with his mind.

Abby stood on the craggy rocks outside of Sorciére for an hour. She stared into the raging river and wondered if Sebastian had been pulled to a watery grave.

At daybreak, Elda insisted that they meet in the kitchen for coffee and regrouping. By then, the alarm was unmistakable and the best efforts of the empaths to calm the group failed. Faustine announced that they must leave

Sorciére and return to Ula.

"Why?" Abby demanded, almost too exhausted to stand, but still ready to fight.

Galla, a Sorciére elder answered.

"Because Sebastian is not in our castle and, if he did somehow get displaced, Elda bewitched him back to Ula."

Abby started to argue, but Elda placed a hand on her arm.

"It's true, Abby. We must return."

When she refused, they forced her to drink a strong tea that Galla had prepared until she became too sleepy to stand. She vaguely remembered Oliver carrying her through the mirror.

****

Dafne moved quickly. She stole into the night at Ula and climbed to the furthest cliff from the castle. The slick rock wall threatened to send her into the icy lake as she carefully threaded her way down the cliff. She slipped into a tiny crevice that offered only enough space for her to lie fully on the earthen ground. She opened her bag, grasping the items tight in her hands, and then she closed her eyes, releasing her astral body.

Indra waited in the caves of the ancients, her purple hair tucked behind her eyes. Her face betrayed none of the fear that Dafne tasted bitterly at the back of her throat. Both Indra and Dafne had participated in the search for Sebastian that morning. In truth, they bumbled the search and misled the other witches at every opportunity. Dafne knew that she had set events in motion that would alter all of their destinies.

Indra gave Dafne a single nod of affirmation and moved forward. She stopped at the center tunnel. They could not enter the tunnel if it had nothing to tell them, but Indra had been studying The Pool of Truth for years and she had uncovered a spell that allowed them through. With her hands she began to draw designs in the stale energy before her. Like carefully aligning a Rubik's cube, she undid the charms that prevented their entrance. Dafne watched her in awe, knowing that each action took them deeper into the betrayal of their covens.

They moved together down the center tunnel, their shadowless astral bodies gliding effortlessly, but Dafne could not deny the trepidation that held her chest in its vice-like grip. It was not thought, for she had turned that off weeks ago when she had embarked on this tumultuous path. However, her instincts, which she had relied on all her life, told her to turn back. She ignored them and continued.

They moved into the silvery light of the cave where water splashed down from the black sky above. The Pool of Truth shone in magnificent waves of starlight and moonlight--not perfectly calm, but slightly turbulent as if it sensed their treachery.

Indra stepped in first and Dafne followed. They stood ankle-deep and linked their arms, both of them tilting back, chests lifting as they began to chant. As their mouths moved in unison, the water swirled and crashed, becoming a stormy sea that bucked around them. Dafne could feel its energy, but dared not look into its depths. Legend told that spells cast against The Pool of Truth brought grave consequences to their creator. Witches knew that some magical spaces and objects were gifts of the divine and to manipulate them was to break sacred law.

"But it's for the greater good," Indra had insisted and Dafne had agreed, of course she had. What witch wouldn't leap to such measures if it meant avoiding the annihilation of her coven and more? Who wouldn't topple the evil before it took hold?

Their voices rose and the sky turned orange and then red until balls of fire rained into the cave and filled the water with bright, putrid light. It burned Dafne's eyes and, though her physical body was not there, she felt her skin begin to blister and cry out. Indra cried as if she too burned and their astral bodies bled together in the firelight.

Indra moved into her power now and water seethed up, forming a dozen cyclones filled with Dafne's fire. The water and fire spun until it broke away from the lagoon and formed a much larger orb above them. Indra looked up into the sphere, her green eyes reflecting the electric colors.

Dafne kneeled on the ground and conjured the clothes that she had clutched in her arms when moving into her astral body. Sebastian's jeans, worn in the knees, a gray Bob Marley t-shirt and even his underpants, blue boxer briefs, appeared before her on the ground. She breathed invisible fire into the clothes and slowly his body emerged. It was not Sebastian, merely an image of him imbued with his essence. The body rose to its feet and then off the ground, pulled by the velocity of the spinning energy above it.

The body lifted and then merged with the pulsing fire and water. Dafne watched the sphere consume the body and then, with a deafening crash, the orb slammed back into the Pool of Truth and sunk to the depths.

****

Candles flickered in the nearly black room. Elda, Faustine, Helena, Max and Bridget stood together in the Magic Circle chanting in unison. Their voices barely registered above a whisper and they had begun to sway gently from side to side. They wore their old cloaks which had grown faded and dusty from years without use. In the center of the circle, the X began to glow. The soft white light grew brighter as they focused their attention upon it, until the entire room was awash. They each closed their eyes, saving themselves from the blinding and mesmerizing light.

"I call upon the energies of the Universe, the spirits of the ancestors," Faustine bellowed. His voice echoed off the concave walls and reverberated around them.

They repeated his words. They called upon the Watch Towers of the north, south, east and west. They called upon their elements, their guides and the white light that infused all things. Their voices merged and flowed like an ellipsis sounding their cries into eternity. Helena began to cry and her tears made the X glow brighter still.

With invisible fingers, Faustine reached into their sphere of power. He searched for the thread, the single radiant filament that would cast out the darkness that had settled upon Ula. A single thread that might show them the path to Sebastian, whose lost soul haunted all of their waking and sleeping moments. Each witch felt Faustine as he probed the sphere of light and retreated, empty, again and again.

Their energies began to fade. They could not conjure the space for much longer. Max dropped to one knee, his mouth slackening as he tried to continue chanting. Bridget squeezed his hand, but she too barely held on. Her body grew hunched and her head lolled from side to side.

Faustine's search became more desperate and erratic, which weakened their circle and dispersed the energy further and further out, so that the concentrated light began to flicker off the walls and bounce away from them.

Finally, in a great flash, the light vanished, taking the meager candle flames with it. Max and Helena fell to the floor, exhausted and overcome by the defeat.

The thread had not been found.

****

Seventy-two hours. Seventy-two hours since Abby had last seen Sebastian. Seventy-two hours since she'd last truly slept, eaten or felt whole. Only in the early morning hours did she leave her room and now, at three am, she walked the castle halls. She went to the dungeons and, zombie-like, slipped in and out of the rooms. She heard sounds behind Dafne's door, but merely walked by without a thought. She returned to the library and lay down on the thick carpet in front of the crackling fire. In the fetal position, she stared into the flames and cried.

When her eyes closed, she did not slip off to sleep, but instead fell into the familiar cave that beckoned to the witch's astral body. She had visited before, several times now and felt unafraid as she glided through the shadowy tunnel. She felt her grief in the cave as palpable as in the castle. Had some part of her thought that solace lay in the cave? No. She knew that only confusion, fear and anger--yes, anger--followed her now.

She neared the fork of the three tunnels, intending to go into the left tunnel where she had yet to travel, but an unseen force pulled her toward the center pathway. She knew what lay in the end of the passage--The Pool of Truth--a gossamer pond that revealed horrific truths to the witches who were called to it. Abby tried to stop, reaching out blindly, fighting to dig her heels into the dirt, but in her astral body, she had no physical form, only a presence less solid than the steam that rose from a tea kettle.

The tunnel had lost all its magic. She had discovered her Aunt Sydney in the Pool. She remembered Sydney's bloated face and the unending heartache of accepting that she would never hear Sydney's laughter again.

Abby could not meet the water a second time but, despite her efforts, she could not flee from her astral body. Usually, she had only to think of her physical form and she would snap, rubber-band like, back into the tangible realm. She tried every tip that Max had taught her. She imagined a pin poking into her flesh. She closed her eyes and pretended to awaken from a long sleep. She muttered the familiar phrase that connected her to mundane reality. "What's for breakfast?" She spoke it again and then she screamed it, but still her body floated forward.

She moved into the opening and the pool gazed back at her, reflecting nothing because she was not really there. She wondered then if any of it was really there--the cave, the Pool of Truth, the tunnels carved into rock. Water flowed from the chasm in the cave ceiling. It trickled and splashed and she bit back a scream as a force carried her over the rock ledge and into the water below.

She did not swim, but floated down as if cement boots were fastened to her legs. She gazed into the crystalline water beneath her, but saw no bottom to the pool. It was an endless watery grave and when she looked back up and saw the soft black curls wafting like a halo, she screamed and bucked, fighting the image of Sebastian, but still the cave did not disappear. As she watched, his body drifted, his gray t-shirt ballooning out and away, and she saw Claire's initials beneath his sleeve. She saw his coarse fingernails and the diamond-shaped mole on his left foot and then his eyes, beautiful, blue, but vacant. She had looked into those eyes and felt the most intense love and fear and desire, but now they were dark and empty, their light extinguished.

****

"Abby, Abby." Lydie screamed and shook Abby as she lay on the floor convulsing, her head snapping from side to side, her gaze fixed on some unseen horror.

Oliver shot through the door, his eyes wild and sleepy. He saw Abby sprawled by the fireplace and a sobbing Lydie over her. He ran to her, pulled Lydie away and shifted her head so that it was in line with her spine. He looked into her eyes and knew that she was astrally-traveling, but to where he could not tell. He sensed danger and went to the fire, dipped one of the metal pokers into the flame and returned.

"I'm sorry, honey," he told the convulsing Abby as he touched the poker to the flesh on her right hand.

In the Pool of Truth, Abby started to reach for Sebastian, wanting intensely to grasp him around the waist and take him with her, but as her fingers took hold of his hand, the pool, Sebastian, and the cave vanished and she returned to her body.

She snapped back, her body rigid and her eyes, bulging with terror, locked on Oliver's before the screams, that she'd been trying to let out, made their way up her vocal chords and into the room. She wailed and rocked and turned on her side, clawing at the carpeting as though it held her hostage.

Elda raced into the room and then Faustine. They stood watching her as she curled into a ball and sobbed like a child. Elda went to her, knelt and rubbed her back. She felt the weight of Faustine's gaze. Elda knew that their call had failed. The energies of the universe granted them no reprieve and now she saw that only more horrors lay ahead.

When they finally calmed her, Helena force-fed her a trauma elixir and Abby told them about Sebastian in the Pool of Truth.

"Please, please," she begged Elda. "It made a mistake, it had to. He's not dead, I know he's not."

Elda sat on a stool across from Abby and patted her knee, shaking her head slowly.

"Oh, Abby, I want so badly to tell you that The Pool makes mistakes. I would give almost anything, but you know that I can't. You know that."

Tears ran down her face and salted her lips and she squeezed her hands together in a fist at her stomach. She felt sick and dizzy and she wanted to rip out her own heart and cast it into the fire if it meant no more pain.

"I can't take this," she said between sobs. "I can't take any more of this."

Oliver stood behind her, his hands resting on her chair back. He had tried to rub her shoulders, but she'd batted him angrily away. She didn't want to be touched and she didn't want to be soothed. She wanted Sebastian. She wanted him to walk into the room and ask Abby to reverse the course of their lives. They would walk backwards out of the castle, row backwards across the lake and, instead of fleeing to Ula after the Vepars attacked them, they would hop on a flight to Australia and live out their days at the beach.

The thought made her cry harder.

"We will find out what happened to Sebastian," Faustine told her feebly. The look of helplessness in his face unnerved them all.

"You have to find out for sure if he's dead," Abby insisted, her eyes going to Faustine's and then back to Elda's. "There must be some way. Can you go to the Pool?"

"It calls out to us, Abby," Elda told her gently. "It's not a choice. It's a doorway that is only open to witches who have a message on the other side."

"But why is he dead?" she wailed, doubling over with an agony she had never known. "Who killed him? Tobias? Did Tobias kill him?"

Elda and Faustine exchanged a look, but neither spoke.

Abby picked up her teacup and threw it across the room where it smashed against one of the bookshelves. She stood from her chair and ran out of the library and out of the castle, welcoming the moonless night.

She walked for hours. She walked the woods, the floating garden with flowers in night bloom, and the edges of both lagoons, up and down the sand dunes. She cried through it all and sometimes she stomped the flowers and kicked the trunks of the trees and twice she sat on the ground and cried so hard that she thought she might actually damage some part of her brain from the sheer force of her sobs.

She crawled down to the outcropping of rock where she and Sebastian had made love only weeks before. She began to talk to him. She asked him about his first kiss and his favorite kind of candy and what he wore for Halloween when he was ten years old. She told him that she once stole panties from a department store because her mother wouldn't let her buy thong underwear. She described how much she hated the third grade because her mother bought a sewing machine from an infomercial and insisted on making all of Abby's clothes herself. Most of her smocks looked like pillow cases with neck and arm-holes cut into them.

"My best memory though?" she continued, growing drowsy, "was the first time that I saw you. I remember your Pink Floyd t-shirt and this huge curl hanging in your eyes and I think the whole world opened for me right then. You know what else? I think you're the reason I found my power. It was you all along..."

She rested her head on the grass and closed her eyes.

****

"We must be able to do something," Oliver said angrily, slopping his coffee onto the tablecloth.

Bridget swept her fingers over the stain and it disappeared. Elda smiled at her apologetically.

"Oliver, you know better than that. We are witches, not gods. Some things must be endured and accepted. Pain is part of the process and..." she held up her hand to silence his interruption, "we all experienced some version of what Abby is experiencing now. You know this."

"Do you hear yourself?" he asked, unable to control his temper. "Someone murdered Sebastian. Something plucked him from a party filled with a thousand witches and murdered him!"

Bridget stood and began to clear their cups from the table. Her eyes were red-rimmed and she seemed close to breaking down. Elda waited until she left to answer him.

"Of course I understand the gravity of our situation Oliver. We all do, but we must not rush. Maybe this is a single incident. Or perhaps Sebastian's death is the tip of an iceberg that has not yet been revealed, but we cripple ourselves with assumptions. Faustine and Max are at Sorciére at this very moment. They will know more when they return and then perhaps we can go forward."

Oliver wanted to argue, to demand, as Abby had done, that the coven do something more, but Elda was right. The calling came with great sacrifice. He had lost much and his loss barely compared to the others. He didn't know the depths of their sacrifice and yet he could not remember a time when he felt as powerless as he did in that moment. Worse yet, he felt guilty because some small part of him had rejoiced in Sebastian's disappearance. Maybe that same part rejoiced in his death. He saw Elda watching him and looked shamefully out the window.

He could not reconcile his growing feelings for Abby. He tried to fight his desire to get closer to her, but it continued to live. Sometimes it felt like the little devil on his shoulder calling out to him to steal her away, but the core of him knew better. In his pure heart, loving Abby meant loving Sebastian because she had chosen him. When love took form, the individual no longer existed without the whole. Any separateness was merely an illusion.

****

After nearly seventy-three cups of tea, Helena pressed her face into her palms and started to cry. For hours she scoured the tea leaves, divining the past and the future. She asked for guidance, but received only jumbled images. Never in her life had the leaves been so unclear.

"Or maybe it's me," she said aloud.

"Or maybe it's Ula," Bridget said from the doorway, startling Helena.

Bridget sat next to Helena at the small kitchen table stacked with cookbooks, but rarely used for eating. She looked at the mound of wet leaves Helena had hurriedly dumped in her quest for the truth.

"You think there's something wrong at Ula?" Helena asked, searching for a moment of stillness to feel the energy of the castle. She expected a buzzing, an aliveness, but a strange silence settled over her.

"Yes, you feel it now. Like a vacuum? It's as if we've been sucked into a black hole..."

Helena nodded and looked again at the cup before her. The leaves had formed a chaotic shape that resembled something like a feather.

"I've seen that," Bridget told her, peering into the cup. "A feather, a black widow spider, a hang-man's noose. I've been getting bad omens for weeks..."

Helena felt a sinking feeling and she turned to face Bridget. She didn't even need to ask the question and Bridget nodded.

"Just like before..."

CHAPTER 8

"Abby, you're naked!" Oliver screamed, rushing through the rain toward her.

She barely registered his voice beneath the water pelting her body. She was naked, naked, covered in goosebumps and writhing beneath the treacherous sky in agony and desperation. She had not returned to the castle all day, but instead stood at the cliff edge and wished to die along with Sebastian. As she attempted to accept that he would never return, the thought of spending another moment at Ula made her skin crawl.

Her heart was heavier than the wet, cumbersome sand beneath her, and split into more pieces than there were grains along the shore. She cried and the rain took it and swept her tears into long snaking rivers down her trembling body.

She could have succumbed to the power. Her spirit would have ripped her from the egoic pain of her loss and catapulted her into a lightning storm of energy. But she refused its beckoning fingers. She refused the thoughtlessness and peace. Instead, she imagined him. She held him in her mind in a perfect memory that can only really exist as a memory and she rocked on her toes beneath the thundering sky.

When Oliver tried to take her hands, she pummeled his chest until he released her. He did not know what to do, but stood, watching her in confused awe.

She was wild, hair wet and ravished and curled around her head. Her body was lean and slick and powerful. He saw her muscles, taut, the veins in her forearms twisted and blue in her translucent flesh. Her brown eyes had taken on the yellow of the storm and they flashed from their teary pools.

He turned to the castle, hoping to see Elda or Faustine running to his aid, but no one came. The castle loomed beyond them, the heavy wood door closed to the lashing winds. He could almost imagine them hovering by windows, staring nervously at the spectacle of Abby at the lagoon edge, naked and raging.

She blamed them. She blamed all of them and her accusations, though not voiced, struck them equally. They could have sedated her, forced her into the library to thaw before the fire, but she was not bound to their coven. She was free, limitless, and her energy rebuked them. Only Oliver could get close and, though she did not fight him with her power, she fought him with her fists.

"Please," he said weakly, holding out his hands to her, palms toward the sky.

She did not even look at them, or at him. She turned and fled into the water, disappearing beneath the cold, gray surface. He nearly chased her in, took a step to do so, but her head popped up and she began to swim vigorously away from him.

"Leave her." The voice, Faustine's, was sharp and cut into his thoughts.

He turned and glared at the tower where he knew Faustine must be, reaching out to him telepathically. Faustine and Max had returned from Sorciére with nothing.

"No," Oliver thought and jerked his head from side to side.

But the voice came again, more insistent.

"She needs this, Oliver. She needs to grieve."

Oliver's jaw tightened and he took another fleeting look into the lagoon. He could see her already on the other side, emerging and running. Her naked body disappeared into the gnarled cherry trees beyond.

She ran and dove off the sand dune on the far side of the island. Her body flew into the pelting rain and she could see nothing, not the dark starless sky above or the black churning waters below. She did not immediately fall, but floated, connecting so deeply with her element that her physical body barely existed. Only when she remembered again her grief did her body regain its weight and allow the force of gravity to drive her into the icy waters below. She hit with full impact, ignoring all of her lessons to lighten herself before the water. Every cell of her body screamed out with the force of the blow and she felt white-hot pain as her lips split open and her head thrust back. The waves crashed and churned, twisting her in their roiling caress. She closed her eyes and let go to the water.

****

Oliver found her floating face up. The rain, now slowed to a steady drizzle, slid over her bruised face. The blood had washed away, but he could see where her skin had torn and already begun to heal. He leaned over the side of the rowboat and hooked his forearms beneath her armpits, pulling her easily into the boat. Her naked body shone in the moon's glow and her wet hair looked oily and dark against her pearl skin. The dive from the cliffs did not mean death for a witch, unless of course they blocked their intuitive shield on the way down and simply hit the water like a human would. He could see that Abby had done just that.

He laid her across his knees and carefully wrapped her in a flannel blanket. She did not stir and, as the boat rocked gently with the waves, her head lolled from side to side.

****

Abby awoke in an unfamiliar room. She watched the shadows from several flickering candles dance along the bulky wooden beams overhead. She could feel her nakedness beneath the heavy comforter and some soreness, but nothing else. Had she expected death? Maybe. At least physical agony, a worthy distraction, but her witch body healed in a special way so she had not even the respite of physical destruction to aid her. The deeper pain blotted out embarrassment, regret and any emotion born of thought.

She turned her head to examine the room. It was large and rectangular and quite different from the one that she occupied. The walls consisted of rough wood, unsanded and knotted. Where windows might have been, the room opened onto a large stone balcony. A gleaming wood burning stove sat in its center surround by black leather chairs. The bed she lay in was propped high, perhaps on a platform and wire cables connected it to the beams overhead. To her left, she saw a wall of Americana with posters of James Dean and Elvis, bookshelves lined with records, CDs, DVDs and even a desk with an enormous desktop computer. The bedside table, an overturned barrel, was jumbled with photo frames and she leaned toward them scanning the unfamiliar faces. She stared at each carefully finally landing on a tall red frame that depicted two young men in kayaks. Their tanned skin and light blond hair made them almost look like twins, but Abby recognized Oliver's wide blue eyes. The other man's eyes were hazel and his chin was softer. Abby realized that Oliver had a brother.

She propped onto her elbows and scanned the room for Oliver, but the meager furnishings left him nowhere to hide. At the base of the bed, he had left a pair of her black stretch pants and a long-sleeved black t-shirt, rightfully assuming that she would be uninterested in anything of color.

She moved slowly, sadly into her clothes, but she did not cry. The sockets of her eyes felt dry and she could not have mustered a tear if she willed it so. She found comfort in Oliver's room and in the small ways that he had held onto pieces of his human self. Since arriving at Ula, her own identity pre-witch had faded, and each day she found less room for her pre-coven hobbies. She suddenly missed her books and her cat Baboon and the ugly purple vase she'd made in pottery class in college. Those thoughts made her long for her mom and her dad and then for Sydney and finally Sebastian. The desert found rain again and her eyes welled up and spilled over. She buried her face in Oliver's pillow and cried until her hiccups subsided and she could find distance again.

****

Had it been hours or whole days since Sebastian had discovered himself at the edge of this wood? And where had he entered? More importantly, why? He could not recall. The walk was fuzzy, like the memory of a dream, and he leaned heavily against the rough bark of a tree. The tree was dead, strangled by a vine that wrapped and crawled from its base to its head. He still did not know how he lost sight of the group or the castle. It didn't make sense. He had been there, drunk and relishing the spectacle...and then what? Had he wandered out a door? Had there even been a door? His eyes itched, but his painted hands made scratching difficult. He wanted to remove the Dragon costume, but feared exposure. Was the costume bewitched? He searched again for the medallion that Elda had given him. A small gold coin that she insisted he carry at all times. She said that if he squeezed it, it would alert the witches of Ula that he needed them. Elda had explained to him that humans could not exist within the coven of Sorciére walls on the night of All Hallow's Eve. The witches ensured this by casting expulsion spells. He wondered if the charms that Elda placed on him somehow wore off. Is that what had happened? He couldn't remember.

When he was a boy of six or seven, he'd fallen very ill. A fever had ravished him for days and he had drifted in and out of dreams. His waking hours were plagued with visions, confusion and fear. He felt that now, the loss of time and the malleability of reality. Was he in France? When he looked down at his body, the costume only confused him more. Great sleek dragon's scales met his searching gaze. Every passing second brought confusion rather than clarity.

****

Dafne stole into Sebastian's room through a secret passageway that opened through his closet. The tunnels within the castle connected nearly every room. In her own room, though, she had bewitched the hole behind her mirror to hold an invisible shield that none but she could walk through. In Sebastian's room, she began to carefully collect all of the items that she had bewitched to ignite his split from Abby. His yearning to avenge Claire's death had offered the perfect bridge into his mind, but now she had to burn it.

She found the box beneath the bed. The shrine-like container missed only a single item, the small silver ring. She searched his drawers, the pockets of discarded clothes and even looked through the books on his shelf, but nothing. She tried to call out to the ring, seeking the magic she had placed upon it, but still it did not appear. She searched beneath the bed again, this time sliding her body under and looking up into the box springs--empty. She started to emerge and then the door to the room swung open and she watched with alarm as a pair of slippered feet walked in. She could see Abby's slim ankles as she moved to the bed and sat down. For several minutes, the room stayed silent and Dafne held her breath, afraid to give herself away, and then she began to hear Abby gently sobbing above her.

"Are you gone?" Abby whispered, her words choked and sticky.

Dafne felt Abby lay back onto the bed and she could almost imagine her wrapping herself around one of Sebastian's old t-shirts and stuffing her face into his pillow. For an instant, the magnitude of all that she had done fell upon her and Dafne thought she might start screaming confessions into the box springs hovering inches from her nose. Then she remembered her own pain and loneliness. She remembered the screams of her friends in the woods and the dark cloud of grief that fell over Ula after three of their witches fell at the hands of Dafne's great love. With a grim finality, she closed a steel door upon her empathy and her guilt. She faced instead the gruesome fate that would have befallen them had she not eradicated Sebastian.

Abby cried for an hour and then she simply stood up and left, as quietly as she had arrived. Dafne wriggled out from under the bed and slipped back into the closet, taking all of the remnants of her deception with her.

****

"Hi," Victor said softly, spooking her in the cave of elders.

Abby had believed that she was alone. She had returned to her room at the castle. She traveled astrally to see Sebastian one last time.

"What are you doing here?" she snapped.

Victor did not look hurt. He merely cocked his head to the side and studied her.

"You're in pain..."

Inside of her, the grief wound tighter, but her astral body could not hold the form. She suddenly felt light, breathless and detached. For the first time since discovering Sebastian's body, her sorrow had abated.

"There, that's better, isn't it?" Victor smiled and reached a hand towards her. He could not touch her, but she felt his energy move through her.

"It is better," she sighed, but shot a furtive glance toward the tunnels behind her.

Unlike her last trip to the cave, the pull towards the center tunnel no longer existed. She didn't want to walk through that passageway--she could barely remember why she had intended to in the first place.

"It's okay to forget," Victor said, "to release the things that are holding us back."

She nodded and relaxed into her spirit body. It felt so good to let go.

"Join us, Abby. Your coven is holding you prisoner. We need you...and you need us." His eyes were intent and riveting. She stared into the sparkling black orbs and felt herself nod.

They need me, she thought and let that roll around in her head for a bit. She liked the way it sounded and strangely could not remember a single time in her entire life when she had felt needed. But, even so, she could not simply abandon all that had happened--Ula, Sebastian, Sydney.

"I'm not finished," she told him, without really thinking the words first, but when she spoke she knew them to be true.

Victor started to protest, but then, seeing something in her eyes, he stopped.

"Then at least let me help you," he sounded determined. "You've been to a Vepar's lair. The location is inside you."

She shook her head.

"I was unconscious when they took me there. I have no idea where it's at."

"Sure you do," he laughed. "You're a witch, Abby. Your body knows things your mind doesn't have a clue about yet and vice versa. We can unlock it, we can find that cave."

"How do you even know about that?" she asked, uncomfortable with what he implied.

"Because Dante saw it at Sorciére. He has this mind-reading thing. It's pretty wild right now and he has no idea when it's going to happen, but he saw the Vepar's lair and he saw that you killed one..."

Abby drifted past him and into the tunnel on the right. At the end of the tunnel, she found the rest of his group. They stood around a glowing fire and she recalled the very first time she traveled to the cave before she even knew that witches existed.

None of them spoke, but their circle broke apart and she and Victor moved into it, closing it again. They did not touch, but their energies became one.

****

Sebastian edged from tree to tree staring through a dense morning fog at an unfamiliar landscape of ripe green valleys, dotted with ramshackle barns. The leaden sky foretold of rain and Sebastian's thin shirt and black spandex pants already left him shivering and drab. His feet were raw and blistered and, when he sat against a large pine tree, the aches of his body immediately clamored for his attention. His legs and back throbbed from days and nights of confused walking. His head swam with tiredness. His hands, feet and elbows stung where blisters and scrapes lay open to the strong winds. He had removed his costume entirely and rubbed his skin raw where the paint had not already been sweated away.

He dared not even think of his predicament in a foreign land with no money, identification or friend to speak of. He still did not know if he was in France or some other unidentified countryside.

Searching his pockets, he emptied the remains in his lap and found little to celebrate. The only thing that he carried was the tiny silver ring he had discovered in Claire's box, the only item he had felt compelled to snatch from his nightstand before readying for the Ball. Not a thought had been given to any human necessity because he was traveling with witches. Who needed passports for magic mirrors or money for booze conjured from thin air? He had brought nothing and now, in the early morning mist of an alien landscape, he had nothing.

His only glimmer of hope was Abby. Surely she was desperately searching for him and insisting that the witches pour all of their energy into that endeavor. It made him feel weak, his terror at being cast out. He had underestimated the security that living with witches brought into his life. For years he had been on his own, struggling and desperate, and then, in a matter of days, that had all reversed and he found himself living with a coven of witches. He didn't have to think of money or food or even...Claire, if he didn't want to. There had even been a few days where her image went mostly unseen. Her memory never died, but the constant itch to avenge her had momentarily subsided. That was until several weeks earlier when suddenly he found himself again consumed by her death. Why had it returned so suddenly?

He still felt it, sort of, as he sat alone and shivering in the morning light. However, mostly he felt troubled. His usual survival skills were slow to kick in. He scanned the horizon, letting his eyes rest on a small shed, blue paint peeling beneath a white hand-painted sign. He could not make out the words but, as he studied them, he grew more convinced that they were in French, which meant that he was still in Bordeaux, somewhere.

He took a deep breath and shuffled to his feet. At the very least, the shed offered sanctuary from the biting wind and an opportunity to shed the remainder of his costume and attempt a presentable appearance. He hoped more that it might contain some food source. He would eat raw eggs, milk, even pigs feed if he had to. He was ravished and scowled each time he thought of the buffets from the party. He had fully intended to gorge half the night away when he'd finally tired of dancing, but he had barely eaten half a sandwich when...what? What had happened?

Why couldn't he remember? He recalled the little girl creating the monster from dust and then a witch. What had her name been?

"Indra," he said aloud triumphantly, and then quickly backed into the trees, It could not have been that loud, but still in the silent valley, who knew how his voice might carry?

Yes, Indra had been her name and she seemed strangely fascinated by him. He had almost asked her if she knew that he was human, but then thought better of it. She might have. He had felt exposed much of the night. Every time a witch's gaze lingered on him, he wondered if they could sense clearly his lack of mystical power. As he grew drunk on champagne, he had stopped caring that he was the odd man out and simply gave in to the pleasure of the night.

****

Abby's bedroom materialized around her and the emptiness found her. For that brief period with Victor and the others, her loneliness had dulled and then disappeared. Returning to her empty room brought the heaviness of solitude back to her.

In the castle halls, she was greeted with silence and she sighed out loud just to hear any sound of life.

She walked to the library, not truly wanting to face everyone, but unable to simply stay in her room and hide. When she heard voices through the door, she paused. They were muffled, but sounded urgent. Abby imagined an enormous rushing waterfall and, as her pulse quickened, she sent the energy into her ear causing her eardrum to vibrate more quickly. She listened.

Elda's voice drifted out.

"I agree that we need to help her, Oliver, but in time, of course. We cannot grieve for her."

"That's not what I'm saying," Oliver said, sounding irritated. "What faith will she have in this coven, or in herself for that matter, if she's forced to sit in her room staring at the sky, while all of her people die?"

"No one else is going to die," Faustine chimed in, his voice high and tense.

"No? And how do you know that? How about her parents, her ex-boyfriend, her old friend's for Pete's sakes. How long until Tobias or some other Vepar decides it's time to even the score for Antonio."

"We must protect the coven, Oliver. That is our first priority. We cannot send her back to France, or anywhere else for that matter. She has not yet honed her skills or even discovered most of them," Elda argued.

"I have to tell her about Sydney," Oliver said suddenly, and Abby heard a chair scrape along the carpeting as if he had stood.

"No," both Elda and Faustine said in unison.

"She cannot handle any more trauma," Faustine's voice commanded.

91

"What she can't handle," Oliver nearly shouted, "is more deception. She needs the truth. The only thing that can free her is knowing everything. I killed Sydney, I killed her, and I have to come clean."

Abby heard the words and began to shake her head no before she even fully processed them. She started to back away from the door just as it flung open.

Oliver stared at her, shocked, and, as their eyes met, he understood that she had heard everything.

"You killed Sydney?" Her heart hurt to say it, but she had to, had to know for sure.

"Oh, Abby, please..." he murmured as tears sprang to his eyes. He grabbed her hands and squeezed them against his chest. "Let me explain."

She bit her lip and refused her own tears, staring with pain and sorrow at the top of his bowed head.

For an instant, she imagined hearing him out. She could listen to his story and then sit down to dinner with all of the other witches, just like every other night and pretend that nothing was wrong, except she couldn't. Before she even understood that staying had already ceased as an option, she had ripped her hands away from him.

"I'm already gone," she said through gritted teeth.

She moved away from him, and again, for a moment, time grew endless and the tick of a second spread into hours and she hoped that he would stop her, that he would rush up behind her and grab her around the waist and tie her to him. Not because she loved him, but because she was terrified at what lay ahead and she was devastated to leave him behind. It was not true that she did not love Oliver. She did love him, but she hated him for Sydney and she hated his coven for Sebastian and she hated herself for all that felt lost to her as she stood in the hallway.

When Abby made it to her bedroom, Victor's face kept dancing into her mind and his image urged her on. She had not intended to actually meet Victor that night. Or had she?

It felt like such a sickly familiar moment, running away. She grabbed a bag and hastily threw together her things. The halls were silent as she strode out of the castle and into the cool evening. She turned only once to see Lydie who lifted a lifeless hand and waved goodbye.

CHAPTER 9

The boat ride was eerily calm and Abby swallowed tears and screams that tormented her chest and eyes. The black night did not disturb her but, for the first time in months, for the first time since leaving Nick and her family, she felt utterly alone, cast out of the new life as if it were merely a dress and the party had come to an end.

She took hours, knowing that Victor would not arrive until well after midnight. She thought of her moonlit boat ride with Sebastian and how they narrowly escaped death by Tobias and the other Vepars. She wondered if they wouldn't have been better off running the other way, fleeing to Mexico and burning Claire's journals rather than following them to the coven of Ula.

When she saw headlights at the mainland, she steered the boat away and then returned on foot through the woods, crouching and watching. When she stood close enough to see Victor's face, she left her concealment and stepped into the car's beams He did not jump, or even flinch, and she understood that he sensed her approach.

He leaned across the seat and pushed the passenger door open.

"Ready for the ride of your life?" he asked, grinning. His eyes, mischievous, danced over her and he raised his eyebrows at her bag. "Bring some snacks along?"

"I've decided to leave Ula for a while," she told him and slid into the seat, pressing the bag between her knees and squeezing it for comfort. She chose not to elaborate.

"A minimalist. I like it," he said with a grin. He did not probe further.

"So how do we do this?" Abby asked. "I really don't remember where the lair was..."

He reached into his pocket and pulled out a small heart-shaped bottle.

"This is a super-special tonic that Kendra makes. I'm embarrassed to admit that we usually use it to find lost keys and other nonsense, but she amped it up for you."

Abby took the bottle and studied it.

"I don't want to start recovering lost memories from my childhood or some craziness."

"That's what this is for."

Victor pulled out a tiny scroll and undid the twine holding it together. A teeny pencil, the size of a push pin, rolled out.

"Write what you're looking for on the paper and drop it in."

Abby took it, leery, but more intrigued. Holding the tiny pencil, she wrote 'The Vepars Lair where I killed Tony'. It barely fit. She carefully unscrewed the top from the bottle and slid the tiny scroll inside. It dissolved instantly.

"Now, you drink while I drive," Victor chuckled.

He gunned the car in reverse and spun around. They tore away from the winding trail that led to Lake Superior. She glimpsed the lake in the rearview mirror as Victor hit the care brakes and the shoreline lit up red and barren behind them.

****

"What's your edge, Abby?" Victor whispered, extending his body another inch over the side of the cliff.

The waterfall rushed beneath them. The water was black, oily and familiar. She remembered the taste, the copper salty flavor like blood. Overhead the moon spooked the shadows and made Victor's teeth glow a vampiric white. A million stars watched, the eyes of the cosmos causing Abby to shiver with delight and fear.

They stood over the Vepar's lair as if on a midnight dare. They might have been high school friends taunting the other to run the light, take the shot...do it, whatever it was. A rock slid away beneath Victor and Abby jumped, startled. Her mind and body were at odds. Goosebumps and trembling flesh told her that fight or flight was at hand. Her spirit, however, drew great heaping gulps from the waterfall below and surged enormous and ready to deal justice to the enemy beneath them.

Abby laughed, scared, but so much more than that. A feeling of aliveness pulsed through her body. She felt alive like no other moment since becoming a witch, alive in a way that reading and casting and conjuring could not imitate. The pain of Sebastian's death lived on another planet, maybe in another galaxy, and she let it stay there.

She held her palms down over the water and she willed it, demanded it to stop. The flow rushed on, but then the water slowed, trickled and dried. The night grew silent beneath the water's absence, but Abby felt the water within her. It surged up and up, waiting for her to cast it out, to channel the energy building.

Victor did not wait, but plummeted over the ledge, his hands claw-like as he climbed the rock surface and swung into the mouth of the cave.

Abby hesitated. She looked at the flowing river beyond and she remembered escaping from the tunnels below her. She remembered plunging the rock into the Vepar Antonio. The squeals of agony and black blood filled her brain like a tumor exploding and then Victor called her name and she plunged after him. She moved down the rock face slowly, planting each foot and hand, searching for the widest ledge and the sharpest outcroppings.

When she reached the tunnel, she nearly slipped on the overhang and Victor did not reach out to help her. He was tap dancing on the remaining pools of water, his eyes shining with moonlight and mischief.

"It's now or never, beautiful." He grinned and heaved her up by the arm.

She cast a final glance at the night sky and together they descended into the darkness.

****

Sebastian rolled onto his back and yawned, stretching his fingers overhead where they brushed an empty trough, the sides dried and rough with dirt. He had slept deeply, much to his surprise, and thanked the gods for his fortune that the shed sat atop a root cellar, full to bursting with jars of pickles, fruit, jams and relishes. He had eaten two jars of peaches and half a jar of pickles before falling into a heap on the ground.

He listened for the sounds of others, but his ears caught nothing beyond his breath and the occasional groans of the shed walls.

Before leaving, he peeked through grimy windows at the field beyond. He saw a tall, dark farmhouse in the distance, flanked by a gnarled orchard. The leaves had fallen and mostly blown away and the house looked empty, possibly abandoned. He had sensed that the jarred food had been in the cellar for years and that perhaps no one saw to the shed on any regular basis. The door hinges were rusted and cried out when he first pushed them in, and everything in the shed, from workbench to rafters, was covered in a light gray dust.

He moved deliberately to a small patch of bushes growing wild in the yard. He stood, waited, and then advanced toward the house. He feigned confidence in case someone did reside there. He would merely pretend that he searched for his missing dog.

He neared the back porch where white paint peeled to gray and noted the boards crisscrossing the backdoor. Two windows revealed broken panes of glass and the overgrowth of weeds confirmed his suspicions that the house stood vacant. Several cars, dead-looking, lazed in the tall grass beside the house. He walked to each, peering through windows at cracked leather seats. They were small cars, European, with steering wheels on the right side. He knew a thing or two about hot-wiring, especially the older cars. His father's best friend had been a mechanic who insisted that Sebastian, as a young man, learn the basics--oil changes, flat tires and hot wiring. He did not feel hopeful, though, as he stared at the clunkers before him. In either direction, the road stretched in an endless line of open fields backed by dense forests. He might walk for miles before he encountered a sign of life, and then what?

He felt a surge of hope at the mere thought of getting behind the wheel. Total helplessness could be remedied by a car. Driving had been important in his life before the coven of Ula. He drove to help Claire get over their parents' death. He drove to clear his mind and to find peace when it all became too much. At Ula, so many of his little cure-alls had dissipated. Gone were his long drives and hours in the kitchen behind a hot stove. His only reprieve had been the coven's library and their extensive collection of books. At Ula, he found material that he had longed for after Claire's death. He had absorbed much, but now, as he stood with his hands on the rusted hood of a four-door Renault, his brain felt void of knowledge. So focused on learning to kill Vepars, he'd all but forgotten what it felt like to survive in the human world.

He found the passenger door unlocked and slid into the musty interior, cringing at the pair of molded fuzzy dice hanging from the rearview mirror. Sebastian surveyed the car's contents. He noticed cardboard boxes filled with records, a couple of bags of musty clothes and pair of old tennis shoes. He fumbled along the visors and beneath the seats, hopeful.

In the glovebox, he discovered a small tool kit and figured that he could at least attempt to start the car with a screwdriver. He pulled the screwdriver out along with a box of matches and, to his delight, he spotted a set of keys tucked snugly between a box of band aids and a roll of duck tape.

"Come on, baby." He immediately started to smooth-talk her as he slipped the key in and turned. Nothing.

****

Victor trotted through the dark tunnels, sliding in the pools of water and casting his dark, twinkling eyes back at her whenever the gap between them started to grow. As they moved deeper into the rock, Abby's cavalier feelings shifted and she found breath harder and harder to come by. The passages narrowed and, when her head nearly scraped the ceiling and Victor had to duck to go on, she laid a hand on the wall beside her and stopped. It felt slimy and wet and she started to recoil and pull her hand away, but then left it. The wall beat a steady thrum of pulses into her hand and with those pulses came flashes of sight.

Victor turned, puzzled.

"What is it?" he asked, returning to where she stood and placing his own hand on the slick wall.

Abby expected him to feel it too, but his face remained perplexed.

"Don't you feel it?" she asked, closing her eyes because she wanted to catch the images as they passed. The water was speaking to her.

At first they came so briefly, she barely saw anything, but then...a flash of blond hair followed by a howling and writhing body on the ground, blood pouring from a wound in the side of its head. Not a Vepar she saw, but a man, his face glistening with sweat, his hands pressed into his temples. The hair again and then a face...Vesta. Then the vision changed and she watched the tunnels as they emptied, Vepars with bloody mouths and heavy feet barreling up out of the earth on a black, moonless night. The dungeons below lay deserted except for...traps. Traps everywhere, spells of evil made stronger through human sacrifice. The room that Toni died in held thousands of black slithering snakes, the poison in their gums filled with the venom of Vepars.

Abby pulled her hand away and teetered on her feet, nearly falling as she attempted to see in the dark passage. Victor caught her, holding her shoulders in his hands and steadying her.

"What did you see?"

"We have to leave here." She choked it out, her throat and mouth bone dry.

She heard his own breathing becoming thinner, whistling through his nose.

"The air," he said. "My power..."

Victor was an air element and, as the air in the cave lessened and grew thicker with...something--Abby didn't know what, only that it smelled noxious and felt thick like gasoline fumes--the color drained from his face.

He shook his head slowly from side to side, and then stumbled into the wall, his eyes starting to bulge.

I can breathe because of the water, she suddenly realized.

Victor started to claw at his shirt and then fell to his knees.

Deep below them, Abby heard an explosion.

****

Dafne hurried through side door of the warehouse and locked it securely behind her. The coven had owned the warehouse for decades and, over time, it had slowly filled. In addition to Oliver's jeep, there were two black sedans rarely used by the elder witches of Ula. Abby's Cavalier occupied a corner next to Dafne's green Eclipse. There were boxes stuffed with clothes, books and memorabilia. Tall shelves held picture albums, television

sets, appliances and toys. Every witch who entered the coven eventually
abandoned their stuff to the warehouse.

The warehouse stood in an isolated stretch of forest at the edge of
Brimley, a small community bordering Lake Superior. The coven owned ten
acres and the warehouse was tucked deep into the trees and surrounded by
barbed wire fencing, which merely served as a deterrent. The repulsion
spells truly kept the humans away.

Dafne had left Ula hours earlier, unable to witness the unraveling of
Abby for fear that Faustine or Elda would sense her involvement. She
moved to the back of the warehouse and then took the metal stairs two at a
time. Her stuff occupied a shadowy upstairs corner, far away from the other
witches' belongings. Dafne grabbed a familiar black tote and pulled it across
the floor. She hesitated and listened, once more checking that no one had
followed her. Satisfied, she began the arduous process of ripping off layers
of the duck tape that criss-crossed the container. She dropped it in sticky
bundles and peeled back the lid, lifting out a heavy metal safe that she
quickly dialed the combo into, despite having not opened it in more than
thirty years.

Inside a jumble of photos and papers greeted her. Not the fodder of
most safes--no cash or expensive family heirlooms lay within the metal
chamber, though there was one piece of jewelry, a small copper band with a
reddish agate stone resting in its center. She lifted it out and slipped it onto
her ring finger where it still fit perfectly. The pictures were not many, but
only a glance and Dafne felt a hundred years vanish. Her hands began to
shake as she touched the worn photos and her heartbeat grew so
thunderous, she thought it might burst and end her suffering once and for
all.

His eyes were the same piercing black but, back then, in the days before
the darkness claimed him, they had a luminous sheen. They shone with
brilliance so intense that sometimes when they walked together in the sun,
she could hardly look at him. He wore his hair long back then, held in place
with a piece of soft leather at the base of his neck. She remembered
brushing it, how the black silky strands flowed over her fingers like water.
He worked on the water, a fisherman, and he always smelled of the dank
scent of fish skins and seaweed. She would file the sand from beneath his
fingers and they would eat fresh salmon, caught just that day, over a fire on
the beach.

In those days, she wasn't allowed to date really. Her minister father and
prudish mother made clear to her at a young age what loose women did,
which, of course, made her nighttime trysts all the more exhilarating. Dafne
had known then that his appeal had nothing to do with rebellion. She loved
him. She loved him from the first moment that he spoke, approaching her
at the market in search of thread and needle for his trousers, which he'd

snagged on a fishing hook the day before.

He courted her, in the days after their first meeting, like the best lovers do. He brought her daisies from the woods and seashells from his fishing nets. He waited weeks to kiss her and even then, he planned it as if it were their first time making love. He lit candles and brought moonshine to his friend's little stone cottage. They cuddled by the fireplace and talked for hours and, when he finally tilted her face to meet his, she let go of everything that she'd kept for herself. Every wall she'd built between them, every secret she harbored, every defense that might have kept her at bay went like smoke in the chimney dancing into the dense night air.

After that, the little cabin became their weekend retreat. 'Nannying the newborn twins across town,' she told her family when she raced from home at dusk. They made love on the thin cot beneath the windows, always open to the lake air. They also began to dream. They dreamed of leaving Trager and finding a big city somewhere. She would sell perfumes and oils and he would fish in the ocean, where real money could be made. They would send their families postcards of the exotic foods they ate and the languages spoken by their immigrant neighbors. New York was the place that they both held in their mind's eye, but they rarely uttered the name of the city. It was too real then and, tucked into the little cabin, their dreams still had wings. Neither of them felt ready to ground the fantasy.

Dafne rotated the ring and looked at the agate stone. It had dulled over the years, but still revealed tiny waves of red and white. 'Lover's ocean' he had called it when he first gave it to her. He said that he had walked the beaches for days finding the perfect one. She imagined him sitting on the boat, polishing and filing the fine stone until it was a tiny round orb that he could fasten to the copper band. He bought the copper from her dear friend Aubrey, and Dafne had been happy then that her closest friend knew of Tobias's proposal. They had all been happy then, before the fire.

CHAPTER 10

August 5, 1908

Aubrey heard the cries in her sleep and when she woke to the silent room, she felt her blood pulsing in her ears. Nothing rustled. The wind had died early that day and not even her curtains shifted in the midnight calm. She closed her eyes and went beyond her ears, probing for the sound that she knew roused her. It came then, a boy's cry, too meek to be audible, but Aubrey felt his anguish tremble through her. She hurried from her bed, threw on a shawl and sandals and ran into the forest.

The trees around her home blocked the light of the moon, but Aubrey did not need to see the forest with her eyes. She moved swiftly around fallen trees and pockets of thorny bushes until the cries became more urgent and loud enough that her ears picked up the sound. She found him in a small clearing, his hands clutching his head and his small body tucked, as if in his mother's womb, on the leafy earth.

"Solomon, Solomon" she whispered the boy's name calmly as she tried to gently pull his hands from his head.

Solomon was the youngest child and only son of her closest neighbor, Jonas Herman. He lived just a half mile down the wooded track that ran to her cottage in the woods. The only boy amongst four sisters, Solomon knew an adventurous spirit and Aubrey often encountered him leaping through the woods in chase of some small rabbit or squirrel. He did not harm the animals, but merely watched and tracked them. He once told her that someday he would farm the land, but instead of chickens, he would raise coyotes.

He looked at her now with a terror that made her blood grow cold. She lifted him into her lap easily, no longer surprised by her unnatural strength. She carried him cradled in her arms and, when they reached her cottage, she laid him in her own bed and covered him with a heavy wool blanket. He shivered despite the fever and his glassy eyes peered out from his sunken face.

She fumbled through her herbs, commanding her trembling hands to steady and quickly mixed a poultice of arrow root, basil and caraway seed. She removed his blanket and rubbed his chest and neck first with warm sesame oil and then began to move the poultice across his skin. He writhed beneath the mixture, his face growing taut as his mouth yawned in a silent scream and Aubrey thought she saw a darkness too great in his gaping mouth to be merely the cavity for his teeth and tongue. He started to rock back and forth, his movements growing violent, and she had to lie upon him to keep him from leaping from the bed.

For an instant, her vision traveled elsewhere and she saw her beloved Henry picking his way through the woods, his heavy boots getting caught in roots and branches. He stumbled and fell on one knee and laughed at his own clumsiness. Henry, not a witch and a rather klutzy human at that, did not have Aubrey's night vision nor her uncanny ability to navigate the Ebony woods with her eyes closed. He'd been gone for two days to Cadillac, a small lumbering town south of Trager where his brother worked as a doctor. Henry assisted his brother in the hospital and in return, his brother gave him free medical supplies for the small clinic that Aubrey and Henry had opened just six months before.

In her mind, Aubrey could see Henry's leather bag nearly bursting and so she ran from the cottage. She did not call his name, for hearing her would only cause him to move faster and he would likely take a more painful spill. He felt her though and so hurried anyway, moving in the direction of her frantic energy.

For three hours, they nursed the boy. Aubrey whispered incantations and commanded Henry to the mortar and pestle where he crushed and mixed until his hands were nearly numb. He had dumped his bag of medical supplies on the floor, but none of the medicine could remove the slithering dark that had entered young Solomon. At dawn another of their coven, Celeste, arrived and then Dafne and five more witches joined their cause. They linked hands and prayed around the boy, calling upon the energies of the earth and rocking from side to side as he too rocked with the power of the monster within him.

When his eyes rolled back into his head and his breath took on the ragged death rattle, Aubrey ran to his father's cottage. The other witches cleaned quickly, shoving their remedies into cupboards before they retired to the woods to wait for their friend. They did not speak. They all knew and loved Solomon and releasing him to death brought them crashing down from the mountains they'd soared to in recent months as together their power grew. Had they failed him? Were they not as strong as they believed? No answers soothed them. They huddled in the dewy, morning woods watching the slanted light of the morning sun as it rose.

They sat in a circle, their hands clasped and eyes closed and when the father's wails found them, they prayed to the source of all light that Solomon's young body be relieved of his suffering and his vibrant soul returned to his home. Aubrey joined them in silence, her brow knitted and her shoulders bowed beneath the weight of her long night.

Chapter 11

Abby thrust her arms beneath Victor and dragged. His head drooped and he felt heavy, as if weighted with cement bricks. Her eyes watered and ran and she started to taste blood as it seeped from her nose. The air was gone, replaced by something poisonous that rolled out from the walls in visible gusts. They had triggered something when they entered the cave and the explosions beneath her and the toxic gas only felt like the beginning. She stumbled and fell over a rock, losing Victor and slamming her head into the hard earth. She could no longer see, and waves of nausea and dizziness coursed through her. She remembered her previous rescue from the Vepar's lair when Faustine found her and Dafne in the ravine beyond the cliffs. She reached for him then, pushing her thoughts towards the castle, holding Faustine desperately in her mind. No images rose up and she felt sure that he could not sense her.

Pressing up on her elbows, she gave one more futile attempt at finding her feet, but made it only to her knees before the floor beneath her cracked from some explosion in the belly of the cliff. She and Victor began to fall.

****

Vesta woke with a gurgling scream, cut off by the rancid smelling palm of the Vepar Wrath. She could see the dirt caked beneath his fingernails and taste the metallic tinge of his last blood thirst. His black eyes did not look at her, but into the distance where the tiniest cloud of dust had begun to rise in the night sky. The ring on her hand pulsed vivid white, faded and then pulsed again. Since Tane's death, its power had changed and it no longer offered reliable signals when a witch moved close by. Now it flashed at strange moments, growing very hot or cold, and at times did nothing for so long that she started to doubt whether its color would ever change again. Tonight it spoke and Vesta knew that Tobias had been right.

Wrath did not even seem to breathe and, after several minutes, Vesta shifted forward slowly, sitting up and then finding her knees. He did not look at her, but she felt his cold fury even as she drifted near him. He hated her, but not because she had foolishly allowed a relic to be created, which later led to the death of the Vepar Tony, but because he hated all things. Unlike most of the other Vepars, even the kill did not satisfy him. He moved through it with a slow, methodical determination that did not betray any joy or frenzy in the death of his victims, but a dead obedience to some devil that even she did not know.

Vesta was devoted to Tobias. She did not attempt to understand the mind state of Tobias. His moods were like the pendulum's swing. In one moment, she felt the sick twist of love between them and at other times, he seemed to delight in her suffering. But those emotions she understood on the most basic human level. Even in the darkness, perhaps more so in the darkness, the animal hunger of emotion reigned supreme. No peace or tranquility existed within her or any other Vepar. Their choice to destroy and consume, betrayed their selfishness, but also their self-loathing. Did she not detest herself as fully as she hated the Vepar Tony whom she hated as much as the witch who murdered him? Did she not hate herself for loving Tobias as he slowly drained the life from her only sibling Tane, or for her weakness in allowing Tane to enter their dark world to begin with? She hated too how visibly she displayed her emotions. She felt Wrath recoiling from her as she trembled beside him.

Every muscle in her body longed to spring animal-like through the forest to the cliff edge where surely their screams could be heard by now. She licked her lips, relishing the thought of the tall blond one, Oliver, writhing in the pit of snakes, his blond hair rich with streaks of dark, coppery red.

"Sit," the Vepar Wrath hissed at her and she realized that she had started to sneak forward onto her haunches, her nails digging into the dirt at her feet. She glared at him, so angry that he should command her that she longed to rip his throat out and drink his black blood. His eyes turned ever so slowly and locked on hers. She no longer hoped to hurt him at all, but merely to survive the next moment and the one after that.

In his eyes, she was already dead and she felt her body lose its vitality and begin to wither and sink into itself. Then she felt the maggots and flies picking at her flesh, their tiny prickling feet on her swollen eyeballs and she tried to scream, but no voice lived in those wasted lungs. She reached up to claw at her rotted face, but the scene before her slid back into focus.. Wrath held her gaze and she turned away afraid that he might conjure the visions again, but he returned his focus to the cliff. Vesta fell back in the dirt and lay silent, staring at the starless sky.

****

Oliver stood on the bank of the river below in shadow. He had watched Abby and Victor go into the cave with a sickness that he confused with guilt. When the explosions began he recognized the sensation for what it was--foreboding--and he bound up the cliff wall like an animal being hunted.

He did not dive into the mouth of the cave, though he wanted to. He paused and peered deep into the dark passage, first listening and then smelling the opening. Before the sulfurous odor entered his nostrils, he saw the tendrils of oily air shining in moonlight, and knew that the lair would be abandoned, but not deserted. The Vepars did not play at vengeance. They destroyed everything if it meant the death of even one of their enemies. He gulped a lungful of fresh air and raced inside, hurtling himself deeper, willing his eyes to see through the blurry mess of gas. He saw Victor and Abby seconds too late as the floor exploded beneath them and they both vanished.

The Vepars had dammed the water flowing above ground into the caverns below, but Oliver found the dam quickly and began to throw the enormous boulders aside as if they were merely pebbles. The water trickled through and then exploded, washing through the tunnels.

****

Tobias joined Vesta and Wrath. They stood in shadows and Vesta bounced from foot to foot, her hunger nearly overpowering her.

"The witches Abby and Oliver?" he asked again, stretching his clownish red lips wide. His black eyes gleamed with pleasure.

"And one more," Wrath added. "The artist from Chicago."

"Interesting," Tobias murmured, lifting his long, pale fingers absently to his right shoulder. Vesta knew that he touched the place where one of Oliver's arrows had ripped through his flesh only months earlier, ruining their sacrifice of Abby.

"But so much has changed since then, my dear," Tobias told Vesta. She shrunk away from him, fearing his new ability to read the minds of those he sired.

Vesta knew little of what had changed in the clan of Tobias. He had stopped consulting her completely and conspired only with Alva. Vesta had fed on nothing but humans for nearly two months. Her bones grew brittle and her skin sallow, but she dared not complain.

Tobias, however, appeared stronger every day. His teeth grew sharper and more pronounced. He moved so swiftly at night, she started to think he could fly. He watched her, amused, and she realized that, again, he read her thoughts.

"Don't think so much my child." He petted her hair gently. "You will hurt yourself."

"What now?" she muttered, praying that he would take pity on her and allow her to feast.

Again he smiled, but his eyes lost their mirthful sheen.

"We are not here to eat tonight, my darling. We are here to collect the snakes..."

****

Oliver did not have to swim far into the hole that Abby and Victor had fallen into. Already their buoyant bodies had begun to rise. He retrieved Abby first. Before his head broke the surface, a chill ran the length of his spine, lighting up at the base, but when he followed the feeling, he felt confident that no Vepars were near. He thrust his head above the surface for an instant, took in a gulp of fresh air and dove back down.

A sharp prick lit up his forearm and then another on his leg. He searched with his hand and clamped down on the slithering body of a snake. He thrust it way and plunged deeper. This time he grabbed Victor as well. He held both witches sandwiched together beneath each arm until he felt Abby begin to wriggle beside him. In her element, she recovered quickly, but he also felt her panicking at their submersion. He locked eyes with her briefly and mouthed "stop." She quit resisting and he sensed the caverns around them. He followed the cave walls until he found a sense of empty space. There he knew they would find air and an opening of some sort. They swam deeper first and Oliver felt more snakes brush against him. Finally, they came into a large circular room where the water had already begun to drain away. He pushed Abby up so that she could breathe. She held onto a hunk of jagged wall. Then he wrenched Victor's face above the water and began to breathe into his slack mouth. He felt the air push into his belly and tasted the oily gas still on his lips. He gagged and spit as some of the water projected out of Victor's mouth and into his own. Soon both Abby and Victor clung to the wall, sputtering and disoriented.

"What's your element, Victor?"

"Air," Victor choked, his throat raspy and swollen.

"Well, I'd say this is the best we can do right now," Oliver sighed, slipping under the water for a moment to find the floor. He re-emerged. "About another two feet and we'll be back on solid ground."

The water level lowered more and soon all three of them could stand. Abby already felt better. She sensed the gashes along her back and arms healing quickly. Victor, on the other hand, grew paler as time passed and a wound on the back of his left thigh bled heavily. Oliver created a tourniquet with his sweatshirt and secured it around Victor's leg. The bleeding slowed, but did not stop.

Despite the water, Abby's strength diminished. The fall and the poisonous air had damaged her and most of her energy went towards detoxifying her lungs and organs. Both she and Victor leaned heavily against the wall.

****

When the car miraculously started, Sebastian could not believe his luck. When it sputtered, stalled and then stopped completely, on a dense, forest road that left little hope in either direction, he couldn't imagine the day getting much worse. He turned the key and listened as the motor cried out a final time. He stepped from the dead car and irrationally kicked the tire before loping off in the direction of the sun.

A half mile down the road, he swore aloud, realizing that he might have fit into some of the clothes piled in the backseat. They likely smelled pretty bad, but they would protect him against the chilly afternoon breeze. He started to turn back and then a wonderful feeling of hope washed over him as he heard the distant sound of an engine.

Sebastian saw the shape of a car in the distance. He stepped into the center of the road and, when the driver drew close enough to see him, he waved his arms eagerly.

The little car drifted to a stop and a young woman with light, hazel eyes rolled down her window.

"Avez-vous briser," she asked, smiling up at him.

"I..." He started to speak and then stopped, suddenly not sure what to say. The words that had been so clear in his mind just moments ago were gone and nothing moved forth to replace them. It was as if someone had reached into his brain and wiped his memory clean.

"Not French?" the woman asked. "American?"

Was he American? He had to think about it, but yes, he felt sure that he was American, but who was he in America? His mind was blank and he felt his chest constrict as he searched the contents and found nothing.

Why was she speaking French? Was he in France? Why would he be in France?

"No? Not American?" she asked again, this time her face growing concerned. Her wide-set eyes took in his strange attire, the remnants of a costume perhaps.

"I can't remember," he told her, rubbing his hand across his forehead like he might be able to bring it back. "I'm American. I think I am, but..."

"Were you in an accident?" She asked, her words heavily accented.

He looked down at his body, shocked by the odd attire clothing him. He wore tight-fitting black stretch pants and a tight black t-shirt. Both pants and shirt were dotted with splotches of paint in hues of red and orange. He rubbed his hands over his torso, along his legs and finally probed his head with his fingers. Nothing hurt and there was no blood, but why couldn't he recall anything?

"What's my name?" he suddenly asked out loud. He looked at her, alarmed. "I don't know my name."

She wrinkled her brow and paused, seeming to consider whether or not she trusted this confused stranger. After a moment, she stepped from the car and guided him around to the passenger side.

"Get in. I will take you to the infirmary."

He sat in her passenger seat and patted his body with growing panic, searching for a wallet, an I.D., anything. He pulled out a tiny silver ring. Strange designs were engraved on the interior, but nothing that might identify him, such as initials.

"Isabelle," the woman told him, holding out her hand.

"I'm sorry," he said shaking her hand hastily. "I don't know what's happening to me."

Chapter 12

August 6, 1908

Dafne sat in the tiny cottage by the water and cried. Solomon's baby face moved in and out of her vision as the tears soaked her soft cotton dress. Dafne's Aunt Patty, the midwife, had delivered the infant Solomon and now it would likely be Dafne's father, the minister, who laid him in the ground. Despite the unseasonably chilly August morning, she felt the heat of their work still coursing through her. How much fire they had conjured trying to burn the demon out of him? But to no avail.

The flimsy door swung in and Tobias walked into the single room, surveying her in silence. She turned her sodden eyes to his, but he looked far away and almost unconcerned with her pain. He turned and left without a word. His behavior, though unusual, did not alarm her. He struggled with great shows of emotion. His own mother had perished at a young age and so he had been raised by men and the sea. The soft freedom that women brought into the lives of boys, rescuing them from the rigidness of their masculinity, was lost on him. Still, she was never left wanting. He supported and loved her with every ounce of his being. He simply showed it in other ways.

Chapter 13

Abby had not told anyone that she was returning to Sydney's house. She had not truly believed it herself, but as she had wandered dazed and embarrassed out of the Vepar's caves, something urged her to do just that. She had left Victor wounded and Oliver watching her in disbelief, but she hadn't cared.

Her escape ended at a bus station where she boarded a bus for Trager City. She traveled to Sydney's home through the woods. The run to her dead aunt's house took only minutes and Abby, so distracted by memories, felt not even a twitch in her hot muscles. Her body was like a machine and she found that she rarely had to direct it--it already knew where to go.

She stood at the forest's edge and watched the house. The autumn leaves lay in heavy dark masses beneath the trees. A large, bright blue sign read 'Ronda's Realty' in tacky red lettering. The dock had been removed and hastily stacked on the shore and the patio furniture was gone, stored by some crew that Abby's mother had likely hired to do a fast job. Overhead the gray sky seeped a cool drizzle onto the earth and Abby, sick of the cold and the forlorn look of Sydney's house, jogged across the lawn and up to the patio door.

It was locked, but one forceful jerk and it shot open, sliding with a crash into the frame. The house was warm; the heat kept on for home showings, but from what Abby's mother Becky had told her, there weren't many potential buyers. It wasn't just a down market. People didn't want to vacation in a house where a woman had been murdered. Nor did everyone in the city believe that Sydney was the victim of her young lover.

According to Becky, a whole cropping of lore and suspicion had arisen after Sydney's death, including the widely held belief that a vampiric cult had killed Devin, Sydney and possibly another young woman several counties away who disappeared without a trace earlier that summer.

Abby dropped her bag on the counter and walked through the house, flicking on lights and breathing through the tightness in her chest. All of the pictures had been removed and much of the house contained new furniture.

Calming beachscapes lined the walls, and the tables and shelves were adorned with glass bowls of seashells and little nautical trinkets. None of the décor reflected Sydney, but the house did. It breathed her. Abby could feel her in the sigh of the floorboards and the groans of the roof overhead.

She walked the interior, pausing in every room, repressing the memories that wanted to greet her. She could not afford to let the agony out--she might create a freak thunderstorm and flood the house. The already gloomy day did not need an additional downpour. The freshly vacuumed carpets and polished wood floors distressed her as she moved through each room. The refrigerator held only gleaming clear shelves and two bottles of white wine. Abby grabbed an open one, plucked the cork with her teeth and took a gulp that drained a quarter of the bottle.

"Ugh, that's good," she told the room and continued outside to the garage.

She was relieved to see that the garage was less together than the rest of the house. Sydney's water skis hung on the wall, along with a frayed badminton set and couple of tennis rackets. Several boxes sat on a small folding table in one corner, a note taped to the side.

This is the last of the personal mementos. Couldn't really organize them, but nothing of value found – Best Ronda

Abby left the note and peeled back the cover on one of the boxes. She lifted out two notepads scribbled with Sydney's small cursive, glancing at grocery lists, which mostly included wine and chocolate, and various phone numbers. The packer of the box had put in a few paperbacks, probably random reads that Sydney had tucked away and forgotten in funky places like behind a box of cereal or on top of a cabinet. There were pictures bound by rubber-band and the first that Abby saw made her stomach lurch painfully. It was Abby as a young girl, maybe five, with her hair twisted in a french braid. She sat on Sydney's lap, her arms tight around her aunt's neck while the woman whispered conspiratorially in her ear. Abby could not see the picture taker, but she guessed it was Harold by the slightly lopsided image, as if he'd taken the shot to capture the boat on the lake behind them, rather than his wife and niece.

Outside, the wind began to pick up and Abby shuddered at the branches scraping across the garage's single window. As a witch, fear felt different. She didn't fear people anymore, but other things, darker things.

As she stood in the lonely garage, Abby realized that she had hoped to encounter Sydney's ghost in the house. Spirits, though still unnerving, at least offered contact. Abby wanted so much to see her aunt, but it was only the memory of Sydney that the house contained. Her spirit had departed.

She had no idea what she was looking for, but the sense that she was close grew inside her. Claire had told her to follow the smoke. Abby did not know what she meant, but she knew that something drew her to Sydney's home.

She pulled out a jumble of keys and looked at the little colored tags attached to each--house, speed boat, storage shed and Rod's loft.

"Rod's loft," she said, touching the key.

Abby had only visited the loft twice. Both were short trips running in to grab Sydney's forgotten bathing suit or sandals.

Now she felt an almost magnetic pull toward the small silver key.

After she pawed the contents of both boxes, she wandered the house aimlessly, fighting the urge to call out. There were guides she knew, guides in the spirit realm, and those energies conjured by the elements, but Elda had explained them in a very peculiar way.

'The spirits are often mischievous, arriving at the most inopportune time with some jumbled message that you spend so much time deciphering, you lose sight of your task. The other energies, those of the earth, arrive only in your most desperate hour, like the lake pulling you during the Vepar's death ritual. It called out to you and your body called back. It doesn't listen to your voice, but to your spirit.'

Elda had been attempting to discourage Abby from too much blind faith in forces beyond herself. The lesson was in self-preservation and Abby had listened closely. Brushing death made one a diligent student.

****

Oliver stared into the fire, sipping his scotch, and ignoring Dafne who'd followed him in. He had not chased Abby into the woods despite every atom in his body screaming to do so. Instead, he had taken Victor safely back to his car and stayed with him until morning. Abby knew that he would, otherwise she never would have abandoned her friend. Oliver tried to talk to Victor, but the witch had been poisoned and, in his groggy state, could barely remember Abby's name. Oliver finally left him when the young witch grew clear and alert and insisted that he was fine.

"She's not gone forever, Oliver. Surely you know that," Dafne said, staring him down from across the room.

He said nothing, but continued to watch the flames dance and pop wildly. He had told his coven nothing about the night before.

"Elda believes that she probably reconnected with some of the witches that she met at Sorciére. Apparently she made some friends there." Dafne snorted as if that were hard to believe.

He shot her a dark look and drained his glass.

"What do you want, Dafne?"

She threw her hands up and walked closer to him.

"I want you to be you again. I want you to stop sulking and obsessing over Abby. I want our life before Abby and Sebastian!" Her voice rose as

111

she spoke and Oliver noted the faintest edge of hysteria.

He could have calmed her. He had done it a thousand times in the past because Dafne lived just one crank away from panic twenty-four/seven. Instead he ignored her.

The library door opened and Lydie walked in. She looked disheartened.

She sat on a pillow between Oliver's legs and rested her head on his knee. He stroked her hair and ignored Dafne who looked even more exasperated.

"Any word?" he asked Lydie who had been hovering around Faustine since Abby left.

"No. He told Elda earlier that he's struggling to make a connection with any of us, even here in the castle. He thought it was All Hallow's, but now..." Lydie trailed off and Oliver heard a tremor in her voice.

"It's okay, Lyds," he reassured her, continuing to pet her hair.

The fluffy orange cat that Lydie had named Garfield jumped from a couch and planted himself in Lydie's lap where it rolled belly up and purred a demand that she pet him.

"Hi, Garfield," she said to the cat lifelessly, running her fingers over his soft fur.

"This is ridiculous," Dafne started again, pacing in front of them. "Witches do this their first year, you guys. They try different things until they find what fits."

"Yeah, but Abby's boyfriend died," Lydie interrupted. "Sebastian died, Dafne. She left because she's sad."

Lydie was not aware that Oliver had killed Sydney, which was also why Abby had left. Faustine and the others would never reveal it. Only Oliver could disclose that secret and the mere mention of Sydney's name made him shudder remembering that night. He tried to shake the memory, but suddenly it fell on him again as it so often did in his nightmares...

At Faustine's urging, Oliver had ventured to Sydney's house to see if the Vepars still lurked nearby. Perhaps they would lie in wait for Abby and Sebastian to return there.

Oliver had watched the woman with blonde hair climb from the lake. She pulled a towel from a chair back, drying off naked beneath the luminous moon. She was older than him, in her forties at least, but a beauty nevertheless. Her breasts were too large to be natural and they tapered down to a smooth, flat stomach and shapely legs. She was short and her blue eyes were piercing, even in the dark. She was related to Abby, he could see that, but there was something darker in her, a shadow that hovered just beneath the surface.

He knew from Elda that Abby's aunt was supposed to be on vacation, but he had no other explanation for this woman, clearly acting as if it were her home that she traipsed around so confidently. He glanced back toward the house, watching each window, but detected no movement inside. Her husband was either sound asleep or gone. Gone, Oliver thought, because he could not detect any other presence there.

The woman strode across the porch and slipped on a sundress. She began to turn toward the house and then paused, meaningfully. She stepped into a stream of moonlight and faced Oliver , staring at him directly as if she could see him clearly despite the leafy shroud of the tree that he waited in. His throat constricted and he bit his lip against the urges that washed over him. He usually had such control, but something about her made his pulse quicken. He felt the blood surging into his temples and he shook his head with a jerk from side to side.

The woman lifted a hand and beckoned to him with a single finger. She turned and disappeared inside.

"What the hell?" he asked out loud. He understood as surely as he knew the earth beneath him that he should not move toward that house. Every fiber in his body was pulling him towards her, but the energy that existed in a realm beyond human desires cautioned him to stay away. Without thinking, he started to move out of the trees toward the house and then caught himself, surprised.

"What are you doing?" he whispered and retreated quickly, hoisting himself into a tree and scampering to the top.

He chewed on a switch of pine, which grounded him. When he felt stable, he turned to gaze at the house. He could see her moving from room to room, turning off lights. She stopped in an upstairs room, drew the curtains wider, and then began to light candles. He saw bits of her as she moved around the space, but already his jaw tightened and he felt his heartbeat grow more rapid. He fought it, calling forth his element and communing with it deeply. In his mind, he softened into the tree, feeling his legs melt into bark and his torso grow strong and sturdy like the trunk. He fixed his eyes on the ground far below him and waited.

Hours passed in silence. Oliver sensed that the woman lay awake in the house waiting for him. He should have left, gone searching for a scent in the woods, but he had been unable to shake the feeling that the woman's home held the answers that he needed.

When her scream pierced the silence, he nearly plummeted to the ground below. A fat branch that he caught with his hand, rather painfully, stopped him and he clutched it only briefly before climbing quickly and silently to the ground. He moved across the yard near the beach, ready to slip into the water for concealment. Nothing raced through the darkness and when he lifted his nose to the air, he did not smell a Vepar nor did he sense the tar-like energy that they oozed into the space around them.

The door was unlocked and, as he crept into the house, he pulled the steel dagger from his pant leg and held it firmly in his fist. He had left his bow and arrow in the forest, knowing that anything he encountered w the house would be a close-range fight. He might not have sensed a Vepar, but they were master concealers and he would show no mercy if one came upon him. He wanted vengeance for the young witch Devin and, more so, for Abby. He wanted to return to Ula and triumphantly tell Abby that he had saved her aunt.

He took the steps two at a time and kicked through the door to the bedroom that the woman had gone into. She stood in a corner, her dress clinging to her body, her blonde hair cascading over her shoulders.

"I called for you," she breathed.

He watched her and tried to maintain control of his body's desire. Something inside of him let go.

He strode across the room and scooped her into his arms, tossing her onto the bed. She released a low guttural moan and he grasped the back of her head, lifting her face to meet his. She kissed him desperately, releasing his belt and forcing his pants down. When she parted her legs and he moved inside her, his entire body trembled with pleasure. His lips sought her breasts and she dug her fingernails into his back as he thrust into her.

His mind had shut down. The witch Oliver, for those several minutes, ceased to exist. When a sharp pain pierced his right side, he barely noticed, so lost in the carnal pleasures of her exquisite body. The second time, alarm bells sounded in his head. He pushed away from her and looked at the blood gushing from the wound below his rib cage.

The woman held his dagger in her hand and her eyes glowed with malice . She sprang from the bed and the knife clattered to the floor. Oliver, dazed, reached for it, not fully grasping that this woman he'd been making love to wanted to kill him. She snatched a bucket from her bedside table and threw it in his face. He recoiled and sputtered as gasoline burned his eyes and coated his lips.

He saw the small box in her hands and her fingers closed on a single red-tipped stick. She started to slide it but, before she could set the match on fire, he thrust his blade into her chest. It went in so easily. It slid through her delicate breast bone. She cried out and dropped her match. Her eyes locked with his and now, again, they were blue and innocent and terrified. She fell to her knees, both hands grasping at the blade.

He reached forward, holding her shoulders as she crumpled back to the floor. Blood began to ooze from the wound and tears fell in thick streams from h̶ ̶ put a bloody, trembling hand into his and, when he ̶ ̶wn throat constricted and he started to pull the knife ̶king irrationality that he might save her. ̶id grip on the slippery handle, a booted foot slammed ̶om behind him and drove the dagger through the ̶it hit the wood floor beneath her. He started to twist ̶ caught him first. He felt the fire lick the back of his shirt. He stood and dove through the open window into the night. He hit the roof and rolled.

Above him, the mysterious Alva, the Vepar who created Tobias, lifted another bucket of gasoline and flung it out over Oliver as he plunged to the earth. The fire seemed to eat him alive. The pain was blinding and deafening and he rolled and twisted, but through it all, he saw the woman's pale blue eyes and the deep sorrow etched into her irises as she faded away.

Oliver stumbled blindly. He screamed and raked at his clothes, trying to pull them away from his skin where the fire consumed him. When he saw Alva moving across the porch towards him, he shut down his senses and he fled. In his confusion, he went in the wrong direction and staggered through woods. He dropped and rolled in pine needles until the fire was extinguished, but still he burned. The blisters on his skin already felt like balloons, expanding outward and ready to burst.

He knew that Alva drew close and with a single, silent thrust, he drove himself towards the water and splashed in. He swam clumsily into deep water. To his horror, a hand grasped his ankle. He looked down to see the dead woman, a gaping hole in her chest and her eyes blazing. She pulled him under the water. He fought her, but her small hands dug into his calves and held until his vision started to fade. A thousand dead things writhed beneath her, waiting to pull him into their pale, almost fleshless arms. He closed his eyes and allowed the darkness to swallow him.

"Ollie...Ollie." Lydie's strained voice came to him and Oliver blinked and then rubbed furiously at his eyes where the image of the woman was still fading away.

"Sorry, hon," he told her. "Got lost in my thoughts, I guess."

Dafne watched him curiously, but said nothing.

****

"Well, she's in tip-top shape," the man told Abby, kicking the tire with his sneaker-clad foot and wincing slightly. "Never died on me once."

Abby surveyed the burgundy two-door Saturn and pretended to consider. In truth, she didn't give a damn about the car so long as it started and got her down the road. She needed a vehicle if she was going to get around the city without creating a rumor of a wild woman living in the woods. Her own car sat in the warehouse near Lake Superior, unavailable to her without the assistance of the coven.

The man, Darcy, had posted the Saturn for sale in Trager's free weekly newspaper and she didn't want to arouse his suspicions by handing over a wad of cash without, at least, appearing to weigh the decision.

"Well, I've been saving for a while and it seems like a pretty good fit," she said. She pulled a stack of hundreds from the Pure Michigan beach bag she had purchased earlier that day at a downtown boutique.

Darcy grinned and Abby tried not to stare at the chocolate smeared across his front tooth. When she'd knocked on his door, he had been scarfing the last of a chocolate doughnut and she saw now that some of it had also made its way to the front of his Fish Whisperer t-shirt.

"Well, you two seem like the perfect pair," he added, taking the money and quickly shuffling through it. She saw that he no longer looked at her at all. Money did that to people. She waved a quick goodbye and got in the car.

She set off down the road, grimacing at the pungent aroma of the air freshener called Black Ice hanging from the rear-view mirror. She plucked it off and shoved it into the glove box, vowing to pick up something a bit less abrasive, like strawberry.

She circled Rod's building twice before she cut the engine a block away and pulled her hood tight over her ball cap. She knew that the outfit was a bit extreme. Hat, sunglasses and hooded sweatshirt, all at once like some paranoid celebrity hiding from crazed fans, but Trager made her uneasy. It wasn't her own near death that unnerved her, but the murder of Sydney and the attack on Oliver that made her skin crawl.

She didn't want to think of Oliver. She knew in her heart that killing Sydney had been an accident, but still, was there no way to avoid it? And why all of the lies? In a coven of witches who supposedly valued honesty, the truth seemed strangely absent.

Next to the car, a group of older women, clutching wine bottles, laughed and moved down the street. They represented the last of the autumn tourists, visiting the wineries outside of Trager and frequenting the downtown shops and stores that had not yet reduced their hours for the coming winter.

She stepped from the car and stuck close to the building, listening keenly to every voice and sound. Her gaze, behind her sunglasses, darted across the street and peered quickly into parked cars, searching for anything out of the ordinary. Nothing aroused her suspicions and, when she finally slid the key into Rod's door and stumbled across the threshold, the vice on her lungs loosened and she sucked in a deep breath of stale air.

The windows were closed tight and the space held an aura of abandonment. The loft's disarray was likely a combination of Rod and Sydney's trip to the Cayman Islands combined with the later police investigation, though Abby had the impression that when Vepars murdered, no real investigation occurred.

She paused and took in the enormous photo collage of Rod and Sydney that hung on a brick wall opposite the door. She felt the flower in her chest bloom and immediately wither. She slid down the closed door and gripped her knees, her eyes spilling over with tears of grief. Sydney was dead and

Sebastian was dead and, in her despair, Abby wished more than anything to join them. She hiccuped and wailed and her nose ran into her sweatshirt. She didn't care if other tenants in the building heard. She had only to jump out the window and run like hell to be gone in minutes. She realized that it was sort of like being a superhero. Right then, she understood their tragic stories much fully than when she'd read comics as a child. They were always plagued by some misfortune that brought loneliness and isolation into their lives. She could feel the pit of that loneliness deep in her stomach.

"Screw them," she whispered aloud. "Screw all of this."

She flung her sunglasses across the room where they landed with a crack on the wooden floor.

She wrung her hands and pressed her face into her knees and sobbed for the loss of the people that she loved. Sydney had been her lifelong comrade and one of the only people in her world that ever truly seemed to understand her. Then Sebastian appeared--that mated soul whom Sydney, somehow inadvertently, had brought into her life. Now they were both gone, their brilliant flames snuffed out by an evil that Abby had not even known existed. Her desperation to find answers suddenly felt pointless and without hope.

Elda had spoken of the witches' burden since Abby first learned of her powers, but she hadn't understood. Those haunted looks that all of the witches seemed to possess, the horrific story of the Lourdes, all foreshadowed that which Abby had refused to recognize. Now she got it, the power, the gift, came with great suffering and she feared that she could not withstand it.

"I don't want this," she cried into the empty room. "I don't want this!"

She slammed her fist onto the wooden floor and a tiny web of cracks appeared beneath her hand.

* * * *

Abby pulled the cork from the bottle of Merlot and poured a heaping portion into a white coffee mug. Sydney and Rod had an entire cupboard of sparkling goblets, but they felt much too festive for Abby's dour mood. She sipped the wine and walked the apartment, silently observing her surroundings.

Elda had told her to shut off her brain and see with her senses.

'Our brains are so efficient," the Elder Witch had explained. 'They create neural pathways to remember things. These pathways are like deep ruts that our thoughts flow through again and again. We stop seeing the tree outside our window and how uniquely beautiful it is every single day. Instead, we see a familiar object and pass it by. We fixate on our lover's flaws because we've trained ourselves to see those patterns rather than acknowledging how gently he's holding the baby or how, today, his eyes are filled with wonder. To see the world through a clean lens, Abby, you must take thought out of the equation. Don't name it or judge it, just see it.'

Abby glanced over pictures, books, artwork and let it merely exist, not allowing any associations or memories to sully the impact.

When she moved into Sydney and Rod's bedroom, she closed her eyes for a moment, feeling the pain of their rumpled sheets and then releasing it.

"There's something here for me," she said to the room. "I can feel that I've been drawn here. Please reveal yourself."

She repeated the words as she walked the perimeter of the room and then into the bathroom. Nothing jumped out, but the hairs on the back of her neck began to tingle. High heels and paperbacks and half smoked cigars, one of Rod's guilty pleasures, slid into focus and then out again. Doorknobs, a wall mural of a Malaysian pool, ceiling fan, wooden floor, black shag rug, ankle weight... She paused, her mind backtracking and she shifted her gaze to the black shag rug. It was small, round and sitting just beyond the foot of the platform bed. Abby had been to the loft several times and she had never seen the rug. On top of the rug stood a small, three-legged table with a mirrored surface. It held two candles, melted nearly to their bases, and a small rock with something etched into the surface. She lifted it close to her face and saw a crudely carved heart. She considered the heart and looked at the rug again, thinking.

She crouched down and slid the table and rug aside and stared at the wooden floor boards. Everything looked right, but something was off. She traced her fingers along the boards and noticed that the grains differed slightly. The variation was barely perceptible, but she began to force her fingernails along the board edges, prying and pushing until one of the boards gave. She lifted and a large square of floor rose up to reveal a trap door.

She sat back on her heels and chewed the end of a fingernail. Rod's body had never been found and the thought of discovering him rotting in the loft floor petrified her. No smell rose from the darkened space.

She took a deep breath and got on her hands and knees, peering into the hole. A wooden ladder led down from the opening. The total drop was no more than five feet and only an empty plank floor greeted her. She could not see what lay beyond the shafts of light illuminating the opening. She grabbed a box of matches and lit one of the melted candles from the table and climbed down.

A secret room existed beneath Sydney and Rod's bedroom. It was rectangular in shape and filled mostly with colored storage totes. Abby had to hunch to keep from hitting her head on the ceiling. A small table stood along one wall and, above it, Abby could see several battery-operated push lights. She clicked three of them and scanned the table. It held a jumble of items from newspaper clippings to keys. She lifted one of the newspapers and gasped at the cover. A picture of a smiling Devin, beneath a headline that read 'Young Trager Artist Found Dead in Ebony Woods,' stared back at her.

"Ebony Woods," she murmured, remembering the name, but not immediately pinpointing where she heard it before. Slowly it dawned on her, the newspaper clipping of Devin's Aunt Aubrey who burned to death in 'the Ebony Woods'.

As Abby studied the dates on the newspaper, her hands began to tremble. The clipping was dated three days after Devin's body had been found. Sydney and Rod had already left for the Cayman Islands.

She spun around, convinced that someone stood behind her, but no one lurked in the shadows. Rattled, she hoisted several boxes out of the hole and closed the trap door.

In the apartment, she set to casting spells over each window and across the door. No spells were absolute, Elda had been clear on that point, but all of them offered some form of protection.

Abby opened Rod's laptop and typed in Sydney1. Rod clearly did not follow safety measures with his electronics. Sydney1 had been his password years earlier when Abby visited. She opened the web browser and searched 'Aubrey Blake witch.' It was the same search that she had performed nearly two months earlier, on the very day that she and Sebastian almost lost their lives.

She found the site History of Magic and clicked it open. The same graphics appeared with stars falling across a black screen and then, pixel by pixel, the image materialized. She saw Aubrey first, her brilliant red hair, black and white in the picture, stuck wildly from her hood. She scanned the other faces. In total, eleven people stood together, their arms linked. Two men flanked Aubrey on her left and right, both grinning beneath their dark hoods. They all stared at the camera with a kind of exuberance that electrified Abby. She laughed in spite of herself and felt their energy travel the distance of time and space to meet her in that modern loft where she sat alone, connecting to them through a computer screen.

She studied each face and when she came to the thin, narrow featured woman who stood four people to Aubrey's left, she grew cold and still. Dafne stared back at her--Dafne of the coven of Ula--not some ancestor, but Dafne herself. Her dark eyes were unmistakable, though different, lighter and filled with joy. She held the same elation as every other witch in the picture and Abby knew that all, but three of them, were witches. She could see an unmistakable aura of glittering light surrounding the witches.

She did not recognize the other faces, and yet she did. She felt the resonance of their bond and, despite the warm room, she shivered and wrapped her arms tightly across her chest.

****

Oliver spent the day in the lake, cutting through the frigid waters between the island and the shore until he grew too exhausted to go on. He stumbled up the sand dune embankment on the north side of the island and fell asleep, his body hot beneath the rising moon.

He awoke to Lydie beside him, gently pooling sand up over his feet, ankles and calves.

"What are you doin,' Lyds?" he asked sleepily, shivering suddenly against the steadily declining temperature.

Lydie wore jeans and a hooded sweatshirt. Oliver wore only his damp swim trunks.

"Heating you up," she said, adding more sand and then starting on his thighs.

The sand felt good, warm, and Oliver knew that Lydie drew on her element of fire to heat the sand. He let his head fall back to the earth and stared up at the night sky.

"Waning moon," Lydie said, holding her index finger and thumb up to the sliver of moon above them. "Waning witch," she added.

She was recalling an old nursery rhyme that spoke of the witch's power waning and waxing with the moon. It might have been a nursery rhyme, but it was very true for many witches, the women especially. Oliver rarely noticed a decrease in power when the moon waned, but he had witnessed it in Dafne on more than one occasion.

"I have to go after Abby, honey," Oliver told her, sitting up and wrapping an arm around Lydie's tiny back.

She gazed into the dark night and he felt her shudder.

"Hurry," she said.

****

Abby checked her mirror one more time. She wore an oversized black coat with a white hooded sweatshirt underneath. Her hair was tucked beneath her hood and a pair of Sydney's gaudy sunglasses covered most of her face. She did not sense danger in Trager, otherwise she never would have risked a trip to the grocery store, but she was starving and wanted a little human contact, even if it only included telling the cashier to have a nice day.

She wandered the aisles in distraction, filling her basket with granola bars and yogurt. She spotted the fruit and hurried over, already craving the sweet produce that Michigan could no longer deliver roadside as winter approached.

She reached for a pomegranate. Her hand brushed against a woman also reaching for the fruit. Abby pulled back abruptly, as if burned. She blushed, embarrassed by her reaction. The other woman had barely touched her, but Abby had felt a jolt just the same.

She turned to the woman and gave her a wan smile, hoping to diminish any concern that her recoil might have caused. The stranger stared at her with intense curiosity. Her clear gray eyes locked on Abby's and she tucked a strand of her short blonde hair behind her ear. The woman opened her mouth, as if to speak, and then a young girl with red curls tugged on her skirt. She jumped, startled, and gave Abby a quick nod before she walked away, holding the child's hand. The woman dropped the pomegranate into her child's small red cart next to a stuffed, purple kangaroo.

"Fruit of babies?" the little girl asked her mother, touching the pomegranate.

"Symbol of rebirth, honey," she told her daughter.

The woman nuzzled the girl and smoothed the curls back away from her forehead. Before they moved down the next aisle, she turned once more to Abby and gazed at her for several long moments.

Abby waited and then she replaced the pomegranate in her own hand and, abandoning her basket, followed the woman. She walked to the front of the grocery store and stood by the drinking fountain, occasionally dipping her head to take a drink.

She closed her thoughts, as Elda had taught her, and acted on intuition alone. If her brain was allowed control, it would demand that she consider every possibility for the shock that this woman's touch had passed to her. She would get lost in fear and paranoia and, in that moment, she needed only to move, to breathe and to move.

When the little redhead squealed in delight that her mother caved and bought her a candy bar, Abby slipped out the side door and jogged quickly to her car. She slid in and turned the key, watching in her rear view as the woman left the store. She bent over and pushed the little girl in her tiny cart across the lot. The child stood in the cart, clutching the sides, her kangaroo dangling from one armpit. The woman pushed her fast and the child's red curls blew out behind her and they both laughed. They stopped at an older blue pickup and the stranger loaded her daughter into a car seat.

The woman drove across town and then turned onto the same winding forest road that Abby had driven a thousand times on her way to her Aunt Sydney's house. However, when they came to Sydney's driveway, the blue truck passed it by, eventually turning into a narrow dirt drive. Abby passed the drive and then circled back once, looking, but seeing only where the weedy path disappeared into trees. A series of mailboxes marked the drive, which meant multiple houses were located there. Abby parked in Sydney's driveway and returned on foot.

She crouched in the woods and watched. Abby observed several small stone cottages along the rocky Lake Michigan shoreline. The cottages formed a half moon around a large fire pit. . Beach chairs and benches lined the pit, despite the late season. Abby could see a few wine bottles nestled in the sand near the chairs and stacks of wood on each of the cottage's porches. She could not tell which home the woman had entered because the driveway simply formed a grassy roundabout with several cars parked along its perimeter.

Abby remembered the cottages, but only vaguely. She recalled Sydney pointing them out from the boat one summer when they were out trolling in the lake with Harold, Sydney's first husband. Harold had mostly dozed off, his pole unattended, while Sydney steered and Abby hung over the bow searching for fish in the clear water.

"They're ripe with history," Sydney had told an eleven years old Abby, veering the boat closer into shore. Abby remembered the strange group of women she had seen that day. They waded in the water, laughing and talking loud, but they wore long dresses that floated on the surface like blue and orange and red lily pads. Several of them waved to Sydney as they passed and, when Abby asked why they were swimming in their clothes, Sydney had told her 'because during the day they can't go naked.'

Abby stood now, almost waiting to see that same group of colorful ladies, like a bouquet of flowers, fanning out into the frigid autumn waters. But the cottages remained silent and still, other than the tendrils of creamy gray smoke that drifted from two of the chimneys and disappeared into the overcast sky.

Abby looked up, startled when a glob of red curls darted across the yard in her direction. The child had barely left the house and, like a blood-hound, she seemed to know exactly where Abby stood. Abby stalled for only a second and then, pushing off with her right foot, practically ran straight up the tall pine tree in front of her. She paused on a series of thin branches fifteen feet in the air and watched the little girl run into the woods below her, stopping immediately. Abby expected her to look up, but she merely gazed deeper into the tress. She hummed a low haunting melody and Abby watched her, mesmerized.

"Ebony, Ebony, where are you?" her mother's voice rang out and Abby recognized the voice of the woman in the grocery store.

Abby returned to Sydney's house, but did not go in. Sydney knew the people in those stone cottages, but how? Abby needed to speak with someone that knew about Sydney's life in Trager City.

Abby rested her forehead against the wall and groaned. She would have to return to Lansing and talk to her mother.

****

Sebastian sat on Isabelle's couch and sipped his tea, heavy with milk and sugar.

The hospital had been a nightmare, considering the staff were busy with people who actually needed their help and could hardly be bothered with a young, clearly healthy, man who'd forgotten his identity. When Sebastian finally made it into a doctor's office, the physician merely asked him a few questions, probed his head for bumps and said that his memory would likely return in twenty-four hours. The doctor further implied that Sebastian was either a con artist or had consumed too much alcohol the night before and would remember clearly when he slept off his hangover.

He stripped down in Isabelle's bathroom, again searching every inch of his clothing for some identification. He found nothing. He put on a pair of sweatpants and a t-shirt that belonged to Isabelle's father. The pants barely reached his shins and the t-shirt hugged too tight around his chest, but stylish clothing was the last thing on his mind.

"I thought I might call around and see about costume parties," Isabelle told him when he returned to her sitting room.

"Costume parties?" he said absently, staring out her window at the small balcony adorned with chimes, ceramic fairies and a single purple lawn chair.

"Yes, your clothes," she trailed off.

He nodded. His clothes were extremely strange. They added yet another element to an already exhausting range of possibilities. In a black room, every corner, crevice and wall offered more space to discover, but also to ram your head or knee against.

"I can't thank you enough," he told her, taking her hand and squeezing it.

She squeezed back and smiled, revealing a dimple on her left check.

"I want to help you," she told him seriously.

Chapter 14

August 7, 1908

"He can't be serious," Dafne told Aubrey, shaking her head knowingly. "He's grieving. No one would possibly believe that tale."

Dafne and Aubrey sat side by side on the porch swing that Henry had fashioned from a fallen maple. The western sun shone through the dense forest, mostly empty of its leaves.

"That's what I'm saying to you, Dafne. People are believing it. They're looking at me cross everywhere I go. I didn't sell a single poultice at the market yesterday or the day before..."

"It's a dry spell, that's all." But Dafne felt her pace quicken as she spoke. They no longer lived in a world of witch accusations and terror, but small communities bred paranoia better than most and, though a life might not be taken, a livelihood easily could.

"I wish to believe that," Aubrey whispered, clasping her hands in her skirt and rocking back in the swing. Worry lines creased her forehead and her bright green eyes shone with fear.

"We're the powerful ones," Dafne told her, urgently squeezing her hand. "If anyone owns this town, it's us."

"You're leaving! You and Tobias are as good as gone."

Dafne bit her lip and shook her head.

"Not yet we're not, and we're all in this together. All of us. We'll see everyone Saturday night and then we will know what to do. Surely Celeste can look into the days ahead and put your mind at ease."

Aubrey shook her head.

"No one has seen Celeste in days. I went by her cottage and not a soul in sight, the doors and windows closed up like the cold season had fully come."

Dafne considered this with a shudder. As a seer, Celeste saw visions of the future. However, she fell frequently into such overwhelming dread that she vanished for months at a time. Her last premonition had occurred just two weeks before the death of her young sister and she still had not fully recovered.

"She would not simply leave though. If she foresaw something bad, she would have told us..."

"Her visions are not helpful right now, anyway," Aubrey continued. "They're too

unclear, there's no focus. I need a source for all this rage directed at us. Something is giving it life."

Aubrey had first complained of the community suspicion a week earlier, five days before Solomon died. She noticed strange looks from neighbors who'd been loyal customers at the weekly market. Henry also noticed fewer patients at their free health clinic.

The situation had grown much more sinister since Solomon's death. Jonas, Solomon's father, had accused Aubrey of creating his son's illness through witchcraft. He had even brought charges against her. This, of course, terrified Aubrey because witch hunts were not all that far in the past and she was, after all, a witch. But it was less the townsmen than the darkness that scared Aubrey. She had told Dafne that she sensed a much larger, much more sinister force at work in Trager and that the evil appeared to be flowing right towards her.

Dafne had been so lost in her reverie with Tobias, she had barely acknowledged Aubrey's stories. Now she realized that Aubrey was right, the issue was escalating.

"Something bad is coming," Aubrey said, pulling her shawl tighter against her body.

"No," Dafne disagreed, hopefully. "This feeling will blow over soon. It's a strange time, that's all."

Chapter 15

"Tell me about Trager," Abby asked her mother. They sat at the same chipped Formica table that Abby had eaten cereal at every morning for the first eighteen or so years of her life.

It was strange returning to her childhood home. Strange, not merely because the train of her life had leaped off the tracks and was now careening across glacial mountains and thorn filled valleys without any tracks to speak of, but also because Sydney's inheritance had clearly left her mother confused. Gone were the spider-webbed dishes with their little blue pastel edges, replaced by heavy Asian themed bowls and plates in smoky blacks and vibrant reds. The dishes looked foreign against the faded sunflower shelving paper in the cupboards. The living room had transformed from a jumble of plaid and floral sofas and chairs to a chaotic menagerie of ultra-modern leather foot stools butted against antique chaise lounges with gilded legs and arms.

Abby had attempted to enter through the garage when she arrived, but nary a footpath existed among the boxes of old and new. There were sagging cardboard boxes, black marker neatly expressing their contents, while other perkier boxes stood upright and revealed new purchases such as the Kessler 89X2000 Super Sucker Vacuum Cleaner. It was unopened, but already collecting dust betrayed by the shafts of sunlight that streaked in through the single unblocked window.

The entire house reflected her mother's conflict over what to get rid of and what to bring in. Even Becky's attire revealed her jumbled state of mind. She wore shiny black leggings with peek-a-boo black heels beneath a heavy moth-eaten purple sweater that Abby had seen her in a thousand times before.

Becky sighed, lit a cigarette, and brushed a hand through her tangled hair. Tired would have been the compliment of the century. She appeared haggard and Abby tried hard to ignore the gnawing guilt that perhaps she had played some part in her mother's unraveling.

"We didn't live there for all that long..." Becky started, less unnerved by

Abby's question than exhausted by the effort of answering it. She took a drag and blew the smoke straight up, watching it curl and fan out beneath a ceiling spotted with watermarks.

"Where's Dad?" Abby asked. She wanted to talk about Trager and get to the issue that had brought her back to Lansing, but she could feel his lack of presence and it didn't seem as though he'd run out for coffee creamer.

Becky looked up at her and her red-rimmed eyes held her gaze for only a moment before she broke away and stared distantly at the small kitchen window.

"He left a week or two ago. Said it wasn't working. Blah, blah, blah," Abby's mother waved her hand dismissively and snorted. "Says I need professional help."

Abby took a deep breath and forced her head to stay steady rather than nod an affirmation to her mother's comment. She had believed that her mother needed psychiatric help for most of her life. Extreme bouts of depression coupled with manic cleaning or buying frenzies had left both Abby and her father in the throes of an emotional tornado that never calmed for more than a few weeks before again gaining momentum and wreaking havoc on everything in its path. Abby's dad had gotten off easy in some regards. As a Realtor, he spent much of his time away. He offered a hundred excuses--showings, schmoozing clients, networking, late at the office. His evasions came so readily that Abby could rattle them off before he even called to say he was going to miss dinner or brunch or that school function that Abby insisted both her parents attend. He wasn't negligent exactly, just unable to face the life that he'd chosen. So he went through the motions, but opted for something else instead--work.

Many times Abby had wondered why he stayed or, more importantly, why he ever signed on to begin with, but hers was not a communicative family. Gleaning the tiniest shard of family history was like tapping a palm tree for maple syrup. Her mother's reactions had generally ranged from suspicion to outright dismissal when Abby probed about her life before her only child was born. Her father offered tidbits here and there, but rarely held a conversation beyond ten minutes and returned his gaze to a television show or newspaper article.

Abby bit her tongue and reached across the table to hold her mother's hand.

"I'm so sorry, Mom. Is there anything that I can do?"

Becky laughed, a dry painful sound, and jerked her head from side to side.

"I'm a big girl, Abby. I may not be superhuman..." she emphasized this last word, but did not look at Abby as she said it, "...but I'm capable of living my own life."

Abby nodded and fought the various suggestions that drifted to the forefront of her mind.

"People can only heal themselves," Elda had told Abby. "And that healing always starts right here." Elda had touched her heart and asked Abby to do the same. She had told Abby these things in response to Sebastian's anxieties over Claire and his desire to avenge her death. But Abby knew that Elda meant it for her as well, and also as a lesson that even witches could only bring help to those ready to receive it .

"Ugh," her mother sighed, heaving herself out of her chair as though her body had grown heavy with age, though Abby estimated her weight at well under one hundred pounds. She watched her mother zigzag through the boxes to the door.

"What are you doing?" Abby asked, wondering if her mother had simply decided to get up and leave in the middle of their conversation.

"What does it look like I'm doing," she snapped, opening the door. Abby heard something scurry inside and she caught a streak of black.

The cat practically dove into Abby's lap when he saw her, his purr loud and desperate as he pawed at her thighs .

"Baboon!" she stared at him, overjoyed and then dismayed. In less than four months, his plump body had become bony and his once sleek fur looked oily and matted.

"Mom? How did you get him?" She nudged her face against his and took her first breath of comfort since walking into her childhood home.

"I didn't get him. Nick dumped him off here. Said he couldn't handle the memories. Left a whole heap of stuff in your old room too." Her mother looked at the cat and grimaced. "I guess you'll be abandoning him along with everything else--another mess for me to clean up."

Abby cringed at her mother's bitterness, but only shook her head and smiled into the sweetly sad eyes of her beloved pet.

"Nope, he is definitely coming with me. I'll look through my stuff too," she added. "And, Mom, if you want, I can get you some help in here, maybe somebody to clear some of this stuff out, donate it?"

"Humph, and have some stranger digging through my things. No thank you! As for your stuff, I don't care what you do with it, but you're gonna do it, not hire some criminal to come in here and sneak my new TV out the back door while he's at it."

Abby held fast to her cat and wished with all her heart that she could breathe love into the wasted body of the woman before her. Her mother had never been an especially kind woman, but the chill that emanated from her felt almost unbearable. Baboon licked her hand and then jumped down, padding across the floor to a mostly empty food dish.

"Trager..." Becky continued, flicking her ash into an expensive-looking marble ashtray and shooting a final scowl at the cat. "It was smaller then, before the tourists and all that--a hick town I guess people called it."

She stood and poured herself a cup of coffee and refilled Abby's half empty mug.

"My mother loved that town, Lord knows why. When my father got the job at the hospital in Lansing and we moved downstate, she just about called the fire department, she was so mad."

Becky didn't sit back down, but instead opened a drawer, one that used to hold kitchen rags, and pulled out a bottle of whiskey, pouring a hefty portion into her mug. Abby grimaced, but again remained silent. Her mother had never been more forthcoming and she wasn't going to ebb the flow with her judgments.

"I must have been about nine when we left Trager. Sydney was eleven or twelve, but she always really loved that place..." She trailed off and her eyes began to pool. She took a drink and wrapped both her hands around the mug. "She was a lot like my mom and I guess I was more like my dad, though even that I'm not so sure."

"Why did Grandma Arlene love Trager so much?"

"I never asked her that," Becky said. "I never asked her much of anything and even now I don't really know why she loved it. Sydney asked her, I'm sure. Sydney followed her around like a puppy when we were girls. She was as in love with our mom as she eventually became with herself." Becky's acrid tone was familiar to Abby. She had heard it most of her life whenever her mother spoke of Sydney or Arlene.

"I was always on the outside with those two. Never included in their little games, not that I wanted to be," she added stiffly, taking a drink and adding more whiskey to her mug.

Abby wondered just how often her mother was drinking, but again left the question unasked.

"For me, Trager was just like any other place. I went to school, swam in the lake, and had a few friends. But Sydney acted like Trager was this spectacular paradise. She barely even came in the house. Her and my mom used to sleep in our tree fort all the time. My dad pretended it drove him wild, but I think he liked it. He watched them from the window with binoculars. He could never understand why I didn't join them."

"Why didn't you?"

Becky cocked an eyebrow and stared at the swirling oils in her coffee.

"I was scared of the dark and I was scared of the woods. Our house was right on the edge of the forest, same forest Sydney's house is on, but on the other side of town, and it always felt off to me. Every time I went in there, I felt this darkness kind of surround me. I wasn't the only one," Becky added quickly as if Abby might doubt her. "A lot of the kids felt that way. The weird ones liked the woods. Sydney and her little friends were in there all the time."

"Were they called the Ebony Woods?" Abby asked.

Becky looked surprised, but removed the expression quickly.

"What's this all about, Abigail?"

It was the first time her mother had referred to her by her full name since she'd been home. Usually she always called her Abigail, but so much of her had changed. She appeared confused as to her place in her own daughter's life. Was she still the mother? Did she have any authority at all? Abby could feel the unasked questions lingering inside her mother's every word.

"You gave me the impression that you didn't want to know..." Abby trailed off, silently hoping that her mother would stick to that original desire and ask for nothing.

Becky pursed her lips and took another drink. For a moment, she looked more like the rigid woman that Abby had known most of her life, but then her face settled and the fine lines reappeared, pulling her small lips into a frown.

"I don't know what I want to know anymore or even what I do know, for that matter. Lately..." she waved a hand around the kitchen, "...nothing feels real. It's like I'm adrift in outer space, don't even have gravity to bring me back."

Abby nodded that she understood, largely because she did. Something about the onset of her powers kept her stable, sane perhaps, but she still had moments where she felt the most intense loneliness as if she existed in an ocean that was void of life. She might spend a hundred years swimming the dark blue depths and never encounter another living soul.

"I think it's best to not go too deeply into all of this right now," Abby started carefully, pulling apart pieces of the paper napkin beneath her mug. "I don't even really know what it all means yet..."

"Sure," Abby's mother laughed. "Don't patronize me."

"Mom, I'm not. I'm really not," she insisted trying to catch her mother's eye. "It would be the blind leading the blind and I don't want to bring any more confusion into your life."

"The Ebony Woods were what the mothers called the woods, only them though--my mom, Peggy Sue's, Lorna's and a couple other girls. They met once a month, it was always very clandestine, but sometimes we spied and a few times we overheard them say Ebony Woods. We never saw where they went. It was like they vanished...poof."

Becky lit another cigarette and blew a white puff into the air.

"Sydney always said that if she ever had a daughter, she would name her Ebony. So much for that plan." But now as she spoke, rather than bitter, Becky sounded unbelievably sad and Abby too felt a great sadness at the thought of Sydney having a child.

Sydney always claimed that she didn't want kids, but Abby had sensed otherwise and her mother had implied on more than one occasion that Sydney had been unable to conceive.

"Ebony because of the woods?" Abby asked.

"Yes. She was almost as obsessed with the woods as she was with our mother."

"How did Grandma Arlene die?" Abby asked. The question had been burning within her since her discovery that her grandmother had been a witch. After all, she lived with witches who were hundreds of years old. Why was her grandmother not among them?

"She died in a car accident. Her and Dad both, you know that."

"There wasn't anything more to it?"

Becky stared at her and Abby shrunk from the anger in her eyes.

"She might have thought she was immortal, but she wasn't. You get hit head on by a semi-truck and you're not coming back."

Abby shuddered, wishing she hadn't asked.

****

On his third day in her apartment, Isabelle had run out of clothing options for Sebastian. When she left for work, she handed him a credit card, much to his surprise, and directed him to a nearby clothing store. Dumbfounded, he attempted to return the card, unwilling to believe that anyone would so openly offer their credit card and their home to a stranger, but she insisted.

He left the apartment wearing shorts and a too small sweatshirt and walked the two blocks on unfamiliar streets to a small department store. By the time he pushed through the double glass doors his legs were rough with goosebumps and his face felt cold and raw. Rather than perusing the clothing racks, he walked to the counter where a tall thin woman absently flipped through a catalog

"Hi?" He asked, not sure if the woman spoke english..

"Hello," she told him, but it sounded like Hallo.

"English?"

"Oui, yes," she replied.

"Is there a thrift store nearby?"

She looked at him quizzically.

"Thrift?"

"Ummm...second-hand, used clothes?"

She wrinkled her nose, but then nodded and smiled.

"Ahh Vintage. Oui, that way, by the café."

He smiled, offered his thanks and started off in the direction she had pointed. He could not stomach the idea of spending Isabelle's money on new clothes.

After nearly a mile, he passed a small bistro adorned with tiny glass tables and iron chairs. Despite the cold, several people, sufficiently bundled, sat outdoors sipping steaming beverages from small white cups. They all watched him with interest, the tall curly-haired man in shorts with chattering teeth.

He pushed into the store, assuming it must be the right place by the mannequins clad in yellowing wedding dresses and puffy-sleeved gowns in the front window. The narrow store smelled of mothballs and stale cigarette smoke.

"Bonjour," a tiny woman with enormous purple spectacles called to him, scurrying from behind a desk nearly as high as she stood. The piles of tattered books that lined it were stacked above her head.

She hurried between the tight racks. Her neck looked heavy with a dozen fake pearl necklaces in various colors.

"Puis-je vous aider," she said brightly, her glasses slipping down to the ends of her nose as she raked up her long silky sleeves and took his wrist in her tiny hand. She immediately started to lead him deeper into the store.

"Umm, Bonjour, sorry I don't speak French," he said to the back of her head where her dark hair was piled and heavily sprayed into place. Barely a strand shifted as she walked.

"English? Fantastic," she told him, glancing back with a grin. "Me too, though I've lived here so long I'm starting to forget."

She laughed, a raspy smoker's laugh, and he felt a sweet internal sigh, grateful for another person who spoke his language. Not only words though, it was the whole demeanor of American, a little less polite and sophisticated, a trait that, in his turmoil, he found enormously comforting.

"Where are you from, honey?" she asked. She turned around and eyed him. "I'm thinking California--you look like a surfer boy to me."

He laughed and started to respond, but realized almost immediately that he had no answer. He had opened his mouth as if it were the most natural question in the world, but nothing came out.

"I don't actually know," he told her, feeling embarrassed. "I seem to have lost my memory."

She shuffled him into a small back room filled with men's clothes.

"Lost your memory?" She stopped and looked him up and down, gauging his size. "You runnin' from something?"

"No," he told her, exasperated. "At least, I don't think so. I was just walking down this road a couple of days ago and before that there's just...nothing."

She started pulling clothes from a rack and he frowned when she held a blue leisure suit up to his chest.

"Well, I've heard of amnesia, but I've never met anyone before that had it, though there's always some handsome hunk in my soap operas that ends up with it." She winked and then frowned sympathetically at the serious look on his face. "Were you in an accident, maybe bumped your head?"

She reached up and ran her hand along his scalp and then down his neck like an overly affectionate grandmother. He realized that he liked her.

"I have no idea, but honestly, I don't think so. I feel like...I feel like I'm not supposed to be here though. I feel like I was in America and then somehow I woke up here."

"Well, how about I.D. or a plane ticket? Have any of that stuff on you?"

"No, I didn't have anything on me at all. No, wait." He slid the small silver ring from his pinky. "I had this."

She took the ring and studied it.

"What's this here on the inside?" she asked. "Some other language?"

He shrugged and she handed the ring back to him.

She held up another hideously ugly suit, this one clearly feasted upon by moths.

"I'm thinking jeans and sweatshirts," he told her quickly, glancing around the room hopefully.

She looked at his current attire.

"Yep, surfer boy all right," she continued gravely, but with a smile. "I keep that stuff in boxes."

She dragged several boxes out from beneath the racks of hanging clothes and started to dig, throwing shirts and pants his way.

"Well, you'll have to contact the authorities and ask them to get some media attention back on you in the States. I'm thinking a picture on all of the major news stations should get you found pretty fast."

He started to agree, but something in his mind immediately constricted at the thought. He couldn't take that route because then someone bad could find him. He stopped, cocking his head to the side and trying to find the root of that fear. Someone bad? Maybe he was on the run?

"I'm Patty," she added, opening another box and heaving out an armful of colorful t-shirts. "I'd ask your name, but..." She laughed and then gave him a sweet motherly smile. "I'm gonna help you though, okay? First with the clothes and then after that, we'll see."

He continued to stare into the distance, desperate to follow the fear that arose at her suggestion of the media. Still no memories surfaced.

"Thank you, really," he told her, taking the clothes into a tiny dressing room that he could barely turn around in. He sat heavily into a small wicker chair crammed into the corner and started untying his shoes.

Patty slipped behind her cluttered desk and dug around in the black hole that she called a purse. She found the tiny blue flip phone that her granddaughter bought her the previous Christmas and quickly punched in the number of a close friend who'd recently come back into her life.

"This is Julian," the man answered.

"Julian, my love," she greeted him, keeping her voice low. "I've just run into a strange man with a very interesting ring."

Chapter 16

August 8, 1908

Dafne held the book in her hand and stared at the message that Tobias had left for her on page thirteen. They nearly always communicated that way, leaving books on each other's doorsteps. They wrote their message on the thirteenth page because they had met on the thirteenth of May. It ensured that her parents would not discover their relationship, but in truth, Dafne loved the romantic secrecy of the gesture.

Tobias had written only one word--Tonight.

She traced her fingers over the word and felt excited and frightened both in equal measure. They had saved for months and already plotted their path by train to New York. A small bag stashed in the cottage by the water held both of their clothes, papers and a handful of items neither could part with.

Dafne thought of Aubrey and the others. The idea of abandoning all of them just days after Solomon's death made her breath catch in her chest and burn furiously. She sat still and felt the pain leave her as she envisioned Tobias carrying her across the doorway into their tiny New York apartment. The others would understand and better, maybe they would join them in the city, though in her heart, she knew that Aubrey belonged to the water and the woods of Trager.

She cleared her thoughts and turned to the task of preparing dinner for her mother and father. At dusk, she would creep out of the cottage of her childhood and meet her future.

When the red moon began to rise, Dafne left her home for the last time. She held a handful of dried lavender clasped in one hand and twirled, laughing as she danced to the stone cottage. She could see a candle burning from within, but when she arrived Tobias was nowhere in sight. Likely walking the beach, she thought, though she could see no silhouette of him in either direction. She settled on the small bed, tucked her feet beneath her and worked on braiding the flowers into her hair. She sang softly and thought of the hastily written letters that she left for her beloved Aubrey and the other witches. Her parents would receive a postcard during the journey. She could not risk a letter for fear they would immediately track her and attempt to bring her home.

Chapter 17

Becky vanished into the basement and Abby waited, trying not to let the feeling of despair, that hung as heavy as the cigarette smoke in her mother's kitchen, drag her down. When she finally returned with a stack of albums, Abby could no longer take it and went to the window over the sink, pushing it open and gulping the fresh crisp air. She watched the tall oak tree in the front yard release some of the last of her brown leaves to the earth below.

Becky dropped the books on the table with a huff and slid the top one to the side, flipping back the cover.

"I haven't looked at these in...well over a decade at least, maybe more. Sydney wanted them a few years back, but I never did get around to giving them to her." Becky sighed and turned the album so that Abby could see it.

"It's not all Trager, there's other stuff mixed in, but here you see all of us out on the lake. Mom, Dad--that's Sydney in the bikini showing off, even at three." She spoke in equal parts anger and sadness. "There's the tree house. My dad built that for Sydney and me, but my mother spent more time in there than I did."

Abby looked at the large structure sitting atop branches that hardly seemed capable of holding it. It was a log-style tree house, complete with little windows adorned with tiny red curtains. A rope ladder hung from its deck.

"Who are they?" Abby gasped. "I mean they look so strange." Abby tried to cover her outburst, but still her mother watched her skeptically.

She pointed to a photo of the stone cottages. Four women stood together on the beach, their arms wrapped around one another. Abby recognized her grandmother in the group.

"That's Lorna's mom, Kate, in the blue dress," Becky told her. "She lived in one of those cottages. Gwen's mom, Denise, has all the necklaces on and she lived there too. Little dumps if you ask me. It was like livin' in a hippie commune, which of course Sydney and Mom thought was a real hoot. No, thank you! That's about one step above a trailer park..."

"A commune? Is that what they were?" She studied the small cottages.

The picture had been taken in the summer and the lawn burst with wildflowers.

"How would I know?" She glowered at Abby.

"Did Grandma say that though?"

Becky shrugged and flipped the page.

"Mom called them love sisters. That was more than enough information for me. I don't know the name of the third woman, but she may have lived there too."

"And Sydney was friends with their daughters?"

"Yep, peas in a pod, that group. Their little houses always smelled like patchouli and, God forbid, you got stuck having dinner over there. Tempeh meatloaf or tofu burgers. Ugh, my stomach turns just thinking of it."

Abby smiled thinking about the roasted Tofurkey Sebastian had made at Ula two weeks before. All of the witches, excluding Dafne, pretended to enjoy it. Helena even asked for seconds, despite the dense soggy texture. It hurt Abby's heart to think of it so she shifted back to the photos.

"What is this?"Abby asked, pulling out a sheet of folded paper that had stuck to the album's page. She began to open it, revealing a drawing of a dark forest with a vibrant red willow tree nestled in the center.

Becky snatched the paper away and balled it in her fist.

"That's private," she hissed and marched out of the room.

Chapter 18

August 9, 1908

Dafne woke to chanting. The haunting murmurs beckoned her out of the cottage and into the warm night. She walked, sleepy, into the Ebony Woods and followed the sounds. Buried deep in the thick foliage, she could see the brilliant light of a fire. Her body began to resist her forward movement. Without warning, her feet simply stopped and she nearly pitched forward. She walked to a tree and rested her palm against the soft white folds of birch bark. The tree emitted an ominous vibration and Dafne pulled away, startled. Then she began to hear the screams.

Aubrey cried out first and then Debra. She heard Henry begging for Aubrey's life. Dafne raced towards the fire, but as she moved into the clearing, she struck a shield of darkness that blasted her back. Her body sprawled on the forest floor. The fire burned an enormous ring around the witches and they were trapped within it. In the center of the circle, shrouded by eerie red light, Tobias stood in rapture. His black eyes reflected the horror of her beautiful magnetic friends. Naked from the waist up, sweat shone on the taught muscles of his chest and arms. Resting on his chest, Dafne saw a gold amulet with a red stone in its center.

"Noooo," Dafne screamed, and she began to draw the fire into her, but it only grew larger around the witches.

Tobias leered at her and threw his hands toward the sky where a ball of blue fire erupted from his fingertips. He turned and cast it towards Evelyn. Evelyn whose beautiful cherub face lit up when she talked to the birds at her feeders each day. Evelyn who'd promised Dafne that when she and Tobias left for New York, she would teach a pigeon to carry their messages. Evelyn burst into flames. She fell to the ground, writhing and screaming in agony.

Dafne saw the other witches trying to help her, but something all-powerful held them rooted in place. She stood and raced into the barrier, but again it shocked her away. A dozen times she tried, but one by one, Tobias burned them all. She slowly understood that he pulled his power from her. With each thrust of fire into the circle, Dafne grew more depleted and Tobias grew stronger. He inhaled the smoke as it rose up from their bodies and he danced in a circle and laughed and cried out in ecstasy. When the entire forest began to burn, Dafne's instincts took over and she fled from the blaze.

Chapter 19

When Abby felt sure that her mother slept soundly, she crept into the basement. It smelled of mildew and kitty litter. The overwhelm of boxes, stacked nearly to the ceiling, made Abby's head pound.

"How am I ever going to find anything in here?" she asked out loud.

"What are we looking for?" a voice asked from a far corner of the room and Abby nearly jumped high enough to hit her head on the ductwork above.

Her eyes adjusted to the darkness and she saw Oliver standing sheepishly in the shadows, his hands tucked into his jean pockets.

"What are you doing here?" she hissed, irritated that he was able to surprise her so easily.

"Sorry," he smiled, and walked into the dim light of the single bulb. "I wanted to warn you, but thought your mom might get pissed if I knocked on the front door."

"And this is better?" Abby asked, grimacing at the cobwebs clinging to Oliver's hair.

"It was effective." He smiled and Abby returned the smile in spite of herself.

She had been so angry when she left Ula. Blinded by her pain over Sebastian's death and the discovery that Oliver had killed Sydney, she had not given Oliver a chance to explain. Made worse when she had fled from him after he saved her and Victor in the Vepar's lair.

"I know you're angry," he said quickly, reading her face and perhaps thinking she might lash out at him. "But I need to tell you what happened and, more than that, I want to help you. I need to help you."

She sighed and sank to the floor, ignoring the cold, damp cement that seeped through her jeans.

"I'm not mad at you," she told him, patting the floor beside her. "I should have heard you out and I'm sorry that I ran. I just...I guess I was embarrassed that Victor and I needed help at all."

Oliver looked uncertain, but then a huge grin drew across his face and, rather than sitting, he plucked her off the floor and held her in a bone-crushing hug. She held him back, pressing her face into his shoulder and letting the tears that never seemed to be far away flow freely. When he pulled back and saw her wet cheeks, he wiped them with his hand and then hugged her once more, kissing her on the forehead.

It felt so good to have a friend. Abby had mostly suppressed her loneliness in the previous days, focusing instead on her search for answers.

"I'm happy I had the chance to save your life, Abby. I, at least, owed you that."

He grabbed two folding chairs and opened them, pressing Abby into one and taking the other.

"And I've missed you," he told her, his green eyes searching hers and she knew that he meant more than the absence of a friend.

She bit back the next wave of tears that rose behind her eyes.

"I missed you too."

They worked in silence, ripping boxes open and casting aside old clothes and household items, piling up the boxes filled with papers, pictures and albums. Abby did not really know what she searched for, only that she had begun to assemble an enormous jigsaw puzzle of which she could see only a corner.

She sensed how unsettled Oliver felt in their mutual silence. He wanted to explain and seek her forgiveness, but she needed to wait until she could offer her full attention. She also wanted to get out of her mother's basement. The space grew more claustrophobic with every passing second.

When they finished, Oliver loaded more than eight boxes stuffed with history into the trunk of her car.

"What did you drive?" she asked, scanning the road.

"I didn't," he smiled and shrugged. "Hitched a ride with a pretty girl from Detroit."

She started to ask how that transpired, but understood that Oliver's charm, combined with a little magic, could have gotten him a police escort if he desired it.

"I have to check my room too. Can you see it there's a cat carrier for Baboon in the basement?"

He grinned, snuggling the black and white cat against his chest.

"Nah, he'll be fine." Oliver winked at her and Abby realized that he could keep the cat calm despite Baboon's usual anxiety in the car. "Take your time. He and I will be right here." He plopped into the passenger seat and laid it back.

She crept up the stairs and opened the door to her old room. She surveyed the neatly stacked storage bins, all labeled, in front of her closet. The ever meticulous Nick had even written a list of the contents on the side. She did not feel any longing as she sat on the carpeted floor, the faces of her past ogling her from the walls. Posters and pictures and old love

letters were tacked and puttied to nearly every surface. She scanned the
containers and read about various items of clothing, choosing to take none
of them with her. Someone else had lived in those clothes and she didn't
want any of that energy following her into her new life. That girl had been
weak and afraid. This one was strong and, if she wanted to stay strong,
especially with all of the pain swirling just below the surface, she had to
close her eyes to the girl who wanted to hide beneath the covers and never
come out.

She opened a tote stacked with albums and frames, pulling out only two.
One held a picture of Abby sandwiched between her mom and dad on a
ferris wheel when she was only five. In the other photo, Sydney and Rod
kissed beneath a bundle of mistletoe that he held above their heads.

"Coffee," she told Oliver when they pulled out of the driveway. She
didn't need the caffeine. When she needed alertness, she only had to dip her
hands in some running water to get a burst, but she loved the smell of the
dark oily beans and the warm surge that came with her first sip.

They stopped at a late night java shop and then drank their coffees in the
car. She had opted for a cup of french-pressed Sumatra and Oliver insisted
on the Works, a caramel double shot latte with extra whipped cream.

"Mmmm," he said, licking off his whip cream mustache.

She laughed and felt grateful for simple joys.

****

For the first hour of their drive, Oliver talked without interruption. He
described the night that Sydney died, but he withheld their lovemaking. He
had not forgiven himself for the indiscretion and knew that Abby would
struggle to accept it as well. Not only had he given in to his lust, his desire
created the perfect opportunity for Alva to strike. He told Abby about
Faustine's theory that Alva had taken control of Sydney's mind and used
her to draw Oliver into the house.

At the end of his long and tragic tale, Abby leaned over and took his
hand. He knew that she struggled to hold back her tears. At a gas station, he
got behind the wheel so that Abby could nap. She curled up on the
passenger seat and faced away from him, nestling Baboon against her belly.
Oliver reached across and rubbed her back gently and eventually the crying
began, not ending until Abby drifted to sleep.

That night they left the boxes in the car and, world weary, took the stairs
to Rod's loft. They slept side-by-side in Sydney and Rod's bed, their breath
lulling the other to sleep as the comfort of their two bodies near to one
another made the long night bearable once more.

****

"Where are you sneaking off to?" Isabelle asked Sebastian , handing him a ceramic to-go mug filled with piping hot tea. "I added honey."

Sebastian had stayed with Isabelle for nearly two weeks. Every day she catered to him and his feelings of desperation grew. Strangely, he sensed that Isabelle was perfectly content to let him live with her, identity-less, forever.

"I'm just going to walk. I'm starting to feel like something's going to come back," Sebastian told her.

"That's great," she said, but her smile looked sad.

He took a sip of his tea and winced as it burned his tongue.

"Thank you again for everything," he told her before he slipped out the door and ambled down the street. For reasons that he did not understand, he wove a strange pattern each time he returned to Patty's store. He doubled back twice and cut through a deli. No matter how many diversions he took before he reached her, he still felt convinced that someone followed him.

Once inside, he closed the door securely behind him and watched through the window for several seconds.

"Got the paranoia on you again today, stranger?" Patty asked, sashaying up to him in a glittery tangerine-colored dress. White tufts of chiffon beneath the skirt combined with knee-high white cowboy boots made the outfit seem more fitting for a five year old whose mother let her pick out her own outfit.

"I like it," he lied, knowing that Patty knew otherwise, but appreciated his compliments just the same.

"Well, I wish I had some good news for you," she told him, walking back to her counter. "But mum's the word on any American disappearances. I've been on the Google for three days and unless you're a teenage girl from Sacramento, I've got nothing."

He moved a pile of clothes from one of her antique chairs and took a seat.

"I'm not surprised," he complained. "It feels weirder than that. Maybe I was a spy or an assassin?" He looked at her hopefully.

She stood on a step-ladder and then perched on the edge of her counter, her boots dangling childlike two feet from the floor.

"Surfer, I'm telling you. You want my opinion? You caught the wave of your life and it washed you all the way to France. I bet you lived in one of those little Winnebagos on the beach and no one even realizes that you're missing yet."

"Ha, yeah," he chuckled, and flipped absently through one of her women's catalogues. "If that's the case, I wish my spaced-out girlfriend would get sick of making her own eggs and come find me."

He glanced down and an advertisement shocked him to silence. The photo depicted a woman in a long silver dress running up a twisted stairway to a medieval castle beyond. In the prison of his mind, a door swung open and, for an instant, he saw a gothic castle towering over a brilliant lagoon. He tried to follow the image, but nothing else came to him.

Patty scooted closer and glanced at the page.

"You just remembered something?"

He nodded and touched the photo. In his memory, he sought a face or a name, but nothing else developed.

"Maybe you're a Prince," Patty teased.

He stood and paced away from her. A terrible fear that he would never remember anything started to wash over him.

Patty sensed his distress and hopped from the counter. She walked to him and, standing on tiptoes, placed her hands on his shoulders.

"I have someone that I want you to meet," she told him.

****

The next day, Abby showed Oliver the room beneath the loft and together they pawed through boxes of newspaper clippings, journal entries and photos.

"Wow," Oliver said, taking a break and stretching his neck from side to side. "There's too much." He held up his hands in surrender.

"I know," Abby agreed. "I felt the same way when I first came down here. I don't even know where to begin with deciphering all of this. And there's more..."

She crawled out of the space and returned with a manila envelope. She opened it and handed him the single sheet of paper inside.

He studied it, at first not seeing, and then a look of surprise took over his features.

"Dafne? What is this?"

Abby pointed to the figure with the wild hair.

"That is Aubrey Blake and this picture was taken a hundred years ago..."

Oliver slowly shook his head from side to side.

"But Dafne never lived in Trager City. Right? I mean, she told me she came from somewhere out east and she couldn't possibly have known Devin's aunt." But he lifted the picture closer to his face, his concern growing.

"I don't know what it means either, but I found this picture right after Devin died. Dafne knew Devin's aunt, Oliver. I don't know why she didn't tell anyone, but that is her..."

"I need to get outside, it's getting hard to breathe in here," Oliver said, pulling at the collar of his shirt.

Abby agreed and they left the apartment, driving her little car out of the city to an old dune trail that Abby remembered from childhood.

"I haven't been out here in years," she told him as they wound through the woods, walking a path that only existed in her memory.

When she was a child, Sydney took her exploring and they found secret forests and beaches tucked all over the Trager Peninsula. Sometimes Sydney had already staked them out and other times they just walked for hours until they found something worthy of their hike. Abby still owned a single pearl earring from one of their expeditions. It sat in a jewelry box in her childhood bedroom.

"Trager," Oliver said, scanning the horizon as they reached the top of a small bluff. What's the pull? You know what I mean? There's something here, I can feel it, but what? And now this thing with Dafne? Is it possible she just passed through here and didn't even remember it?"

"Dafne doesn't seem like the forgetful type," Abby told him.

He nodded, reluctantly, but knew she spoke the truth. Dafne had been keeping secrets for a very long time.

Abby pointed towards an opening in the dune grass. Lake Michigan lay beyond and, as they started down the slope toward the water, Abby began to feel lighter, even buoyant

Oliver looked at her sideways.

"Well, I see what all this water does for you..."

She smiled and a shiver of pleasure ran through her at the intensity of the lake's energy.

"I understand what you're saying," she murmured. "I've always felt connected to this space. When I left Lansing, I didn't think about a single other spot on earth. Trager was the only refuge. It was almost like I didn't even make the decision."

"And that's what happens," he told her. "One day you're waking up every morning and punching the clock, kissing your girlfriend goodbye like you mean it, and the next day you're driving like a fiend toward some destination that suddenly feels more real than every person and experience of the previous seventeen years of your life."

"Did you have a girlfriend?" Abby asked. "Before?"

Oliver chuckled and ran a hand through his shaggy blond hair. Color appeared high on his checks, but only for an instant and then it washed away as if he willed it so.

"Jamie," he said smiling. "Jamie with the sleepiest brown eyes you've ever seen and this ridiculous hair like silk almost down to her waist. I used to brush it and it made me..."

"So in love?" Abby asked, losing herself for a moment.

"So horny is more like it."

They both started laughing and then the shoreline met their feet and a peaceful lull spread over them. The lake undulated in ripples of green and blue. The gray sky made the sandbars and drop-offs more visible and Abby recalled how it felt to look upon the lake as a child. Standing in that exact same spot with Sydney close at her side, she felt that all of the secrets of the universe lay in that sometimes tranquil, sometimes furious, water.

Oliver took her hand and squeezed .

****

Love of another is beautiful, but it is not wholly pure. It is dirtied with the mind, with possession, desire, fear and attachment. It is the darkness in that light that makes it the perfect portal for evil to enter. It is so easy to take the enormity of that emotion and feed the shadow. The shadow grows and grows until it swallows the light and the love disappears all together.

Dafne had never spoken of her love affair with Tobias to Elda or Faustine. They did not probe--it was not their way--and she hid her past beneath an impenetrable shield of thought. Only Oliver had ever brought her to the edge of revealing her heart-wrenching story, but then Abby had arrived and with her, Sebastian, and the past had flooded back with excruciating clarity.

Dafne walked the cliff edge, the castle rising behind her like the ominous all-knowing eye in the sky. She felt Faustine's curious gaze from his tower, but she did not look back. She braced her face into the cold November wind and allowed her thoughts to flow freely. Faustine could not read her. She had cut herself away from his searching mind, but allowed simple thoughts to float at the periphery to distract him. More deeply, she considered Sebastian.

Indra had voiced concerns that the spells had failed and his memory had begun to return. Nothing concrete had arrived, but Isabelle claimed that he acted strangely, disappeared for hours at a time and had become rather guarded with her. Dafne did not question her own abilities, but she did question Sebastian's natural power. Both Elda and Faustine had alluded to an unnatural strength in Sebastian, comments that had only driven Dafne deeper into her belief that he was destined to be the next to rise in the Vepar Clan.

He could not return. Her deception of the coven was unforgivable, and placing Sebastian dead in the Pool of Truth...well she preferred not to think what might transpire if her coven knew.

She thought then of the Lourdes of Warning, exiled to her underground prison, tethered by an ancient spell of darkness and her own delirium. None of the others knew of her relationship with the Lourdes. Her web, now spun, could not be disentangled, only annihilated and what destruction would befall all of them if that occurred?

Chapter 20

August 1908: After the Fire

Dafne wandered the beach like a soul trapped between this world and the next. She hadn't eaten in days. Her already thin body had grown gaunt and sunken. Her eyes looked out from two gray holes and the bottom of her tattered dress was still black with soot from the fire that stole the life of her best friend, all of her friends. She felt less than utterly alone, she felt dead, as if someone had sliced her down the middle and plucked her heart out, but replaced it with some dead thing that kept her body moving, but nothing else. The waves crashed or they lulled, the tide surged and retracted. Her bare feet crunched over shells and seaweed and dead fish and she walked on, oblivious to the blood and the soreness and the infections beginning to cause the fever that made sweat pop along her hairline.

The sun rose and it fell and if she passed other beings in the land of the living, she did not see them or hear them or notice how they took a wide berth to the sickly girl at the water's edge. Her dark hair grew tangled and sand-filled in the wind.

When Faustine and Elda found her, the walking had ended. She lay nearly dead in the tall dune grass so that if Faustine had not connected with her telepathically, they might never have discovered her there on the beach. She had no recollection of her saviors when she woke four days later in the healing room at Ula, swathed in sheer gauze and breathing the scent of some strange oil burning at her bedside. Elda had barely left her and she sat now, a book balanced on her knees and her eyes watching the young woman with interest and hope.

Dafne blinked and, when she remembered, a long tremble rolled through her body and she started to gag and to cry. She flung herself off the bed and she clawed at the stone floor and wailed as Elda wrapped strong arms around her and cooed in her ear as if she were only a baby. When the crying finally ended, Dafne stared into the deep well of her pain and her past and saw a heavy iron lid swing down upon it, sealing it off as if it never existed at all. As Elda helped her back into the bed, a cool numbness fell over her. Deep in the pit of her belly, a tiny life shifted, but she shut her heart to it and fell asleep.

Chapter 21

Lydie wrapped her wool blanket more tightly around her shoulders and climbed the cold sand. At the dune ridge, she glanced back at the castle in the distance, hoping that no one watched her. Even if the other witches saw her, they would merely think that she was napping, though, they would likely find it strange that she napped outside on a cold November afternoon. She settled onto the sand, snuggling deeper into her blanket as the cold wind whipped across the water.

She closed her eyes and waited.

She woke again at another sand dune and began to drift down towards her childhood home. Suddenly the world whipped passed her in a blur. A thousand trees sped by and she found herself in an unfamiliar forest. Bright green ferns tittered on the ground beneath her. She heard voices and moved toward the sound. A woman's scratchy whispers pricked at some sensitive piece of her and she paused, scared. For a second, she wanted to flee back to her physical body, but a need to know urged her forward.

In the distance, a bloom of bright red stood in stark contrast to the greens and browns of the forest. A red, sinister-looking weeping willow rose up from the earth with a cascade of scarlet branches reaching toward the ground.

Lydie saw Dafne at the edge of the willow. Beneath her, stretched along a mossy red floor, Lydie noticed a woman. She moved closer, knowing that they could not see her in her astral form, but terrified still. Flesh hung form the woman's face and she propped her torso high on her hands like a Sphynx. Lydie wanted to look away, but could not seem to rip her gaze from the woman-creature's bent body. The bones along her spine jutted out through a soiled-looking pink dress. Her honey colored hair, out of place on her skeletal form, was pushed over one shoulder.

"I fear that my spells have been unsuccessful. I have removed his memory, but it seems to be coming back. Indra and I placed him in the Pool of Truth, but..." Dafne's voice trembled as she spoke. Though she gazed at the woman, her eyes darted into the forest as if she could only take the sight in small doses.

"Blach." The creature held up a gnarled hand and coughed twice before continuing.

Her gravelly voice crawled through Lydie's brain and she fought the urge to scream. The voice did not belong to a woman, but something ancient and terrifying. "Fools," she continued. "Such little fools you were a hundred years ago and you are even now. That's what happens to witches in covens, you know?"

The woman turned slightly and Lydie glimpsed more of her face. She clenched her eyes shut against the vision. The ghastly face of a corpse sat upon the woman's slender neck. Her blackened lips curled back into the cavity of her mouth and, when she spoke, the hole opened to reveal a yawning emptiness.

"You get weak, turn to mush." She shifted, her body pitching forward, and grabbed a handful of the slimy red moss that jelled between her fingers. "You don't defend evil from your stone palace, little witch. You let it in the front door." She began to cackle and the sound reverberated through the forest.

"Drink Lourdes, you're time is short," Dafne told the woman, shrinking away. She looked as revolted as Lydie felt, but seemed to be trying to hide it.

"Scared of the truth, are you?" the woman screeched. "Scared of this old dead face? What do you think you look like under all that magic? With that black soul eating you away?" She laughed again and then lurched to her feet.

The woman-creature plucked a bottle from Dafne's hand and held it to her lips, drinking thirstily, her dark tongue lashing out at the mouth of the bottle like a lizard. The woman's face began to transform.

As Lydie watched, the creature's face melted and reformed. The sagging skin grew pink and luminous. Full, sensual lips replaced her thin, wrinkled mouth. Her entire body shuddered and shifted until she became painfully beautiful. Lydie found the beautiful woman almost as impossible to look at as the creature.

The witch, now stunning, cocked her head to the side and turned, her eyes roving over the spot where Lydie stood.

'She can see me,' Lydie thought with horror.

But the woman said nothing.

"I need your help, Lourdes. I know that you don't want this anymore than I do. This curse will destroy us all. Their numbers here are already weakening us. Have you yourself not found your strength diminishing?"

"It is not the Vepars you should fear," the woman told Dafne, smiling maliciously. "It's Kanti."

Lydie saw confusion cross Dafne's face and she too wondered - Who or what was Kanti.

She heard the question begin on Dafne's lips, but already the scene began to fade and she felt her astral form called back to Ula.

****

Sebastian had been surprised when the man sitting in the chair opposite him, reached across the table and plucked a cigarette from his pack, lit it and casually leaned back in his seat.

"Do I know you?" Sebastian asked hopefully, not minding the man's strange behavior if it meant a clue to his identity.

"Yes, and I you," the man told him, his unnerving dark eyes settled on Sebastian's. He rested his oddly short arms on the table before him, clasping his long skeletal fingers together.

The hair on the back of Sebastian's neck stood on end and he shifted in his seat, suddenly itching to be somewhere else.

The man simply watched him, a curious smirk playing across his amused face.

"So you do not remember me?" the man asked, taking a drag on his cigarette and releasing it through his nose.

"He looks like a devil," Sebastian thought, and then chased the image away, unwilling to let go of any opportunity to find answers.

"Everyone has missed you so much," the man said, suddenly leaning forward. His face changed from fascination to kindness and Sebastian forced a smile. This person truly did know him.

The man cocked his head to the side as if picking up a sound from far away.

"We should go," the man told him, standing abruptly and stubbing his cigarette on the table's edge. He dropped the butt on the ground and Sebastian started to pick it up, but the man stopped him.

"Like this." He waved his hand over the butt and it vanished.

Sebastian's jaw dropped and he started to look for it, but the man laughed and took Sebastian's shoulders in his hands, guiding him down the street.

"I should tell Isabelle," Sebastian said, but the man encouraged him forward and Sebastian no longer felt like resisting. He followed the man to his car.

****

"So you think the people in those cottages are involved in this?" he asked Abby, opening a large envelope stuffed with old yellowing pictures. "Why would they be keeping this stuff in Sydney's loft?"

"That's what I don't understand. Unless they put it here so that I would find it? Something drew me here, Oliver. When I walked into this room, I

151

felt a message waiting to be discovered."

"How can Dafne possibly be a part of all this?" He looked again at the photo that Abby had shown him that included Dafne in the throng of witches standing in the night-time field. Though she looked much younger, and far happier than he'd ever seen her, she was unmistakable. "I just can't believe that she's intentionally deceiving us, Abby. There must be some other explanation." But his tone betrayed his suspicions. Dafne had been acting strangely ever since Abby and Sebastian arrived at Ula.

"Do you think she had something to do with Sebastian's death?" Abby asked, her voice much smaller as she spoke his name. Baboon purred from a nest in the center of the bed and Abby stroked his ears lovingly.

Oliver wanted to say no, but his heart knew better.

"I hope not, Abby, I really do." He took her hands in his own and kissed them, surprising them both. A tear slid down her face and she turned her head so that he could not see her eyes.

He wanted to draw her to him, bury his face in her hair and pull the pain from her heart, but her body warned him to stay away . He returned to the stack of papers and wondered why Dafne had loathed Sebastian so completely.

"I've been asking the wrong questions all along," Abby said, lifting the box that her grandmother had left for her and holding it in her lap. "I just got lost in this idea that I was a witch and, I needed to know something, I would just know it. I went on that wild goose chase and almost got killed, and all along it's been right here. This history, it's buried here. When I first started searching for Devin's killer, I found this picture on the internet. Something led me to that and I totally disregarded it. I should have tried to understand why Dafne hated Sebastian. I should have questioned how all of this past played into what was happening."

"You can't know until you know," Oliver told her, smiling wryly. "It's one of those things you learn to accept. The world is unfolding exactly as it has to, regret is wasted. The point now is to ask those questions and to follow them all the way in, find out what's hiding in the shadows."

"I want to, but I still feel lost in this. Like it's right in front of my face, but I'm just not seeing it."

"Well, we are witches." He smiled at her and winked. "Let's see what the universe is willing to tell us." He gathered up a bunch of the papers and set them on the bed. Then he proceeded to light candles, each from the flame of the last, and walked the room in a circle counter-clockwise, placing candles along the floor.

He left the room and returned carrying two small crystal paperweights. He set them on the floor in the center of the circle.

"Let's raise the vibration in here, huh?"

He held out his hand and they settled on either side of the circle.

"No mantras, no chanting. I'm thinking just a simple intention of guidance, yeah?"

Abby opened her palms on her knees. Elda had taught her about meditation and lightening the self to connect with the less dense aspects of reality. Until that moment, she had almost forgotten that she was even a witch and that she and Oliver were not merely helpless pawns in the game of some faceless evil.

They each closed their eyes. Abby felt pulled by her thoughts, but focused on a single white light at her third eye. She imagined the word guidance, spoke it in her mind, and visualized it before her. Eventually the meditation lost sight of its intention and she drifted, feeling her body sway from side to side. Somewhere far away a clock tower chimed and pulled them both back to the room.

"Our closing gong," Oliver said, standing and stretching for a moment. "Now for our answer."

He picked up the pile of papers from the bed, as many as he could hold, and briefly closed his eyes. Then he threw the papers out before him over the circle. They flew in all directions, floating toward the floor and Abby almost reached out, fearing that some of them might catch fire. Then, incredibly, their flight slowed and they began to organize themselves in midair until they had layered into several distinct piles.

"Wow," Abby said.

"Yeah, it takes a while in the beginning to remember that we have the whole universe to call on when we're confused."

Abby grabbed the first stack of papers.

"Look at the cover of all three first," Oliver told her. "Those are the places to start. If they're on the top, they need our immediate attention."

On the top of the first stack, Abby saw a news article published just five weeks earlier claiming that the Trager City deaths were the work of a vampire cult. The next stack held the picture of all of the witches grouped together, Dafne and Aubrey nestled amongst them. The final sheet held an advertisement ripped from a magazine.

"American Spirits?" Oliver held up the advertisement, which portrayed the black and white image of a Native American man smoking a peace pipe.

Abby shrugged and picked up the newspaper article from the first stack. Oliver scanned the title. "That's the first pile, so I think we need to track that guy down first."

"The reporter?" Abby asked skeptically. "He's offering a pretty funky story here. Do you really think he knows anything?"

"Were you not here for all of this?" He gestured toward the candles and the neat stacks of paper. "He knows something."

****

Isabelle hung up the phone and walked to the tiny french doors that opened to the balcony. Beyond, she watched Sebastian as he lit a cigarette and coughed uncomfortably with each inhale. He sat at a small bistro table in a cafe across the street, his eyes scanning stacks of newspapers that he discarded on the chair beside him. She regretted giving him a pack of her cigarettes the week before because he now smoked nearly a whole pack whenever he sat at the cafe across the street. She watched him ash into his empty cup of coffee, his brow furrowed as he read.

Before she even hung up the phone with Indra, she knew that she had to tell him. Isabelle wished to turn back the clock and refuse her great aunt's pleading that she participate in this debacle. Indra had insisted that she and this other witch, Dafne, knew of a great catastrophe that would befall their covens if Sebastian continued to live at the coven of Ula. However, Isabelle no longer trusted Indra's intuition, witch or not, and she felt unbelievably guilty at her role in his deception.

In the weeks since she had picked him up on the side of the road, Isabelle had begun to fall in love with Sebastian. Foolish she knew, but still the feelings did not go away. She had little knowledge of his lover in the States, only that she was a new witch, and Isabelle hated the thought of him returning. However, beyond her fear of losing him, she could not live with his hatred and if he learned the truth, he would surely hate her.

Indra had made it all sound so simple. Isabelle would greet Sebastian and, at the sound of her voice, he would lose all connection to his prior self. His life had been filled with pain and heartache, Indra told her. Isabelle would be saving him. He would stay with her for one month and then Isabelle would travel with him to New Zealand where Dafne would have created a new identity. Sebastian would be enchanted to retrieve memories that did not actually exist. Then he would return to his so-called previous life in New Zealand and the Great Curse, as Indra called it, would end once and for all. Unfortunately, Sebastian had already begun to chase the tendrils of his life that had supposedly been wiped clean.

Isabelle turned away from the window and went to the kitchen to start dinner. In the market, she had purchased duck and fresh herbs, and planned to make a final meal to celebrate her last night with him before he knew the truth. She would call into work sick the next day and spend the morning telling him all that she knew. Not a witch, Isabelle would be unable to reverse his memory loss but, when he reconnected with his love, she would reverse the spells and return him to his life before.

Isabelle sighed and wished, not for the first time, that she too had become a witch. Her Great-Aunt Indra, who looked no older than she, had hoped for such a miracle, but another generation passed without a new witch in the Chaput family. Isabelle's brother, Dominic, had one child, a son named Court, who Indra now hoped would claim the witch's blood. Dominic would not be pleased if his son were a witch. Unlike many of the other Chaput family, Dominic abhorred magic and followed a strict Catholic faith, denouncing the witch ancestry that ran in his blood. Isabelle, on the contrary, had dreamed her entire life of one day discovering her powers, only to face disappointment year after year when they did not manifest. She hoped now to someday have a child of her own who might be a witch.

She basted the duck and flipped through her recipe index searching for the perfect dessert, believing perhaps that food really was the way to a man's heart. She decided on lemon soufflés with blueberry sauce. Sebastian had been at the newspapers for nearly three hours, longer than usual, and she returned again to the window to see if he might be soon wrapping up.

Sebastian's seat sat empty and the newspapers, abandoned, rustled in the wind. On the sidewalk next to his chair, she could see the pack of cigarettes she had bought for him that morning.

Chapter 22

"Who did you say you were with?" the nervous intern behind the front desk asked when they entered the office for the Trager City Herald. She glanced anxiously back toward the cubicles as if she hoped someone might save her from the serious duties of answering the questions of total strangers.

"We're from the Lansing News," Abby told her again, this time standing taller and attempting to look professional. She might have thought of that before her and Oliver decided to leave the loft both dressed in ratty jeans and sweatshirts. Her hair was shoved loosely under a ball cap and they both wore dark sunglasses. Flimsy disguises surely, but better than nothing.

"We're on vacation," Oliver chimed in, locking his blue eyes on the girl's much beadier brown ones. He leaned into the desk and flashed her a smile. "Technically we're doing a bit of work and play, but we really hoped to meet with Stephen Kramer--he's highly esteemed in the news world."

The girl looked a bit mushy as she stared up at Oliver. She smiled shyly and started to fumble with the phone. "He's not here, but can I ask the editor?"

"We'd love that," Oliver told her. "Take your time." He reached forward and patted her hand. She softened even more, lavishing in his attention.

"Umm, hi, Ms. Cooper. Hi. Yeah, it's me, Regina at the front. Yeah. Oh sure, sorry, no problem. There's just two journalists here. No, not our journalists. No, not a story on the Thanksgiving parade. Actually, they're looking for Mr. Kramer. Oh. Oh, I see, and he's...oh, okay. ye."

Abby and Oliver did not need the girl to tell them that Mr. Kramer had taken an extended leave of absence with no return date set. Their excellent hearing, combined with the boisterous voice of Ms. Cooper, made the entire conversation audible to all the parties involved. To be polite, they waited for Regina to explain.

"Huh. Well, that is really unfortunate," Oliver told her after she finished. "You know there was talk of a prize in journalism, but if he's unavailable..."

Regina's eyes lit up at the mention of a prize.

"Well, he'd want to know that," she whispered, this time clacking at her computer keys and then jotting down a piece of information on a lime green sticky note. She glanced behind her again and, when she felt sure that no one watched, she slid the paper across the desk.

"This is where he lives. Please pretend you found the information somewhere else."

"Of course," both Abby and Oliver said in unison.

They left the building and returned to Abby's car, both knowing that Mr. Kramer's leave of absence did not bode well for the reporter or their search for information.

Abby found the house easily. He lived in town in a small, off-white bungalow with a neglected yard. They observed a pile of newspapers yellowing on his front porch.

"Should we go in?" she asked, passing the house and circling back around.

The dark windows looked ominous and the house clearly had not been occupied in weeks.

"Yeah, I think we have to."

Abby parked on the road several houses down. They walked to the house through the neighbor's backyard. The screen door that opened at the back of Kramer's house hung by its hinges.

Abby walked to a small rusted bird bath and stuck her hands into the icy water, absorbing the rush of energy that fled up her fingertips. Oliver tried the door handle and found it unlocked. He opened it slowly, standing back and wrinkling his nose in disgust at the rancid smell that drifted out.

"Something dead," he said.

Abby froze, not sure if she could face what lay inside.

"Not a human," Oliver reassured her. "At least, not that smell. More like rotting food, chicken maybe."

Abby nodded, but stayed close to Oliver. The faded kitchen linoleum creaked when they walked across. Clearly the house had been abandoned in a hurry. Cupboards were flung open and plastic bags littered the floor. The house did not reveal destruction like Sydney's house had after the Vepars trashed it, but instead the kind of panicky mess left by someone rushing to get out.

The living room lay dark and musty, smelling of cat pee and cigarettes. However, it was mostly undisturbed. They moved upstairs, pausing to train their senses to any possible danger. Abby knew that Oliver could sense Vepars and felt slightly more at ease knowing that his alarms were not sounding.

They continued to the upstairs hall. Both of the second story rooms held a disaster similar to the kitchen. In a small study, papers were strewn across a large work desk and a visible dust square showed the place where a computer had once been. Abby opened the desk drawers and found a small three-ring notebook. She flipped through it. There was writing on nearly every page. Most of it appeared to be outlines for various stories, but she stopped when her eyes passed over the name Dafne. She studied the page which held a series of comments without organization. The word 'curse' was written beneath Dafne's name. Several more names were listed below hers. Abby showed the page to Oliver and then tucked the notebook into his bag.

The bedroom across the hall revealed clothes pulled quickly from the closet, some items still dangling haphazardly from their hangers. The unmade bed held piles of bags and suitcases as if they'd been pulled out for packing and then abandoned in the process. The curtains were open wide and the blinds lifted to reveal the driveway below.

"I don't think something attacked him," Oliver said, walking the room and kicking at little piles of clothes. "I think he got scared and ran."

Abby glanced briefly at several pictures on the nightstand. In one, a much younger Kramer beamed from the deck of a cruise ship, his arm wrapped tightly around the waist of a slim brunette in a brightly colored sarong. In another, the journalist sat on his front steps, with a small dog resting in his lap. A woman occupied a chair adjacent to him and Abby recognized her immediately.

"She's the one from the grocery store." Abby picked up the photo and looked closer. "I don't think this was taken that long ago."

Oliver peeked in the closet and then returned.

"Whoa, look at this one," he said. He'd plucked a photo from the back of the table. The journalist, again off duty, sat comfortably on the end of a boat dock. A familiar house rose up in the distance behind them--Sydney's house. Next to him sat a young man with narrow dark eyes. He held a lit sparkler in his hand, which created a wave of light flecks in front of his body.

"Victor," Abby whispered.

****

It happened so quickly that he barely had time to register it. One moment he was walking down the street with the man who claimed to know him and in the next, he was speeding across the city in the back of a van, getting tossed from side to side as the van careened around corners in the cramped French streets. He remembered one thing clearly. When the van door opened and strong hands reached out to pull him inside, the man he had been walking with ceased to be a man. His face transformed into something monstrous. Sebastian swore that he saw fangs in his mouth, but before he could decipher the changing face, the door slammed and the man was left behind.

"What is this, what's happening?" Sebastian scrambled to a low squat and stared at the person who'd hauled him into the moving vehicle. He expected to see an enormous meat-head, but a tiny and strangely familiar woman with striking green eyes looked back at him.

She studied his face and then sighed as if accepting some foregone conclusion.

"I know you?" he asked, feeling oddly hopeful at the sight of his captor.

She smiled, seemingly appeased, and nodded.

"Yes, you do. Unfortunately, your memory has been tampered with and now I'm going to have to retrieve it." She looked mildly irritated at this, but also determined.

He glanced at the door and thought that he should flee, tumble out onto the road and run, but he found that...he didn't want to.

"Hi, Sebastian," a man's voice called from the front of the van.

"Sebastian?" Sebastian asked, but again something familiar in that name. "Am I Sebastian?"

"Well, that's your name, anyway..." the woman told him, shooting a dirty look towards the man at the front, "...though I'd hoped to work into that a bit more gradually."

"Sorry, Adora," the man called."

"It's okay, Roderick," she replied curtly.

"Rod," he shot back, but she only rolled her eyes.

"So what the hell is going on here? Have I just been kidnapped?"

"Ha," Adora smirked. "No, you were just about to be kidnapped back there." She pointed out the back windows that were blacked out with paint. The man that you were having an afternoon stroll with did not have your best interests at heart."

"Why, what do you mean?"

Adora smiled and patted his knee.

"Trust me. You just avoided a truly horrible fate my friend, but for now let's get started with bringing you back to you. Take these." She held out two small greenish capsules.

He shrunk away and shook his head.

"No, I don't think so. I mean you may be someone that I know, but I'm not taking some pills so that I can wake up in a bathtub tomorrow without a liver."

Rod laughed, but Adora only looked concerned.

"Sebastian, I don't want to overwhelm you with your life right now because, frankly, it's probably going to scare you, a lot. Not only that, it will just be words. Until we start to clear out whatever is blocking you in there...," she pointed at his head, "...none of it will make any sense. These pills are not going to knock you out. They're not poison. They're herbs.

They help to purify, and once you take them, whatever toxic energy that's in your body will begin to dissolve at least a little. There's no way that I can help you if you refuse my remedies."

Sebastian stared at her and then at the pills. Fear did not prevent him from taking the pills. Instead, he felt plagued by a sudden and strange desire to simply choose the blissful ignorance of previous weeks. If he took those pills, what would he discover?

"It's okay, man," Rod called from the front of the van. "I promise you, we're friends. You'll remember soon enough."

Sebastian took one more second to consider and then, before he could change his mind, he grabbed the pills and threw them to the back of his throat, swallowing without water. Adora handed him a thermos.

"Tea," she said. "Wash them down."

He did and they drove on in silence.

They arrived at a secluded sandy brick colonial-style house. Its gabled roof was dotted with moss that glowed in the setting sun.

Rod held open the door as Adora led Sebastian into the foyer, which smelled sweet and homey. A fire burned in a kitchen hearth and an older man stood at a block of wood, cutting vegetables and humming some barely audible tune. He glanced up as they walked in and then returned to his cutting.

"So you found him then? You are a clever sleuth." He did not direct his comment at anyone in particular, but Sebastian sensed that he spoke to Adora. "And you've given him the Anamnesis?"

"Yes on both accounts, though we arrived only in the nick of time," Adora added, opening a cupboard and pulling out a tea kettle, which she filled with water and set on the stove.

"I thought so," the man told her, still not addressing Sebastian at all, but concentrating on the garlic bulb beneath his fingers. "When Patty told me of a meeting in the afternoon, I suspected that we would be too late. And how about you, Roderick? Beginning to question your desire to know more?"

Rod only grinned and shook his head.

"Not for a minute. My Sydney didn't die in vain." He still smiled as he spoke, but a hard gleam had come into his eyes and something like sorrow crept into his voice.

Julian nodded and sighed.

"Well, you have something in common then." He nodded toward Sebastian as he spoke.

"I would love to join this conversation but, honestly, I don't know who the hell any of you are," Sebastian retorted, suddenly sick of the cat and mouse. "Did you drive me to this house in the middle of nowhere just for kicks, because at least back at Isabelle's I didn't feel like anyone was toying with me."

"No, man, it's not like that," Rod told him quickly. "I
though. They just can't tell you everything until your me
back."

Sebastian rolled his eyes. "And you think some pill is g
magically happen? I've been wandering around a foreign
and have yet to remember my own damn name, which yo
Sebastian, and I don't have much choice other than to take it. Right? For all
I know, you guys don't have a clue who I am and this whole weird ass thing
is some kind of set-up."

Adora took the kettle off the stove as it started to whistle. She took four
mugs out of the cupboard.

"Your name is Sebastian," she said sternly. "And to be truthful, I barely
know you, and Julian doesn't know you at all." She pointed at the older
man. "But Roderick does know you and, more importantly, we know of
you. We know where you came from and we know that every minute you
remain in this forgetful haze, you are in grave danger."

"It's Rod," Rod told her, before turning to Sebastian. "Those pills will
work. Think of this guy as an alchemical genius okay?" He nudged an elbow
toward Julian. "And her..." waving at Adora now, "...as something of a saint.
Right? She saved me, now she's going to save you too."

Adora looked uncomfortable at this comparison, but remained silent.

"The pills are magic, Sebastian. That's why they work," Julian said, this
time looking directly into Sebastian's eyes. Julian's eyes were such a light
blue that they appeared white. "But they're not instantaneous. Prepare to
have a very vivid night in the dreamscape. You will be encountering
yourself."

Chapter 23

"He likes to call us Urban Guerilla Witches," Kendra told Abby as the three of them stepped off the elevator. She slid the metal grate closed behind them and gestured to a funky wooden coat rack.

"I like it," Oliver said, surveying the apartment.

Kendra grinned and looked at Victor who'd barely turned from the enormous flat screen computer monitor hanging in one side of the loft. Steel cables held it firmly in place. Victor's fingers flew across a large glowing tablet that hung below the monitor. On the screen, Abby watched different areas on a city grid lighting up.

She had not seen Victor since the night that Oliver rescued them from the Vepar's lair. She had apologized to him for running, but he insisted that he understood. Abby did not intend to bring it up--at least, not right away.

"So what does that mean?" Abby asked Kendra, following her into the open kitchen resplendent in black and stainless steel. "To be an Urban Guerilla Witch?" Kendra pulled them each shots of espresso.

"Well," Kendra said, taking out a small frothing wand and adding steamed milk to their espresso. "It's all about motion in meaningful ways. Too many covens have become these petrified power centers. They're filled with ancient potent witches who have slowly withdrawn from society and all of their work happens within their coven instead of the world. We spare little, if any, energy on our group. We come and go as we please. There's no constant ritual keeping us together. Instead we expend our energy in communities that need it. We're also plugged into modern reality." She cocked her head toward the computer as she handed an espresso to Victor and Sebastian. "We use the internet, cell phones, tablets, GPS--you know, all that technology that witches think they're supposed to live without because of their superior intuition. It seems more like pride than productivity that lies at the heart of this refusal to participate in the world as it is now."

"Exactly," Victor chimed in. "How can we do good in the world if we can't even communicate regularly at the most basic level. There are three year olds in contact with their cousins in Spain. We're an advanced species of witches and we can while away days sitting in a cave waiting for another witch to show up with information."

Abby sensed that Victor and his group had spent a great deal of time trying to understand and define their purpose in the world. She appreciated it, but always felt a bit taken aback by any group that elevated themselves too high over others. Especially when the others had spent thousands of years creating the world that they believed in.

"What about learning?" Oliver asked, intrigued. "How did you learn what you could do?"

"How could we not?" Kendra retorted, smiling. "I started manipulating air when I was sixteen. I could shift storms before I turned twenty. But let me not pretend that we didn't have help. We were all discovered by elder witches tracking our blood lines."

"I believe we'd have discovered it for ourselves, anyway," Victor said simply, turning away from the computer.

"Maybe," Kendra said carefully, "but I can't imagine how difficult it would have been to make sense of it all."

"We stand on the shoulders of giants," Oliver said, watching Victor's response.

Abby knew that Oliver held a fierce loyalty to Ula, and specifically to Helena, for discovering him and introducing him to the coven. Victor's obvious disdain for the elder witches did not sit well.

"Yes, exactly," Kendra jumped in, also sensing the rising tension. "Our progress has been greatly influenced by the witches who came before us and paved the way. Our tinctures alone are hundreds, if not thousands, of years in the making. To begin from nothing...well, I don't even want to think about it."

Victor nodded, but returned to his tablet.

"This is Chicago," he said pointing towards the screen. "We've created this grid so that we can see the separate areas where we're working. Everything from planting gardens, with a bit of magic of course, to opening free clinics for basic healthcare. Everything is run by residents, non-witches, but we use spells to bring it all together and ultimately hold it all together."

"Urban farming?" Oliver asked, tuning into a video on the tablet of a giant community farm surrounded by high-rises. "I've been reading a lot about that. It looks like you guys have done a great job with it."

"It's real," Victor said. "It's not hiding from the world and wasting decades chasing Vepars."

"Not that those aren't legitimate too." Again Kendra kept the peace. "But we don't want to be reactionary and fear-based. We're trying to make a difference in real time, you know?"

"Huh. It's great, but I'm curious then why you felt the need to take Abby back to that Vepar's lair? I mean if you're not interested in hunting them and all?" Oliver's acidic tone left Abby momentarily speechless.

Kendra gave Victor a funny look, but said nothing.

"That's a long story," Victor replied, looking apologetically toward Kendra. "And I didn't mean to insult you, Oliver."

Oliver looked vaguely mollified.

"I guess I'm still curious how you protect yourself and your community?"

"The same instincts run in our blood that run in yours," Victor told him.

Abby realized that Victor's pride may have been more injured in their late night outing than his body.

"We do our best," Kendra interrupted him. She took his hand and slipped him a small turquoise stone.

Abby recognized it--Amazonite. It was only one of the hundreds of stones that she'd sifted through at Ula, recording their properties and trying to experience their affects first-hand. When Sebastian had been acting strangely, she even tried putting Amazonite under his pillow to calm him and open the lines of communication.

Victor did not look at the stone, but Abby noticed his hand tighten around it and then he nodded and gave her a little smile.

"The truth is that we want to make a difference, that's it. We're like every other person stumbling around out there trying to find their purpose and improve the world some in the process."

Abby nodded, agreeing completely. She wanted nothing more than to help in some way. She hadn't felt useless at Ula because she'd only just discovered her gifts months earlier, but another year or two and the status quo may have become an issue.

Oliver rubbed his jaw. His eyes lit up with excitement and maybe even envy as he looked at the enormous digital grid, but she also saw his continued reluctance to get on board.

"But you're not here to learn about us," said Victor. "You need help."

"Yes, we do," Abby agreed. "We're in the middle of something that we can't quite understand and we need information."

"That is our specialty," Victor told her, wiping his hand across the tablet so that the monitor showed only a blank white page and a small search box. "What are we looking for?"

"A connection, or maybe a curse," Oliver began, grabbing his bag from the coat rack and pulling out several newspaper clippings. "It's at least one hundred years old and it originated, we think, in Trager. There's some kind of group up there who knows about witches and is writing about their findings and have been for a long time. We're trying to find out who they are and what this curse is all about."

Kendra walked beside Victor and placed a hand gently on his back. He turned and kissed her lightly on the forehead and Abby felt a twinge of sadness. She could not afford to think of Sebastian in that moment--it hurt too much--but she found the pain, always dormant, waiting to rear its ugly head at the slightest show of affection.

The elevator slid open and the other three witches, who Abby had met at Sorciére, ambled off. Their loud voices echoed around the apartment. They knew that Abby and Oliver would be there and had brought sustenance.

"Pizza and beer," Dante chimed in his high feminine voice.

Kendra cleared an enormous round coffee table and the witches gathered around it to eat and discuss. Abby and Oliver spoke first, explaining everything they'd learned and what they searched for. The other witches looked intrigued and excited. Only Victor appeared mysterious in his thoughts, his expression rarely giving him away. His secretiveness was not lost on Abby or Oliver.

"I met Sebastian," Marcus said out of nowhere. "Only briefly but, yes, I remember him and you know, I did sense some cloak hiding him. I didn't probe it. He seemed very happy, Abby."

He smiled at her warmly and Dante squeezed his knee. She realized that they were lovers.

"Where did you see him? Was he with anyone?"

"By the wishing fountain," Marcus continued. "The one in the smaller Ballroom. When you dropped your wish in, a star floated up and imbedded in the sky overhead. It was really spectacular."

"I saw the wishing fountain too," Oliver added, "but he wasn't there then."

Abby took a drink of beer and closed her eyes tightly for a moment.

"I know that his death..." her voice choked a bit at this word, "...is a part of this. I know it, but I don't understand how..."

Ezra slid close to her and rubbed her shoulder gently. Abby struggled for a moment not to cry and then, with a long exhale, she released the grief clamoring for her attention.

"Well, let's find out then, shall we?" Victor said. He called a voice command to the giant computer and it came back to life. From across the room he directed it to find any pieces of news from Trager City in the previous three months and then every piece of news from the year 1908. He then added a command that the computer intelligence system, which he referred to as Jax, find correlations. "While Jax is working on that, let's get started on this."

He began grabbing boxes of paperwork and hauling them to the table. Abby and Oliver had brought many of the totes from Rod's crawl space, along with information that Abby had gathered from her mother's basement. Victor handed each person a box. Then he walked to a large silver drafting table, rolling up plans and stacking them on the side.

"Find the links. You come across the same name, pile them together.

Let's start to make sense of this."

Oliver nudged Abby and smiled his approval. He'd been apprehensive about coming to Victor's apartment, especially after the incident with the Vepar caves, but he gave in when Abby insisted that they needed back-up, not to mention fresh eyes. She could see his relief at having help.

The first hour passed and no one spoke. On the computer screen, words whizzed by, pages flashed and disappeared. At one point, Abby looked up and saw Devin's wide green eyes for only a moment before the photo vanished, replaced by a map and then another news article.

She trudged through a box from her mother's basement that held family memorabilia. Photos lay strewn about, tucked between old receipts and greeting cards. When she passed a postcard, she almost passed it by, but the word 'curse' popped out at her as it had in Stephen's home. The postcard showed a Native American man, a medicine man perhaps, drawing images in the sky. On the back, only a single line was written. The curse is buried.

****

Sebastian hoisted himself onto the tall loft bed at the very front of the house. It pressed against a wide window that looked out on the choppy waters of the sea. The white caps frothed and rolled over the gray rocky shore and, as he watched, he felt the first stirrings of familiarity. Not a memory per se, but a sense of calm that all of the mysteries of his life lived in such water and that, as he drifted off to sleep that night, some water nymph or magical sprite would come to his room and whisper the tales of his forgotten life. He felt sort of giddy at the thought and laughed out loud, not minding the sound of his voice as he lay alone in the bedroom. For the first time since standing on that deserted road, he did not feel lost, but found. As though the three people whom he had only met hours earlier genuinely did hold the key to the locked doorway of his mind.

"Sebastian." He said his name and stared at a lighthouse perched at the end of a craggy pier beyond the house. "Sebastian, Sebastian, Sebastian." It didn't feel like it belonged to him, but then again, maybe it did.

He heard the floors creaking in the hallway outside his room. The man named Rod called out 'good night' to his other house mates. Rod did not fit with the other two. His goofy demeanor had an edge. Rod harbored some kind of anguish, a grief that Sebastian sensed in his own heart when he turned the full light of his awareness towards it.

****

Sebastian woke and fought the covers away from his neck. They seemed to be strangling him. The thick embroidered fabric felt heavy like the sand that Claire used to pile on top of him when they would go to the beach. She would dig a long hole and insist that he lay in it and then proceed to scoop plastic bucketfuls of sand onto his legs and torso and arms until only his head emerged from the shore. She must have turned the heat up in their apartment. He stumbled out of his bedroom and into the hallway, but then the hallway was gone and he realized he'd been sleeping on Sydney's couch. He stared up the stairway to where Abby slept. Photos lined the stairway wall and he looked at them quickly as he walked up to Abby's room. He could hear her crying and he pushed the bedroom door open, starting to step in, but caught himself just in the nick of time. Beyond the doorway, the world fell away. A hundred or more feet below, along a jagged rock cliff, water crashed. He teetered for a moment, grasping the wooden door frame and feeling it give, splinter, and then let go. He plunged into the starry night sky, arms and legs flailing, as the water rushed up to meet him.

He woke in the house by the sea and again tore away covers and sheets, heaving them to the floor and stumbling down from the high loft bed, landing funny on his right leg so that his ankle twisted and he cried out in pain. Confusion and exhaustion coursed through him and, for a time, he grasped it all--Claire, Abby, the coven of Ula, All Hallow's Eve, Adora and Rod--and then he opened the doorway of his room and stood, not in a hallway, but in a dense, black forest. The leering face of Tobias stared back at him, his mouth rimmed with blood and a twisted figure at his feet. The figure kept changing, long red curls became Claire's short black bob and then Abby's baseball cap the morning that she found Devin's body. He stared at his own body writhing on the earth, black snakes coiling around his arms and legs. Now dozens of Vepars surrounded him and they chanted into the night sky, their arms rising in worship to some invisible demon. He turned from the image and the woods were gone, replaced by a cliff of wildflowers, and Abby stood in the center, her long brown curls blowing in a lake breeze and her smile like the sweetest honey. He ran across the field but, as Abby turned, he saw that it was not Abby at all, but Dafne, her dark eyes looking angry and her face twisted into a grotesque and hateful grin. She lifted a finger and pointed.

Sebastian fell through a doorway and found he had somehow made it downstairs in the strange house he'd been brought to the day before. His hands and knees hit the cobblestone pathway outside of the front door and pain shot through his limbs. He crawled toward the water, sweat pouring down his face and dripping from his armpits. Dizziness and nausea wracked his body and he teetered to the side, landing in a barren thorny bush that clawed at his face. The bush held its shape, but the rest of the world shifted and now he lay on a soft blanket with surging lake water caressing the cliffs beneath him. He groaned with pleasure as Abby guided him inside her. She pressed her naked breasts against his chest and began to slide back and forth on top of him. He pulled her hips down and laughed as he came, but when he sought her sweet brown eyes, they'd been replaced by oozing black holes. Long flaxen hair flowed from the ghastly face of the monster than held him beneath her. He wrenched away from her and fell from the cliff edge, landing in a circle of fire. The Vepars again surrounded him. Their eyes held black glassy stares and their bloody lips moved in unison. Somewhere in the woods, a young boy cried, and then the cry became Claire's and he called out to her.

Julian watched Sebastian and carefully stirred the boiling liquid that he had placed on the stove when he first heard the young man crash from his bed upstairs. Julian had only used the Anamnesis twice, but twice was enough. The concoction would aid Sebastian in his shock, but also begin to repair the damage done. To remove an entire memory took ancient magic, the sort of magic that, if done poorly, left lasting damage.

Julian allowed Sebastian another half hour before he went to the beach to retrieve him. He did not intend cruelty by this delay, but understood the delicate mechanisms at work in Sebastian's mind. Julian knew that his own interjection would only prolong the process. He found Sebastian near the water, his body tucked into a ball and his face wracked with grief.

"Sebastian, come out. You're safe, you're safe," Julian told him, kneeling on the rocky shore and placing a warm water bottle against Sebastian's icy skin.

Sebastian heard a disembodied voice from the sky and then from the darkness as the forest too fell away. He followed it out and back into the present where he lay on the beach and Julian's face loomed before him.

He blinked wildly around, straining for breath, but struggling more to piece a lifetime back together. The blank mind afflicting him for the previous weeks had vanished. All of the pain and joy that had transpired to make him the man that he was slid back into place with the force of a hurricane. Tears poured from his eyes and he closed them and relished their salty taste. He had never been so grateful to remember the long tragic tale of his life.

Chapter 24

That night, Abby and Oliver walked the streets of Chicago and talked about their findings. The city had already begun its relentless pursuit of holiday buyers and every storefront held dazzling Christmas displays with elaborate trees and red-cheeked mannequins. Garland-wrapped street lamps lined the sidewalks and passersby huddled close to their loved ones, hats tucked tightly over their ears and hands shoved into their pockets. Despite the cold, the city was romantic, and Abby felt a smile curve her lips when they passed a man playing a saxophone along the Grand River. Oliver dropped several bills into his open case and took Abby's hand in his own.

His warmth felt so good that she drifted in the fantasy of lovers strolling the haunted Chicago streets with no greater problem than whether to get cocoa or coffee that night.

He spoke and her momentary reverie dissipated with the cold halo of his breath.

"Do you feel like we're getting closer to this?"

Abby considered his question, flashing back on the day's discoveries.

"Maybe. I want to find Stephen Kramer. He's clearly hinting at something happening in Trager City. Of course that concerns me for his whereabouts..."

"Yeah, me too. I think he ran, though. The question is from what?"

"Exactly. I'm also curious about that fire in 1908. The reports were conflicting. I mean, you have witnesses saying that more than eight people died, but the paper only reported one. Not to mention the cities attempt to demolish those woods and build a parking lot. What's that all about?"

"I suspect," Oliver said, "that the person who wrote that Aubrey was the only fatality, also had a hand in lobbying for the destruction of the woods. Maybe they wanted to hide something?"

"Or," Abby interjected. "Maybe Alva was playing puppet master even then. I told you how he orchestrated the arrest of Devin's adopted brother. I think he either got into the heads of those working the case, or he just went in there and did it himself."

"Yeah, that sounds about right."

"Have you told anyone at Ula about all of this?" Abby asked.

"I haven't spoken with anyone at the coven in nearly five days."

"Not even Faustine?" Abby was surprised. She assumed that he still connected with Faustine telepathically.

"No. Our connection dissolved before I left, but since then, no communication from him at all. What's worse is that I feel so free and yet completely guilty at the same time."

Abby squeezed his hand.

"I understand that. When I left Nick and my family and went to Trager, I felt more liberated than I ever had, but beneath that lived this huge ball of shame just eating away at me. It's still there most days."

Oliver sighed and shook his head sadly.

"They have been so much more than a family to me, Abby. They saved my life. Before Helena found me, I was just...lost. I had even considered suicide. Can you believe that? Taking my own life because I just couldn't handle what was happening to me."

Abby stopped and hugged Oliver hard, wrapping her arms tightly behind his back and letting her breath warm his neck. He hugged her back and they stood that way, allowing the world to move around them as they comforted each other for things that they didn't even know.

When she finally pulled away, the heat abandoned them and they both grew cold.

"Let's go in there." Oliver pointed to a tiny pub, tucked between two glowing store fronts. Inside they slid into a small half-moon booth with cracked and faded red leather seats. Abby leaned her head back and took a long breath, not minding the musty, dank air. Only a few people occupied the other tables. Several of them laughed too loudly as they drank enormous glasses of beer. The bartender looked tired and Abby watched her eyes drift repeatedly to the clock. Her blonde hair showed gray roots and she wore a low-cut, black t-shirt that revealed sagging breasts and the edge of some rose-patterned tattoo.

"My lovely friend here and I will each have coffees, with Irish Cream," Oliver told the bartender when she shuffled over to the table, not bothering to pull out a pen and paper.

"I.D.s," she grumbled, again her eyes flickering toward the clock.

Absolutely," Oliver told her warmly, removing his and then taking her hand in his own as he pressed his driver's license into her palm.

Abby saw the slightest shift as warmth traveled from Oliver into the woman, lighting up her body from within. When the flush reached her face, she smiled brightly and her eyes grew wide and alive.

"What's your name, honey?" Oliver asked her, still holding her hand.

"Janis," she responded kindly. The depth of her smile took ten years from her face.

Abby marveled at the change and, even when Oliver took his hand away, the woman's cheery disposition held. She whistled as she walked away and playfully flicked the ear of one of her regulars as she returned to the bar. He laughed and threw a sugar packet at her.

"That's a gift," Abby said, feeling lighter herself.

"Yes, it is," Oliver agreed, and though he still smiled toward the woman, his eyes looked sad. "A gift that I rarely use. You know what? Victor is right. I don't want him to be right, but we're wasted at Ula. I have these powers and what do I do with them? I hunt Vepars. I use Helena's magical tinctures when I have a headache or when my past feels too heavy a load to bear. I could count on one hand how many times I've done that in the last year."

Abby continued to watch the bartender as she flitted behind the counter, now like a tiny hummingbird. The weight of the world had vanished, not only from her shoulders, but from the energy around her. She delivered their drinks with a flourish, sliding Oliver's across the table so it just touched the edge, laughing merrily when he leaned down and took a sip.

"Delicious, best I've ever had," he told her with a wink.

"Thank you," Abby added, and the woman floated away, stopping at another table with three men who all whistled as she took a chair.

"I agree with you," Abby said, "but I also think we need time at the coven to learn. It's like you said, they saved you. We shouldn't take that for granted."

She spoke the words, but just barely believed them. After all, she'd felt stifled at Ula and angry at the way the witches seemed to shut out Sebastian. In her heart, she could never truly give herself to any group who cut out the people that she loved for being different.

"Lydie too," Oliver continued. "She's brilliant and, when she gets a little bit older, she will be able to do the most amazing things. If she stays at Ula, I'm so afraid that she'll become like Dafne, this bitter angry woman who lives in a constant state of fear and agitation."

"Do you think Ula did that to her?"

"No, but it hasn't helped. The coven is supposed to support and help you grow. It's not meant to be a hideaway where witches avoid and escape from the problems of the world. Even Buddha spoke about how enlightenment is not avoiding life, but finding peace within life. I never wanted to be a monk tucked away in a mountain cave. I want to bring my light into the world."

Abby took his hand and kissed it, moved by his words.

"Me, too. I've always felt so damn simple, so not extraordinary and now I am. I can do crazy things that no one can do. I want to make a real difference with these powers, with this life."

"That's what they're doing, Victor and Kendra and the others. They're like hippie witches, they're revolutionaries. The coven's are the past and they are creating the future."

Oliver's words frightened Abby, but they also excited her. She didn't necessarily want to live Victor's life, but she wanted her own version and something about the coven seemed to warn against such things.

"What would Elda say if you told her that? And Faustine? Would they try to stop you?"

Oliver thought about it, slowly draining his glass and signaling to Janis for another.

"I honestly have no idea. I really don't. This is the first time in years that I've even thought about leaving Ula. When Julian left, I almost followed him. He told me the same thing as Victor--in his own way, of course. He felt that the witches of Ula had retreated and were no longer living a creative life. They punished him by forcing him out of the coven."

"Really?" Despite Abby's apprehensions, she found it hard to believe that Elda and Faustine would throw anyone out of the coven.

****

Sebastian held his head in his hands and crinkled his nose at the bitter smelling mug that Julian had placed before him.

"I know," Julian said kindly. "It's pretty ripe, especially when you're feeling like that."

Sebastian nodded and took a sip, studying Julian, and for the first time realized that he knew him from somewhere.

"Have I met you?" Sebastian asked, not totally hating the muddy tea once its warmth spread through his chest.

"No," Julian told him without hesitation. "I would remember."

Sebastian continued to stare at him, perplexed, and then he remembered a photo from the library at Ula. Eight people dressed in formal attire stood in front of a painting. The men wore tuxedos and the women ball gowns, but of an era long past. Julian had been in that photograph, his hair long, nearly past his shoulders, and darker. His arm had been draped along the shoulders of a beautiful woman with large oval eyes and a pile of light-colored hair twisted on top of her head.

"It was a picture at Ula," Sebastian told him, "on the fireplace mantel in the library."

Julian smiled sadly.

"I see. Then, yes, I guess that I am familiar to you."

"Did you live at Ula?"

Julian sighed and refilled Sebastian's cup.

"Yes, for many years."

"How about Adora? How is it that she's here? She helped my sister Claire, but I thought maybe she had died...she just disappeared."

"And she feels extremely guilty about that," Julian replied. "She had an emergency and left abruptly. She did not intend to abandon your sister and had she known what would befall her, she never would have left. In her haste, she even left a Book of Shadows, which she fears may have fallen into the hands of the Vepars and caused the death of the witch Devin."

"No, I had the book. First Claire and then, after Claire died, me. They killed Devin, but they didn't use the book to find her."

Julian looked thoughtful.

"Hmmm, that's interesting and will be welcome information to Adora. She suffers daily with the burden that she inadvertently caused the death of two witches and perhaps more. Who has the Astral Book of Shadows now?"

"Elda. I gave it to her, along with Claire's journals when Abby and I first arrived at the island. Right before the All Hallow's Ball, I went into the dungeons and found some of the journals. I suddenly felt like I had to avenge Claire, as if she called out to me to even the score. What's strange is that I don't feel any of that anger now."

Julian shook his head.

"Witches are not vengeful creatures, Sebastian. I believe that your Claire rests peacefully."

"How can you possibly know that?"

"Because agitated spirits are easy to detect, especially when you've been around as long as I have..."

"It felt so real. She came to me in my dreams and she asked me to find her. She wanted me to kill Tobias."

"I know that you believed it to be real," Julian conceded. "But I also think that some other entity hoped to poison you with such thoughts."

"Have you told them that you found me? Abby must be freaking out." Sebastian asked, realizing how terrifying his disappearance must have been for the witches at Ula.

Julian paced to the window and looked into the night.

"She is, I'm sure," Julian told him. "But no, I have not been in contact with the witches of Ula for more than ten years."

"What? Why? We have to tell them." Sebastian stood up, faltered and sat back down.

Julian turned back to Sebastian and looked at him seriously.

"First you need to understand what's happening."

"Okay, tell me then."

"Let me begin by saying that I don't have the whole picture yet and that is why I have not reached out to Elda or Faustine. What I do know is that Dafne has masterminded this entire mess--your disappearance from the All

Hallow's Ball, your memory loss and, if I'm right, the misconception that you have died."

"Died?" Sebastian spat and then quickly lowered his voice, not wanting to wake the others. "Abby thinks I'm dead?"

"I believe so, though on that point I'm not positive. However, this information comes to me from a very reliable source."

"Dafne," Sebastian frowned as he spoke her name. "She has hated me since day one, but why would she do this?"

"The answer to that is very complex and, again, I have only pieces of this much larger picture. Dafne was part of what appears to be a horrible curse that originated in Trager City. This curse occurs only once every century. You and Abigail arrived at the coven of Ula just days after the one hundred year mark. It is a strange curse, one that I still do not fully comprehend, but I have experienced first-hand the path of its destruction, as has Dafne. She believed that she could prevent the return of the curse by removing you from Ula."

"A curse on what?" Sebastian asked. He took another drink of the tea and shuddered as the house moaned in the strong shifting winds.

"A curse on the human lover of a new witch. It is tied to Trager City in some way. It appears to affect only one witch and her human counterpart. Of course, nothing truly happens only to one. We are intricately connected, what happens to one happens to all."

"I still don't understand. What kind of curse? Is that why I lost my memory?"

"No, I do not believe that the curse has begun. Adora and I have searched for dates, but they are inconsistent. The last witch who suffered this curse was Dafne and, in a span of only hours, her entire life fragmented. She lost her great love, her dearest friends and all that she had known in the world up to that point."

"How is the curse on the lover then? Did he die?"

"He was Tobias, Sebastian."

Sebastian did not feel. First, numbness spread through him. The mere mention of Tobias's name brought such searingly painful memories that he felt unable to move or think. When his voice finally returned, he chose not to speak, fearing that he would scream.

"It's true, Sebastian. I know it's hard to believe, but it's true."

Sebastian picked up his mug and, before he could think, he slammed it back onto the counter and watched it shatter into tiny pieces. A shard cut deep into his hand, just below his thumb. The pain felt good and he glared at the blood gushing onto the white tiles.

Julian said nothing, but handed him a clean rag and left the room. He returned with a brown leather bag and sifted through the contents, withdrawing a small glass bottle, similar to the tinctures at Ula.

"Soak the rag in this and hold it on the wound," Julian told him.

Sebastian did and the blood soon slowed and then stopped. The skin around the cut grew very hot and then it turned white and started to tingle.

He stared at the puddle of blood that had pooled on the floor and let his thoughts run like wild dogs in his head. Their teeth gnashed and they howled in disbelief and he thought, if he were magic, he would throw Dafne in there and let her contend with the devils in his mind.

"So what then? Is she a bad witch? They're in this together?"

"No, not at all," Julian said quietly, ignoring the blood and taking a seat on one of the other stools. "One hundred years ago she and Tobias were in love and then in an instant he was pulled to the evil. He decimated her sister and brother witches, he burned them alive and he became the Tobias that we know today."

Sebastian sat back down, the fight suddenly gone from him.

"How is that possible? You're telling me that Tobias lived a normal life? That he wasn't always evil?"

"Evil is not a natural state. It's like hate and greed and envy, we learn those realities. Evil gets a foothold here in the world of form because it's so dense and we're so confused by these bodies and brains. It can plant a seed and grow into this monstrous organism because there's a lot of fertile soil in the darkness of our hearts. Something reached out to Tobias because he loved a powerful witch. Love is energy like everything else. Transform that passion into hate and now it's powerful in a destructive way."

"I need a drink," Sebastian muttered and started for the pantry door.

"Scotch," Julian said. "To the right of the bread box. Make it two."

Sebastian poured them each a small glass and threw in a few ice cubes.

He savored the heat that flowed into his belly, grateful for anything to dull the information he'd just received.

"The curse did not end with Dafne, though. Somehow she brought it with her to Ula and it nearly destroyed us as well."

"You? That's when you lived at Ula, a hundred years ago?"

Sebastian looked again at Julian. The man didn't look to be a day over sixty, but then again, Abby had told him that she suspected Faustine to be hundreds, if not thousands, of years old.

"Yes, I lived there and many other witches as well. My wife Miranda..." he took a long drink at the mention of her name and his eyes briefly closed. "She died just five days after Faustine and Elda brought Dafne to our coven."

"How? Did Dafne do something?"

"No. At least, not that I'm aware of, but Dafne and Tobias were somehow linked. This is part of the story that I don't yet understand, but the coven of Ula knew great power then. We were fifteen witches strong and we thrived as a coven and in the world. Tobias penetrated our fortress.

He used Dafne to get in and for one very long night, he..." Julian's voice shook and his hand trembled on his glass. "Another time for the recounting of all that. Tonight we talk about the present."

Sebastian did not press him.

"So why does she think I'm going to be part of this?"

"Because Abby is a new witch and you are her epic love. It's not as simple as all that, but that's where it begins."

"She thinks that I'm going to become evil and destroy the coven of Ula?"

"I would never claim to know Dafne's thoughts. She is a complicated individual, but yes, I believe that she felt so strongly that you and Abby were going to be the next to fall to this curse that she created an elaborate plan to not simply get you away from Ula, but out of the picture for good."

****

In the morning, Abby and Oliver shared coffee and pastries with the Guerilla witches before they each left for their various projects around the city. Only Victor remained.

"Victor, I need a favor," Oliver told him, downing the last of his espresso and quickly washing his cup. "I dreamed of my coven last night and I have to go there today."

"You need some wheels?" Victor asked.

Abby nodded.

"I have some investigating to do otherwise I would give him mine," she added. She hated to refuse Oliver the car--not that he'd asked for it--but she was desperate to speak to the woman at the stone cottage.

"It's no problem at all," Victor offered. "We have five cars in the basement parking garage of this place and we never even drive them." He laughed. "The public transportation is just too good."

"And one more thing," Abby told him.

She walked to her jacket and pulled the photo of Victor sitting with Stephen Kramer from her pocket. She laid the picture on the table in front of Victor. He touched the photo and his face softened as if recalling a fond memory.

"Time to come clean," he sighed. He propped his legs on the coffee table in front of him and considered where to begin. "I dreamed of you before the Ball, Abby. I didn't know where you would come from, but I knew to look for Melusine and then there you were..."

"You dreamed of me," Abby crinkled her forehead and tried to make sense of Victor's explanation.

"But long before I dreamed of you, I dreamed of her." He pulled a neat leather notebook from his satchel and flipped it open to the first page and then the second and the third.

Abby studied the same face again and again. At first, the rudimentary drawing revealed only the shadow of a woman. Her dark hair hid the contours of her face. Then Victor's pictures grew more elaborate. Wide brown eyes bore from the face of a young Native American woman, barely older than a child really, with sensuous lips and smooth honey skin. She looked angry and afraid.

Abby recognized the woman from Sorciére. She saw that Victor had even captured her in the same costume she'd worn that night. Deerskin robes and thick rabbits-fur boots. Her hair hung in a single heavy braid over one shoulder and she clutched a child to her breast.

"She guided me to you. I never questioned her, Abby."

"But who is she?" Abby asked, not liking the way the drawing's eyes seemed to hold her own in their steely gaze.

"Okay, wait," Oliver interrupted. "Your dreams don't explain this picture. Why are you sitting on Sydney's dock?

"Stephen Kramer invited me there. I met him at a paranormal seminar in Chicago when I was twelve years old. Crazy, right? You know, I think one of my favorite parts of being a witch is synchronicity." He started to hop up, excited, and then winced in pain at his leg, still healing from the Vepar's lair. "It seriously blows my mind. I didn't even know of Abby until I dreamed of her and then after we met and she told me about Trager, I realized that I had met her Aunt Sydney."

"Why did you lie about it?" Oliver challenged.

"I didn't lie," Victor said slowly. "I refrained from talking about it because I was shocked myself and I wanted to understand what it all meant."

"Why didn't you say more at Sorciére, though? I mean, you sought me out, Victor, and even after I agreed to meet you, you didn't say that you had dreamed of me."

Abby could not stop staring at the picture of the Native American girl.

"I'm sorry for that, sincerely. I can't give you a satisfying explanation," he paused. "If it helps, I haven't even told Kendra that I knew your aunt or that we went into the lair that night..."

"I don't get it," Oliver chimed in. "You're recruiting Abby like you want her in your coven."

"We're not a coven," Victor interrupted.

"Okay, your housemate," Oliver said exasperated. "Still, why would you pursue her and not be completely honest about why you're interested in her to begin with?"

Victor pointed to the drawing of the woman.

"Because Kanti didn't want me to."

Chapter 25

"Rod. It's really good to see you, man," Sebastian told him when they finally had a few minutes alone.

Their day had been a flurry of preparations to leave France and return to the United States. Now, as they sat waiting to board their flight, Sebastian gave Rod a hug and gestured to an empty seat.

"You too, Sebastian. Really and truly, I'm so happy to have a friend around." Rod grinned and rolled his eyes toward Julian and Adora who stood talking quietly. "After they brought me to France, I started to think I might go flippin' crazy."

"Yeah, I know the feeling. I've spent the last two weeks not having a clue what my own name was. You wanna talk crazy..."

Rod patted him on the back and smiled, settling back into the stiff airport chair.

"Sometimes I wish I could be so lucky," he murmured.

"What happened?" Sebastian asked gently. "I mean, after you guys got back from the Cayman's? If it's sensitive, you don't have to talk about it."

"Damn," Rod started, and then he pulled a pint of Jack Daniels from his carry-on bag and poured a hefty serving into his styrofoam cup of coffee. "Duty-free." He grinned. "Want some?"

Sebastian held out his own cup and let Rod pour him a shot, more out of solidarity than any real desire to get drunk.

"I need to talk about it, except that every time I say her name I feel like someone's squeezing me really hard. I'm beginning to wonder if my body is trying to let go, but my mind really wants to hang on."

"As if there are hands on your throat and around your heart and reaching up inside of you and pulling out everything that ever mattered..." Sebastian trailed off. He knew that pain. He knew it almost as well as he'd known the love when his family was still alive.

"Exactly," Rod sighed. "It's kind of blurry now and I guess that's because I didn't want to face it. For the first couple of weeks, I just got drunk a lot..."

Through the wall of glass before them, an airplane taxied down the runway and took off into the cloudless sky.

"We went back to Trager because Sydney had this horrible dream that Abby was dead. It was so vivid that she couldn't shake it and then she got online and looked at the Trager news and realized that a woman had been found murdered."

"Devin."

"Yeah, Devin, but her name hadn't been released and Sydney just panicked. She packed all of her bags and bailed. We couldn't get on the same flight because it was so last minute. She got back in the evening and I didn't get into town until the next morning. Of course, by the time I got there..."

"She was already dead."

Rod closed his eyes and shook his head in disbelief.

"I still don't understand, Sebastian. Sydney knew things about witches. Maybe she even knew about Abby, but I never really questioned all of that. Part of me honestly felt like it was just a fantasy that her and these other people played at. Sometimes I wonder if this all happened because I didn't believe--like God cursed me for doubting."

Sebastian hated how well he understood Rod's pain. He experienced similar thoughts after Claire's death and still wondered if he might have stopped it.

"You couldn't have saved her, Rod, and no amount of belief could change that. How did she know though? I mean, who told her about witches?"

Rod shrugged his shoulders and he looked exasperated. "Fuck if I know. She lived and breathed all of that when I first met her. I think she dove into the lore to escape her marriage with Harold. She tried to bring me in a few times, but I didn't really connect with it all. She claimed that these magical people existed, but I never saw any real proof. It was just her getting together with these other believers and stringing up all this evidence to make it true."

"She was in a group?"

"Yeah, I think they even referred to themselves as a secret society. I met most of them. They sat around and drank wine and wrote in journals by candlelight. I found it pretty sexy and mysterious, but that was about it. When I got home and went to the lake house, it was just a nightmare. Her pictures were smashed, half the yard was burned black and she...well, Adora got to her first and covered the body, but I know she went painfully. I just know it."

Rod cried openly. He pulled a wad of toilet paper from his pocket and blew his nose.

Sebastian smiled in spite of himself. As a child, he'd always imagined

Sydney with a man like Rod--a tan, chiseled, marshmallow that would love her, no matter what. He never understood her marriage to Harold who seemed more interested in his tie collection than his beautiful eccentric wife.

"She was lucky to have you, Rod. She loved you a lot."

Rod smiled and shook his head. "Yeah, she was a real piece of work. I couldn't have loved her more though. I'm lucky that Adora beat me there. She practically threw me in her trunk and hauled me off to some safe house where they kept me pretty well drugged and boozed up for Lord knows how long. And then I met that old windbag, Julian." He laughed as he spoke and Sebastian appreciated his ability to bounce back.

"So you've been in hiding ever since?"

"Yeah, for a lot of reasons from what Adora has said. For one, the Trager police more or less pinned Sydney's murder on me, which had me about ready to go into the precinct with a shotgun and give them a piece of my mind, but then she started to fill me in on the history of Trager and those evil fucks that killed my wife. Vepars she calls them. Since then I've taken my medicine like a good boy."

Sebastian detected a note of resentment.

"They're right. I know it's miserable feeling helpless--I get it, I really do--but the Vepars are...sick. Sick in the head, sick in the heart. I've been researching them for the past couple of months. I never used to believe in the devil, but I do now."

****

Sebastian stared at the skyline of New York City.

They had arrived that morning and checked into a tall faceless hotel that mirrored every other building in the city. They shared two connecting rooms, each equipped with overly firm double beds and paintings of the Statue of Liberty.

"Rod, it's for your own protection. If the authorities recognize you, you'll be arrested."

"I should be able to show my face in my own damn town. That's my home. My wife grew up there, for Christ sakes."

Adora looked to Sebastian for help as she tried to make Rod stand still.

"It's not permanent, man, it's just to make things easier for right now. Cool?"

Rod looked irritated that Sebastian had sided with Adora.

"Fine," he said.

Adora had already died his blond hair black and now she intended to change the color of his eyes and modify the structure of his face, softening his chin and making his nose larger.

Sebastian was struck by the bizarre scene before him. Rod stood with his eyes clenched closed, his chin shrinking back into his face as Adora, resplendent in a long magenta robe, crunched handfuls of herbs into a plastic cup inches from Rod's nose. Julian sat on the bed, his back pressed against the headboard and his legs neatly crossed as he flipped through an outdated issue of Mother Earth News.

"I suddenly feel so unprepared," Sebastian said to no one in particular. "I feel like I'm ten all over again getting ready to jump off my roof with a rain jacket because I couldn't find my mom's umbrella."

Julian chuckled and flipped the page.

"There's no such thing as prepared," he said calmly.

Little more than forty-eight hours since Adora and Rod had plucked him off the streets of France, Sebastian could hardly believe that his life was being returned to him. He felt giddy and alarmed and disoriented. Though his memory had returned intact, he couldn't shake the impression that his whole world had been flipped upside down.

He paced into the room and studied himself in the mirror, a habit he'd developed after recovering his memory. He studied his blue eyes and tan face. He touched the black curls that were so long he had to tuck them behind his ears to keep them out of his eyes. He wore a rather ugly Hawaiian shirt of Rod's on top of a long-sleeved white t-shirt and a pair of tapered jeans. Claire would have called them 'pancake butt jeans'. He looked foolish, but that didn't bother him. What concerned him was how he kept seeing something wicked in his face. No, that wasn't quite it either. He kept seeing Tobias in the mirrored face staring back at him.

Chapter 26

"I dreamed of Miranda last night," Elda told Faustine, her eyes tired and aching from her tormented sleep. "I fear that..."

Faustine held up a hand to silence her and nodded his head toward the door. Beyond, Elda could see the shadows of two small feet--Lydie.

She whispered a muting incantation to block Lydie from hearing them.

When he knew that Lydie would not hear him, he spoke. "I too have dreamed of Miranda, and the others as well. I wanted to believe that something else was giving life to these phantoms in slumber."

It's been more than a century," Elda responded.

"Yes, and did we not wonder a hundred years ago if that horror would cycle through again? We all sensed it, didn't we?"

She nodded gravely and laid her hands on the table in front of them. Etched with symbols and words, the table was meant for spell casting, but even here in the coven's center, Elda felt the disrupted flow of energies.

"It has already begun," she sighed.

Elda closed her eyes tightly and when she exhaled, her shoulders slumped further. Faustine noticed, perhaps for the first time, how gaunt she had grown.

We are aging, he thought, not with sadness or fear, but a small reluctance. He understood that the passage of time allowed the coven to slip into complacency. They still functioned, but only on the defense. They hadn't actively brought their energy into the world beyond the island in years. He had felt both Oliver and Lydie's frustration with the seemingly dulled world of Ula.

The coven had once thrived. They moved in and out of the world like phantoms, or perhaps the term 'angels' was more appropriate. Helena and Elda were rarely found in the castle walls, too busy at the hospitals sneaking healing elixirs to the ill and remedying the faltering humanity of those who had lost hope. In those days, Faustine's long hours in the tower did not involve spying on his coven, but communicating danger, need and news to the witches who sometimes scattered across the whole of Gaia to do their bidding.

The ruin of their coven happened in nineteen hundred and eight and they never referred to it as such. They called it many things in the midst of their fall--primarily the dark times, but later they abandoned words and, with it, they slowly abandoned the memories. They agreed that they must do more than release the energy of that time. They must eradicate the memory as if it had not happened at all. Faustine presented it as a powerful tool to rewrite the past and thus change the future, but even he, an ancient and powerful witch, underestimated the influence of that violence in all their lives and, perhaps more, in their hearts. He foolishly believed himself immune to the lasting effects of the tragedy that befell his coven. He thought that his witches could simply will it away. Instead, they buried it, and it rose from the dead, reminding them that those who forget their history are doomed to repeat it.

He communicated his pain to Elda with a gentle touch on her wrist and he felt her great sadness.

"We have already lost so much," she told him desperately, shaking her head from side to side. "Now we must face this evil again?"

"We never faced it," he told her. "We tucked away and hid. We cast Julian out and he may have been the only one of us running towards the face of this thing."

"Do you think that Julian lives?" Elda asked. The shadows at the door had disappeared.

Faustine sighed and scratched his head.

"I once believed that I would always know if one of my witches lived or died, that the threads between us would never fray, but now...now I cannot feel my own coven. You sit here next to me and I can barely feel you."

Elda put her hand in Faustine's.

"Should we go to the cave then?"

"I think that we must."

****

Sebastian closed the bathroom door and quickly shuffled through Rod's coat pockets. He found a money clip with nearly six hundred dollars in cash. Equipped with the fake passport and identification procured by Julian in France and Rod's money, Sebastian told Adora that he wanted to check out the pool and he left the hotel room.

In the hallway, he began to run. He had known that the moment he landed in the States, he would try to break away from the group and find Abby. Every time he thought of her, a terrifying sense of doom washed over him. The frustration at not having a phone number to reach her, or a damned e-mail address even, so disturbed him that he wanted to punch every single person he passed on his race to the airport. He boarded the first flight to Trager City, which cost him nearly all of the cash he'd stolen from Rod. He didn't care. He would rob someone to get to Abby if it came to that.

During his flight to Trager City, Sebastian furiously scribbled everything that Julian had told him about Dafne and the curse. He wanted to remember every detail and, after weeks of not even recalling his own name, he held a secret fear of somehow losing it all again.

****

"There's something out here," Lydie squeaked, and Helena tightened her hold on the little girl's hand.

When had she ever really thought of Lydie as a little girl? Not in a long time, but in that moment it rang true, as true as her tiny voice lost in the night wind and her fingers clenching Helena's so that her own grew sore.

"It's okay, Lydie," Helena assured her, battling her own unease as the wind whistled in the trees. Helena suggested the night stroll because the castle felt too cold and empty with the other witches far off in their astral travel or just gone altogether. She had planned to walk Lydie to the enchanted garden where they would inhale the flower scents and spell cast under the nearly full moon. But, distracted, she had instead steered her towards the far northern tip of the island where few of the Ula witches ever wandered. The barren woods in that area knew a dark history and Helena halted when they came upon them.

The full moon no longer cast them in its warm glow, but slid behind a gray cloud. The sky, clear when they departed the castle, now gave way to something marred with thick streams of cloud and an electric feel like rain.

"Can we go back?" Lydie whimpered, her eyes darting into the trees.

Helena inhaled and exhaled very slowly. She ground her feet into the earth and called silently to her power source, feeling it ignite briefly and then fizzle as if she did not stand in the open air, surrounded by her element.

"Lydie, draw strength from your element," Helena told her, immediately regretting her strained tone.

Lydie's fingers tightened in her hand.

Lydie closed her eyes and Helena felt her reaching out. She knew that Lydie's fear worked against her, but so did the lack of sunlight. Neither Helena nor Lydie had the hunter's instincts. They were healers by nature and, without the other witches, a crippling vulnerability began to descend.

A twig snapped nearby and Lydie spun around, crying out, and simultaneously sending a jagged bolt of flame across the dry earth below them. It lit the woods for an instant and, to Helena's horror, a shape loomed in the distance. The man wore a dark hood, but Helena caught the red glow of his eyes.

"Lydie, run," she commanded , pushing Lydie with the force of her power toward the castle. Lydie took flight, running so fast that her legs carried her into the air, but then she touched down and disappeared into the trees. Helena again called upon her element and then she whispered an incantation to the moon that it light the island, but darken her. She felt her own shape dim as the woods and water beyond lit up. Where the man stood, she now saw only a gnarled tree.

She felt nothing, no presence, but also no lack of presence. The transmitter that endlessly sent signals into her body had grown silent. She thought of the nothing and then she remembered Lydie and fled to the castle.

****

Lydie raced through the castle doors and slammed them behind her, running halfway down the hall before the darkness hit her. Every candle in the castle had been extinguished. She started to scream, but instead shoved her fist into her mouth and pressed her back against the wall, sliding towards the library where she might disappear into a secret passageway and hide from whomever or whatever had breached the coven's barriers.

In the familiar terrifying darkness, all the fear of her childhood rushed back at her.

She sat again in the tiny cubby the night her mother and father were murdered. She heard their cries and pleas as the Vepars dragged them from the cottage and ransacked the house in search of her. She smelled her parent's blood as it filled the air and mixed with scents of pine and the cinnamon cookies her mother had baked just that evening.

Like that night, when the fear became more than she could face, Lydie closed her eyes. The darkness, like an old friend, wrapped close around her.

****

"I will light the fire. Might you fan the smoke?" Faustine asked Elda who stood in the cave staring up at the stars. She looked younger in the moonlight and he felt an old desire awakening in his body.

Once upon a time, they had loved each other with a passion that he believed would endure all things. They never chose to reveal their intimacy to others, but instead kept it as a beautiful treasure meant only for their two hearts. In those days, they both put Ula before themselves. They agreed that physical love could not interfere with their work as witches. He wondered now if they would have been better off marrying and wrapping the whole of their coven within their love instead.

"Yes, I will go up," she told him and began to float up toward the sky, perching on the rock ledge.

He blew fire into the cave floor and its flames danced up into the heavens, concealing Elda from his view. He knew that she would be calling out now to the other five witches, the smoke signals reaching to them at the far corners of the earth.

When Elda returned, they rocked together, their energies feeding the fire. It grew bigger and brighter and eventually witches began to traipse out of the tunnel behind them. All five arrived, their black cloaks billowing as they merged into a circle around the flames, their arms linked and their heads bowed. Faustine did not have to describe the unrest at his coven. The other witches had only to pick it out of the flames.

No one spoke. They communicated through the fire and both Elda and Faustine paid keen attention to the thoughts of the ancient witches who had come to offer their wisdom. The witch who spoke to the spirit of the Great Mother knew that the deception had come from within their coven, and Faustine felt tremendous pain as he accepted this truth. He realized that Elda had already suspected as much and, furthermore, she knew that it was Dafne who had deceived them

****

Helena felt along the castle walls, her bare feet sticking to the floor beneath her.. She wanted to call out to Lydie, but her body vibrated with a message of danger. She bit her tongue and moved slowly through the darkness. Never in all of her years at Ula had all the candles extinguished.

When she found the door to the tincture room, she slipped inside, closing it softly behind her. She whispered an incantation, sealing the door with darkness, so that when she created light within the room, it would not be seen from outside.

"Fire of sun, light of moon I call you
Light of moon, fire of sun I call you
Let this room illumine, let this room illumine"

She held fast to the stone about her neck as she spoke, willing the power of the air to send her call into the elements. Gradually the room lit until she could see the bottles of tinctures lining the walls.

She searched quickly, grabbing several, including the venom antidote, an invisibility potion and a poultice, which could be ripped and thrown into the face of an enemy to render them temporarily blind. She filled a small satchel with several poisonous tinctures and tied it about her waist. She grabbed a calming elixir and drank it quickly, welcoming the immediate sensation of peace that fell over her. Death came swiftly to those who panicked.

Lydie's scream pierced her thoughts and Helena darkened the room before running into the hallway and smacking into something large. She fell back and hit her head against the stone wall, crashing to the floor where several tinctures smashed as she landed upon them. The glass from the bottles cut into her back and, for a moment, she felt paralyzed as the liquids merged with her blood.

The dark figure paused and something wriggled in its arms. Helena sensed Lydie directly in front of her, thrashing in the arms of her captor. The young witch tried to scream, but her cries were muffled. Helena struggled to sit, her hands mashing into glass and blood, but her body had grown heavy. She heard Lydie's strangled screams grow further away and she felt the poison race towards her heart.

Chapter 27

Abby knocked on the door of the stone cottage, noticing the darkened windows. All of the cottages looked vacant. No one answered.

She went to another cottage and then another. She knocked on doors and peeked in windows. In the cottage where she'd seen the woman with the child Ebony the week before, she saw darkened rooms.

Still, she sensed human life nearby, and something else--fear. Abby tried the door--locked. The door appeared old and heavy so Abby picked a lake-facing window near the rear of the cottage. She took off her sweater and wrapped it around her elbow, slamming it hard against the glass. It shattered easily and stung Abby's arm for only a moment before the pain subsided. She crawled through the window and into a child's bedroom painted with fairies and strung with garlands of pink and green lace.

"Is anyone home?" Abby called out. She moved cautiously, stopping to listen and feel what lay ahead. The cottage held another bedroom--the mother's--a tiny kitchen and living room combined, and one small bathroom. No attic. She continued to call out as she walked, but no one called back.

She started to leave, thinking that perhaps she had sensed the remnants of the people there instead of an actual person when she heard the tiniest sigh from below her. It barely registered and any human brain would have written it off as the sounds of the house or the wind outside, but Abby knew it to be breath. There was a basement beneath the cottage and someone was in it.

She moved back through the cottage lifting rugs and looking beneath furniture. She found the trap door in Ebony's bedroom concealed beneath a large wooden doll house. When she lifted the door, she heard the unmistakable sound of footsteps scurrying away. She also felt the woman's fear as she dropped into the space.

The woman from the grocery store cowered in the far corner of the crawl space, a single candle clutched in her white-knuckled hand. She opened her mouth as if to scream and Abby held up her hands.

"Please don't be afraid of me. I swear, I'm here to help. Let me help you."

The woman did not scream, but her gaze darted around the small space as if seeking an escape route.

"My name is Abby," Abby told her, extending a hand.

At the mention of her name, the woman's gray eyes grew larger and less afraid.

"Abigail Daniels?" the woman asked in a husky voice that sounded like she had been crying.

Abby cocked her head to the side and studied the woman.

"You know me?"

The woman nodded.

"Of you. I knew Sydney. Sydney was a very close friend."

Abby smiled and relaxed as the woman finally began to make her way, hunched, over to the floor opening.

"Let's get out of here," Abby said. "It's creepy."

The woman laughed quietly.

"That's exactly how Sydney described it."

Abby hoisted herself out of the space. The woman carefully replaced the door and slid the doll house over it.

"Why were you hiding?" Abby asked, walking back toward the kitchen with the woman behind her.

The woman looked around nervously and then stared out the window for a long time, watching the woods.

"I don't believe that we're safe here," she said at last.

"Has someone tried to hurt you? And I hope you don't mind my asking, but where is your child?"

Dismay colored the woman's features, but then she seemed to think better of it.

"I have not been attacked, but I'm sure that others have. My daughter was taken to a safe place where she will be protected."

"Protected from whom? And what others?"

"I don't think we should discuss it here. We're not safe."

Abby sighed, exasperated, and was tempted to tell the woman of her powers so that she might rest easy.

"I know you're not ordinary," the woman replied. "But your enemies are mine as well."

"Where is safe then?" Abby asked finally. "And what is your name?"

"Gwen," the woman said, running a hand nervously through her tousled blonde hair and glancing again toward the forest.

"I kept hearing things in there last night. Screams and then this strange crying, but not like a human cry--an animal cry."

Abby wondered if the woman might be losing her mind, but knew that she only wanted to believe that.

"Do you think someone was hurt in there?"

"No," the woman whispered. "I think it was the cries of the dead."

****

Elda picked up the message first.

'There's something wrong at your coven,' the elder witch, Hatha, projected the thought to Elda and Faustine.

Faustine brushed over it. He already knew as much, but Elda recognized it for what it was--an urgent warning.

"Now?"

The witch nodded gravely and immediately the fire began to die as Elda and then Faustine allowed themselves to be pulled back to their astral bodies. They came to on the floor of the dungeon in complete darkness.

"Where is the light? The candles have all been extinguished," Faustine whispered, sitting up and immediately casting a glow in front of them. He allowed it to fill the room and they followed it into the hallway and up the dungeon stairs. The castle lay quiet, but the air felt chilled and disturbed. Something malevolent had been in the castle and its vestige remained.

Faustine reached out to the spell that lit the candles. Someone or something had tampered with the coven's protective barriers. He sought the missing pieces and began to pull the energy back together. A few of the candles lit and then went out.

"Forget the spell, Faustine. Just give them fire."

He did so and the hallway grew bright, the lights flickering and at times going out. Far down the hall, they both saw the pool of red spreading on the stone floor.

Elda ran to the spot where it trailed into the room of elixirs and pushed the door in, nearly falling over Helena who had crawled back to the door before slipping into unconsciousness. Elda could see the weak rise and fall of her chest.

"I will take her to the Healing Room. You must go to the tower and find Lydie." Elda's voice cracked on Lydie's name. She scooped Helena into her arms and rushed out of the room. Faustine stood paralyzed, his eyes taking in broken bottles and blood spatter, his brain trying to wrench him back one hundred years to a similar scene.

"There's no time for such nonsense," he chastised himself, and hurried towards the tower, searching for Lydie's presence behind every closed door that he passed, but knowing in his heart that every room lay empty.

****

Abby and Gwen drove. They did not have a destination in mind. Gwen insisted movement was their safest choice so Abby filled her little car with gas and chose a long stretch of country road.

"My heart has been broken since Sydney's death," Gwen started, clasping her knees and leaning her head toward the dashboard. She shook it from side to side as if still in disbelief.

"Mine too."

Abby stared ahead and tried to forget the image of Sydney's dead, bloated face.

"Sydney started the group. I mean, technically it started long before her, but she restarted it, if you will. She was definitely the longest standing member and the most knowledgeable."

"The group?" Abby asked.

"Yeah, the Asemaa. I'm not exactly sure what it means--something to do with tobacco."

"A smoker's group? Really?"

Gwen laughed.

"No, a group that studies witches."

Abby turned and looked sharply at Gwen, but could see that the woman was entirely serious.

"What does that mean?"

"It means that I know that you are a witch, Abby. I know that Sydney's mother was a witch. I know about the coven of Ula, though not very much. Sydney devoted her life to compiling information about your...kind. Sorry, I just don't know what else to call you. Anyway, she wasn't the first and she didn't make up the name Asemaa. It came from a man who knew of witches and of their connection with Trager. She never told me much about him. She called him Gibbs, though that was his last name. Gibbs told Sydney that the men who founded the group were tobacco traders and they used their routes to meet and share information."

"Why would this man be interested in witches?"

"I don't really know. Sydney spent a lot of time trying to trace the group's beginnings, but never found any more than Gibbs had told her. She devoted a lot of time to her research, but you know Sydney, she didn't exactly savor sitting in a dark library reading all day."

"To tell you the truth, I can't believe I never knew about any of this. I spent time with Sydney every summer and I never got even a whiff of this group."

Gwen waved the comment away.

"Sydney took a lot of pains to hide it. Not from you per se, but from Harold especially. She intended to tell you. She wanted to wait until she felt that you were ready and, after she met Rod, she got pretty distracted for a while. For a couple of years the group cooled off and our meetings became a lot more sporadic. But she got really excited about it all again last year.

She had a dream about your grandmother. Arlene demanded that she return to the witch studies and implied that something very important was going to happen."

Abby drew in a deep breath and watched silently as the bare trees whizzed by.

"She kept a lot of her information at the loft. In fact, she bought the loft for Rod because of that secret room. She thought it was perfect. Before that she kept it all in a storage unit, but that scared her because anyone could break in and take it. Rod didn't even know about the room. I think it was the only thing that she ever lied to him about..."

"Why would she need to protect it? I mean, other than the obvious reasons like who the Hell believes in witches to begin with and if they found out she was researching them they'd all think she was bat shit crazy."

Gwen smiled.

"Well, she was, but that's hardly the point. She knew that Vepars hunted witches and could trace bloodlines. It was the curse more than anything though. The curse on Trager that was valuable, and if that information got into the wrong hands then witches would die and humans would die and Vepars would have access to power greater than they'd ever known."

Abby realized that she'd begun to press hard on the gas and let up. She took a couple of slow breaths and cleared her running thoughts.

"After the dream, Sydney insisted we return to twice monthly meetings and hinted about a big 'tell all' with you. I think she decided that if you carried the witches' blood, then telling you might begin the process of discovery and, if you didn't, you could become part of the Asemaa."

"She planned to tell me?"

Abby wondered how differently things might have gone if Sydney had only told her. She clenched her teeth to keep from crying. Gwen reached over and rested a warm hand on her knee.

"I'm sorry, honey. You meant so much to Sydney, I hope you know that."

Abby nodded through her tears and then wiped them hard with her sleeve and continued.

"So you're saying that Sydney discovered a curse on Trager that has something to do with me?"

"I think so, yes. I think that the Asemaa originally discovered the curse, but I believe something bad happened to most of them." The woman shuddered.

"How long ago did Sydney form this group?"

"I knew her when we were little girls. We played in the woods between our houses. Even then Sydney knew stuff, weird stuff that I only half believed. When she came back later, I was the first she let in on her secret and then slowly we added four more. We had six in all. Two of them, Karl and Meghan, live in the cottages with me. Stephen lives in town and Lorna is further north. We met twice a month usually at the cottages and shared what we had uncovered in the previous weeks. In the beginning I didn't take it very seriously. You know, I thought that Sydney was probably embellishing some of it, but then she introduced me to Adora."

"Adora?" Abby asked, startled by the name of the witch who had helped Sebastian's sister Claire.

"Yes, she had come to Sydney, believe it or not, looking for information about the curse. Most of Sydney's documents came from her predecessor and, though she'd read all of it and taken a library of notes, she still didn't really understand it. In fact, we've spent most of the last five years trying to unearth the origin of the curse."

"So what happened with Adora then?"

"Well, Sydney brought her to the cottages and she performed some parade magic, she called it, to convince us of her legitimacy. She created a lightning storm and then she flew into one of the trees and made all the leaves turn purple. Nothing too brilliant according to her, but let me tell you, my whole life changed that night. I suddenly saw the world as it is really is, this insane mystery. All my doubts died in an instant. Of course that meant a whole new level of fear too, because now there was real evil in the world and I was a part of defending against it in my own little way, which scared me for Ebony and for the others."

"And where are the others now?"

Gwen closed her eyes.

"I don't know where Stephen and Lorna are. Their homes were abandoned and none of us have heard from them in weeks. Karl and Meghan took Ebony..."

"Why didn't you go?"

"Because of you."

Abby slowed and pulled off to the side of the road, turning to face Gwen.

"What do you mean by that?"

"Stephen found something important a few weeks ago and he wouldn't explain it over the phone, but he told me that you, Abby, are the next in line. That's it, that's all he said, but I knew what he meant. You're the next in line for the curse."

Chapter 28

Oliver stood on the shore and looked into the choppy, gray waters of Lake Superior. The path he had swum to the castle a thousand times before lived in his muscle memory but, without Helena's pepper plants, he couldn't make the swim in the bitter November weather. He didn't feel cold, he rarely did. His body naturally ran hot and, even on the most frigid of nights, with snow piling around the castle, he'd often gone for barefoot walks and marveled at how the snow melted away from his feet. Small, seemingly irrelevant memories kept coming back to him. He remembered how Lydie used to demand to sit in his lap at breakfast while grumpily munching her cereal in the years after her parents' deaths. She rarely spoke then and when she did, her words held an accusatory edge for everyone, but him.

The winter sun shone its pale light on the water and reflected the almost cloudless sky above. If he looked hard at the water, he could see Lydie in it. The look on her face terrified him--a look that had woken him in the dead of night and signaled that something felt terribly wrong and he had to return to Ula.

Now he fought the urge to dive into the icy waters and sprint to the island. It was faster, but not safe. So he searched the shore until he found the row boat discarded by Abby weeks before. As he cut through the rough waters, he felt the tiny shiver of the spells cast around Ula, but they barely registered. The spells never blocked him, nor did they appear to him as they did to strangers. He'd helped place them, after all. However, they usually jolted him. When he passed through the barrier, he normally felt a mild electric shock. Today he felt nothing.

He came into view of the castle, but still he did not feel Faustine. He moved through the tunnel into the island lagoon and sprang from the boat to the dock.

The emptiness surrounding the castle was palpable and Oliver's world rolled. He looked at the earth, still steady beneath him, and realized he felt the energy of what had moved in that space. Oliver bolted up the steps and met the castle door with a hard thud. Not only locked, the door had been sealed and when he struck it, a shock blasted him away and he sprawled on the stone terrace. He ran around the side of the castle, jumping onto one of the tiny stone ledges that barely left room for his toes. He scaled the castle wall, glancing down when the ground fell away and was replaced by jagged cliffs plummeting to the roiling water below. He moved slowly along the edge. He would likely survive a fall, but wasn't in the mood to find out. When he finally made it around to the dining room balcony, he bounded over the small stone railing and raced to the door where again he struck some kind of electric shield that tossed him away. He was ready for it this time and landed on his feet.

He started to yell and then to scream, waving his arms and hoping that someone within would see him. No faces appeared behind the dark windows. He kicked the stone railing until it began to break apart and started to fling the pieces. He grabbed the first chunk and threw it at the library window where it jerked away before touching the glass. Three more hunks of stone met the same resistance. Only when he threw a piece as high as he possibly could muster, at one of the tiny windows in Faustine's tower, did he connect. He heard the ping as the stone struck glass.

Carefully channeling the adrenaline that coursed through him, he started up the tower. The stones had few spaces between them and even fewer cracks in which to wedge his feet, so Oliver plastered his body flat against the wall using his palms to suction the face of it while squeezing with his arms and legs around the curve of the turret. Within minutes, his entire body ached from the exertion, and the sweat breaking out on his body, made the stone slippery and harder to hold. Halfway up the tower, he started to lose his grip. His inner thighs spasmed and he closed his eyes, clenching back the images of the rocks far below him. He could survive a lot, but a thousand foot fall onto pointed slabs of granite would likely kill him.

He started to yell again, hating to waste any bit of energy, but realizing with a cold certainty that he would never make the window. He clenched his eyes shut and instead started to move back down the tower. Every time he inched lower, his whole body started to lift away from the castle wall. He froze, clinging to the tower and trying desperately to find Faustine with his mind. When he could hold it no longer, he again started his descent but, as s he shifted down, his legs went slack and he began to fall. Despite his connection to the stone wall, his powers failed him. He flailed his arms and legs, screaming as the rocks rushed up to meet him, but an instant before impact, he felt something slow him down. His body began to float lazily upward. As he passed the terrace outside the dining area, he saw Elda, her face purple with strain. She reached out, took hold of his arms and pulled him to her and then she collapsed.

Oliver could not stand. He lay next to an unconscious Elda and then slowly moved onto his hands and knees. He vomited, feeling his stomach churning sourly, and then wiped his mouth on his sleeve, before standing and gently lifting Elda into his arms. The door to the dining area stood open and he walked through hesitantly, not entirely sure they wouldn't both be blasted away.

Inside the castle, an eerie silence greeted him. He did not call out, but laid Elda gently onto a rug and moved into the main hallway. Only some of the candles flickered, casting the hall in shadows, which taunted him as he searched for movement along the corridor. He tried to feel the presence of the other witches, but found only a great void.

He went first to the library and then to the kitchen. He raced up the tower in search of Faustine, but every room lay empty. He finally moved into the dungeons, and there he heard the first sounds of life. Voices rang out from the Healing Room.

He burst through the door and both Faustine and Max swung around to face him. Their hands and clothes were matted with blood and sweat ran down their faces in streams. Faustine looked wild-eyed and Max on the edge of defeat.

"Oh, you're okay. Thank the heavens that you're okay," Max said, wiping a bloody hand across his forehead.

Oliver began to ask who they were tending to and then he spotted Helena on the bed just beyond them.

She looked so pale that he recognized her only by her auburn hair streaked a coppery brown. She rested on her stomach, her face turned towards him and clenched with pain though she didn't appear to be conscious.

"What happened?" He moved to her side, grimacing at the open wounds that streaked across her back. Several of them continued to ooze blood while others emitted different colors. One especially deep gash, released a grayish puss.

"We were invaded," Faustine said grimly, gently mopping Helena's skin with a damp cloth. She moaned in her sleep and shifted, but did not wake up.

"Something got into the castle. It appears that she fell on some tinctures, poisonous tinctures," Max's voice broke as he talked. He returned to the long table of herbs, hurriedly mixing another in what appeared to be, twenty or thirty poultices that were already soaked in Helena's blood. He handed the satchel to Faustine who placed it on her wounds.

"Where's Lydie?" Oliver demanded. He swept around the room searching under the beds as if she might be hiding there, though he knew in his heart he would not find Lydie anywhere in the Healing Room or in the castle.

"We don't know." Faustine spoke so quietly that Oliver almost missed it.

"We've searched the entire castle..." He placed his hands on the edge of Helena's bed and stared down at her. Oliver sensed how far he'd fallen and, though his guts screamed at him to be angry at Faustine, his heart could not.

"Elda saved me upstairs. I nearly died trying to scale the building. Now I, at least, understand why. If Lydie has been taken, who is out looking for her?"

"We arrived less than an hour ago, Oliver. Elda was resealing the castle while we..." He gestured at Helena.

"Where are Bridget and Dafne?"

"Bridget left more than a week ago to stay with her daughter in Florida and Dafne..." Faustine closed his eyes for a moment. "She's been missing for several days."

****

"I went to the loft earlier this week. I planned to tell you everything, but you weren't there," Gwen told Abby.

"I have all of the Asemaa's journals. You can read them. I'm not sure if there's much in there that might help. A lot of times it seemed like we chased pointless leads. One thing appeared important and then would just fizzle out. You see, we had information about that horrible fire in Ebony Woods. And you know what? If I'd known about that fire I never would have named my child Ebony. I feel foolish now because I love the name and, to tell you the truth, Sydney picked it, but later when Sydney showed me the newspaper clippings about Aubrey Blake and then we discovered all those other people died, I just felt like I'd cursed my own child."

"It is a beautiful name," Abby said, remembering her mother mentioning Sydney's hope to someday have a daughter and name her Ebony. "I'm sure that you blessed her with that choice and nothing else."

Gwen smiled thankfully and continued. "In the months before Sydney left for vacation, we met every single week. Stephen told us he found a lead and scheduled a trip to Houston to meet this person. I know he told Sydney more about it, but I missed the meeting with him before his trip. Sydney knew something, Abby. In fact, I'm not entirely sure that she didn't foresee her own death."

"What? How?"

"Again a dream. She had such vivid dreams and, a lot of times, they turned out to be true though you couldn't see it until later. About two weeks before she left, she told me she dreamed again of your grandmother, but this time, Arlene and your grandfather and all of these people from Sydney's life who had died were hugging her and saying Welcome."

For a moment, Abby felt all of it. She felt the deaths of Sydney and

Sebastian, the strange undulating powers coursing through her like an electric current, the fear and awe of the woman beside her, the knowledge that Sydney was not alone and so neither would be Sebastian. For him on the other side, were Claire and his parents and untold other loves that she had never learned about in her short span of time with him. She felt fully how unfair it was and yet how, as Elda said, beautifully orchestrated.

"Tell me about the curse."

****

Oliver stood in the doorway of Lydie's room, unable to walk in. The room's enormous bay window let in a flood of sunlight that washed everything in color and made Lydie's room look too happy and sparkly to be real. His eyes scanned the books and stuffed animals tossed on the window seat and the yellow beanbag chair with the dents of her body still pressed into the surface. Her bed was unmade with the turquoise gem bedspread shoved halfway down and her fuzzy big foot slippers on her pillow as if she slept with her feet at the top of the bed.

A soft mewling came from Lydie's closet. He strode across the room and got down on his knees, pushing aside clothes and old discarded books. In the back of the closet, Lydie's new kitten, Garfield, peeked out from Lydie's old doll house, a toy that Max had laboriously carved for Lydie's seventh birthday. Though she never admitted to playing with the house, everyone in the coven knew that she loved it and now, years later, Oliver could see where her toys had scraped the perfectly sanded wooden floors and her play dough had gotten stuck in the tiny furniture.

"Hi, Garfield," Oliver cooed, pulling the kitten out gently and holding it against his chest.

Faustine entered the room behind him and stood silently.

"I have thrown the Ink of Revealing into the sky and there is a clear path away from here. It is going south and likely fading every minute," he said finally.

Oliver set the kitten down and stood abruptly.

"We should leave at once," Faustine told him.

"I think that I should go alone. Elda and Max are not safe here with Helena in such bad shape. I can find her and bring her back."

Faustine shook his head no, but then Elda came in behind them, her face revealing that Helena had turned for the worse.

"She's slipping away. I can't seem to bring her back." Her face was pinched with worry and Faustine seemed to come to a decision.

"Fine then, go now, but you must keep contact. There are fresh medallions in the library--take two of them. Place one around your neck, close to your heart. I should be able to feel you that way."

Oliver left quickly, grabbing the medallions and racing out to the dock where Faustine's small Boston Whaler sat ready. Overhead he could see streaks of silver in the sky. The silver illuminated the dark energy that had entered the castle and then escaped back across the water.

****

"The curse began more than two hundred years ago, maybe longer. We know of only two hundred years and not all that much about those. What we think is that approximately every one hundred years a new witch somehow triggers this curse. What we know about the last time is only that there was a loose coven of young witches in Trager in nineteen hundred and eight. Aubrey was one of them and there were probably five or more others. We've struggled to track them all. One witch, her name was Dafne, drew the curse. She had a human lover called Tobias and you may have heard of him because he is now a Vepar."

"What did you just say?" Abby asked stunned. "Tobias was Dafne's lover?"

"You know him then? And her too? We thought she may have died in the fire..."

Abby placed her palms together, as if in prayer, and held them to her lips. She suddenly feared for Oliver and the others at Ula.

"She did not die. But please tell me all of it. I need to know everything that you know."

"I'm not sure where the curse came from or even how we know about it exactly. Dafne and this Tobias meant to run away together, but instead he used his connection with Dafne to become a very powerful Vepar. In order to make this transition, he had to harness the power of many witches, which meant they had to die. We all thought Dafne probably had to die too, but now you're saying she's alive so I guess we didn't understand that part. Somehow Tobias burned all of them in the Ebony Woods. What we know is that this also happened in eighteen hundred and eight in Trager to a witch named Milda."

Milda? The name rang familiar and Abby frowned trying to remember. Had she met a Milda at All Hallow's? No - where then? It came to her slowly and with horror. Elda had been sitting in the library describing the sad tale of a witch seduced by black magic only after being deceived by her human lover, The Lourdes of Warning.

"You know of her too?" Gwen asked.

"Worse," Abby mumbled, trembling at the memory of the wasted body in her self-made prison beneath the earth.

"This doesn't apply to me," Abby said suddenly. "My...person, my lover-- he died."

The color drained from Gwen's face.

"Not Sebastian? Sebastian died?"

Abby closed her eyes at the sound of his name and nodded.

"Yes."

Gwen hung her head.

"I can't believe it. I don't want to."

"You knew him?" Abby asked.

"Only through Sydney." She looked far away suddenly, remembering. "I spent a lifetime hearing stories about him and his sister from Sydney, looking at pictures. The way his family died and then Claire. Oh, it's wrong how much heartache can be visited upon one life."

A horn startled them and Abby looked up as a large hay truck passed dangerously close to the car. The driver's face glowered at them and then he disappeared in a puff of exhaust. Gwen jumped and then laughed, embarrassed.

"I get spooked pretty easy these days," she said.

"Yeah, me too," Abby replied, turning the car back on and pulling onto the road.

"So who knows about this curse? The Vepars? Do they know? Does Tobias know?"

Gwen glanced nervously out the window and shook her head.

"I don't know. I wish Stephen were here. He was better at this. He took it really seriously like Sydney. I'm just...I'm just a part of it. I never really meant to be, but I am, and Stephen's been investigating disappearances for the last three months. At least ten, but maybe more people who have just vanished. Some of them were wanderers, vagrants, and so they mostly went unnoticed, but a few had families, husbands, wives, kids. Stephen was onto a lot that I didn't know about."

"We went to Stephen's, my friend and I, and it looked like he left. It didn't look like someone took him," Abby said, trying to soothe Gwen.

"Did Stephen say he thought the Vepars were behind the missing people?"

"Yes. I mean he didn't say that, but yes. He wouldn't have made a point of calling to tell me about it otherwise. He also thought that someone was following him. This all happened within weeks of Devin's murder. Everything got really bizarre and scary."

"Had it ever been scary before? Did you ever suspect that the Vepars knew of the Asemaa?"

"No. Even after I met Adora and knew that all of the stories were true, I still felt removed from it. If I'd have thought that we were in real danger, I would have stepped away from it for my child's sake. I would never knowingly put Ebony at risk and now..." Gwen stammered and reached unconsciously for the small gold rose around her neck, "...now I'm afraid

I've done exactly that."

"But she's safe right now?"

"Yes, no, I think so. I'm scared Abby. I'm so scared that I haven't even really thought about how scared I am. When you found me in that crawl-space today, I'd been down there since last night. I slept down there. I just felt sure something would take me in the night."

Abby took Gwen's hand and allowed a rush of gratitude to flow into her.

"You're not alone, okay? I'm a witch and I have friends and we won't let anything happen to you or to Ebony." Abby grew stronger from her own words and, deep down, she believed them. She would get the others from the coven and she would stop blaming them for Sebastian and for Sydney and they would end this thing. Tobias would not steal anyone else that she loved and as for Dafne--Elda and Faustine would know how to deal with her.

"I want to see your journals," Abby said. "All of it, everything you've got. And I've pored over Sydney's stuff and only found a little bit about the curse. Is there more?"

"Yes, it's in the cottage—the one nearest the woods with the little iron rooster on top? We have a bookshelf in there with a secret compartment behind it. I stashed all of the material in there."

"Clever."

"Not really. I mean, considering secret bookshelves are basically the hiding place in every movie and book nowadays, but the guy who originally built the cottages created a bunch of funny little spots like that."

"I'll find them," Abby reassured her.

"Oh, you don't have to worry about that. I'll show you right where they are."

Abby shook her head no.

"I'm going to take you to a bus station and get you out of town. You're right that it's not safe here. I have to return to Ula, but first I need those journals."

Gwen looked like she might argue and then nodded slowly.

"Okay, but please stay in contact with me? I have to know what's happening and my friends are missing, Abby. I can't just let that go. For Ebony's sake I'll leave right now, but I'm not abandoning this. The Asemaa began with Sydney and it won't die with her, you understand? I won't let it die."

Abby did understand and she knew in her heart that Sydney would want her to keep the group alive. It had apparently been her life's work and Abby had never known it existed.

****

After the lake, the trail moved south in a nearly straight line. The Vepar must have carried Lydie through the woods rather than driving, which hardly made sense. Vepars could move quickly, but not nearly as fast as a car, and surely he would have tired at some point.

This forced Oliver to abandon his car fifty miles into the trip and travel on foot so as not to lose sight of the trail. He ran as fast as his body allowed, but still he could see the stream beginning to fade. He had run for nearly two hours when the last remnants disappeared from the sky.

He approached a tree and laid his hands on the bark. He pressed his face close trying to catch the Vepar's scent, but found barely a trace. At the base of a very tall birch, he caught the first very subtle smell of something dark. He crawled up the tree and, strangely, found that the scent grew much stronger near the top. It was as if the Vepar had traveled through the trees or, he suddenly realized, above the trees. Somehow it had flown.

He jumped from tree to tree, painstakingly pausing in each one to see which way the scent moved. Twice he jumped to the wrong tree and had to backtrack when he lost the smell. Finally, it moved downward and he followed it to the forest floor. He stood only a few miles outside of Trager City. Somewhere along the way, he heard Faustine speaking to him. His thoughts were muffled, but Oliver understood that Helena had stabilized.

As he followed the Vepar's path, he perceived danger. He knew that he was close and sprang back into the trees to avoid detection while he searched the earth below. He nearly missed the cellar door, so concealed by leaves that it looked merely like another mound, but a small flash of silver caught his eye and he recognized a handle.

He watched it for several minutes, waiting to see if any of the vile things emerged, but the door stayed closed. Finally he crawled down and, treading softly, walked toward the door. He pressed his ear to the earth and listened.

Chapter 29

Sebastian went to the bus terminal near the airport with his last twenty-five dollars. The next bus wouldn't arrive for seventeen minutes. He sat down to wait, munching a bag of pretzels he'd bought from the vending machine.

He watched the terminal doors and studied the faces of every person who walked through them. He wore a hooded sweatshirt that he had dug out of an airport 'lost and found' to conceal his hair and face. He knew that Abby was in Trager. He felt her more strongly with each passing second, but he didn't know where.

The doors opened and, with a gust of cold air, a petite woman with short golden hair blew into the terminal. She looked frazzled and upset, clutching only a handful of cash in her hand as she made her way to the ticket counter. She paid, took her ticket and then turned to the row of seats, her eyes lighting for a moment on Sebastian before she turned away, but then slowly she turned back and stared.

Sebastian broke the stare, tucked his hood lower over his face and started to get up, but already the woman began to approach him. Before he could escape through the door, she grabbed his sleeve and turned him towards her.

"Sebastian?" she asked, and he wondered suddenly if maybe all of his memory had not returned because he did not recognize this woman who spoke to him.

He started to shake his head no, but as he looked into her eyes, he felt her pain and also a deep need to know that yes, he was Sebastian.

He nodded.

"Oh, my God, you're alive! Abby told me you died, she thinks that you are dead," the words poured out of her and she looked like she might begin to cry.

"You've seen Abby? Where is she?" he asked her urgently.

The woman looked around anxiously and then she looked back into his eyes and stared at him for a long time.

Seemingly satisfied, she said "Abby has gone to the stone cottages by the lake. I should have gone with her, I'm sorry."

"Wait, what cottages?"

"The circle of stone cottages past the woods north of Sydney's house."

Sebastian vaguely recalled them. He immediately turned to leave and then remembered his bus ticket.

"I'm sorry to ask this, but I have to get to Abby and I'm out of money. I need you to help me."

"Here," the woman thrust most of her money into his hands. "Yes, go now," she said anxiously , and threw her arms around him, hugging him tight. "I'm so happy that you're alive."

He didn't wait to hear more. He rushed from the bus station and ran across the parking lot to a grubby little car rental agency that boasted rentals as low as ten dollars a day. Without a credit card, Sebastian had to pay the kid at the desk nearly two-hundred dollars to take the rustiest car on the lot. He squealed out of the parking lot, trying to outrun the sense of doom growing within him.

****

Oliver opened the door easily, knowing that leaving it unlatched may not have been an accident, and stared into the black hole below him. Vepars lived in squalor. They played at a certain sleek humanness in the above-ground world, but in their lairs they resided in filth. The walls on either side of the tunnel were dirt, but wet-looking and slimy to the touch. Before entering, he'd sprayed one of Helena's scent neutralizers over his entire body. Vepars did not always smell witches, but the more powerful ones had the capacity and, in their dungeons, they were much more likely to catch the scent.

The floor moved downward steeply and then leveled off. The walls became smooth and small oil lamps lit the tunnel. The silence grew thick and unease began to set in. Oliver did not spook easily and, beneath the earth, literally embedded in his element, he could not have been stronger, but still he knew a trap and he was walking right into one.

****

Abby used Gwen's key to open the door to the cottage with the rooster on top. The musty odor of mothballs greeted her and she saw a light film of dust on nearly every surface. She maneuvered around piles of furniture and boxes stacked with tattered books and ancient-looking picture frames.

Gwen had told her that they used the cottage for storage, which was why she had chosen to hide the journals there. In the sea of stuff, most people

would quickly give up and look elsewhere. Abby found the built-in book
shelf. She knelt on the floor and sought the small lever Gwen had
described. The simple metal hook jutted from beneath a rug and Abby
pulled up on it hard, jumping out of the way as the shelf swung out. The
bookshelf lurched into a stack of lawn chairs and they crashed to the
ground, startling Abby and dislodging several books.

"Relax," she whispered and took a couple of deep breaths. The space
behind the door was roughly the size of a broom closet and, stacked within
it, from floor to ceiling, were journals, binders and accordion files. She
grabbed a stack and walked them to the trunk of her car, carefully closing it
between each trip and returning the key to her pocket.

Halfway through the pile, she caught a shift in the air around her. Her
senses sharpened. Every sound and movement grew distinct and separate.
The water lapped the shore, washing over each tiny grain of sand, and she
heard it all with acute clarity. In the woods, not far away, something rustled.
She breathed deeply and tried to get a sense of the thing. An animal? Not
exactly, but not human either.

All at once her skin began to crawl and her pulse quickened. She wanted
to run to the water, but even as she thought it, she detected something
beneath the surface, some darkness that lay in wait for her.

She slammed her trunk and ran to the woods, hoping to escape into a
tree, but found the trees bare of their leaves and hardly a good hiding place.
In her terror, she discovered that, despite her sharpened faculties, the world
seemed distant as though she watched the scene unfold on a movie screen
instead of in real time. Her eyes scanned gnarly branches and heavy stones,
searching for a suitable weapon.

Abby started to run and in her mind's eye she saw the thing sense her
movement and begin to follow. She fled, moving fast, faster than ever
before, but still it gained on her. She could not see it or hear it. It seemed to
come from everywhere. She ran into a bush and screamed, pushing the
branches away, hurling her body through and into another space only to
again run full-faced into a sharp bush of thorns. They caught and held her
and she fought them, furious and terrified and crying now. She ripped out
of her jacket and the thorns released her. She ran into a field. It lay empty
and enormous and she hated to run across it and expose herself, but the
thing behind her still bore down. Halfway across, she struck a log hidden in
the high dead grass and toppled over it. She swore and struggled to her feet.

It seemed to fall from the sky, the black oily monster with fangs barred.
It landed on Abby's back and, before she could fling her body to the side,
its long fingernails sank deep into her shoulder, warm blood spurting from
the wounds as its teeth sought her neck. She reached back and found its
hair and, with all her strength, tried to rip the creature from her, but already
her power had begun to drain as the teeth broke through the skin and the

venom found her blood, racing like wildfire to her heart and her brain. She started to collapse beneath the weight of it and then the heaviness vanished, lifted from her by some unseen force.

She fell, first to her knees as her legs buckled beneath her. She made a feeble attempt at throwing her hands out to break her fall, but none of her limbs obeyed and she hit the cold ground with a thud and felt her head snap to the side.

When she saw him, she knew that she dreamed or had died because Sebastian could not be beating the evil thing that had fallen upon her. In the pale light of the moon, she watched him lower blow after blow upon the black figure at his feet. The creature suddenly reared back and Abby thought it would envelop Sebastian in its huge hair wings. Instead it took to the sky, rising up and away before Sebastian strike it again.

She opened her mouth to call to him, but made no sound. She closed her eyes and thanked the Gods for a final glimpse of her love, knowing in some broken part of her that he was merely an illusion and, if she ever woke up, she would be alone again.

****

Lydie sat cross-legged on a pile of dirty pillows and blankets streaked with blood. She held a rough-looking gray puppy in her lap. The dog whined fearfully when Oliver entered the room.

"Lydie!" He ran to her, reaching down to scoop her up, but the puppy snarled and bit viciously at his outstretched hand. She looked up at him with glassy eyes and frowned.

"You shouldn't be here, Oliver."

Oliver? She never called him Oliver.

"Lydie, I'm here to spring you, hon. You've got to put the puppy down."

It didn't look like a puppy anymore with yellowed bloodshot eyes and a jaw hanging slack, but ready to spring closed at any moment.

She shut her eyes tight and shook her head no.

"They're coming back today. I can't leave until they come back."

"Who's coming back, sweetie," he asked, trying to keep the alarm from his voice. She looked catatonic. He inched a little closer to her, with every intention of snatching her and racing from the room the moment he could get within arm's reach. His ears were perked for any sound, but again, maddeningly, only silence greeted him, and every part of him knew that he'd walked into a trap and that Lydie, sitting alone in the room, was bait.

Lydie ran her mostly limp hand over the dog's matted hair and rocked slightly back and forth.

Oliver took another step.

"Who's coming back, Lyds?"

She looked at him as if she'd forgotten he was there.

"Mom and Dad." She gazed into the dirt wall as if she could see something beyond and a small smile lit her face. "Coming back today." She sang it and Oliver hated the sound, wanting to clamp his hands over his ears because Lydie sounded insane. He feared that if he spent another second in the room with the snarling dog and the bloody sheets he would go insane too.

Finally, close enough, he reached for her. As his hand brushed the sleeve of her soiled jacket, the dog clamped its teeth onto Oliver's wrist. He muffled his yell and went to jerk his arm away, but the jaws sunk deeper into his flesh and the venom burned as it oozed into his bloodstream. Impossibly, the dog started to thrash and convulse. Its face grew a long snout that warped into a gargoyle-like head with tiny black eyes and a gaping mouth. The dog's spine twisted and popped and wings flapped out for an instant before they were sucked back in, and the skin of the thing ripped open and a larger being started to emerge, all the while holding Oliver's broken and bleeding arm in its mouth. Oliver had dropped to his knees and wanted to beat at the thing's head, but his whole body began to lose strength and his other arm felt like an anvil resting on the ground. The face now looking back at him belonged to Tobias. Black eyes grew larger and white skin streaked with blood as the carcass of the animal fell away from the Vepar's body.

Tobias released Oliver's arm and smiled, moving to a squat beside Lydie who looked at the dog's corpse with the same dazed expression she had offered to Oliver.

Oliver fell onto his back, his arm gushing while black spots dotted his vision. His head struck the earth, but his body no longer seemed solid. Instead, he fell into a bottomless black pit. As he plummeted, Tobias and Lydie and the scene in the room grew further and further away until they vanished completely.

Chapter 30

"Sebastian." His name barely sounded from her parched lips. His beautiful perfect face peered down at her, but her visits with the dead had made even her great love suspect as he leaned over her.

"You're nearly healed beautiful, " Sebastian told Abby as she began to come to. He sat in a chair pulled to the edge of the bed, his hands clutching one of hers as it lay mostly lifeless on the sheet.

She wiggled her fingers and gazed at the room. They appeared to be in a tiny cabin.

"How are you alive?" She took her hand from his and reached to touch his face. She rubbed her thumb across his prickly chin and then over his soft lips, all the while staring incredulously into his achingly familiar blue eyes.

"I am. Right now that's the only thing that you have to know. I'm alive and I've been dying every day that we've been apart."

She nodded and, leaning in, he kissed her mouth and then her wet cheeks, pulling her head into his shoulder.

"Where are we?"

"The Chateau," he whispered, nuzzling his face into the palm of her hand. "My dad brought me here when I was a kid, although back then this place was filled with bunk beds, card tables and an old wood-burning stove. I guess the owner's remodeled."

Abby glanced around the room. It was sparsely finished, but tasteful. A tiny alcove held a sink and mini refrigerator, but otherwise the bed and two wing-back chairs were the only furnishings. A single painting of a Lake Michigan sunset hung over the fireplace where Sebastian had built a crackling fire.

"There's so much that we have to talk about. So many questions that I have, and that you have. I can already feel them dying to get out, but let's save that for tomorrow? Okay? Let's just be together tonight because I swear it feels like it's been an eternity..."

She smiled and pressed one of his hands against her cheek. It felt too good to be true. In the weeks since his death, she'd slowly assembled a wall around her grief and encapsulated it in a tiny dark room. In that room lived the impossibility of him ever holding her like this again, but he was, and she could barely stop from biting and clawing and mashing against every piece of him just to prove that he was not a figment of her mind.

He tilted her face up and crushed his mouth against her. They were not careful as they pulled her shirt over her head, ignoring the bandage that covered her left shoulder. She didn't even grimace at the flash of pain, but instead relished it as she tugged at his pants, which he kicked off with a grin before burying his face in her neck. She pushed the blankets away and ripped open his ugly Hawaiian shirt, laughing as the buttons skidded across the floor.

She reached for him and guided him inside her, letting out a sob of pain and pleasure.

"I love you," he whispered.

****

"We have to leave this place," Faustine told Elda and his gaunt face frightened her.

Elda looked at Helena who slept peacefully, the strong medicine stealing her away from even her nightmares.

"How can we?" she asked, helplessly.

"We'll call to Sorciére. It has only been twenty-two days. The doorway can be opened for thirty days after All-Hallows. They will do it for us."

Elda nodded, but looked again, fearfully, at Helena. The doorway took a great deal of strength to pass through and witches could be lost in the space between. Helena could die.

"I will carry her through myself," Faustine said.

****

Abby lay in bed, frozen as she'd done in childhood when some unknown terror pulled her from sleep and left her paralyzed, straining to hear the tiniest sound which might betray some evil lurking close by. She wrapped her arms across her chest so tightly that she could barely breathe and then Sebastian moved next to her. The fingers of his right hand fluttered against her thigh as he shifted in sleep and she nearly screamed at the sensation. The black writhing monster whose eyes had locked onto hers for only a moment rose up in her mind and then faded away.

As her eyes adjusted to the room and her mind remembered the man that she loved lay beside her, the beating of her heart slowed and cooled. Watching the gentle rise and fall of his naked chest soothed her.

Somewhere far away a bird cried out, but otherwise the night lay silent. The room felt thick and hot and she struggled from beneath the heavy feather comforter and sat on the edge of the bed, her feet dangling above the wooden floor. A fire still glowed in the stone fireplace, mostly dying embers and, for a brief hysterical moment, she wanted to douse it in water and suffocate the heat pouring forth. Instead, she stumbled into her tennis shoes and, wearing only Sebastian's Hawaiian shirt, crept out of the cabin and stood on the porch. The cool night stole away the last of her sleepy confusion and chilled her instantly.

Overhead the black sky held the tiny pinpricks of a billion stars, but she could barely see them. The stars always seemed to slip further and further into the cosmos as summer gave way to fall and then to winter. Her breath blew a white halo and she took huge gulps of air, but could not seem to satisfy her body's longing for a deeper, fuller breath. She pressed her hands against the porch rail and stared hard into the night, trying with all her power to grasp that Sebastian had not died. He did not rot somewhere in an unmarked grave, ravaged by their shared enemy. Still, she could not shake the terrifying gloom that held her captive in its dark palm. It was if an enormous evil had taken hold of their lives and set into motion events that she could not hope to stop.

She left the porch and walked into the woods, shivering, but needing the cold to soothe her achy body and clear her tired mind. She thought of Oliver and hoped desperately that he lay safe in his bed at Ula having prepared the coven for what surely lay ahead. He would be so happy that Sebastian lived, but would he also be tormented? Abby knew that Oliver's feelings for her moved beyond friendship and she too had felt the stirrings of such things, but none of that seemed real in comparison to her Sebastian.

"I vow to protect him," she said to the silent night. "I will never lose him again."

Through the skeletal trees, she could see the luminescent moon. She jumped onto a low tree branch and crawled all the way to the top, nesting in the crook of a large branch. The bark scraped her bare legs, but she leaned her head against the tree and let her mind wander.

A thousand questions plagued her. Where had he been since All Hallow's Eve? Had the Vepars held him captive and he somehow escaped? Were they, at that very moment, hunting them both? She decided that she would wake him as soon as she returned and they would talk about everything.

When his scream pierced the otherwise quiet night, she nearly fell from the tree. Instead, without a thought, she swung down three branches and then dropped straight to the earth twenty feet below. She landed and ran.

The door to the cabin hung from its hinges. She raced through the doorway, not caring about the danger within. The comforter lay on the floor and the sheets were smeared with mud and several dots of blood.

"Sebastian!" She screamed his name and tore the room apart, but he was gone. She ran back onto the porch and, like before, the monster fell from the sky. It dove at her and reached with taloned claws as if might grab her and carry her away, but she fell back and its claws caught her stomach, ripping through her shirt and into her flesh.

She grabbed for anything and her hand found a ceramic pelican that decorated the front porch. She brought the pelican onto the creature's head. Blood splattered across her face, but the thing swooped away and soared into the night sky.

Abby did not wait. She ran for the forest.

****

The mirror, still concealed behind the heavy velvet draperies, glinted as if cleaned that very day. Its surface swooned in the firelight and Elda kissed Helena gently on the forehead as Faustine cradled her in his arms. He took a deep a breath and fell through the surface of the glass.

Elda pulled a stool in front of the fire and sat, gazing steadily into the lapping flames and praying for their safe passage. Max stood at the window, watching and waiting.

When Faustine returned, he brought three additional witches from Sorciére with him. They stumbled into the room, all disoriented from the gateway, and alert for danger.

Elda knew the three witches, though none of them well. She had not known if Faustine would be successful in bringing help. Though the family of witches knew no boundaries, covens rarely involved themselves deeply in the affairs of others. The fates aligned each witches' life accordingly. To muddle in the life of another might change that witch's destiny.

"Elda." The oldest witch, Galla, crossed the room and clasped Elda's hands tightly in her own. "Our Indra has disappeared as well."

"Indra?" Elda spoke her name and then remembered the volatile Sorciére witch who'd grown so close to Dafne. "They are together then?" Elda wondered aloud.

"There was a human witness. Isabelle," the Sorciére witch Thomas interrupted. "She said that Dafne and Indra were at her home. They left in search of the human called Sebastian. The last this Isabelle saw them, they were walking into a café and a tall very pale man with dark eyes seemed to be following them in."

Elda frowned.

"Not Tobias? How could he follow them to France? How could they not sense him?"

"And why on earth were they looking for Sebastian?" Faustine asked.

"Without telling us first?" But Faustine's questions were rhetorical. Elda knew that Faustine did not want to reveal their knowledge of Dafne's deception.

"We must go to the place that Faustine lost Oliver," Galla said. "Though I fear that our fate may already be sealed."

"There are many fates," Faustine replied, unwilling to accept powerlessness.

"Did you know that Indra was hiding something?" Elda asked her.

Galla keenly sensed falseness in witches, but she shook her head no.

"We thought it was All Hallow's, and Indra is always so distant we barely gave it a thought. My first sense happened when Sebastian disappeared. I saw him for a moment very clearly in her mind and then felt her cover the thought. I brushed it off..."

"We all did," the third witch, Demetrius, added. He wore his customary tweed blazer and brown slacks. He clearly had not intended for the day's venture. "It's very clever of them, I think, to put on this craftiness during All Hallow's."

"Treachery is what it is," Thomas snapped, his face growing red.

Galla put her hand on his arm.

"I ignored it in Dafne," Faustine said, bowing his head slightly. "I still cannot condemn her, not without knowing..."

"What is there to know?" Thomas retorted. "Can there ever be a story good enough? A reason valid enough to lie and deceive her own coven? To break the most sacred bond of trust?"

Elda knew that Faustine felt as passionately as Thomas did, but she also knew that he loved Dafne. The bonds that held the coven together were not merely an issue of trust, but mutual love and respect. Faustine never turned against his own, never.

"I think we must move from this place," Galla said. "I feel what came in here, the darkness is still heavy on this castle. And your spells have fallen short. They are not protecting us."

"Should we try to strengthen them?" Elda asked. "Might we create a secure space again?"

Galla looked at Elda with sympathy.

"Dafne compromised your coven, dear, she broke the spells down first. We cannot override something that began from within..."

Elda nodded, trying to hide the hurt from the prying thoughts of the witches around her. She knew they felt it though.

****

Abby stopped at the water's edge. The moon reflected a pale halo in the dark blue surface. She knew that the creature stalked her and would soon come into the lake opening and see her there, vulnerable and nearing death. The warmth in her hand spread out away from her torn stomach and each breath grew harder to take in. She could feel the softness of her insides spilling against her shirt which terrified her, but each time her mind tried to grab hold of the image of organs falling from her ripped body, she chased them away and focused instead on her breath.

Remembering a spell from the Astral Coven's Book of Shadows, she started to whisper the incantation as she recalled it. Knowing that her words were imperfect, but the power of the water would help her, she dropped to her knees in the wet sand. Gradually, the few clouds in the sky began to shift, guided by a soft, cold breeze. Abby felt the sting of air against her hot skin. Slowly the lake grew dark and the moon was all but hidden behind the accumulating clouds of gray. She then shifted her focus to the waters itself, envisioning the hardening of the surface. Her strength had begun to abandon her so that the singular focus Elda had been so insistent she find in previous lessons, kept getting lost in the feverish dreams of a slipping mind. She crawled closer to the water until it lapped her knees and shins. Only then did she start to see it wobble and take form. It was barely solid when she began to crawl across it. The surface dipped and undulated beneath her as she squirmed. Slowly she found the center of the lake and collapsed upon it. She lay very still because, in the woods behind her, she heard the winged monster crashing through branches knowing that it had mortally wounded her and did not need to conceal itself.

The water held her and she cloaked herself the way that Oliver had taught her. She imagined that she became the water. Every piece of her body took on the misty blue that surrounded her.

It searched for hours, flying back and forth overhead, swooping close to the water and in and out of the forest. It had begun to make garbled cries that sometimes sounded like a whimpering dog and other times more human. All the while, she felt the blood leaking out of her body and dissipating into the water around her. She thought that she might die at any moment, and thought worse that Sebastian might already have died and, in the stark night, relived his death again and cried soundlessly for the unfairness of the world. After a while, she wished for death, but it did not come and nor could she sleep because if she broke her concentration, the water would become liquid and she had no strength to swim. Eventually the creature went away and, unable to turn over, she pulled herself to the shore using her elbows and scooting her feet. She did not make it, but lost consciousness and the water swallowed her whole.

Chapter 31

"How many are missing?" Galla asked.

"Four. Abby left first. Dafne disappeared two days ago. At first we didn't even realize she'd gone as she often avoids breakfast and has been keeping to herself lately. At dinner, her absence was noticed and, when we went in search of her, one of the row boats was missing as were some of her things. Oliver left to find Abby more than a week ago, but came back today when he dreamed of Lydie. Lydie was taken this morning when Helena was attacked."

Galla looked grim.

Outside a raven soared through the early morning sky. Elda looked around the library at the towering shelves and the thick oriental rugs and wondered why everything around her felt so old and near to death.

She felt Galla's inquisitive eyes and she let her mind fall open, for an instant, to the secret dread that lived inside her. Galla gave her a small nod of understanding and then returned to Thomas who had begun to rattle off a plan of action.

Galla interrupted him. "Before we leave, gather an item from each of the four. It should be something very personal otherwise I will be unable to get a read."

"I will go to Lydie and Oliver's rooms," Faustine said. "You can secure items for Abby and Dafne."

"And Sebastian," Galla added. "I want to try to understand what happened to him..."

"Of course." Elda and Faustine left the three witches in the library.

****

They traveled by boat to the small coastal city where Ula housed their cars and other affects. At the warehouse they chose two separate vehicles. Elda also went quickly to the upper level and saw Dafne's secured trunks lying open with items strewn about the floor. She snatched up a small copper ring and dropped it in her pocket.

Galla was an air element and wanted a peak or a cliff to catch the mid-day breeze. They parked the two cars at the base of a rocky outcrop and the six of them climbed to the top. They sat together in a circle, their jackets whipping roughly back and forth. Elda's long hair splayed out behind her and she closed her eyes against the chill, inviting the sweet freedom that called to her.

Galla took Lydie's tattered baby blanket in her hands. The yellow fabric had faded and worn bald in spots. Elda could still see the ghostly images of once bright orange and purple ducks, now mostly edges of feet and beaks. She leaned her head on Faustine's shoulder and remembered how good it felt to be comforted by someone that she loved.

Galla closed her eyes. Her hands clutched the blanket and her mouth turned down, but she made no sounds at all. When she finally opened her eyes, they looked troubled.

"Tormented child," she said. "Images of a sand dune, an old dilapidated house, her house as a child maybe, a strange tree, a willow, but bright red in color, a dark soul there with your witch Dafne, talk of a curse. Who took Lydie? A Vepar, yes and no, a mutant, human in it and an animal..."

They all listened closely. Galla did not receive a story when she read the energy of another being, but instead bits of images, words and feelings, which together they would attempt to make sense of.

"Lydie's childhood home, I'd imagine. It was near the base of a sand dune in the woods. It is quite fallen now and she hasn't been there since she was very young," Faustine said.

"I'm sure she has gone recently," Galla replied, staring at the blanket. "But maybe not in her body. In her astral body, I think. Yes, I'm sure."

"She can't travel in her astral body," Elda told them, but knew in that moment that she was wrong.

"She can and she hid it from you. I feel the cloak of secrecy now," Galla continued.

"A red willow? Are you sure?" Faustine asked, concerned.

Galla nodded.

"The Lourdes of Warning," Elda completed his thought.

"Why would she astral travel there? And how?" Max asked, clearly upset. As Lydie's teacher, he felt responsible for the young witch.

"Called, I would imagine," Thomas replied. "The astral body is easily guided, especially when something is amiss. I have been called to strange places in my astral journeys. Places filled with purpose if I could only see them correctly."

"Why didn't she tell us?" Max looked toward the ground as if an answer might be found there.

"You said the person that took Lydie was part human or animal? What does that mean?" Faustine asked Galla, shifting the discussion.

Galla stared at the distant clouds. They moved quickly across the light sky.

"I didn't see it, I felt it and it felt...different. Not like a Vepar..." She held her hands up in frustration. "I don't know."

"Go on." Faustine handed her a soft leather bracelet of Oliver's. Helena had made it for him not long after he arrived at Ula.

Galla took it and closed her eyes. Her features softened and she did not drift for long.

"Oliver has been with Abby on some kind of search." She smiled. "I think that he loves Abby. They seemed to be discovering something big, perhaps. Yes, there are other witches, young ones like themselves. I feel him going down into the earth, but then all is lost for me."

She shook the images away and held her hand out for the next item. She rarely got more than a fleeting idea of what went on in the individual's life over the previous days or possibly weeks if she could make a really strong connection. The wind did not seem to be boosting her power a great deal.

"It's Abby's hair," Elda said handing her a small satchel with an inch of Abby's hair tied with a purple string. "Helena cut a piece for the ritual in the Circle, but it never came to pass."

None of the other witches spoke, but Elda suspected that they disapproved of a witch living in the coven who had not spoken the vows.

Galla took the hair from the satchel and the color drained from her face. She swayed from side to side. A tear fell from her tightly-closed eyes and, when she returned to her body, she looked dazed.

"Abby is near death." Galla started to fall to the side and Thomas steadied her. She pulled heavily on his arm and stood. "Something attacked her in the night, she and Sebastian both. He lives! I can find her."

Before they could protest or ask for more, she began to fumble her way down the rocks, leaning heavily on Thomas as if the visions had depleted her.

"Sebastian is alive? You saw him?"

"Yes, or he was alive, but something terrible has happened. Blood and Abby," Galla clutched at her stomach.

Elda knew that Galla could feel Abby's injury and grew cold wondering if they might find her dead.

"Tell us what you saw, Galla?" Faustine asked urgently.

Galla mumbled and started to fall to one knee.

"It's the hair. Take the bloody hair out of her hand," Thomas growled.

Faustine jerked the hair away and Galla shut her eyes. When she opened them, she had regained some of her composure

"It attacked them in the night, but Abby was not in the bed. She found the bed empty and bloody," Galla's eyes were far away again. "It's like a bird, it ripped her open. She is nearing death."

When they reached the cars, Galla held up a hand to stop them.

"Faustine, you must take Demetrius and Max and go to Oliver. It is unsafe to go into the lair because they trapped him, I am sure of it. But you must go and watch the hole. He is alive and they are saving him and Lydie both for something, which is why they must not know we are near because they will do something extreme. We will go to Abby." She gestured to Elda and Thomas. "Be vigilant. This thing is new, and it will not be predictable."

Thomas drove and Galla tried to tell them more, but already the images had lost their potency and she struggled to describe the feelings that overpowered her.

"First grief," Galla told them. "Her heart so broken and then he was there. Sebastian lived. But then I saw her coming into the room and the comforter on the floor streaked with blood and the sheets and when she emerged from this cabin... yes, it was a cabin..." she said slowly, thinking, "...it fell upon her and it tore at her." She groaned as if she still could feel the pain.

"But she's alive, you're sure she's alive?" Elda asked.

Galla did not answer right away.

"I believe that she was still alive five minutes ago when I held her hair."

****

Galla directed them to a secluded stretch of woods almost seventy miles north of Trager. Why Abby and Sebastian had chosen that location, no one knew but, as they turned onto a two-track road and began to bounce over roots and rocks, Elda grew concerned. When they finally stopped in front of a tidy log cabin, a rusted Buick parked near the shed, Elda almost jumped out of the car.

She walked to the steps and saw a pool of blood beginning to dry. The blood dotted the dried grass and disappeared into the trees. She followed it, without waiting. It was too much blood. That was the first thing that she knew without a doubt. A person died when they lost that much blood.

They found Abby, floating face up, in the glassy lake. Her hair fanned out from her face in a dark halo and the angelic, waxen smoothness of her skin made Elda's breath catch in her throat. She splashed into the water, barely registering the icy shock. Before she could grasp Abby's broken body and pull her to the shore, Thomas's voice rang out.

"Wait. Look at her stomach, Elda!" he cried.

Elda did, and reeled away in horror at the twelve inch gash running horizontally across Abby's mid-section. Her shirt had been ripped open as had her skin and, it seemed, the organs beneath her skin. Elda saw the raw inflamed edges of Abby's intestines. Her body no longer hemorrhaged blood as it surely had when the wound was first created, but that only made Elda more terrified.

She stood, cemented to the marshy lake floor, until Thomas strode into the water beside her.

"Lay hands upon her," Elda implored him, knowing that he, a gifted-healer, might have the power to save the young witch.

Thomas placed his hands on each of Abby's temples.

"She's in there," he said. "She's alive."

With Thomas's words, Elda found the energy to move.

"We can't keep her here," Galla said, surveying the small cabin that Sebastian had been abducted from. The air felt electric with the violence of the previous night and all three elder witches shifted uncomfortably, their eyes darting into the trees around them.

Elda, flustered, tried to think of safe havens and grew embarrassed at their lack of connections on the shore. It served as yet another reminder of how disengaged Ula had become from the living world.

Thomas had tucked Abby carefully into the back seat after suturing her belly closed with a crude thread and needle they had found in the cabin's little bathroom. They had also found a small backpack with Sebastian's things, but seemingly nothing of Abby's except a pair of dirtied jeans hanging over the shower and a ripped, bloody sweatshirt. Galla had touched these items and retrieved fragments of Abby's first attack the day before.

"There is Lydie's home," Elda said, hesitating. "From your vision, Galla. Her mother was a great witch, an herbalist. The plants around the cottage are surely still teeming with useful remedies."

"How far?" Thomas asked, knowing that they needed to begin healing Abby soon or she would be dead by nightfall.

"It's near Trager City in the Sleeping Bear Forest. I think half an hour from here."

"Let's go."

****

"I am at fault," Julian sighed, maneuvering into the left lane and passing a slow-moving semi.

They had realized, after more than an hour, that Sebastian had never returned from 'checking out the pool.' Rod claimed ignorance and Adora would have been reluctant to believe him except that she knew he wanted to leave as badly as Sebastian, not to mention Sebastian had taken all of Rod's money. If Rod had known, he would likely have insisted that he join.

"I was thinking aloud to myself before we left France and he heard me. He must have feared for her life."

"Well, now he's put us all in jeopardy," Adora said, trying to keep her hands steady in her lap, but unable to stop their shaking.

She knew how to appear calm in every circumstance, but her steely resolve grew more tenuous every minute. Once upon a time, curses did not exist. Of course, Adora had been a witch too long to suffer in such blissful ignorance. As she and Julian uncovered bits of evidence, her unease had doubled and then tripled. She wanted to believe that it did not exist and that they would find Sebastian anxiously rowing his way to Ula, but unable to break through the coven's barriers.

Julian cocked his head to the side and then slowed the car, exiting the freeway.

"I need you to drive, Adora," he told her.

They changed seats and Julian took a moment to dig a bag of crystals from his small leather suitcase. He held them in his lap and closed his eyes.

"I have just had the most vivid image of Faustine come into my sight," he whispered, mostly talking to himself. "He needs us..."

Adora returned to the freeway, pushing the car over one hundred miles per hour while simultaneously cloaking the car in a spell of concealment. They were not invisible per se, but merely under the radar.

After several minutes in deep concentration, Julian came back.

"Elda is at the Nook," he said, looking curious.

"The Nook?"

"Yes, Lydie's childhood home. It's been years since I've been there. I'm amazed it's still standing."

****

Sebastian threw up and rolled onto his side on the cold steel floor. He pressed his forehead, on fire, to the metal and tried not to throw up again when his stomach heaved at the smell of the vomit spreading out beside him. Overhead a fan whirred and something sucked and sputtered, like water caught in a hose. He opened his eyes and stared to his right where the shiny floor was marred by the black clawed legs of a table draped in dark sheets.

His head swam with whatever rushed through his veins and his vision grew blurry, focused and then blurry again. The sucking sound tried to draw his eyes up, above the table, but when he shifted his gaze, the world tilted with him and he vomited again. He felt as if he'd just stumbled off the Gravitron, Claire's favorite fair ride when they were children.

He thought of Abby and tried desperately to remember what had transpired after they'd fallen, sweaty and elated, into bed. He knew that one moment his hand rested on the small of her back as she lay beside him, and the next, something dark and foul had taken hold of him and dragged him into the black night. He felt sure that the creature had bitten him and lighted briefly on waves of green leaves flashing by as if they were above the trees, flying.

He planted both palms on the floor and pushed, rolling onto his back with a gasp as pain coursed through his entire body. Bodies hung from every available wall, held in place by thick black straps. Tubes ran from their noses and mouths. Some of their heads were shaved, making their nakedness seem even more complete, and complex helmets, streaming with wires, were fitted to each of their heads. The tubes fed into an enormous metal cylinder that sounded like a washing machine. Sebastian could see a lifeless hand dangling over the edge of the black gurney.

Chapter 32

Abby stumbled through the woods, the snow falling in thick layers and blotting out the world around her. She waded, more than walked, and twice fell forward into the deep drifts, almost wishing that the hard earth would greet her and put an end to the writhing in her belly. It was time. She could feel the wetness spreading out from within her. It saturated her thighs and made the skin raw beneath her fabrics. Her tears froze hard and glass-like in the whipping winds. When she saw the tiny stone cottage, she cried out in relief. The frozen door would not give and she threw her weight against it again and again. Finally it cracked and then inched open. She pushed again and this time it swung into the tiny room, barren except for a pile of hay and dusty wool blankets in one corner.

She slammed the door and dropped to her hands and knees. She crawled to the bed of blankets and fell onto her side as another wave of pain rushed through her abdomen. She felt the hands of a giant clamped tightly on her belly trying to squeeze her empty.

She cried and gasped and fought her damp and frozen clothes from her body. Blood immediately began to seep into the straw. She shuffled onto the blankets, screaming, and biting the glove that she'd pulled from her hand when another storm of contractions coursed through her.

The baby came quickly. She pushed and felt its slippery weight gush into her hands, barely able to reach it, before it slid onto the makeshift bed. She had seen at least a dozen births, but the new mothers were always surrounded by her circle of women. She had no one to help her and no tools to sever the life cord. She raised the baby toward her face and bit the cord, barely acknowledging the stream of hot liquid that rushed out. In her tribe, the liquid would have been preserved and the mother would have consumed it, bringing the power back into her own body, but Kanti spat it out and thrust the cord away from her face.

She stared at the oddly silent infant through exhausted eyes and thought, briefly, that it had died. But then the child, a girl, blinked and let out a feeble mewl. She held the baby to her chest and felt the girl's tiny mouth easily find her breast and attach to the nipple. She laid her head back and drifted away.

* * * *

Abby woke with her hands pressed against her belly expecting to feel the weight of the child from her dreams--but not her dreams, Kanti's dreams.

Slowly, her own life materialized and she blinked the room into focus. Elda's solemn face peered down at her.

Elda clasped one of her hands and held it to her heart.

"Thank you," she whispered, her eyes shifting toward the heavens before her gaze returned to Abby. "Just now you seemed to go away. I thought we had lost you."

Abby didn't speak, but pressed her hands into the bed beneath her and started to sit.

Elda pushed her back down.

"You can't get up, Abby. You were gravely injured."

Abby looked down at the place her hands had been and saw thick gauze layered across her stomach. It was soaked with blood. For a moment she thought that the dream had been real and then she remembered the creature attacking her. Its claws had ripped her open.

"Sebastian?"

"He's not here. We found the cabin, but someone took him Abby. I was hoping that you might be able to help us. We know that he lives and that he was taken from you in the night, but that is all..."

"It wasn't a Vepar," Abby said, surveying the room. They were not at Ula, or anyplace else that Abby recognized. In fact, they seemed to be in an old cottage. Leaves and twigs were brushed against the base of the walls.

"We're in Lydie's childhood home," Elda told her. "Ula has been compromised and we cannot return there."

* * * *

Sebastian took in the faces. Lydie, Oliver, Isabelle and then others that he did not know. People barely shackled, but hanging lifeless to the walls, something being drawn out of them and into the vat in the center. He braced his hands on either side and looked in. The fluid that poured in from the various bodies looked clear and very bright, almost like liquid light, but it did not pool. The metal interior funneled into a small black hole the disappeared into the floor beneath him.

He needed a plan and fast. His body ached, but the nausea had abated. He felt sticky wetness where claws had ripped into his skin and he remembered again the monster that took him. Its wolfish face had leered at him with knowing eyes, familiar eyes. When it bit him, Sebastian felt fire moving through his bloodstream and then the world had faded to black.

He turned slowly, wishing desperately for water to quench his thirst, but hoping at least for a weapon or some means of escape. The large room had only one opening, a small trap door in the ceiling, but no ladder was in sight. He began to move among the bodies, checking for pulses. Everyone was alive, though several people had pulses so weak he wasn't sure he'd felt one at all. He had the feeling that they'd been in the room for days, if not weeks.

He considered unhooking them, but he knew that he operated on borrowed time and at any moment the beast might return. He stared at Oliver hanging limply from the wall, his blond head resting on his chest. If anyone could help him, it was Oliver, and the creatures probably would not notice if a single stream stopped moving into the basin. His ego wanted to do it alone. However, he knew that his humanness made him weak. He had no element to draw on, no storage of ancient wisdom to unlock the mystery surrounding him.

He took the tube moving into Oliver's arm and pulled gently, grimacing at the spurt of blood that poured out when he drew it from his flesh. He removed the tube from his right arm and then went about carefully, slowly, extracting the tiny metal filaments poking into his skull. They were long and copper and each time he removed one, he expected the trap door to fling open and the wolf beast to pounce on him. When he had removed all of the wires, he put his arms beneath Oliver's armpits and lifted him gently from the wall.

Oliver was an earth element and Sebastian knew that they were underground, which meant Oliver should have access to power. Sebastian pressed Oliver's palms flat against the ground. He remembered the small pouch that Julian had given him. He'd hung it around his neck and when he reached inside of his shirt, he was shocked to feel it still intact. He pulled it out and loosened the tiny leather strap. Inside, Julian had placed four stones. He had labeled them protection, power, healing and wisdom. He placed the stones of protection and healing on the tops of Oliver's hands. In his own hands, he held tightly the stones of wisdom and power. He closed his eyes and imagined his body growing lighter. In his mind, a long suture split the ground above them and a brilliant shaft of light snaked through the crevice into the earth and filled their bodies with light. Minutes passed, but he no longer felt the pressure of time. The world had ceased its heaviness and buoyancy overtook him He felt like a bubble floating just above a tranquil ocean. He imagined dropping into the ocean and being absorbed by the powerful sea. He started to feel the muscles in his body vibrating, communicating with his brain. Without thinking, he stood and walked the room, soundlessly tapping each wall. His palm met thickness on every wall except one. Near Lydie's tiny form, he found the hollow echo that told him he could break through.

"Ugghhhhh..." The moan startled him and broke his concentration. His heart skipped in his chest.

Oliver groaned again.

"Shh." Sebastian knelt beside him. The stones had fallen onto the floor and he placed them in Oliver's palms. Oliver's eyes, unfocused, blinked rapidly and then the film that drew across them started to dissolve.

"Water." he croaked.

"I wish I could," Sebastian told him. "But I think I've found a way out. I'm going to need you, though."

Oliver squeezed his eyes shut in pain. When he opened them, he lifted the healing stone and pressed it against his forehead. He did not move for several minutes and Sebastian started to grow impatient.

Finally, Oliver set the stones on the floor and, with great effort, pushed up to sitting. He teetered back and forth and Sebastian placed a hand on his shoulder to steady him. His hair was disheveled and prickled with bits of dried blood. His face looked swollen and scratched and his bare torso was a puzzle of cuts and wounds, but Sebastian could see them growing less vibrant and sore with each moment. Oliver took the stone and pressed it to each wound, wincing, but also sighing with relief. His right arm was mangled and mostly useless. He held it tight to his body.

"This is powerful," he whispered hoarsely as he examined the stone.

"Julian gave it to me."

"Julian?"

Sebastian nodded and Oliver understood. There was no time to discuss it.

Oliver's eyes drifted over to Lydie and he shot to his feet, making it halfway across the room before his legs gave out. He would have crashed into the swirling vat of fluid had Sebastian not caught him. He held him around the waist and waited until Oliver seemed capable of standing.

"What is this?" Oliver's eyes darted around the room, taking in the others. Sebastian saw fear.

Suddenly Oliver grabbed his head and tipped to the side, crashing to the floor. Sebastian scooped him back up.

"There was something in there," Oliver whispered as if the 'something' might hear him. "It knows I'm disconnected." He looked puzzled as he spoke.

Sebastian understood. The metal in Oliver's brain had connected him to someone or something.

"But Faustine was in there too... I saw his face and this other thing—it saw Faustine's face too..." Oliver's speech slurred and a small trickle of blood seeped out of his left nostril.

Sebastian hated to look at it. He had not realized until that moment how much he needed to believe in the witches' immortality.

Oliver took a deep breath and then moved into a kneeling position. He pressed his forehead against the ground and began to murmur.

"There's no time for that," Sebastian said, but only half-heartedly.

Oliver did not speak and Sebastian realized that he was praying and, as he whispered his incantations, the color slowly returned to his skin. When he stood, he was sturdy, and the glassiness in his eyes had dissipated completely.

"Faustine and one, maybe two, other witches have tracked us. The Vepars know it. That's why they haven't come in here. They're planning an attack."

"How do you know all that?"

"Whatever doorway that thing opened to get into my brain left me open to theirs too. I didn't get a lot, but I caught that."

Sebastian walked to the hollow wall.

"We can get through here, I'm almost sure of it."

Oliver pressed his palms against it and nodded.

Oliver took a deep breath and scanned the room one more time.

"We're going to smash the wall and then you're going to run like hell. I have to get Lydie. I'll be right behind you."

"I'll carry Lydie," Sebastian said, gesturing towards Oliver's arm.

"Okay. Then on three," Oliver whispered. "One, two, three..."

They both barreled into the wall with their full strength. It crumbled forward. Before them lay a long dark tunnel, dimly lit by small oil burning lamps.

Before he could turn to grasp Lydie, the trap door flung open and a Vepar dropped onto the floor behind them.

Oliver struggled with the ugly creature whose wide forehead and jaw reminded him of the Neanderthal pictures he had seen in anthropology classes in college. The Vepar was strong and he lifted Oliver and flung him into the wall. Then he strode across the room and knelt beside him, baring his fangs.

Sebastian had no weapon. He moved quickly, wrapping his forearm around the Vepar's neck and pressing. The creature pushed away from Oliver and his strength nearly toppled Sebastian backwards, but he held on. In his mind, the Vepar struggled and then lost consciousness. He focused every ounce of energy he could muster into that single image. But it was no use, the creature's arms flew wildly about and one cracked Sebastian in the face, splitting his nose and lip and sending him over backwards. The Vepar's eyes grew wide at the blood and he fell upon it, lapping it from the floor and then training his eyes on Sebastian's bloody face.

He turned to run, but before the creature could reach out and grab him, he saw Oliver rise up behind him. He held a hunk of the wall they'd smashed. He brought it down on the Vepar's head with all his might, hearing the skull crack, and the creature fell with a sickening thump onto the floor. Black blood oozed out of his greasy hair.

"He's not dead," Oliver said, beginning to remove the menagerie of tubes and wires from Lydie's body.

Sebastian cradled her in his arms and they ran from the room.

They did not have time to consider the others. They would come back for them.

****

Galla built a fire outside the cottage and the flames rose high, nearly licking the low branches of the trees. She called upon the spirits of her ancestors and the energies of the earth, wind, fire and water. With each gust of wind, more knowledge passed through her. She sent the growing power around her to all of her witches and she prayed that the breeze carried it swiftly.

A small SUV pulled down the rutty trail and stopped near the house. Two witches and one human emerged from it. Galla recognized Julian, but continued casting, knowing that if she broke the spell, the energies would quickly vanish and she felt sure that Demetrius, Faustine and Max needed her assistance.

Adora pushed open the door into the abandoned cottage. It creaked and swung in to reveal a cozy, but ramshackle space that had clearly been neglected for a long time. She saw Elda tending to Abby who looked near death, her skin as pale and iridescent as sugar.

"Julian," Elda murmured, fighting tears, as she stood and walked into his embrace. They held each other for a long time.

Rod went to Abby, crouching down to give her an awkward hug.

"You're alive?" she asked incredulously.

"Unfortunately," he teased, but she saw his heartsick expression. "And it seems you're just barely alive as well."

She nodded and grimaced at the throbbing sensation in her belly.

"What happened to you?" She asked touching his chin and then smoothing back his black hair.

"Witch disguise. I told them a good ole fake mustache and spectacles would do the trick, but they love to show off."

She smiled and winced.

"I've missed your sense of humor. It's been so long, it feels like a thousand years."

"I know," he agreed. "It's been ages since I've felt anything remotely normal."

He sighed and looked around the room.

"This is the best they could do? Witches with unlimited resources and power?"

Abby held up a hand.

"We're alive, right? I mean sometimes that's got to be enough."

He nodded and sat down fully, crossing his long legs.

Elda and the others returned. Adora began digging in her bag for tinctures as Julian laid his hand on Abby's forehead and then gently felt her hands and her feet.

"She's healing unusually fast," he said to no one in particular. "It's amazing."

"Yes," Elda agreed. "We discovered that this is her gift. It seems that she gets to test it again and again." The others chuckled, but their laughter was forced.

****

They raced through the underground tunnel and Oliver felt them all around him--Vepars with their black souls and the stink of their rottenness. He knew that some cavern beneath them held something so powerful it could topple all of the witches of Ula with a single breath, but it was dormant. It slept and grew stronger. In front of him Sebastian slid to a stop. Oliver walked to the edge where the ground suddenly dropped away. The gap in the floor was no more than four feet, but the chasm disappeared into blackness. Sebastian pulled a rock from the floor and dropped it. They did not hear it land.

Then they did hear something--nails scrabbling against dirt and stone. Something was crawling up from the darkness. Sebastian recoiled, but Oliver placed a firm hand on his back.

"Go now, jump." And as Sebastian leapt, Oliver mustered the energy around him and blew, giving Sebastian an extra boost that landed him several feet beyond the other side. Oliver did not hesitate. He jumped and nearly crashed into Sebastian and Lydie.

Neither stopped then, both knowing that whatever climbed out of that hole was not human, probably not even a Vepar exactly, but intent on reaching them before they fled the underground prison.

The chasms appeared more frequently and every fifteen feet they again had to leap over the startling blackness. Oliver sensed that there was light ahead and ran harder, but then one of the creatures scrambled from the earth in front of them, blocking their path. It had once been human, but now bore more resemblance to Night of the Living Dead. Rotted flesh hung from the man's jowls and his teeth showed through where chunks of lips were gone. Bones stuck at weird angles through his withered t-shirt, but he moved with speed. He darted toward them and, before Sebastian could think to defend himself, the creature slammed into him and Lydie with the force of a freight train. He flew backward, smashing into Oliver. With horror, Oliver felt, not earth rising up to meet them, but emptiness as they tumbled into one of the black holes.

Chapter 33

Galla walked into the cottage and collapsed onto the wasted sofa. It blew a puff of black feathers into the air where some bird had nested in the old fabric. The others waited for her to speak.

"Demetrius and Faustine have found the lair. It is heavy with Vepars, but it is not Vepars that makes them worry. There's something ancient inside and it seems be growing strong."

"It is the curse," Julian said. "Somehow it's being kept there. Whatever gives it life must be in that lair."

"What curse? What are you talking about Julian?" The lines in Elda's face seemed to grow deeper and more pronounced as she spoke.

Julian sighed and gazed around them.

"You have Dafne's ring?" he asked Elda.

She looked surprised and wondered how Julian sensed it. She had forgotten about the ring.

"Give it to Galla and let her read it. We must move quickly, but all of the pieces have not fallen into place," he said.

"I can help," Abby said, grasping Rod as she lifted herself to sitting. Elda tried to protest, but she waved her away. "Oliver and I have been studying it too."

Julian nodded and looked relieved.

Elda pulled the ring from her pocket and walked it to Galla who eyed it wearily. She held out her hand and Elda pressed the small band into her palm.

Immediately, Galla felt herself thrown back against the gaunt frame of the couch. In an instant a thousand memories and emotions coursed through her. She felt Dafne's epic love and then equally the horrors of the betrayal. She saw the woods burning and the witches writhing and screaming, but unable to escape. Tobias flickered in and out in a million shades of love and hate as Dafne's wasted body walked the cold beach. She felt the rumblings of a child inside her belly and later, the slick surge as the child burst into the world and was whisked away while Dafne turned her head and screamed into a pillow.

When the room re-emerged before her, Thomas was at her side, his hand prying open her fingers to pull the ring away. Then he pressed his hand against her heart and she felt the beating start to slow and the tension that had pulled her body rigid gradually eased away.

Galla told them what she saw and Elda shook her head in disbelief.

"Tobias could not have been her lover, and a child? Dafne never had a child. She lived with us. I nursed her back to life myself. I would have sensed the being inside her. I would have..." but her voice wavered and she could not look Galla in the eye.

"I knew something," Julian said. "I knew she had a vault of secrets inside her the very first day you and Faustine brought her to the castle. I tried to divine them. Miranda and I both did. It was like a game we played those first few days and then..." He did not talk about the night that Miranda died, but it was in his eyes.

"It started before Dafne," Abby told them. "And I think I've been dreaming of her, the original, the creator of the curse."

"Her? You believe it started with one woman?" Adora asked.

"Yes, and I saw her. At All Hallow's I met another witch who has been contacted by her. His name is Victor."

"Okay, wait," Galla interrupted. "We need this to make sense so let's start with Abby. Tell us everything you know."

Abby began. She talked about the Asemaa and all of the information that they had gathered. She told of Sydney's secret room filled with legends and news stories and journals. She described the trip that she and Oliver took to Chicago to see Victor and how Victor told her that the Native American girl, Kanti, had been contacting him for most of his life. She came to him in dreams and sometimes he saw wisps of her on streets and in forests, but she always vanished before he could reach her. She told them of the dreams she'd had where the girl gave birth to a child.

"There are hundreds of journals and countless boxes filled with information compiled by the Asemaa, but something has happened to the group. They started disappearing after Sydney died. I found one of them-- Gwen--and she is on the run now. Somehow the Vepars discovered the Asemaa and they must have wanted their information. I think they're in the dark too."

Is this what you have discovered, Julian?" Galla asked. She had regained her strength and paced the room near the fireplace.

"Yes, though Abby has a direct connection that I have clearly lacked. I know that the Vepars are more active players in this. I don't know how, but this curse seems to help them. Tobias was born of it. And Dafne fears that Sebastian is next in line. All of her efforts, deceitful as they may be, were to protect her coven." He looked pointedly at Elda when he said this and she nodded her thanks.

"Of course, we all know how the fates operate. It's like King Laius hearing the oracle's tale that his child would kill him and marry his mother. He ordered his son's death, thus creating the perfect narrative for Oedipus to fulfill the destiny that his father conspired to destroy. I fear that Dafne's scheming has brought us to the exact crux that she so wanted to thwart," Julian finished.

"No." Abby winced as she struggled to her feet, pushing Rod away when he tried to stop her. "Sebastian will not become one of them. There is no evil in him. We have to save them because when they realize that he won't join them, they'll kill him."

The other witches looked less convinced. Only Rod seemed to agree with her, bobbing his head up and down.

"It is his longing for vengeance that makes him vulnerable," Galla said. "I know this from you, Abby. I feel it. I know that you believe it's true"

Abby's face grew pale and she felt complete rage that her mind had been violated in that way. But Galla was right. Sebastian wanted to kill Tobias. No darker desire existed in the hearts of men.

"The time has come now for action," Julian announced. "I have known this day would come. We all did, I'm sure, and for every second that passes we grow weaker while they grow strong."

"Abby and Rod stay behind. I think we need..." Elda started.

"No," both Abby and Rod shouted at the same time. "Don't try to control this, Elda," Abby said gently. "I won't stay here and you will put me in greater danger by not including me and Rod," she added, taking his hand.

"Don't underestimate me," he said to Elda with a shrug. "I have nothing to live for."

Elda looked sad, but also resigned, as none of the other witches stepped in to support her.

****

"They will arrive soon," Faustine whispered to Max and Demetrius.

They gathered together in a thicket of pine trees, half a mile from the Vepar's lair.

"Galla has asked that we wait for them."

"To give the Vepars more time to prepare? More time to kill Lydie and Oliver?" Max looked aghast.

"I agree with Max," Demetrius said. "Your connection with Galla is strong right now. If we go in, we will give her and the others an advantage. If we wait, everyone is in the dark."

Faustine pressed his palms together and stared up at the sky. He felt genuinely conflicted. There were too many lives hanging in the balance to make a mistake.

"Okay, we will go in first," he told them. "But not all at once. First, I will go and then, Demetrius, you follow after five minutes and, Max, you come five minutes after that."

****

"No," Galla shouted in the back seat.

"What is it?" Abby asked, twisting around to face her.

"They're going in without us."

Elda grabbed her hand and held it tightly. The two elder witches huddled together. It frightened Abby to see them so shaken. Rod kept his eyes focused on the road and Abby appreciated his presence in the car. Unlike the witches, he seemed to be completely unafraid of what lay ahead.

****

Faustine did not enter the cellar door that Oliver had gone through. In the hours since their arrival, he, Demetrius and Max had scoured the woods and surrounding area searching for another way in. They had discovered a deserted farm with an old well, crumbling at the edge of the property only a mile south. When Faustine hovered near the top, he became convinced that it would lead them to the intricate underground tunnels that the Vepars called home.

"I'm not confident about this pulley system," Demetrius said, giving the old rope a tug. The rusted contraption looked ready to crumble.

"I believe that I can float down. However, I will take the rope just in case. Let's tie it off over there." Faustine pointed to an old tractor. The seat and wheels were corroded, but the frame looked heavy enough to hold him.

They tied it off quickly and Faustine prepared to go in.

"Are you comfortable with levitation, Demetrius?"

"Of course."

"Okay, then. We will levitate ourselves and we will not waste energy on each other. Once I am in the tunnel, I will move forward and send images back to you both. It is possible that our connection will be weak once we are underground."

They all agreed.

Faustine climbed over the edge of the stone well and several rocks displaced and tumbled away. He began to chant and soon his body floated just above the opening. As he dropped into the tunnel, he held the slack rope knowing that if he lost his connection, the rope might not hold him. As he floated down, he noticed claw marks scratched into the rock wall. He pressed his fingers against a deep gash. The contact jolted him and he lost his concentration. His body began to plummet and then suddenly he steadied. Max had floated him a rush of upward moving energy.

"Thank you," he called up. "Don't touch the walls," he added, knowing that Max and Demetrius would have also felt the shock.

Faustine refocused and Max eased his control. Almost fifty feet down, Faustine saw a half moon opening, large enough to fit a man, cut into the bedrock. He planted his feet on the edge and stepped forward, scanning the passageway before him. Demetrius and Max sent him silent confirmation that they would follow.

The passageway had been blown out and then meticulously formed. The earthen path was smooth and damp. Faustine began to rapidly descend less than twenty feet into the tunnel. Soon the slope turned into rudimentary stairs carved into the floor. Oil lamps hung from metal stakes driven into the wall. Despite the lamps, he walked through pockets of darkness. He perked his ears for any strange sounds, but heard nothing. He sensed that Demetrius had entered the well.

The stairs grew steeper and Faustine braced his hands on the narrowing tunnel walls to maintain balance. The steps ended abruptly and Faustine estimated his depth at more than three hundred feet underground. The water flowing through the bedrock helped him maintain his connection with Galla.

He continued forward on even ground until he came upon a mass of boulders completely blocking the path before him. Knowing that Demetrius and Max were close behind, he waited.

****

Sebastian plunged through darkness. Even as they fell, he held tight to Lydie, knowing that death might come at any moment. As he waited for the impact, he felt his body slowing and growing lighter. He realized that Oliver was easing their descent.

Before his body slammed into the mass beneath him, Sebastian smelled the dead. The stench filled his lungs with a scent of metallic rot. His stomach rolled. He felt his body smash into bone and flesh. It gelled beneath him. He and Lydie did not merely land--they sank. The hole that their forms created, closed as the body parts tumbled together. Sebastian held his breath and kicked and clawed out of the jumble of corpses. He felt his mouth and nose fill with blood and bodily fluids and he started to gag.

Only when his head emerged from the foul pit did he realize that he was howling.

"Stop," Oliver seethed and clamped a disgustingly slimy hand over his mouth. Sebastian slapped it away. He grabbed Lydie with both hands and trudged through the bodies to solid ground. He deposited her on the earth and fell to his knees, retching uncontrollably.

He tried to suck in a fresh breath, but the smell overpowered him and he gagged.

Oliver squatted beside him. He held a clump of dirt to Sebastian's face. "Breathe," he said.

Sebastian leaned into the dirt, half expecting to inhale a clump and choke, but only clean air entered his lungs.

"Hold your breath," Oliver told him, dropping the dirt and picking up another handful and then another.

"You're going to have to breathe through your mouth now," Oliver said. "Otherwise, you're going to get sick again."

Sebastian did as Oliver asked. The thought of inhaling the decayed remains made him nauseous, but he didn't smell it anymore.

"What the hell is this?" Sebastian asked finally.

He surveyed the mound of bodies stacked in the underground hole. There were a hundred, at least, in varying levels of decomposition.

Oliver shook his head and swiped at his watery eyes.

"I've never seen anything like it."

They had fallen into an enormous cavern. At least three hundred feet deep, the walls were a honeycomb of tunnels. As they watched, a creature, not unlike the one that pushed them into the pit, crawled out of one of the tunnels, scurried along the wall and entered another tunnel. A high-pitched cackle greeted them from an opening less than fifteen feet above their heads.

Sebastian scrambled to his feet.

"We're screwed," he whispered, staring in horror as another of the undead things fell from one of the crevices in the ceiling. It landed with a sickening thud.

"I'm not sure if it's dead," Oliver said with surprising calm. He watched the bodies wearily, but the creature did not emerge.

"I think it was already dead," Sebastian replied, accepting that even his worst nightmares had not prepared him for this moment.

"Faustine," Oliver whispered suddenly. "Faustine is down here."

"Where?" Sebastian scanned the room, searching the tunnels for Faustine's face.

"He's in a pathway that has been blocked off. This way, I think." Oliver started to walk the perimeter of the cavern, trying not to step on the dead, but unable to avoid them completely. His eyes kept wandering toward the faces. Some of the bodies were still intact and their faces had not morphed into the ghoulish undead that appeared to be travelling through the underground lair.

"Stephen," Oliver said startled. The journalist that he and Abby had been searching for lay at the edge of the mass. His glazed eyes stared at nothing, but his mouth was parted in an 'o' of horror as if his last visions had literally scared him to death.

"What is it?" Sebastian called out quietly.

Oliver waved him away and put a finger to his lips. He could hear scurrying from one of the tunnels. He continued around the bodies and then a shriek near Sebastian sent him running back.

One of the fiends leered at them. Its black tongue lashed out from its, once feminine, face. The creature's hair fell in black clumps around her wasted scalp. With talon-like fingers, she scrambled onto the wall and then jumped to the earth below. Sebastian kicked desperately at a rock, trying to unearth it. He snatched it up and bent his knees low.

Oliver too grabbed a rock and focused on harnessing the powerful energy of the limestone surrounding him.

The fiend lunged forward, reaching for Sebastian with skeletal fingers. Before Oliver could heave the rock in his own hand, the creature burst into flames. She let out a single, high-pitched squeal and then collapsed, squirming and then growing still.

"What the..." Sebastian started, but Oliver saw that Lydie had returned to consciousness.

Though she still laid flat on her back, her eyes were open and her hands, shaking, pointed toward the charred monster at Sebastian's feet.

Oliver rushed over, awkwardly hugging her with his single good arm. Sebastian joined them.

"When life gives you lemons, make barbecue," Lydie rasped with a hollow grin.

Sebastian shook his head and smiled, in spite of himself.

"Only you could make this shit funny," Sebastian said, sitting down roughly against the wall.

Lydie reached a hand over to him and patted his foot.

"Thanks for rescuing me, guys."

Oliver laughed and didn't bother trying to wipe his tears.

Lydie struggled up to sitting position and pressed her face into her palms.

"I think I'm going to puke," she mumbled, and some of the little girl had replaced her hardness. Oliver let her go and she doubled over, throwing up and then dry heaving until she collapsed back onto the ground, her face close to the dirt.

Oliver rubbed her back.

"Sebastian, there's a passageway somewhere on the other side of those bodies. It's filled in with rocks. We have to move them. Faustine is on the other side."

"Faustine." Lydie perked up and Sebastian immediately sprang to his feet at the hopeful sheen in Lydie's eyes.

"I'm on it," he said.

He walked around the mound of bodies and found the only tunnel at ground level. It was large, at least ten feet tall, and packed with huge rocks. He grabbed one and pulled. It didn't budge.

Chapter 34

Demetrius came upon Faustine and then Max arrived several minutes later. Demetrius, an earth element, had the most power to influence the rocks. He placed his hands on the boulders, feeling their mass and slowly growing in tune with their vibrations.

"I can move them," he said finally, "but it will take some time."

"We may not have time," Max whispered, hearing the far-off sounds of heavy footfalls. As an air element, Max was at an additional disadvantage, but he also knew that Lydie lay somewhere inside and he would die to get her out.

"I will retreat," Faustine said. "Let me be the first line of defense."

Max began to argue, but Faustine silenced him. "There's no more time."

As Faustine ran back down the tunnel, Demetrius grew very quiet. He spread himself across the boulders, pressing his forehead, torso and legs against every possible surface. His body began to tremble and then shake.

****

They parked the cars along a wide shoulder and took to the woods by foot. Abby, not fully recovered, and Rod, a non-witch , slowed the group down, adding to the already strained energies. Fear, tension, exhilaration and impatience were, but a few of the waves of emotion passing through all of them collectively.

As they walked, Galla reported the images from Faustine. Elda, too, had begun to pick up his signals and Julian as well. When Faustine back-tracked to face the Vepars, Elda's face grew tight with worry. She started to walk faster.

"We can't all go in," Julian reminded them. "We need reinforcements at the well. I think two should go down here and two should stay above the ground..."

Abby wanted to go in, but she knew that they would not allow it. Her abdomen continued to throb and a fever had washed over her, causing sweat to stand out along her brow line. Each step radiated up her legs and into her core. A dizzy spell overcame her and she started to fall sideways, but Adora caught her and held her steady.

"You have to go back to the car," Elda insisted, taking Abby's clammy hands in her own. "I know that you are strong, Abby. But we're going to need you because if anyone gets hurt, your blood is going heal them..."

Elda had never talked about Abby's blood being healing for other witches. She started to argue, fearing that Elda intended to trick Abby to keep her out of danger. Instead, she grew woozy and nearly fell a second time.

"It's decided then," Julian agreed. "Abby returns to the car. Rod?"

"No. I'm sorry, Abby," he pecked her on the cheek. "But I'm going down there."

Julian turned up his palms in surrender and looked at Adora.

"I will walk her to the car," Adora said, resigned. "And then I will stay in the trees. If any of those demons come out, they're mine."

****

It took a moment for the nausea to pass, but once Lydie could stand, she hurried with Oliver to the blocked tunnel. They could not tell how far the boulders went in.

"Fire is not going do us a lot of good, hon," Olive told Lydie. "But it will take care of those dead things when they come in."

"Great," she said. "Sounds like more fun than a barrel of monkeys."

Oliver bit his tongue and did not comment on the return of the clichés. He realized that she needed them to make it all less scary and, in truth, he appreciated the humor.

Sebastian walked to the pile of bodies and, plugging his nose, he reached into the mess. He wrestled two large thigh bones from a mostly decomposed skeleton.

"It's better than nothing," he told them dryly.

Oliver returned his attention to the rocks. He could feel Demetrius somewhere on the other side, slowly breaking them down. He chose a different tact. Pulling a surge of energy from the ground beneath him, he grabbed a boulder with invisible hands and inched it away. It stayed put and then, miraculously, it shifted. As he took hold with his mind, it gained momentum and rolled back.

"Yes," Sebastian whistled behind him.

"Three o'clock," Oliver shouted, gesturing towards one of the undead, standing in a tunnel above them.

"That one's been beat with the ugly stick," Lydie said, opening her arms wide and, in a rush, slamming them back together. As her hands connected, a fireball shot from between them. It launched up and struck the hollow-eyed beast. It screamed once as it fell from the hole and landed in the bodies below. Immediately another appeared behind it and then two more tunnels filled with ghoulish faces.

Oliver returned to the rocks, knowing that help and a way out was close at hand.

He focused on a low boulder. With all his might, he drew it towards him. It moved, barely, but still it moved. He gritted his teeth and fought with it. His eyes itched and his brain felt ready to explode. Finally, it shot backwards, nearly striking him. The five boulders supported by it, tumbled away. One struck Lydie and she flew forward, landing on her hands and knees, too shocked to cry out.

"I've got her," Sebastian shouted, running over and helping her to her feet.

Oliver saw the fiends crawling down the walls. The next boulder, he levitated and, with a force that nearly blew out his right eye, he flung the boulder into the wall, smashing one of the creatures. From the corner of his eye, he saw Lydie blast a feeble bolt of fire towards another of the fiends, but it did not reach.

"A chain is only as strong as its weakest link," she announced, closing her eyes and trying again.

She reached the creature but, as it started to burn, another lunged from above her. It struck her shoulder and she pitched to the ground, striking her head.

Sebastian fell upon it with the bone. He struck it in the face, grimacing as the soft flesh caved in and the teeth broke away. Even after it stopped moving, he continued to strike it.

Lydie pressed her fingers to her scalp and felt the mash of hair and blood.

"Ouch," she whimpered, teetering on the verge of a full break-down.

Sebastian scooped her up and carried her behind one of the large boulders that Oliver had dislodged.

"Take a breather, little fire goddess," he told her. "I can take care of these guys."

She nodded grimly, pressing her face into her knees to cry.

****

Faustine became clear like water and melded into the limestone wall. He knew that there were two and that they were not small. Their footfalls sent thundering vibrations up his legs. A human might not have sensed the impact of their movements, but Faustine discerned their every shift. They paused halfway down the stairs and he wondered if the other witches had arrived. Only one continued forward.

He reached for Galla in his mind and warned her about the Vepar lying in wait. His focus on transparency pulled him away from his telepathic connection and he could not be sure that she received his message.

As the Vepar came into view, Faustine studied him for recognition. His huge blockish head sat atop an equally thick neck, giving him the appearance of having no neck at all. Black curly hair surrounded his large chapped mouth. His tongue stuck between a gap in his front teeth and his eyes held a looking of cunning determination. He looked dim-witted, but he was not. Tobias was sending in heavy artillery.

The Vepar stopped and scanned the tunnel. Faustine felt the demon's eyes rove across him and pass by, but they paused. The hesitation was barely perceptible, but Faustine understood that he had been discovered.

Before the Vepar could rush him, Faustine reached into the body of the dark thing before him. With phantom hands, he seized the Vepar's brain, an organ composed mostly of water.

The Vepar charged him, smashing him back into the rock wall and knocking the breath from his body. He lost his hold and crumpled to the earth. The Vepar snatched him by the collar of his shirt and flung him into the ceiling. He could not shield himself and reach back into the Vepar's skull. His body struck the earth and he felt the bones in his right shoulder shatter. He glared into the demon's eyes as he hardened the water within the thick skull to ice. The brute's eyes widened and he staggered back, clutching at his head and wailing in agony. Faustine concentrated on the ice. As it hardened, he envisioned it splitting and spider webbing. The demon's eyes began to ooze black blood and he fell forward on his hands and knees. He made a final attempt at Faustine, lunging forward before he buckled to the floor.

****

Julian and Elda went to the well. Though they did not receive Faustine's message of the Vepars below, Julian perceived them before they reached the farm property. He handed Elda a sack of black powder and a steel stake.

He dropped in first, quickly using the rope to slide down the well. At the lip of the tunnel, before swinging in, he pulled out his own bag of black powder and flung a handful into the opening.

Julian had created the powder. To it he added ground rosary peas, frankincense and the ashes of a thousand candles burned on the altar of his lost wife Miranda. He then sat with the powder for a hundred nights, invoking the greatest Vepar hunter the world of witches had ever known. The powder affected every Vepar differently, but it never failed to debilitate the demons in some capacity.

When no sound returned, he swung into the tunnel to wait for Elda. The Vepar rose from a crouch and, even in the far-off darkness, Julian saw the red glow in its eyes. He reached for the bag of powder and started to warn Elda, but the demon moved like thunder. It struck him and drove him back into the well and they fell. Their tangled mass hit the walls and brought a shower of rock with them as they twisted in the air. The Vepar sunk its huge jaws into Julian's wrist.

Elda dropped, focusing on buoyancy, but also speed. She slowed when she heard them splash into the bottom of the well. Pulling the bag of powder from the pocket of her cloak, she grasped a handful and prepared to rain it upon them. Above her, something slid across the well opening casting them into darkness.

"Just throw it, Elda," Julian screamed from beneath her and she could hear them thrashing in the water.

She opened the bag and flung it back and forth, praying that it would not hurt Julian as well.

The Vepar took hold of Julian's neck and thrust him beneath the water. Julian grasped the sharp fingernails digging into his flesh. He couldn't breathe and conjuring a faculty of his power ceased to be possible as spots of white began to dance behind his eyelids.

Elda pulled energy from the water and called upon the spirit of the sun to cast out the darkness. A brilliant white light illuminated the water and she saw the demon holding Julian beneath the surface, but his grip had loosened. The Vepar's eyes were clenched together and a stream of black foam dripped from the corner of his mouth.

Julian rose and shoved the beast away. It swayed drunkenly, but did not fall. Julian pulled a dagger from his belt and, using his good arm, he thrust the dagger into the beast's abdomen, driving the blade in and up and until he felt the familiar burst. The Vepar collapsed and a rush of black blood filled the water.

****

Adora tucked Abby into the backseat and stood outside. She walked the perimeter of the car sprinkling salt and grated osha root. She called upon the elements of earth, wind, fire and air to protect the young witch and to conceal her from searching eyes. Abby fell into a feverish sleep.

She shivered and rolled over, feeling soft fur beneath her cheek. She tried to pull her blanket closer, but someone tugged it away. The blanket lifted and she stared at the naked back of a young woman. The woman pulled the fur throw--it looked like bear--up to her neck. She stood and walked toward the triangle of light coming through the single opening in the enormous leather tent. Abby scanned the tepee that she'd woken in, counting at least three more dozing bodies buried beneath heaps of blankets and furs. The young woman's long black hair caught the sunlight as she walked into the clearing where the previous night's fire still smoldered, leaking out wisps of gray smoke. The woman, Kanti, turned and Abby saw that she was barely more than a child really. A halo of breath stole from her small red mouth and her dark eyes glittered. She lifted a stick from the earth and began to poke the fire, then bent close to it and seemed to coo and whisper until the flames started to grow and dance. She shuffled out of sight and Abby stood and walked to the tent's opening.

The girl sang softly as she gathered two logs from a stack of firewood and returned to the growing blaze. Then she reached into a small pouch that hung from her waist. She sprinkled something into the fire that made it crackle and laugh, and she laughed with it. In the dark forest behind the girl, movement caught Abby's eye. She watched a hulking shape, a beast of some sort, pacing within the shadows of the trees. Abby started to call out to the girl, but only silence emerged where her warning cries should have been. Abby lifted a hand to her throat, but felt nothing. It was if she were not there at all. In the forest, the shadow broke away from the trees. It was a very large man, well over six feet tall, laden with oily-looking black furs. Despite his size he moved quickly and, worse, quietly. The girl continued to sing and flirt with the fire, unaware of the man closing in. He took her in a single swipe. His huge arms enveloped her body, one across her face, silencing her screams and then he disappeared back into the woods. Abby stared at the stick that had fallen from the girl's hands and she watched the flames grow huge and bright and then, as quickly, they died again and only the smoldering embers remained.

Chapter 35

Galla, Thomas and Rod moved through the tunnel that Oliver had entered earlier that day. Galla conjured a dense shield of green light that shone out of her chest and surrounded them completely.

Thomas walked in front and, as tunnels began to appear on either side, he stopped and consulted with Galla before moving forward. Galla no longer had contact with Faustine. The impenetrable earth and forces, that she preferred not to consider, put a stop to the visions.

Rod walked between the two witches. In his hands he held a dagger and a fistful of Julian's powder. Of the three, Rod was the least afraid. His heart beat steadily and every muscle in his body reassured him that it was time to fight.

When the Vepars appeared, blocking either direction, Galla knew that they would not all make it out alive.

****

Demetrius and Max burst through the last of the boulders and rushed into the cavern. Oliver crouched on his knees, his eyes bloodshot and his face dripping sweat. The elder witches recoiled at the stench and covered their faces with their hands.

"Good God, what is it?" Demetrius hissed, stripping out of his jacket and covering his nose. He didn't need an answer. He could see the mountain of rotted bodies rising up from the earth.

Sebastian and Lydie stood in the center of a fire ring that Lydie had created. Charred bodies were laid around the circle, the hair of one fiend continuing to burn.

"It's a dumping site," Max whispered, shaking his head in disgust. He went to Oliver and laid hands on his back. He sent radiant light into the young witch and allowed his own energy to be depleted as Oliver healed.

Lydie released the fire ring and ran to Max. She nearly knocked him down. He bent over and hugged her fiercely.

243

"You're okay now," he whispered into the top of her head. She cried openly, balling his shirt in her fists and pressing her face into the fabric.

****

The first Vepar struck the shield and blew the energy apart. The blast rocked them all. Before Galla could try to recreate it, Rod rushed forward and attacked the Vepar who lay stunned on the ground. He stabbed at the demon, sinking his blade into its neck and chest.

Thomas raced to his aid, knowing that Rod did not have the strength to thrust the stake through the Vepar's chest plate. He pushed Rod out of the way and slammed his fist hard into the handle.

Vesta emerged from the shadows and fell upon Thomas. She sank her teeth into the soft flesh of his neck. She did not merely bite to anesthetize, but to kill. As his neck opened, she drank the witch's blood and felt her overpowering thirst finally quenched.

Galla could only watch in horror as Thomas buckled beneath the succubus. Beyond Vesta, the Vepar Wrath watched Galla with cold dark eyes and it took all of the power within her to hold him back. She held her palms toward him and created a wind strong enough to stop him from moving forward.

As Vesta drank, Rod threw the black powder into her face. She hacked and spit and turned on him.

"He's mine," she growled to another Vepar, also a woman, but a smaller pixie-ish thing with pointed spikes for hair and rings sticking from nearly every orifice in her face.

Vesta grabbed for him, but her hand froze in mid-air. She started to tremble and convulse. She turned back to the smaller Vepar, but the demon backed away and hissed when Rod reached for another handful of the powder. She retreated further into the tunnel. Vesta's head shook mechanically to the side as if trying to rid her ears of water. Thomas's blood flowed from her lips.

Rod pulled the stake from the chest of the fallen Vepar and plunged it into Vesta. She did not cry out, but sank to the ground. Her body slowed and then stopped shaking. He pushed it deeper and, when it still did not break through, he stood and, with precision, jumped and landed on the handle. It slammed into the Vepar and her eyes shot open and locked on his. She let out a gurgling scream and then the black thing that she'd traded for her soul exploded within her.

****

Elda drove the stake into the Vepar that lay unconscious near Faustine.

"My old friend," Faustine sighed as Julian offered his hand. "And I see that we are in similar positions." He gestured at his limp arm.

"Yes, and damn, does this anti-venom make my blood feel like ice," Julian complained, offering Faustine a one-armed hug.

Elda put the blade in her cloak and walked to Faustine. Gently, she took his face in her hands and kissed him.

"I prayed for this moment," she told him, fighting back tears. "I was not sure..."

"Shh...I know, darling. Let's celebrate like the old days when we get out of this pit of despair."

Together they moved quickly down the long stairway. They did not speak, each on high alert for any disturbance in their energy field.

They smelled the departed before they reached the bottom of the stairs. As they entered the cavern, Elda stopped, causing Julian and Faustine to nearly walk into her.

"Oh," she placed a hand over her mouth and shook her head as if she might deny the savagery. Her heart broke in equal measure for the dead, the dying and for her coven. Oliver looked dazed and leaned heavily against a boulder as he spoke with Demetrius and Sebastian. Max sat on the ground with Lydie's head cradled in his lap.

Elda went to them and helped Lydie to her feet. She hugged her close and apologized for her terror. Both Faustine and Elda took Sebastian in a long embrace. Sebastian fought the urge to ask about Abby. Demetrius had already told him that she waited for him above the earth.

Max shook Julian's hand.

"It's been too long," Max told him.

"And what terrible circumstances for a reunion," Julian added. He could barely take his eyes from the mound of bodies. "I have never seen anything like this."

"Nor have I," Max agreed, but he looked away from the dead. He felt the suffering still palpable in the room and it exhausted him to endure it.

"Julian," Oliver hugged him with his good arm and laughed when Julian returned his own clumsy one-armed hug. "They must be trying to turn us into a coven of cripples."

"Or eat us all together," Julian added wryly, immediately sorry when he saw the tear-stained cheeks of Lydie.

"The dead people have stopped attacking us for now, but I'd rather not wait for another freak show," Oliver announced. "Let's get out of here."

"The dead people?" Faustine and Julian asked in unison.

"Yeah, Zombies," Sebastian said.

"This is a charnel ground," Faustine spoke, drawing again on the ground water to bring him strength. He asked the water to speak with the dirt and rock and he listened to the language of life and death. "They're not only animating these beings, they are drawing power from them."

"I want to leave," Lydie choked. The crying had stopped and her face had returned to her world-weary expression.

"I agree," Sebastian added. He could not help, but think of Claire or Sydney lying in the pile of the dead. He imagined all of the people whose hearts would break when their loved ones never came home.

"We need to consider our best way out," Elda said.

"But where did you just come from?" Oliver asked. "Why can't we go that way?"

"Because something shut us in," Elda told him uneasily.

****

With Vesta's death, the tides started to turn and then Wrath, as if cued, charged Galla with all of his force. He drove beyond the wind pressing him back. His face held no expression at all. His eyes were two black holes that Galla could not look away from. Beyond him, something huge and black began to fill the cave. Rod shot forward and threw a handful of the black dust, but Galla's wind blew it passed Wrath and he fought on. She lost her hold and, with a final burst, she turned to Rod and screamed, "Run."

But it was too late to run. The Vepar took hold of Galla with supernatural force . He grasped her hair and raked her to a stop. Rod seized her hands and tried to pull her out of the Vepar's grip, but he might as well have been a child fighting a toy from a tornado.

Beyond Rod, a hulking black shadow fell upon them. Galla saw giant twisted wings and human eyes--no, not human, Vepar's eyes in the wolfish face. With huge taloned feet, the creature seized Rod by the throat and dragged him back down the tunnel. Galla lost her hold on his hands and screamed in agony as the monster crushed Rod's neck and then disappeared into the tunnel's darkness.

Wrath wrestled her onto the ground and pressed one grimy hand into her face and another into her chest. His breath smelled foul and saliva dripped from his pointed teeth. He kneeled on her legs, trapping her. She felt the upsurge of panic, but beat it back, focusing on the dagger concealed beneath her left sleeve. She thrashed and blew gusts of wind into his face to prevent him from lowering his teeth into her neck. He shifted further down her body and she screamed as his teeth pierced her thigh. He gnashed through two layers of pants and, in a single bite, pierced her skin and muscle.

An excruciating heat poured through her whole body, but her hand released the dagger and she slammed it into the Vepar's temple as he drank. His mouth continued to suck even as his body grew slack. She shoved him and drove the dagger into his abdomen and up into his place of power. He died silently and his mouth shone with her blood. She scrambled for the anti-venom in the pouch secured around her waist. Already her vision grew blurry. She poured it into the wound and then began to drag herself back out of the tunnel.

****

Abby came to in the car. She pushed the quilt that Adora had wrapped her in to the floor. Sweat made her shirt cling to her torn stomach. She lifted it and stared at the blood-soaked bandage.

Images from her dream continued to course through her muddled brain. She saw the girl, Kanti, stolen from her tribe. She saw the fear in her eyes as the giant dragged her away. Suddenly a chill settled upon her and she wrapped the quilt around her again.

A cold gray sky began to transform as Abby watched the first snow of the year. Fat white flakes grew into a sea of dazzling white beyond the windows. She stepped from the car and tilted her face into the snow. It started to fall harder, coating Abby's eyelashes and hair. Soon she could barely see the woods at the edge of the road.

A vicious shriek broke the wintry silence. Abby ducked, afraid that the winged monster circled the sky above her. She pushed away from the car and stumbled blindly through the storm. Gusts of snow hit her in waves, attempting to drive her back as she continued forward into the woods. She prayed for her inner knowing to guide her because her eyes surely could not.

In a thicket of pines she stopped and placed a hand on her belly. Something stirred deep in the center of her being. She sank to her knees and felt the fluttering in her womb. A sudden vicious wave of nausea coursed through her and she leaned over and vomited. She rested her back against a tree and closed her eyes.

****

The fire came all at once and from everywhere. The boulders that Oliver had lodged in the tunnels blew into the cavern. The crevices above them poured liquid fire, igniting the tower of bodies. The undead that still crawled through the underground lair began to wail in grotesque agony. Several Vepars fell from the tunnels overhead, their bodies twisted in the flames.

There was no time to think and barely time to act. Max threw a shield over Lydie and himself. Demetrius, Oliver, Elda, Faustine and Julian locked hands and created a bubble of earth and air and rain. Sebastian cowered in the center, astonished, as beyond the bubble, the fire ravaged everything.

The witches fought the blaze with earth and water. Water spewed from the walls and roof of the cavern soaking the bodies and the earthen floor beneath them. Mixed with the soil, the water created a deluge of mud that dripped from the ceiling and flowed down the cavern's walls. Their bubble grew black with smoke and dirt and the slimy entrails of the bodies that fell from above. The air grew thinner in the bubble as the temperature climbed. Sebastian coughed and stuffed his face close to the earth.

Something rumbled inside of Sebastian and suddenly he couldn't stay within the bubble. He felt as though he might explode. He burst from their protective canopy. Pressing his hands against his ears, he began to wail. The sound pierced the air and grew so loud that it drowned out the raging fire. The ground began to shake and above them the earth split. Rocks and dirt and trees rained into the crevice as it opened to the sky. The snow, falling in waves, slowly muted the fire.

The circle of witches fell to the floor gasping. Oliver bled from his nose and ears. Elda's silver hair had been mostly singed away and patches of her scalp showed angry red welts. Faustine collapsed completely. Oliver rolled him over and felt for a pulse. It was there, but faint, and he barely breathed. Oliver adjusted his head and neck and started CPR. He pounded on his chest and blew breath into his mouth.

"Let me," Julian rasped, pushing Oliver out of the way. He pressed both palms against Faustine's chest. His body convulsed as if Julian had shocked him. He did it again and Faustine groaned. His eyes fluttered and then closed, but his chest began to rise and fall as he took in breath.

Lydie began to sob and Oliver, barely able to stand, lurched to her side. She crawled out from under Max whose head and back had blistered purple. He had died protecting her.

Slowly, they all turned and looked at Sebastian, whose screams had somehow ripped the earth in two.

Chapter 36

They found Abby unconscious in the snow. In her hand, she held a familiar antique bottle. Sebastian remembered it from the Vepar's ritual--a bottle that held the blood of some ancient Vepar. They made their witch sacrifices drink it. It was empty. He pried it from her fingers and threw it into the woods. He lifted her and carried her to the car.

The witches trudged together through the forest. The tempest had calmed, but hid the earth in a layer of soft white. Elda and Faustine leaned heavily on one another, cringing against the harsh cold on their raw skin. Oliver carried Lydie whose silence scared them more than her cries. Julian and Demetrius carried Max's body.

Adora did not greet them in the trees and a bloody trail led ominously from the well, suggesting a violent end for the cautious witch. With each new discovery, the devastation grew. They found Galla in the car with both relief and sadness when they learned the fates of Thomas and Rod.

"They've become skin-walkers," Galla told them shuddering. "The Vepars can change forms..."

****

They did not return to Ula. Together, the seven witches and one human, traveled to the coven of Sorciére.

The Sorciére witches doted on the injured and grieving of Ula. They too mourned the loss of their beloved Thomas and, equally, the disappearance of Indra. Neither she or Dafne had been found and many of the witches feared that their corpses were merely two of dozens buried in the Vepar's charnel ground.

Abby and Sebastian occupied a single room in a sunny part of Sorciére's north tower. For their first three days at Sorciére, they spoke very little and then, one night after a wonderful dinner prepared by Bridget and Sorciére's Jacque,the flood gates finally opened. They talked, almost without pause, for two days. Sebastian told Abby about losing his memory, the woman,

249

Isabelle, whose body he saw in the Vepar's lair, and his insane escape from Julian, Adora and Rod. Sebastian teared up at the mention of Rod's name, but they both agreed that Sydney had welcomed him into the after-life so that the two could continue their shenanigans for eternity. Abby described her quest for answers. She told Sebastian about Victor and his intentional witch community in Chicago and promised that Sebastian would meet them soon. Sebastian tried to describe what happened in the Vepar's dumping ground, but he found it impossible to reconstruct. He knew that Elda intended to help him investigate the power when they visited the concrete slabs of Ula.

Oliver spent every waking moment with Lydie who lapsed into long silences punctuated by clichés or total melt-downs. She slept in Oliver's room every night, curled at the foot of his bed. The Sorciére witches swarmed around her. They brought her sweets and performed exotic magic, turning parrots into bunnies and changing the color of Oliver's hair to a pink Mohawk and then long orange dreadlocks. She smiled when they paraded Andromeda's seventy-five cats through one of the banquet halls, but she rarely laughed. Sometimes she sat with Abby, and Sebastian told her stories about Claire. She seemed to relish the anecdotes from the young witch's life and perhaps relate them to her own.

Elda and Faustine were a single unit. They moved as a powerful entity and they talked incessantly about Ula's rebirth. Galla, Demetrius and the other Sorciére witches vowed to help in the rebuilding of their coven. Helena too was exhilarated at the thought of Ula's revival. However, her injuries left her weak and plagued by bouts of dizziness. Sorciére's healing witch, Yia, insisted that Helena would recover when her coven was whole again and that gave everyone additional motivation to see Ula rise from the ashes.

In the end, Abby and Sebastian decided that they would not return to Ula. Neither Abby or Sebastian could stomach the thought of living again within the repressive stone walls. Instead they would return monthly to discuss the curse. A time that would also allow Abby to continue her studies and training.

The witches of Ula gathered together in Sorciére's Chambre des Reves, or Room of Dreams, on their last night at the coven. The room's ceiling was enchanted into a twilight sky. One half of the dome ceiling revealed a glowing red sun disappearing into the horizon, but as their eyes drifted up, the sky merged into pinks and purples and finally blue with a tiny sliver of moon on the other half of the dome. The floor appeared to be a forest. However, the leaves and grass were thick soft carpeting and the stumps and giant flowers were pillows and bean bags. Holographic trees rose up in the center of the room, releasing vibrant lavender-colored flowers. Hummingbirds darted into imaginary rose bushes.

Oliver settled on an enormous daffodil and Lydie folded into his lap. Sebastian and Abby opted for a mushroom that squished as they sank into it and they laughed, almost toppling out. Faustine, Helena and Elda all chose the carpeting beneath the falling leaves. Bridget stretched out on a long pillow log and watched the shooting stars overhead.

"We will meet four weeks from today?" Faustine asked, though it had already been decided. "And we will share all of the information that we have discovered about the curse and about this Kanti woman."

"And we will celebrate a new Ula as well. With a feast!" Bridget chirped. "We must not forget about the food."

"Never forget the food," Helena added, laughing.

"We need one of these rooms at Ula," Lydie sighed and Helena agreed.

"You can have anything you want," Elda said seriously. "We're creating a whole new world..."

Sebastian kissed the top of Abby's head and hugged her close. After all of the tragedy in his life, he suddenly felt hopeful again.

"Yes, four weeks from today," Abby chimed in. "But first we're going to buy a house."

Elda smiled and held her hand out for a darting hummingbird.

"Do you already have something in mind, Abby?" she asked.

None of the Ula witches argued when Abby and Sebastian insisted that they wanted to create a life beyond the coven. Oliver, however, looked crestfallen at the news.

"Yes and no," Abby replied. "We both love the Sleeping Bear Lake shore and we want to be near the water and the forests, so..."

"And Trager too," Helena added darkly. "Are you sure that you want to be near that city?"

"Yes," both Abby and Sebastian answered together.

"It's not the city that's evil, Helena," Oliver added in their defense. "It's the Vepars and I think they're pretty well cleared out for now."

All of them hung on the 'for now' because they knew that both Alva and Tobias had escaped the lair. Not only did they escape, but their new ability to transform into flying creatures of the night meant they were far more lethal than before.

"Do you think they have Dafne and Indra?" Lydie asked, reading their minds.

"If they do," Faustine told her, "we will rescue them. That is our first priority, dear, I promise." He placed his hand on his heart, but Lydie did not look convinced.

Chapter 37

"I don't think we won," Lydie murmured, pulling Baboon into her lap and stroking his ears. He purred and nuzzled her fingertips.

"Why do you say that, Lyd Pie?" Oliver asked her. He was still sorting journals into dates and fighting the urge to eavesdrop on Sebastian and Abby in the kitchen.

Oliver and Lydie were staying with Abby and Sebastian in their new house for several weeks while Faustine, Elda and the witches of Sorciére cast new spells to protect Ula.

"Because I think Kanti, the spirit, won. I think she wanted some of us to die and some of us to live, maybe just to let us believe that we'd survived something."

Oliver paused and looked at Lydie, whose tiny body was nearly lost in the silver throw that she snuggled in. She looked old--not simply older, but old. Small lines flecked her mouth and the crease between her eyes held thoughts that he didn't want to consider in her young mind. Worse still, her words revealed some of his fears.

He considered reassuring her. He almost felt obligated to do so, but he knew that he would lose her if he followed the lead of the elder witches and continued to treat her like a child. He sat on the floor in front of her.

"I know what you mean, Lyds. I wish I didn't, but I do."

"So does Abby," she said. "I saw it in her eyes at Sorciére. It's not over and she knows it."

Again, Oliver marveled at how adult Lydie seemed, terrifyingly so.

"I know, but we have knowledge on our side now. Before we were all in the dark and that gave her an advantage. This time..." he pointed at the boxes of journals, "...we're going to do our research and we'll be ready, not to mention Victor and his crew will join us for our monthly meetings at Ula."

"The Chicago witches?"

"Yes, and you're going to love them, I promise. They're pretty unconventional and that's exactly what Ula needs."

Lydie glanced at the windows facing the lake. The blue sky was marred by distant dark clouds moving in.

****

"I love this house so much," Abby told Sebastian for the hundredth time, standing on tiptoe to kiss him. They had signed the contract the week before and Abby could barely contain her excitement.

They walked from the kitchen onto the sunlit porch, heavy with the morning's fresh snowfall. The snow caught the sun and dazzled her eyes in a wave of sparkling grandeur. She lifted a hand to shield her face and looked out at the iron gray waters of Lake Michigan. The lake never froze completely, but along the shoreline sheaths of ice formed and created outcroppings of twisted glassy structures that reached into the lake.

The vast house behind them towered over Lake Michigan and sat at the tip of a long wooded peninsula. The Gothic Revival structure boasted a single turret, an elaborate widow's walk and a porch that wrapped around the entire base of the house.

Sebastian and Abby bought the entire peninsula along with the house, which included more than two hundred acres of dense northern Michigan forest. The color, Japanese Indigo according to the real estate agent,reminded Abby of the dark blue waters of the lake. The intricate wood work along the gabled roof and widow's walk was a lighter shade of green. Fireplaces warmed every bedroom, the sitting room, the library and even the kitchen. Sebastian loved the kitchen with glistening marble counter tops and a commercial-sized gas stove. His eyes glittered when he talked of Christmas dinner at their home. It invited you, this house.

They both embraced the dawning of a new day. The home held an air of possibility that Abby had never genuinely experienced. She turned and gazed back at the house. She could see rose-colored silk curtains hanging in the tower window just above the porch. She loved that room most of all. The circular shape and soft edges made it the perfect space for a nursery.

As if the child sensed her thoughts, she felt the tiniest shift deep in her womb. She smiled up at Sebastian and wondered again why she had not told him about the new life growing inside her.

AUTHOR'S NOTE

I love characters. For me that's the heart of writing and reading. I would love to hear about your experience with my characters and what other fictional characters you love. Reading has truly shaped my life and there's nothing more amazing than connecting with other readers who share passions similar to my own. I write as J.R. Erickson, though my legal name is Jacki Riegle. I live in Northern Michigan with my excavator husband and my beautiful little boy.

Don't forget to check out the next book in the Born of Shadows Series: Kanti. Visit my author website www.jrericksonauthor.com for more information about upcoming book releases.

Proof

Made in the USA
Columbia, SC
15 November 2017